STORM OF DESIRE

"Pooh on marriage." Storm waved a disparaging hand. "Who needs it? I think it's an institution that's highly overrated." Her chin tilted belligerently and she taunted, "Why haven't you embraced the hallowed state of matrimony if it's so important? Can't you find a woman who measures up to your ideal of a wife?"

Wade caught the pain in Storm's voice and felt pain in his own heart. He had deeply hurt this young woman whom he loved more than life itself. If only she knew that a day never went by that he didn't think of her, that too much drink and too many women hadn't put a dent in his longing to see her, to hold her in his arms again.

His eyes soft, he leaned from the saddle and gently stroked a finger down Storm's cheek. "I guess I'm like Becky," he said. "Marriage isn't in the cards for me either."

Unaware of the pleading quality in her voice, in her blue eyes, Storm asked, "But why, Wade?"

Wade's answer was to swear softly under his breath, grab her by the shoulders and pull her toward him. As she blinked in surprise, his head came down and his lips clung to hers like a man who had thirsted for a long time.

Storm
NORAH HESS

LEISURE BOOKS **NEW YORK CITY**

To Dr. "Jay" Janardhan, my friend,
who helped me research Huntington's Chorea.

A LEISURE BOOK®

September 1994

Published by

Dorchester Publishing Co., Inc.
276 Fifth Avenue
New York, NY 10001

The name "Leisure Books" and the stylized "L" with design are trademarks of Dorchester Publishing Co., Inc.

Printed in the United States of America.

Prologue

"Here you are, Wade." The bald-headed postmaster finally slid a bundle across the worn
counter to the broad-shouldered, narrow-
hipped man who waited impatiently for his
mail. "It piled up pretty good in a week."

Wade Magallen pushed the sweat-stained
Stetson to the back of his head, ignoring the
question implied in the postmaster's tone as he
glanced down at the seven *Daily Argus* newspapers, out of Cheyenne, which were folded
around the other mail. He flipped through the
pile quickly; there were circulars advertising
beer and whiskey, a magazine about cattle, and
a few white envelopes bearing business names
in the left-hand corner.

"Thanks, Pete," he said, pulling his hat back in place and striding out of the post office, his spurs jangling as his heels came down on the scarred floorboards. He was in a hurry to get home, to dive into the Platte and scrub away a week's accumulation of sweat and grime. He had just returned from driving 200 head of cattle to Fort Reno, some 160 miles from Laramie.

He was stopped several times on the three-block walk to Laramie's only livery. Wade was a man's man, as well as a ladies'; his easygoing, reckless ways appealed to both sexes. That he was a bit wild was overlooked: He'd settle down once he got married and had a family, everyone said.

Wade slowed his pace when he came to the Longhorn saloon to glance in at his father, standing behind the long bar. Jake Magallen had owned the saloon as long as his son could remember. As usual, there were several men leaning against the bar, and a poker game was going on off to one side. But there was no tinny piano music here to offend the ears, and no whores propositioned the customers. A man could sit in peace in the Longhorn as he had a drink alone or relaxed in the company of friends, solving the problems of the world.

When Jake first opened the Longhorn he was told that he would never be able to make a go of it without light-skirts to entertain his male customers. But he had clung to his plan, and in the end the doubters had been proven wrong. From the beginning, when Laramie was only a town of tents with no streets to speak of—only well-trodden paths—the drinking place had been popular with the rough miners and cowhands who came to the males-only saloon. If any of the drinkers got the urge to while away his time with a whore for an hour or so, he had only to go a few feet to the large tent next door to find a willing partner.

As a general rule, Jake ran the place in the daytime, with Wade and a hired bartender taking over at night. There was also a fill-in man for those nights when Wade was away. His main interest, and the job that made him the happiest, was the partnership he had with his boyhood friend, Kane Roemer. Kane raised the cattle and Jake and his cowhands drove them to Fort Reno, where he sold them to an army agent out of Kansas City. He had just returned from such a trip.

His stallion, Renegade, whistled a greeting from his stall when Wade entered the livery. Wade never rode the handsome animal when he drove a herd of ornery longhorns. He would never risk the thoroughbred, who might get gored, or even killed, a sharp-tipped horn ripping through his belly. On a trail drive, and while working the cattle, Wade rode a fast little quarter horse, wise to cattle and aware of how to keep away from the deadly horns.

It took only a few minutes to throw a saddle on the black; then the two of them were galloping out of town, hitting the rutted road that would take Wade to the old log house on the Platte where he had been born.

Renegade needed no guiding; he well knew the way home, and Wade was free to dwell on what he was going to do tonight. Before the August evening was over he was going to propose marriage to the most beautiful girl in all of Wyoming Territory. He was finally relinquishing his bachelorhood and all that went with it. There would be no more carousing and woman chasing. He had had his fill of all that while waiting for this special girl to grow up. She'd had her eighteenth birthday last week.

Gray eyes flashed and white teeth gleamed in a darkly tanned face as Wade smiled in anticipation. The lovely Storm Roemer was all the woman he'd ever want.

When Renegade came to a halt in front of the barn Wade slid from the saddle and led the animal into his stall. Wade stripped the saddle off the horse's broad back after removing his mail from the saddlebag. When he had removed the bridle from the black's proud head he picked up the mail he had laid on the oat bin and walked toward the cabin. As he mounted the two steps to the wide porch, he wondered how long a time should elapse between an engagement and the marriage. Six months? A month? Possibly only a week? He grinned to himself. He had waited so long to possess the long-legged, blonde-headed Storm. Storm, named so by her parents because she had been born on the night of the worst storm the county had ever known.

The door slapped behind Wade as he entered the cool, dim interior of the log house. On the way to his bedroom, he tossed the papers and mail on a cluttered table next to a rawhide-covered couch. It spread out as it landed, and he paused to peer closely at a white envelope half hidden beneath a circular. He fished it free from the others and frowned. It was addressed to him.

Unease shot through him and he was gripped with a premonition that once he read the contents of the letter his life would change forever, that all his planning and daydreams would have been in vain.

His fingers shook slightly as he tore open the envelope and withdrew two sheets of paper. He looked first at the last page, his eyes dropping down to see the signature of the writer; then he groped for the chair behind him as he began to read the letter. His face grew ashen and his fingers tightened on the pages as his eyes flew over the words. Then, as though in a daze, he dropped the letter and rose to move across the room and stare out the window.

He stared without seeing at the Platte as it flowed past the cabin, didn't hear the meadowlark singing in the small pasture behind the barn. His stomach muscles knotted and his eyes squeezed shut as though he was in pain, and a delicate, lovely face swam before his eyes. With a deep groan he dropped his head on his folded arms, hoarse, dry sobs racking his body.

13

*   *   *

Wade stood in front of the window, thinking, until the setting sun threw a red glare on the river. He gathered up the sheets of paper and envelope then, and laid to rest all his wonderful plans for the future with his beautiful, golden girl. He was supposed to take her to a dance tonight, ask her to marry him. He would, instead, take another girl. Storm's pride would take care of the rest. He hoped she would leave the big ranch a few miles from Laramie, maybe go to Cheyenne and become the schoolteacher she had always wanted to be. He couldn't leave the area himself—Pa depended on him too much.

His steps shuffling like those of an old man, Wade walked into his bedroom.

Chapter One

Wyoming, 1878

The hot August sun beat down on the tall,
rangy man leaning against the weather-beaten
building housing the ticket office. A stranger
seeing him for the first time would never
guess by his garb—woolen trousers shoved
into worn, scuffed boots, a faded flannel shirt,
and a loosely knotted handkerchief—that he
owned a 1000-acre ranch. But the truth was
that Kane Roemer ran 3000 steers, and often
had as many as 15 men working for him.

As the handsome ranch owner waited for the
afternoon stagecoach from Cheyenne to pull
in, he let his gaze wander over the sprawl-
ing town of Laramie. It was an ugly place
in the daylight, he thought, his eyes moving

15

over miserable-looking shacks and sun-faded, false-fronted buildings, the sun striking lights off the empty whiskey bottles littering the street of ankle-deep dust. A man lay in front of a saloon, sleeping off the whiskey he had consumed, and he didn't move a muscle when two dogs came up and sniffed at his face, then gave a shake of their heads and trotted away. I guess the whiskey fumes were too much for them, the rancher thought in amusement.

He looked down to the end of the street, where the plains stretched away to the horizon, and wished he was back at his ranch where it was clean, and the land was still wild and beautiful.

Pulling a small white bag of tobacco and a thin slip of paper from his vest pocket, Kane Roemer deftly rolled a cigarette. Striking a match off the sole of his boot and holding the flame to the rolled smoke, he looked toward the other end of the street. The coach should be pulling in shortly. It seemed he had been standing here baking for over an hour, but he admitted, as thin spirals of smoke drifted from his nostrils, that he had ridden into town an hour early.

But his sister, Storm, his only living relative, would be on the rocking, bumping four-wheel monster, and he couldn't wait to see her step out of the big contraption.

Storm had been teaching school in Cheyenne for the past four years. In all that time she hadn't come back to the ranch once. It had been up to him to make the 50-mile trip to see her. And though she seemed content with her new way of life, she was always pitifully glad to see him. She asked dozens of questions about the ranch: How were Maria and old Jeb, and the cowboys? Was her mare, Beauty, being exercised every day?

He would pressure her to come home, to see the people she asked about, to take care of Beauty herself. And though deep in her blue eyes there was a sadness, she always insisted that she was happy where she was.

Each time she told her obvious lie, he wanted to shake her, make her tell him why she had left everything and everyone she loved to hide herself away in a crowded city that was alien to what she was used to.

Kane was brought back to the present when he heard the distant rumble of galloping hooves and the creaking of iron-rimmed wheels. Suddenly he wasn't alone anymore. When the swaying coach came into view at the far end of the deeply rutted street, the stores and saloons emptied out. Everyone wanted to see who would step out of the cumbersome vehicle, and then to take note of who would board it on its return trip to Cheyenne.

With the popping of a long black whip and loud swearing, the driver pulled the horses to a stop in front of the ticket office in a swirl of dust. He set the brakes, then jumped down from his high perch, a box in his hand. He placed the box just below the heavy coach door, and then swung it open. Laramie's leading banker stepped out, then lifted a hand to assist his female companion to the street.

As Kane stepped off the uneven boardwalk and hurried to sweep the slender blonde woman into a great bear hug, he heard snatches of comments from those behind him. "Why, I believe it's Storm Roemer"; "Ain't she a beauty"; "I wonder if she's home to stay."

A shining happiness was visible through the tears that glimmered in the eyes of the young woman who was causing so much excitement among the watching men. How good it felt to be back in familiar surroundings, to be with people she loved and who loved her in return. Her four years of self-enforced absence from all that was dear to her were over. For better or worse, she was home.

Their exuberant greeting over, brother and sister watched the driver toss three carpetbags, two leather-bound trunks, and six boxes to the ground.

"All yours?" Kane asked in some awe.

"All mine," Storm agreed, a twinkle in her eyes.

When Kane felt a steady pressure at his back he looked over his shoulder and shook his head, a smile twitching at the corners of his lips. Several men were pushing and jostling each other, trying to get a better look at Storm. He glanced down at her and wasn't surprised that his sister was oblivious to the flattering looks turned on her.

18

She had never been aware of her beauty, he remembered. This blindness of hers had caused him much concern when their father had given his permission for young men to come calling on her. At that time Kane had taken her aside and laid down some rules for her to follow. As he looked back, he realized that some of those rules had been a little ridiculous.

She was always to stay within sight of the ranch house if she went horseback riding with a young man, he had told her. And God help her if he should ever hear that she let some randy youth park his conveyance in a secluded spot away from prying eyes.

Storm had given him such an indignant look at that last rule, he had muttered that he really didn't think she would be so foolish.

Kane slapped a broad-brimmed hat on his head, covering hair as pale as his sister's, and walked over to the pile of luggage. He tossed a bag into the back of the lightweight wagon he had driven into town; when he bent to pick up another, many hands were there to help him.

"Well, thank you." He grinned and stepped back to let the others finish the job. He looked down on his sister's head and teased, "I see the men still stare at you, Storm. I'd hoped that by now you'd have grown warts on your nose or something like that. Anything that would keep the male population in the territory from tearing up the road to the ranch."

When Storm ignored him Kane feigned a regretful sigh. "From the way those yahoos are ogling you, I'm afraid the past four years have only put frosting on the cake. I can see that the peace and serenity of the old homestead will be a thing of the past."

Having had enough of Kane's foolishness, Storm jabbed a sharp elbow into her brother's side, causing him to grunt loudly. "You're getting your share of looks from those silly, gawking women, so just hush up. And I doubt very much that the *old homestead* will be overrun with panting men."

"We'll see," Kane said. Seeing that all Storm's bags had been stowed into the wagon by the smitten men, he put a hand on either side of her waist and boosted her onto the well-sprung wagon seat, her skirt ballooning up past her knees.

"Kane," she hissed, smoothing the dress down to her ankles, "watch what you're doing. I'm not a sack of grain to be tossed about."

"Sorry, Sis." Kane bit his tongue to keep from laughing at her red, flustered face. He turned to the men and repeated, "Thank you kindly, fellows." Then he climbed into the vehicle and picked up the reins. But the helpers hardly heard him through the blood pounding in their ears from the bright smile of thanks Storm had given them.

Kane snapped the lead reins on the team's fat rumps and they leaned into the traces. As the wagon began to roll, starting the ten-mile trip to the ranch, he picked up the subject they had been discussing.

"You could be right about the men not comin' to the ranch," he began. "Most of your old beaux are married now." He gave Storm a sidewise look and added, "Most of your friends are married too. I think you're the only one who hasn't married and started a family."

"Are you trying to tell me something, big brother?" Storm grinned at the sober-faced man who now looked straight ahead into the westward-moving sun that would set shortly after they arrived home. "Are you hankering to be an uncle?"

"You are twenty-two years old," Kane pointed out. "You should at least be plannin' on gettin' married."

"What about you?" Storm sent him an impatient look. "You're thirty-two yourself. According to your calculations, you should have been married ages ago. When are you going to take that walk down the church aisle? Aren't any of the local women good enough for you?"

Kane gave her a look that said she was talking nonsense. "Of course they are, but you know that most men don't get married until later in life. A man has to sow his wild oats, settle down, before he makes good husband material."

Storm hooted with laughter. "You men can think up more crazy reasons to hang on to your freedom. I wonder how you figure that a girl should get married almost as soon as she develops breasts."

When Storm only received a grunt in response she gave an exaggerated sigh and said,

"If it's so important to you, I promise I'll make you an uncle someday."

Kane sent her a mock frown and growled, "Marriage first."

"Oh, by all means," Storm answered with the same sham seriousness.

No more was said as Kane gave his attention to steering the team through a press of wagons, light carriages with well-dressed women, and men on horseback, all of them craning their necks at Storm.

As they weaved their way down the street, Storm scanned the faces they passed, looking for familiar ones. She saw none. Laramie had grown in her absence, bringing in many new people.

Once clear of town and rolling along the Old Oregon Trail, Storm broke the silence. "How are Maria and old Jeb? Anything new at the ranch?"

"Maria and Jeb are fine, I guess. Maria is a little heavier, and Jeb, the old coot, talks as much as ever. They're both anxious to see you. I've got five head of pure-bred Arabian mares and a stallion to breed them with."

Storm gave him a startled look. "Are you going to switch from raising cattle to raising horses?"

Kane shook his head. "It's going to be a little sideline for me. A man gets tired of lookin' at longhorns all day. There's no beauty in them."

"You always did like horses."

22

"From the time Dad sat me on top of one. But the big money is in cattle, and I could never afford to raise horses for a living. I'll be content just raising a few. Now, how about you? Are you content to be comin' home?"

"More than content, Kane." Storm turned a glowing face to him. "You can't imagine how happy I am."

A pleased smile curved Kane's lips. "I wasn't sure," he said as the wagon bumped along. "You always seemed happy, there in Cheyenne." A reproachful note crept into his voice as he added, "And you never came home for a visit. You always claimed to be so busy with your teachin', with your new life."

Storm stared ahead of her. She'd had her reasons for not visiting the ranch, reasons that only she knew. But she would not linger on that, she thought, and turned her head to Kane.

"I'm sorry about that, but I *was* very busy, what with teaching regular school during the year and then private tutoring for slower students during the summer."

She kicked off her soft slippers and propped her feet on the wagon's splashboard, then pulled her skirt up to her knees. Giving Kane a sly look that made him laugh, she added, "Not to mention all my men friends."

Kane squeezed her hand. "I'm glad you've been happy, Storm."

Oh, Kane, Storm thought bitterly, if only you knew how *unhappy* I've been. How homesick I was in the beginning, my first time away from home, missing you and the ranch. Worst of all was living with the pain that sent me away from you.

Her thoughts went back four years. Kane had gone with her to Cheyenne that August, and he had stayed to see her settled into three furnished rooms over a drugstore. The place was neat and clean and within walking distance of the school that had hired her through correspondence.

She recalled the morning Kane had prepared to step into the coach that would take him back to Laramie. As she bit her lip to keep from crying, he had pressed some money into her hand and, with an unnatural roughness in his voice, said, "There's enough there to see you through until the school starts paying you." He must have seen the glitter of tears in her eyes then, for he had smiled and teased, "That is, if you don't spend it all on boyfriends."

She had slipped a hand to his waist and pinched the flesh above his belt. He had yelped, "Ouch," and laughed before stepping into the waiting coach. When it pulled away she had felt more alone than ever before in her life.

Her loneliness had continued through the rest of the month as she acquainted herself with Cheyenne.

Then the days had grown shorter and cooler, and September had arrived. A week into the month, school had started. Storm had gradually made friends with the teachers, both male and female, but she discouraged her male acquaintances from courting her. It wasn't worth the guilt she always felt when she stopped letting them come around because they were showing signs of becoming too serious about her.

Looking back now, she was almost sorry she hadn't given one of those men a chance. They might have been quite sincere in their displays of affection. She might have learned to trust one, to return his feelings for her.

But at the time she couldn't have chanced opening herself to pain again. She had experienced the duplicity of man, his pretense, his deception, and it had taken years for her torn heart and mind to heal. And she intended that they would both remain healthy.

Yet I want children, Storm thought, *and a man is necessary to that end.* Could there be a man out there somewhere whose main interest in marriage is to have a family, a son; an ordinary man who might be a little dull, but one that she could depend on? Such a man she believed she could marry.

Storm looked unseeingly at the passing scenery, missing the white-tailed deer that bounded across the plain. She was thinking that she would have to give some serious thought to a marriage without love. Could respect be enough between a husband and a wife? she wondered. Was a heart-pounding, throbbing desire to make love necessary in a marriage? Surely there were many couples living in harmony who came together only to perform a duty.

Storm withheld a sigh. If she wanted a family, she would probably have to settle for mediocrity. Otherwise lonely years stretched ahead of her. Chances were she would never teach again.

During the past two years, she had pushed herself too much, had worked too hard with her students. Those hours spent with the children, both winter and summer, had caught up with her. She had lost weight, become irritable, continually felt tired.

Two weeks before, when summer school let out for the day, she had been called into her superior's office and gently told that she had all the symptoms of a nervous collapse about to happen.

"Storm," the kindly, middle-aged woman had said, "I want you to go home for a long rest. Enjoy that ranch of yours, take long rides on that mare you are always talking about. Do anything that will take your mind off teaching."

When she had tried to protest, to argue that there was nothing wrong with her, Mrs. Wilson had shaken her head and said firmly, "No, Storm. I have been involved in teaching children more than half my life, starting when I was sixteen. I know all the telltale signs." She stood up, signaling that the discussion was over. "Don't look so devastated, my dear," she said, walking to the door. "It's not the end of the world. You're a beautiful young woman. You should get married and have children of your own to teach. Otherwise you're going to end up an old maid like me."

Storm had gone back to her three rooms and cried off and on for two days. Then she finally accepted the inevitable and wrote to Kane. She had received a letter from him by return mail. All he had written was, "Come home, honey. Let me know when to meet the stagecoach."

She had fired back an equally short message. "Will be in on Thursday's coach." She had said good-bye to friends and packed her clothes and the pictures and knickknacks she had bought to add a personal touch to the rented rooms. Then there was nothing to do but wait for Thursday to arrive, and all the while she was filled with dread and eager anticipation.

Immersed in the past, Storm didn't realize immediately that Kane had turned the team onto a rutted secondary road that would, before long, lead them to the ranch house.

She dropped her feet to the floor and sat forward, her hands clasped in her lap. When the team topped a small rise Kane pulled the horses to a halt and smiled when she stood up. He was silent as she hungrily feasted her eyes on the sweep of the plains, the low valleys, the distant mountains, the longhorn cattle browsing between them and the Platte River. Wyoming Territory was still little more than a wilderness, inhabited mostly by unfriendly Indians. But oh, how she loved this big country.

In its vastness and solemn silence she felt her raw nerves begin to heal and a contented sigh feathered through her lips. She would be all right now. She dragged a deep breath of pine-scented air into her lungs and looked at Kane with tears shimmering in her eyes.

"I tried to fit in with my new friends, to involve myself in the doings around Cheyenne, but I always felt like a spectator, a stranger who stood to one side watching a very discontented young woman struggling blindly along. It is so good to be back where I belong."

"So I finally get the truth out of you," Kane said gruffly, realizing just how unhappy she had been. He wished he could get his hands on a certain man right this minute—the one he was sure had sent Storm running away from her home and family.

When Storm sat back down he clicked to the team and they started down the short incline. "The past four years are behind you, Storm," he said. "You're back where you belong. There isn't anything, or anyone, ever goin' to make you leave again."

Storm shot Kane a startled look but made no response to his surprising remark. She wondered if he suspected why she had left in the first place.

She decided on second thought that he couldn't know. She had always been careful that nobody except her best friend, Becky Hadler, knew about her hopeless love.

The road bent sharply, stretching through a glade of cottonwood, and Storm caught her breath. A hundred yards away stood the ranch house, just as she had left it, just as she had dreamed about it so often.

In the beginning the house had been a two-room affair, built by her father from stones he had hauled from the banks of the Platte. When time permitted, for he worked long, hard hours rounding up wild longhorn cattle, getting his ranch started, he had added a room off the kitchen and moved his and Mama's bed into it.

Then Kane had come along, and when Mama was expecting again two more rooms were built on top of the original two. That baby boy had died of pneumonia in his first winter. A miscarriage had followed three years later, and Kane had been ten years old when Storm was born and the room that had been empty for so long was at last put to use.

Pulling back on the reins, Kane brought the wagon to a halt in front of the wide porch that had been added when she was around five years old. Storm sat and gazed at the house as if she couldn't fill her eyes enough. She had always taken her home for granted, but it held a new significance for her now. She loved every stone, every board in it. She loved the Laramie foothills that sheltered it from the fierce winter winds. It was sturdy; it was dependable; it would never let her down.

The front door suddenly flew open and a short, plump woman in her late forties hurried across the porch, calling Storm's name. "Maria," Storm yelled back, scrambling out of the wagon. She threw herself into the wide-spread arms held out to her, exclaiming, "It's so good to see you!"

The years rolled backward and Storm was a teenager again, crying out her grief for her lost parents on those comforting breasts. Through the years Maria had been surrogate mother, friend, and confidante, sharing good times and bad and all her secrets . . . almost all of them, Storm amended, returning the housekeeper's fierce hug.

After a final squeeze Maria held Storm away from her, scanning her face. In a slightly accented voice she said, "It's time you came home. You've been gone too long."

"It's good to be home again, Maria." Storm's gaze went to the house again, then to the flower beds lining the porch. A remembered aroma wafted through the door and she sniffed appreciatively. "You're making my favorite meal, aren't you?" She grinned at Maria, her mouth watering.

"*Sí.*" Maria smiled widely, then frowned when a voice cracked with age called out to Storm.

Storm turned around, then with a glad cry ran to meet an old, bowlegged, white-haired man hurrying toward her.

Theirs was a silent greeting, only the fierce hug expressing their joy at seeing each other. Jeb pulled away first, as though embarrassed at the emotions working on his wrinkled face.

"You ain't lookin' too good, Stormie," he said after studying her face closely. "You're too thin, and them circles under your eyes make you look like a little hoot-owl. You been sick?"

"No; just a little tired lately. I'll be fine now that I'm home."

"You shouldn't have left in the first place." There was an angry tone in Jeb's voice. "Ain't nothin' nor nobody worth leavin' your family for."

How much did old Jeb know about her rush to Cheyenne? Storm wondered. Did he know her secret? She shook her head. He would have no way of knowing.

"Will you be having supper with us?" she asked when Kane called impatiently, wanting to know if she intended to jaw with that old coot the rest of the day.

"Can't tonight, Stormie," Jeb said, ignoring Kane's less than flattering description of him. "I been pesterin' Cookie for a month to make bread puddin'. Today, that mean son of a gun made it. If I'm not there to eat it, he'll never make it again."

"Well then, I'll see you tomorrow," Storm said, and walked back to where Maria waited for her on the porch.

Linking her arm with Storm's, Maria led her into the dim, cool family room, stopping at the foot of the stairs that led to the bedrooms above. "By the time you wash up and change your clothes, enchiladas, refried beans and a big salad from our own garden will be on the table."

31

Storm was almost at the top of the stairs when a loud snort made her look over her shoulder. Kane stood below, glaring up at her. With a heavy bag in each hand and a smaller one tucked under one arm, he griped, "You might help me with some of your luggage."

"But, Kane," she said, smiling helplessly at him, "you know how delicate I am."

"Hah!" Kane grunted. "You're about as delicate as a piece of rawhide, even if you do look like a gentle breeze would blow you away."

He followed a grinning Storm up the stairs and into her room. He dumped the bags in the middle of the floor and started to stomp back downstairs, and Storm's grin widened as she called after him, "My shoes are still in the wagon. Bring them along, too, will you?" She paid no attention to Kane's muttering as he went, but she could imagine what he was saying.

With a soft sigh, Storm looked around her old room, thinking that it was just as she had left it. She crossed the floor to stand at the window, looking up at the mountain. She stood there a minute, listening to a bird in the tall lodgepole pines. She had known both happiness and extreme anguish within these four walls. There were so many memories.

Turning from the window, she walked about the room, smoothing a hand over the bright patchwork quilt on the spindle bed, lightly touching the blue muslin curtains she and Maria had stitched shortly before she left for

Cheyenne. She trailed loving fingers over a pine dresser, a matching wardrobe, a rocking chair, and the small table beside her bed, all made by a local carpenter.

She opened the window to let the mountain breeze into the room, then sat down in the chair. With a push of her foot she set it to rocking. Closing her eyes, she soaked up the comfort of the room.

"What are you doin', sittin' there like the Queen of Sheba?" Kane asked, startling Storm as he thumped a trunk onto the floor. When she opened her eyes and gazed at him, he tossed her shoes at her feet and warned, "You'd better go wash up. Maria is about ready to put supper on the table."

"I'll be right down." Storm rose and picked up the smallest bag and placed it on the bed. As she undid the straps and took clean undergarments from it, then filled the hand-painted basin with water from a matching pitcher, she heard Maria come in.

"It's good to have her home again, huh, Kane?"

Her lips curled in a smile when Kane answered. "Yeah, but we mustn't let her know it. She'll walk all over us if she finds out."

"I heard that, Kane Roemer," she called out, then hurriedly began to wash up.

Maria had lit the kerosene lamp suspended over the table in the big kitchen, turning its wick up high so that a soft glow was spread

33

over the steaming Mexican dishes she had prepared especially for Storm.

As the spicy food was consumed with much gusto, Maria and Kane filled Storm in on happenings around the ranch and in Laramie during her absence. There were no radical changes on the ranch, but Laramie had experienced quite a growth. There was now a butcher shop, with Kane providing its beef, a bakery run by a German couple, and, of course, a new saloon.

"Just what Laramie needs." Storm laughed. "Another saloon."

"Ain't it the truth," Maria snorted, and began to gather up the dirty dishes.

Kane pushed away from the table, remarking with a devilish grin, "The new place has some good-lookin' women workin' in it, though."

Maria swatted him on the arm as he walked past her on his way outside. "You stay away from them good-lookin' women."

"Oh, I will, Maria, I will," Kane said just before he walked out the door. "You know I never go 'round wild women."

"Hah!" Maria grunted; then she handed Storm a dish towel and started washing the panful of dirty dishes and flatware.

With the two women working together everything was soon washed, dried, and put away. Storm was sweeping the floor, immersed in plans for the next day, when Maria spoke.

"I'm sorry, Maria," she said. "I'm afraid I was wool-gathering. What did you say?"

"I said that Becky Hadler has come back."

For a moment Storm was too stunned to speak. Then the words came pouring out as she put down the broom. "That makes my home-coming complete, Maria! How does she look? Has she changed? I can't wait to see her. We have so much to catch up on."

"Slow down, Storm, before you swallow your tongue," Maria cautioned with a half smile. "Becky looks pretty much the same as ever. Same curly black hair, same big brown eyes." After a pause Maria said, "She has changed, though. I noticed the last time I talked to her that the laughing, carefree girl you used to know is gone. I'm afraid life hasn't been too good to her."

Storm looked questioningly at Maria. "How do you mean, she's changed? Has something happened to her?"

Maria drew a deep breath and sat down at the table. "I guess you could say that," she said as Storm sat down across from her, a worried frown creasing her forehead. After a short pause she said bluntly, "Becky is now a high-priced whore."

Storm gaped at Maria, struck dumb. If she had been told that Becky had turned into a horse, she couldn't have been more incredulous.

Maria reached across the table and patted her hand when Storm continued to sit in silence. "Don't feel bad, Storm. Becky doesn't seem to."

Suddenly, words of denial spilled from Storm's mouth. "Who tells these lies about

Becky?" she demanded, on the verge of tears. "What old busybody started such an ugly rumor?"

"Look, honey," Maria said quietly, "I know you don't want to believe it. I didn't want to either, but I'm afraid it's true. I'll give you the facts and you can make up your own mind. All right?"

Storm nodded and Maria began. "Three months ago Becky got off the stagecoach one afternoon all dressed up fancy. She went across the street to the Plains Hotel and rented their most expensive room. The next day she rented a horse and buggy from the livery and rode out of town, and she didn't come back until near sunset. She did the same thing the next day and the day after that. Then the following day she went to the bank and drew out enough money to buy that old place out on the river road. You know the place; the one you kids used to make up ghost stories about, past the Magallen cabin."

Storm nodded again, and Maria continued. "Before Becky moved in she had the old place fixed up; a new roof, a new porch, and a coat of paint. As you can imagine, a lot of gossip began to circulate. How did Becky Hadler, a penniless orphan, come by so much money?

"It was noted then that every Friday afternoon Becky caught the coach to Cheyenne and didn't return until Sunday afternoon. And," Maria said on a long sigh, "it leaked out at the bank that every Monday morning

Becky deposited large sums of money into her savings account.

"But the rumor was really proved when Reverend Miles and his wife were visiting friends in Cheyenne. They saw Becky and a man go into one of the fancy hotels there. They didn't think much about it until the next day, when they happened to see her go into the same hotel. Only this time she was hanging on the arm of a different man. Both men were in their fifties and looked very well to do."

Maria gave Storm a sober, questioning look. "Does it all add up for you, Storm?"

Storm reluctantly nodded her head. The evidence against her childhood friend didn't look good. There was only one way Becky could make that kind of money, other than striking gold.

Still, she couldn't say it out loud. She got to her feet, said good night to Maria, and went upstairs to her room and to bed. But she was still wide awake when the mantel clock downstairs struck midnight. The big pine outside her window cast spiky shadows against the wall as she tried to come to terms with what she'd learned.

Chapter Two

Kane folded the newspaper he had received from Cheyenne the day before and laid it on the floor beside his chair. He had read with interest that steers were bringing the highest prices in history. It was time he set in motion a plan he'd had for some time.

He looked across the table at his sister. Amusement twitched at his lips as he watched her polishing off steak and eggs, along with a generous helping of fried potatoes and hot biscuits.

Storm had always had the appetite of a ranch hand, he remembered, rising to take the coffee-pot off the black range. He poured the fragrant brew into a mug with the word *Boss* painted on one side of it. The ranch hands had presented it to him shortly after his parents' deaths, and he treasured the simple gift. The act had told him that the men would give him the same respect and allegiance the older Roemers had received from them.

Placing the pot back on the stove, he sat back down. As he pulled the sugar bowl toward him, he asked, "What are your plans for the day, Storm? To get reacquainted with the ranch, I suppose."

Her face devoid of expression, Storm gave great attention to chewing a mouthful of food before answering. She knew better than to say what she had decided last night before falling asleep; she was going to visit Becky. It was an almost sure thing that he would forbid her to go, and then they would have a big argument.

It was only natural that Kane would feel that way, Storm supposed. And maybe he would be right in more than one way. Maybe the gulf between herself and Becky would be too wide to span. For all she knew, Becky might not want to renew their friendship. After all, six years had passed since they had seen each other, and no doubt both had changed some over the years. But the sisterly closeness they had shared since childhood wasn't to be ignored. Today she was going to learn just how Becky felt about a lot of things.

She opened her mouth to answer Kane but was spared from replying when the sound of thundering hooves pulled his attention away from her. He rose and walked to the kitchen window, which gave a view of the river road some 50 yards away. When he sat down a minute later his face wore a frown of disapproval.

"That idiot, Wade, is gonna break his neck one of these days, racin' his stallion like some wild Indian," he said. "He's been out carousin' all night, just gettin' in from . . ." Kane's face reddened at what he had almost said.

Storm raised her cup to her lips, and after taking a cautious sip of the steaming brew she said caustically, "So, the randy tomcat is still chasing women. You'd think by now he'd have found one who suited him. He's tried enough to know."

Kane frowned at his sister's frank talk, then remembered that she was no longer a teenager, but a woman grown. "I'm afraid so," he said, "although he's pretty much settled down to Josie Sales."

"I bet that makes ole Josie happy." Storm's lips curled. "She's been after him as long as I can remember. Maybe she'll finally get him into her bed legally."

Josie Sales, the same age as Kane and Wade Magallen, was the proprietress of a dress shop in Laramie, and lived in a room in the rear of the store. Storm had never liked the cat-faced woman.

Kane grinned at her remark and said, "No chance of that happenin'. Wade's only interested in . . ." Again he didn't finish his sentence.

"Has he ever been serious about any woman, ever loved one?" Storm asked after a while.

Kane stared into his cup for several seconds before saying quietly, "Yes, Wade did love once. I'm sure of it. I think it damn near killed him when things didn't work out the way he wanted them to. He hasn't been the same man since."

Storm gave her brother a startled look. This was news to her. "What happened between him and this woman?"

"I never knew." Kane gazed out the window, cradling his coffee cup in his hands. "Wade's not the sort you question about personal things."

Storm told herself that she didn't care how many women Wade Magallen had loved. Still, she asked a moment later, "Did this woman marry another man?"

"No, she never married. She left Laramie."

Storm set down her cup, picked up her spoon, and looked into the concave side of it, gazing at her upside-down face. "Do you think Wade still loves her?" She put the spoon down.

Kane shrugged. "I don't know. I hope so."

"Why do you say that?" There was a hint of shrillness in the question.

"I think they belong together. I hope more than anything in the world that they will get together someday."

There was a definite peevish note in Storm's voice when she asked, "Do I know this woman you speak of so highly?"

When Kane's face tightened she knew he was about to put an end to this particular conversation. When he said firmly, "No more questions,

Storm," she accepted the futility of pressing the matter.

Kane did, however, add a few more words concerning Wade. "I want your promise that you'll never speak to anyone of what I've just said to you."

"I would never do that, Kane Roemer." Storm scowled, wishing that he *hadn't* mentioned Wade's lost love. His words had caused a tightness in her chest that she hadn't felt in a long time.

"Sorry, Sis." Kane pushed himself away from the table. "I thought you might talk to Maria about it." As he stood up, he gave her shoulder an affectionate squeeze. "I'll see you at lunch."

He started to leave, then paused at the door. "If you should go riding today, stay away from the eastern range. Some of the men spotted a wild stallion and his harem grazing out there one day last week. That rogue wouldn't hesitate to go after your little mare."

Storm assured Kane that she wouldn't go near the wild horse's territory, and when the door closed behind him, she began clearing the table. The voices of Maria and her adolescent nephew, who did odd chores around the ranch, came from outside, and she hurried to carry the dishes to the sink and wipe the table. Maria would be full of chatter this morning, and Storm hoped to slip away from her.

She gathered her gown and robe up past her knees and took the stairs to the rooms above two at a time. In her bedroom she took clean underclothing from her dresser, then opened the double doors of the wardrobe and flipped through the clothes hanging there, clothes she hadn't worn since she was eighteen. She took down a divided riding skirt of dark blue twill and a white shirt. When she had put on the clothing she sat down in the rocker and tugged on a pair of scuffed boots.

After she pulled a brush through her shoulder-length, loosely curling hair, she slapped a black, broad-brimmed hat on her head and left the room, closing the door quietly behind her. She stood at the top of the stairs a moment, listening. Maria and her nephew were still talking in the front yard, Maria giving the boy his duties for the day. Good, she thought, and slipped down the stairs and hurried out the back door.

There was no one around the stables as Storm greeted the little mare she had missed so dreadfully. The trim little horse whinnied a greeting and nudged her soft muzzle against her mistress's shoulder. "I've missed you too." Storm kissed the wide space between the soft brown eyes.

She found her saddle—the one her parents had given her on her sixteenth birthday—on its usual peg. Running her palm over the handcrafted leather and finding it soft and pliable, she smiled, picturing old Jeb rubbing tallow into it, keeping it ready in case she came home someday.

With swift, sure motions, Storm soon had Beauty ready. Then she led her outside to be mounted. The mare danced about, eager for a run. Storm put her left foot into the stirrup and swung onto the mare's back. Settling herself comfortably, she touched her heels to the eager mare, and the little animal sprang into a full gallop.

As they flew past the house, headed for the river road, Storm caught a glimpse of Maria, still standing in the yard. Her hands were on her ample hips, and her face wore a fierce frown. Storm grimaced. She'd get an ear full from that quarter when she returned home. The housekeeper knew where she was going, and she heartily disapproved.

When Beauty's dainty hooves hit the river road it was as if the past four years had never been. To Storm it seemed only yesterday she had ridden along in the shade of the willows arching over the well-trodden road. Sometimes she had ridden alone, once in a while with Kane or Wade, but mostly she had ridden with Becky.

Had Becky changed so much? Storm wondered. Maria had said that she wasn't as she used to be. What if they found nothing to talk about? What if they no longer shared the same interests? Their reunion could be very awkward.

Storm Roemer and Becky Hadler had known each other almost from infancy, living as they had on neighboring ranches only a short distance apart. The Roemers and Hadlers had been close friends, visiting each other often. In their childhood the two girls had shared secrets and dreamed aloud their plans for the future. Becky, with her love of animals, would be a veterinarian, and Storm, loving children, would be a teacher, if ever a school was built in Laramie. They, like all the other ranch children, learned to read, write, and do simple sums from their mothers.

The carefree days slipped by, and then the girls were young women. As they swam the Platte or took horseback rides, their long, confidential talks were about boys. Both were popular with the opposite sex, but while dark-haired Becky allowed her young men a few liberties, Storm's were lucky to receive a short good-night kiss.

Storm had chosen her man a long time ago.

Life had been sweet for the girls until they turned sixteen. A spasm of pain stabbed Storm's chest as she remembered the turning point in her and Becky's lives.

One hot summer day, six years earlier, the two sets of parents had climbed into a boat and gone fishing on the Platte. A sudden storm had come up, with lightning flashing and thunder rolling. Before the men could row the boat ashore, a zigzagging streak struck the boat, electrocuting all four aboard.

A shudder ran through Storm as she remembered the funerals, the closed coffins buried side by side on top of a gentle hill situated between the two ranches. She and Becky had clung to Kane as the hard clods of dirt rattled on the coffins, shoveled there by friends. When they had sobbed until they were ill, Kane, bowed down with his own grief, led them away.

Everything had gone against Becky then. The mother and father from whom Becky had inherited her reckless, carefree ways had left their only child penniless and homeless. The bank in Laramie held a large mortgage on the Hadler ranch, which would have to be sold. Storm had felt a sense of guilt that Becky had nothing, while she could continue to live in her debt-free home with an older brother to watch over and care for her.

A week after the bank foreclosed on the Hadler ranch, both girls fell into a deep depression. Since no relatives had stepped forward to offer Becky a home it was automatically assumed she would live with Storm and Kane. Then the church had stepped in, declaring that it wasn't proper for a young girl to live in a home where the head of the household was a young bachelor.

Becky had been placed with a squatter family 20 miles away. Devastated at losing each other, the girls had corresponded at first, and Kane had taken Storm to visit Becky a couple of times.

Neither visit had been a happy one. It had broken Storm's heart to see her friend living in a four-room shack overrun with six children.

Becky had looked so miserable and unhappy that Storm had cried all the way home.

After that Becky had been shuffled from one home to another. The unhappy girl had ceased writing, and they had lost touch with each other.

Becky slipped from Storm's mind as the Magallen place appeared up ahead. Slowing Beauty to a walk, she swept her gaze over the large, sturdy log cabin. There was no sign of a tall, rangy man with black, black hair and slate-gray eyes. She wondered sourly if Wade was sleeping off the debauchery of the previous night.

With an unconscious sigh, Storm pressed Beauty into a canter and rode on, telling herself that one day soon she would pay a visit to the elder Magallen, Jake. Wade's kind and loving father had never done anything to hurt her.

Storm's heart began to thud when Beauty followed a bend in the road and a big farmhouse, its new paint gleaming beneath the sun, appeared some 20 yards off the road. She turned Beauty onto the gravel path that led to a hitching post beneath a large cottonwood. Would Becky be as nervous as she was? she wondered as she slipped out of the saddle and flipped the reins over the post.

She stood uncertainly a moment, taking in the peaceful surroundings of Becky's neat home. Only the distant sound of a meadowlark broke the silence. Her eyes ranged over the flower beds bordering the path to the wide porch. Geraniums, marigolds, larkspurs, and different shades of zinnias made a blaze of color against a freshly mowed lawn. The windows were so sparkling clean, the panes reflected parts of the yard like a mirror.

It certainly didn't look like the home of a fallen dove, Storm thought. She half expected to see a bunch of kids come bursting through the door any minute.

It wasn't until she had stepped up on the porch and rapped on the door that it occurred to Storm that Becky might still be sleeping. Then she smelled the aroma of coffee and decided that Becky must be up and about. "She must be around here someplace," Storm muttered to herself after knocking for the third time and getting no response. For one thing, the place didn't have that sense of sleeping, waiting for a human to stir it to life.

Maybe she was in the backyard. Storm stepped off the porch and walked alongside the house.

The only thing to greet her was more shorn grass, more flowers, a well-tended vegetable garden, a bird feeder and bath, an apple tree, and a large shed under a tall pine.

The door of the shed stood open, and the noise coming from inside it sounded like that of a small zoo. Storm approached cautiously, calling Becky's name as she stepped inside.

She stood peering into the gloom, which was broken only a little by the light from a good-sized window facing the east. Objects were beginning to take shape when she gave a startled gasp. Something soft and furry had wound around her leg. Then the mewling of a kitten brought an embarrassed smile to Storm's lips. She glanced around the room and saw a young doe with a bandage across its rump, and a nondescript bitch with four pups lying in a wicker basket. Four more kittens came and scampered around her feet, and she wasn't surprised when a black-and-white mother joined them.

Storm moved farther into the shed, then gave a smothered squeal when a young bobcat in a wire cage arched its back and hissed at her. "Oh, you poor thing," she murmured, seeing the splint on its left hind leg.

It became clear to Storm as she followed the sound of hungry peeping birds why Becky had chosen a place in the country instead of in town. Where else could she have such a menagerie?

The peeping led Storm behind a tall pile of hay. She stopped and gazed at the small, dark-haired woman sitting at a rickety table, patiently feeding a pair of baby meadowlarks. Love for her longtime friend rose up and threatened to choke her. She took a step forward, saying softly, "I see you haven't lost your love of animals, Becky."

The small head snapped up. Then, with a delighted squeal, Becky was off her stool and hurling herself across the small space that separated them. As they hugged each other, Becky's head not quite coming to Storm's chin, Storm thought crazily, she's not grown very much since I last saw her.

They released each other, and Becky cried, "Oh, but it's good to see you again!" They hugged again, Storm echoing the same words. When they broke apart once more Becky asked, "Are you home for good or just a visit?"

"I'm home to stay." Storm smiled through happy tears, thinking that Maria was mistaken about Becky being changed. Becky didn't look or act much different from the way she'd been during those happy days they had spent together. The brown eyes were still clear, still shining as though with eager anticipation of a new day and what it would bring. If her profession bothered her, it certainly didn't show on the outside.

"Home to stay. Don't the words have a nice ring to them?" Becky's voice wavered a bit, then strengthened as she added, "I'll bet Kane is as happy as he can be. When I ran into him in town a few weeks back he said glumly that you loved teaching and would probably never come back to the ranch to live."

She cocked a questioning eyebrow at Storm. "Are you tired of teaching, or did something else bring you back?"

It's not what you're thinking, Becky, Storm wanted to say, but she kept the words to herself. "I still love teaching," she said. "I just need a little rest from it."

Becky started to say something, changed her mind, and then turned back to the peeping birds. "Let me finish feeding these babies, then we'll go to the house and have some coffee and talk up a Wyoming storm."

Storm watched Becky pick up a short twig about the size of her little finger and dip it into a small bowl at her elbow. When she lifted it out a tiny piece of water-soaked bread clung to its tip. As Becky directed it to a wide, gaping mouth, she explained, "I found these two fellows abandoned out in the meadow back of the shed."

She dipped the stick back into the bowl and, lifting it to the second hungry mouth, added, "They keep me busy. Seems like they're hungry all the time."

Storm stared down at the hungry fledglings and made a face. God, they're ugly, she thought. Skinny, no feathers, eyes closed, and those awful-looking yellow rimmed . . . lips?

When Becky asked, "Aren't they beautiful?" all she could manage was a weak nod of her head.

"Where did you get the hound and the company over there in the corner?" Storm changed the subject, fearing Becky might offer to let her feed one of the birds.

"Those poor things." Becky pulled a cloth over the birds, whose hunger was sated for the time being. "I found them along the road a couple of weeks ago. Some heartless coyote had just dumped them out to starve to death." Her eyes sparked fire. "If I could get my hands on the person who did it, I think I might kill him."

Storm sympathized with her, then asked, "How did you get the bobcat and the doe?"

"Young Tommy Hayes brought them to me. His folks have a small farm a few miles from here, and he's always finding a bird or some animal that's been hurt." She chuckled. "I told him he could bring me anything but snakes. I can't stand the slithering things."

Becky stood up and took Storm's arm. "Let's go have that coffee and catch up on each other."

Becky held open the screen door and Storm walked into a spotlessly clean kitchen. The first thing that caught her eye was the table, with a red cloth spread over it, and the four chairs sitting beneath a window. A tall vase filled with flowers sat in the table's center. Matching red curtains were tied back to give a view of the backyard. A black stove sat against the opposite wall, a filled wood box next to it, and there was a dry sink with a small water pump. On the wall across from the window were three shelves, each beneath the other, and two tall cupboards. There wasn't a speck of dirt on the wooden floor; only a woven, multicolored rug lay before the sink.

"Go into the parlor and I'll bring the coffee in directly," Becky said. "It's probably still hot."

Storm nodded and went through the door near the shelves. She found this room equally neat and clean and very pretty. A settee flanked the fieldstone fireplace, a long, low table placed before it. A big, comfortable-looking chair and a rocker sat opposite the couch and table, a square pinewood table sitting between them.

Against the wall, behind this grouping, was a long, narrow table, a bowl of flowers on one end, a milk glass kerosene lamp on the other. A large expanse of the floor was covered with a rug braided from strips of cloth that matched the two small pillows on the couch. No doubt made by an Indian woman, Storm thought.

Over the mantel was stretched a bright Indian blanket, a backdrop for the clock that ticked quietly below it. There was a framed painting of Becky's parents hanging on one wall. A photograph of herself and Becky when they were children was hanging beside it.

Storm sat down on the couch and picked up a veterinary magazine from a plentiful supply spread on the low table. As she leafed through it, she wondered if Becky still dreamed of becoming a veterinarian someday.

"Well, how do you like it?" Becky entered the room carrying a wooden tray bearing a coffeepot, two mugs, a bowl of sugar, and a pitcher of cream.

"I love it, Becky. It's just like you, warm and lovely."

Becky's eyes glowed with pleasure as she placed the tray on the table. "Thank you, Storm. I've planned this room for a long time. If you could have seen some of the awful . . ." Her voice trailed off, but Storm had glimpsed some of the remembered suffering that flickered in Becky's eyes.

"The past years haven't been kind to you, have they, Becky?" she asked quietly as Becky poured a mug of coffee and handed it to her.

The dark-haired girl shook her head, her blue eyes clouding over. Then, in the blinking of an eye, Becky's lips tilted in their old way, and the sparkle returned to their depths. "Those days are behind me, Storm," she said firmly, "and I never look back."

She kicked off her shoes and, tucking her bare feet beneath her, she picked up her own coffee, grinned at Storm, and said, "Now, tell me all that's happened to you in the past six years. How did you like living in Cheyenne? How's your love life? Anybody special in it?"

Storm's tickled laughter rang out at the questions fired at her, then answered them in order of the way they were asked. Leaving out the reason she had fled to Cheyenne, she lied and said she had liked Cheyenne very much and that her love life at the present was nil; no, there was no special man in her life.

She sat beside the empty fireplace, surprised at just how dull and empty those years spent away from the ranch had been. She had covered the events of four years in less than ten minutes.

But at the end of Becky's story, Storm was thankful for those uneventful years. Her friend's past had nothing in it that appealed to her.

Calmly and matter-of-factly, Becky spoke of the many homes she had lived in after leaving the squatter family. Three had been in Cheyenne, where she had worked night and day, scrubbing floors, fetching and carrying.

Finally she had been placed with a couple living on a ranch. "They were still young, somewhere in their midthirties, and childless. The woman was sickly and spent most of her time in bed, complaining. Each had his own bedroom, and not once did I see Marcus enter his wife's room.

"I guess it was loneliness on both our parts that drew us together. He's a good-looking man, strong and virile, and before I knew what was happening, we were lovers." Becky took a sip of her coffee, then placed the cup back on the table. "Although I enjoyed making love with Marcus, I didn't love him. I wouldn't allow myself to do so because he had a wife—a wife he no longer loved, but one he couldn't leave.

"So when my eighteenth birthday arrived and I was allowed to go off on my own, I packed my few duds and Marcus reluctantly took me to Cheyenne." Becky's lips curved in a soft smile. "He stayed with me until I found a job waiting on tables in a hotel dining room and was settled in a small room in a boardinghouse. Before he left me he pressed some money in my hand and made me promise that if I couldn't make it on my own I would come back to the ranch.

"But I knew there was no future for me there and I was determined to make it on my own. But my pay was small, and the tips were scarce. My biggest ones came from the whores who wandered in once in a while. It was when they'd open their reticules and I'd see all the bills inside them that I began to get an idea. I had given my body to one man, so why not be paid for the use of it? I asked myself. A week later, my mind made up, I went to the fanciest pleasure house in town, and within an hour I was working at my new trade.

"I realized early on that the nameless men who visited my room weren't for me. I had to know and like the men who shared my bed for a short time. So I learned the names of those men who were kind, generous, and wealthy. After a couple of weeks I rented a small house at the outskirts of town and told five men, all of them in their fifties, where they could find me.

"I should have been happy then," Becky said, after a pause. "My gentlemen friends were very generous with the money they left on the bedside table, and before long I had more money in the bank than I had ever dreamed of.

"But all the time I was missing the place where I had enjoyed life the most. It nagged at my brain until one morning I woke up and knew that I was going home. I made arrangements to see the three men I liked most on the weekends and told the other two I had gone out of business. I withdrew my money from the bank and caught the coach to Laramie. I bought this house, and guess what else?" Becky's eyes sparkled.

"I can't imagine," Storm said weakly, stunned by Becky's story. "You've probably turned outlaw."

Becky's laughter rang out. "I wish I'd thought of doing that instead of entertaining men." Her demeanor turned serious. "Every afternoon I go to work with Doc Stevens, the veterinarian. He's teaching me how to doctor animals."

"Becky! That's wonderful!" Storm grabbed her small hands and squeezed them. "It's what you've always wanted to do."

"I know." Becky's eyes fairly jumped out of her head. "I can't believe it's finally happening. I—"

An old familar male voice spoke behind them. "I saw Beauty tied up outside and wondered if Kane had finally sold Storm's mare."

Chapter Three

For a moment everything around Storm became blurred. She had just heard the voice of the man who had driven her away from all that was dear to her four years earlier. As from a distance she heard Becky's cry of welcome.

"Wade, come on in. You'll never guess who's here. Someone you haven't seen for a while, I'll bet."

Storm still had enough wits about her to know that she couldn't continue to sit like a rock in the road. Taking a deep breath, she leaned around Becky and said, "Hello, Wade."

The man who had turned her life upside down four years before leaned lazily in the doorway. Then the laxness of his body stiffened as he stared at Storm, a mingling of shocked disbelief and absolute joy flashing in his pewter-colored eyes. But Storm, in her own dazed state, didn't see the latter. She saw only the impersonal politeness that had hurriedly replaced the momentarily jubilant expression.

Sharp-eyed Becky had caught the pulsing nerve in the strong jaw and knew how shaken the big man was as he moved into the room. She scooted away from Storm and, patting the space between them, invited, "Sit down, Wade, and have some coffee with us. We were just talking about old times. I bet you could add a lot to our memories."

Wade settled his lean body between them, and when Becky made as if to go for another mug, he shook his head at her. "Maybe you'd like something stronger then," Becky suggested. "A glass of whiskey?"

"God, no." Wade scowled, drawing up his leg and resting the ankle on the opposite knee. "So how have you been?" He looked at Storm coolly.

"Oh, just fine. And you?"

Storm had no idea what Wade answered. She had suddenly become aware of her indolent sprawl on the settee, her legs slightly spread, and Wade's gaze, fastened on the area below her waist. She felt an answering response to the raw desire that flared in his eyes and sat up straight, bringing her knees together. His face flushed slightly, Wade pulled his eyes back to her face.

"How long will you be visitin'?" He spoke huskily.

Before Storm could answer, Becky broke in excitedly. "She's not visiting; she's home to stay. Isn't that wonderful?"

Storm felt Wade's body stiffen and wondered why. When no reasonable answer came to mind she decided she had imagined the quickening of his muscles. After all, why should he be affected one way or the other by her permanent presence in the area? It never had before, she had finally realized.

Wade made no response to Becky's enthusiasm, only scorched a glance over Storm's breasts before saying with a sardonic twist of his lips, "Ol' Kane is gonna have his hands full, keeping the men away from you." His eyes narrowed on her face. "I bet you had a high old time in Cheyenne; all those men and no big brother to scare them off."

While Storm choked back hurt, shocked tears, Becky flew to her friend's defense. "What's gotten into you, Wade Magallen? You're not here a minute and you're picking on Storm."

Storm looked fully and clearly at Wade for the first time. He'd aged a lot, she thought, seeing the liberal sprinkling of gray in the sides of the black hair that needed cutting, the lines of hard living on his face. Which only made him more attractive, she added sourly to herself.

When she answered his mocking question she managed to keep her tone light and easy. "Of course there have been men in my life these past four years. After all, I am a healthy, normal woman."

Wade's face tightened and his lips hardened. "Big brother will soon curb those *normal, healthy* inclinations you've acquired." His eyes bored into Storm. "You'll be headin' back to Cheyenne in about a month."

All the fight suddenly went out of Storm. It was all she could do not to lay her head on her bent knees and cry. Wade's attack confused her; there was no reason for it. He acted as though she had somehow let him down, disappointed him.

She leaned her head back on the settee and said dully, "I see no point in discussing it. Let's wait and see if anyone's interested in me first."

"Oh, there'll be plenty interested in you," Wade said with a barking laugh. "The gravel will fly from the galloping hooves racing to the Roemer ranch house."

Storm looked helplessly at Becky, and her little friend jumped to her defense again. "Why don't you stop jawing at Storm, Wade. Your mood is so rotten today, I'm beginning to think Josie is slipping. Can't she keep up with you anymore?"

A dull red surged over Wade's face. "Damn you, Becky," he said furiously, darting a glance at Storm, "keep your opinion to yourself."

"For Pete's sake, Wade, why are you so riled up?" Becky demanded in sham innocence, her eyes flashing devilishly. "Storm has always known that you're an alley-prowling tomcat."

"I mean it, Becky!" Wade jumped to his feet. "Keep it up and I'll give that runty rear of yours a couple of good whacks."

Becky relented at Wade's obvious agitation. Giving him her most winning smile, she said, "I'm sorry, Wade. I was only teasing, you know. But you've been razing Storm pretty hard." She stood up too. "It's lunch time. I'll go make us some sandwiches."

"Oh dear, is it noon already?" Storm exclaimed, all three of them standing now. "I hadn't meant to stay so long. Kane probably has the men out hunting the range for me. He's concerned about a wild stallion that's been hanging around."

Wade moved toward the door, muttering that he had to get back to the river; he had some things to do. Becky followed them out onto the porch, and she and Storm watched Wade walk down the path to where he had tethered his black stallion a safe distance from Storm's little mare.

"Hey, Wade," Becky called after him, "why are you limping? Did you hurt your leg?"

His only answer was a dismissive wave of his hand.

Storm and Becky looked at each other and shrugged; then Becky asked, "When will I see you again?"

Storm hesitated a moment, then threw caution to the wind. "I plan on visiting Mama and Papa's graves one day next week. Do you want to come with me?"

"That sounds fine. I've been up there several times since I've been back. We can bring some flowers with us. When do you want to go?"

"What about next Tuesday, around two o'clock? I have to get settled in, visit with Kane and Maria."

Becky nodded. "I'll meet you there."

Giving Becky a quick hug, Storm hurried to swing into the saddle and send Beauty off at a canter. Kane might be worried, and for sure he wouldn't like it that she had visited Becky.

As Storm rounded a bend in the road, she saw Wade up ahead, waiting for her. Her heart gave a glad leap. Did he want to ride along with her, laugh and talk like they used to . . . before that afternoon when she had foolishly thought he felt more than friendship for her?

When she came up even with him he kicked the stallion into motion and rode alongside her. "Slow down to a walk," he grunted. "My head feels like it's goin' to roll off my shoulders."

"Good," Storm snapped, keeping Beauty at the same gait. "A man your age still carousing, I hope your head splits wide open."

"And what's wrong with my age?" Wade yelled, then he grabbed his head. "Storm," he groaned, "you never used to be so heartless."

"That's because I used to be a silly little girl," she retorted, but she pulled Beauty to a walk. "You grow up; you toughen up."

"You don't look so tough to me," Wade said, his eyes sliding over her. "You look all soft and silky. Just like . . ."

"I guess this is where you leave me," Storm interrupted him, reining in the mare where the well-trodden path to the Magallen cabin branched off. She had listened to his sweet talk once before, and the results had been disastrous.

Wade looked at her, a hint of a frown on his handsome face. "Storm," he said gravely, "you understand, don't you, that you and Becky can't go back to how it used to be between you."

Storm's eyes flashed defiance. "If you think I'm going to turn my back on Becky, you are badly mistaken. You don't know her whole story, what led her to the life she's leading now. She was only eighteen when she was put out on her own."

"She didn't have to be on her own. She knew she had friends back here. Kane and I would have helped her out gladly. We'd have seen to it that she learned how to become an animal doctor if she still wanted to be one."

"She has pride, you know. It's not her way to take charity from her friends. Anyway, she's learning how to become a veterinarian all on her own."

Surprise jumped into Wade's eyes. "I'm glad to hear that," he said after a pause, "but in the meantime she's ruined her reputation. If she stays around here, she'll never find a man who will marry her, give her children."

"Pooh on marriage." Storm waved a disparaging hand. "Who needs it? I think it's an institution that's highly overrated." Her chin tilted belligerently and she taunted him, "Why haven't you embraced the hallowed state of matrimony if it's so important? Can't you find a woman who measures up to your ideal of a wife?"

Wade caught the pain in Storm's voice and felt pain in his own heart. He had deeply hurt this young woman whom he loved more than life itself. If only she knew that a day never went by that he didn't think of her, that too much drink and too many women hadn't put a dent in his longing to see her, to hold her in his arms again.

His eyes soft, he leaned from the saddle and gently stroked a finger down Storm's cheek. "I guess I'm like Becky," he said. "Marriage isn't in the cards for me either."

Unaware of the pleading quality in her voice, in her blue eyes, Storm asked, "But why, Wade?"

Wade's answer was to swear softly under his breath, grab her by the shoulders, and pull her toward him. As she blinked in surprise, his head came down and his lips clung to hers like a man who had thirsted for a long time.

At first Storm was so stunned, her lips lay passive beneath Wade's. Then, as the pressure of his mouth increased, licking flames of passion swept through her and her own began to move under his.

Wade groaned and pulled her closer, bringing her almost out of the saddle. But when her arms came up around his shoulders he lifted his head abruptly and straightened away from her. Without a word he picked up the reins and, turning the stallion's head in the direction of his cabin, he rode away.

Storm sat a moment, staring after him; then she jabbed a heel into Beauty and the little mare sprang away. Self-scorning tears spilled down her cheeks. Why had she responded to him? she railed at herself. Didn't she have any pride? How many times was she going to let him make a fool of her?

Wade dismounted at the stables and walked past the cabin, moving toward the slowly flowing Platte. His hands shoved into the back pockets of his trousers, he gazed blindly at the river.

"God," he groaned, "why did she have to come back?" He closed his eyes, trying to shut out Storm's face. Wouldn't a person think that after so many years a man could get over his love and yearning for a woman, he asked himself, put her from his mind?

He sighed raggedly. It hadn't been that way in his case. Time hadn't even put a dent in the way he felt about Storm Roemer.

What was he going to do? He stared down into the water. Could he bear living in the same town as her, see other men courting her? He knew beyond a doubt that every single man in the county would come calling at the

Roemer ranch now. Storm had been a beautiful eighteen-year-old, but beautiful didn't half describe the woman into whom she had grown. She made a man melt just to look at her.

His broad shoulders drooped. Somehow he'd have to live with seeing her with other men. He couldn't go off and leave Pa . . . not until he had to. He moved a hand from his pocket and massaged his right thigh. More and more it bothered him.

Chapter Four

Kane placed his knife and fork beside his empty plate, which had, a short time ago, held a steak, a baked potato, and string beans from the Roemer garden. He stood up, and as he passed his sister, sitting across the table from him, he lightly squeezed her shoulder.

"I'll be comin' home late tonight," he said, "so don't wait up for me."

Storm patted his hand affectionately. "Then I'll say good night now."

When the kitchen door closed behind her brother Storm hungrily attacked her steak, which was growing cold. She had barely touched her supper as she waited nervously for Kane to bring up the subject of how she had spent her day.

But to her relief he hadn't thought to ask

her, and he hadn't been home for lunch, when her whereabouts might have crossed his mind. Had he asked, however, she had made up her mind that she would tell him the truth, even though she would have had to listen to much the same thing Wade had said. The only difference would have been that Kane would have ordered her not to go out to the little white house on the river road again. And then they would have had words. In the past she had almost always obeyed Kane's dicta, trusting his judgment. But in the case of Becky, she would do what her conscience directed. Seeing her old friend today, laughing and talking about the good times they'd had growing up, had acted as a tonic to her, and she was willing to face any censure from man or woman to spend time with Becky again.

Storm's lips twisted wryly as she swallowed the last of the meat and vegetables. Although she had been lucky with Kane, that hadn't been the case with Maria. The housekeeper had started in on her the moment she walked into the kitchen and sat down at the table.

"Storm," she'd said sternly, slapping a bowl of soup in front of her, "I know you've been out on the river road visiting Becky this morning." When Storm would have interrupted her Maria held up a silencing hand. "I also know how close the two of you were before you lost touch with one another. But Becky has chosen a way of life that makes it impossible for the two of you to go back to the way it used to be.

You can no longer socialize with Becky."

"Maria, how can you say that?" Storm had protested angrily. "I can understand that Kane might think that way, but you always loved Becky, felt sorry for what happened to her after her parents died."

"Storm, I still love Becky, and at my age I can visit her, talk to her if I run into her in town. But you're young. If you should be seen in her company, you know how people would talk. The story would spread that you were no better than Becky."

Storm knew that Maria was right. There was always someone ready to start a rumor, to sling mud. She hadn't responded to Maria's words, but her lips had firmed in a determined line. She wasn't going to give up her friendship with Becky. A few people might believe the gossip, but those who knew and liked Storm Roemer would know that it wasn't true.

Storm sat on at the table, unrelated subjects jumping about in her mind: students she had taught, friends in Cheyenne, a beloved dog that had been trampled to death in a stampede when she was eight years old.

When the kitchen became shadowed she rose, lit the lamp that sat in the middle of the table, and began gathering up the dirty dishes. She grinned ruefully as she carried them to the dry sink. It had been almost as if the past four years hadn't existed when Maria told her just before supper that the beds needed changing tomorrow, and that there was a basket of clothing waiting to be ironed.

Dusk had turned into night by the time Storm had washed and dried the dishes and swept the kitchen floor. She walked into the big sitting room and lit two more lamps, thinking that it was going to be a long, lonely night for her. Maria was visiting her sister in Laramie, and no doubt Kane would be coming home long after she had gone to bed. She had the feeling that his trip into town had been to see a woman. She wondered if her brother finally had settled down to one woman. There had been a time when his reputation with the ladies had been almost as bad as Wade's.

The large, comfortable room had always been the gathering place for the Roemers, where happenings of the day were discussed and plans for the future were made. Storm was gripped with nostalgia as she moved about, running a hand across the top of the leather chair her father had always favored, doing the same thing to the rocking chair her mother had always taken.

She stood a moment in front of the fireplace, looking up at the trophies on the mantel, trophies her father and Kane had won for riding broncs and rifle-shooting. They were both experts at shooting and riding. She, too, was handy with firearms, as had been her mother. Her father had thought it necessary that they both learn to handle a gun and rifle, and to be able to hit what they aimed at. A week hadn't gone by that some man riding the grub line stopped by, looking for a meal. Some of them hadn't been all that honorable and would have been quick to take advantage of unprotected women. There was also an occasional renegade Indian skulking about, ready to make off with anything he could get his hands on, especially horses.

The room was warm, still holding the heat of the day, and Storm stepped out onto the porch, hoping to catch a cool breeze off the Platte. She sat down in a weathered rocking chair and leaned back her head, remembering the many tears she had shed over Wade Magallen here in the darkness, where no one could see.

Her idolization of Wade had started at a very young age, lasting up until the day she had left the ranch and gone to Cheyenne. Only Becky had known her secret, had known that the many callow youths who chased her were compared to Wade and found wanting.

Wade had become even more handsome as he matured. He had a magnetism about him that had the unmarried women in the area chasing him shamelessly. It had hurt Storm dreadfully to hear people laugh and say that Wade Magallen seldom turned down what was offered to him. He was a young man, it was said, who didn't have to go to the whorehouse next door to his father's saloon and pay for his pleasurin'; he got more free stuff than he could handle.

What hurt almost as much was that Wade more or less ignored her. It was almost insulting, the way he avoided her.

Storm

Then, right after her eighteenth birthday, Storm had glimpsed heaven. One hot summer day she had saddled Beauty—the mare had been a birthday present from Kane—and had headed out across the plains, headed for the shady river trail. She had been riding for about ten minutes when she spotted Wade on his big black stallion, some distance ahead of her. She had called his name and lifted the little mount into a gallop, coming up alongside him. She had given him an uncertain smile, and was happy beyond belief when he returned it. It had been years since he had smiled at her like that. "Do you think that little mare of yours can beat my stallion in a race?" he had teased.

They both knew Beauty couldn't beat Renegade—the big black horse was the fastest in the county—but they lined up the mounts, and when Wade shouted, "Go," the earth had trembled with thudding hooves.

She had lost the race, of course, but when Wade had helped her to dismount, dusty and sweaty, she had smiled up at him, declaring that someday she would outrun his stallion.

The flow of the Platte, only a few yards away, had beckoned with its murmuring, reminding them how cool the water was. "Let's take a dip," Wade had said, "get some of the grime and sweat off us."

Storm agreed readily, having gone swimming in the river with Wade and Kane countless times. Of course, she hadn't been allowed to swim with them after she turned twelve, a fact she couldn't understand until Mama had pointed out that her budding breasts could be seen clearly through the thin material of her undershirt.

But, Storm had reminded herself, she wore a camisole now, which should reveal very little. So, without further thought, she had scrambled out of her riding skirt and shrugged out of her shirt. She stood poised on the riverbank, ready to dive into the cool, flowing water, when a raspy, indrawn breath turned her head around.

Wade stood staring at her, his eyes heavy with desire as they moved over her breasts and hips. She drew in a shuddering breath, and Wade responded with glittering eyes and reaching arms. She was hauled into them and crushed against his chest, the hardness of his arousal grinding against her stomach as his head swept down, his lips taking hers.

The kiss was tender at first, as though he was afraid of frightening her. But as she eagerly responded, her lips clinging to his, it grew hard, demanding. When his tongue probed her mouth she moaned and slid her arms around his neck.

The kiss had continued, Wade's hands moving restlessly on Storm's back, sliding down to her waist, molding it for a moment, then moving up to her rib cage, his fingers hesitating just under her breasts, then sliding back down to her waist.

Storm

She was staring up at him with dazed eyes when he put her away from him. Her fingers clenched on his hard forearms in response to the burning need inside her, she had asked huskily, "What's wrong, Wade? Don't you like kissing me?"

"I like it too much," he'd answered.

Now Storm jerked impatiently to her feet. "Stop living in the past," she muttered fiercely. "All that happened a long time ago and should be forgotten by now." She walked into the house.

She had started upstairs to her bedroom when she heard galloping hooves coming up the gravel road. Why was Kane coming home so early? she wondered. Had he argued with the woman he had ridden into town to visit?

Her eyes twinkled mischievously as the horse swung by the house, headed for the barn. She would stay up a little longer to bait her tall, handsome brother a bit.

She curled up in the corner of the sofa, and a few minutes later the kitchen door opened and Kane walked into the room, stepping quietly so as not to awaken the household. He had gone to the sideboard and poured himself a glass of whiskey before he spotted his sister, grinning at him like a Cheshire cat.

"Well, big brother," she teased, "since you're home so early, I take it you didn't have much luck with your lady tonight."

"When did you start thinking such things about me, missy?" Kane gave her hair a tug

75

as he sat down beside her.

"Oh, I don't know." Storm grinned at him. "When I was around fourteen, I guess. I just got around to saying it tonight."

"So, all these years that innocent-looking face has been hiding unwholesome thoughts?"

"Well, it wouldn't take a very smart person to come to the conclusion that you didn't get all dressed up just to ride into town."

"Just like a woman," Kane grumbled, "always condemning a man without a particle of truth. I didn't get all dressed up, as you put it; I only changed into clean clothes and shaved. I had no intention of seeing a woman; I went to the Stag to talk to Wade."

Uneasiness gripped Storm. Had Wade mentioned seeing her at Becky's house? She realized in the next breath that he hadn't. Kane would have faced her with it the moment he saw her.

With a sigh of relief, she asked, "How is the big oaf?"

Kane shrugged, frowning a little. "All right, I guess. He was drinkin' a little more than usual; seemed to have somethin' on his mind. I don't think he heard half of what I said to him."

He tossed the whiskey down his throat and placed the empty glass on the table at his elbow. "He said he'd be over one of these days to welcome you home. Don't hold your breath, though. He probably won't give it another thought for weeks."

Storm didn't doubt that for a moment. "He's not likely to give much thought to a female he watched grow up," she said finally.

Kane didn't agree or disagree. He said instead, "Me and Wade are hittin' the trail in a week or so. I've been talkin' to a farmer who's breeding shorthorn cattle, and I hope to buy some."

"For heaven's sake, why? You're already running over a thousand head of cattle."

"Yeah, longhorns, with their tough, stringy meat. Shorthorns are broad-chested brutes with much more meat on them than the longhorns, and way more tender. If they can take our Wyoming winters, I intend to gradually get rid of my present wild, ornery steers."

"How long will you be gone?"

"Probably a couple of weeks, if everything goes well."

"I'm surprised Wade can drag himself away from Josie for so long a time," Storm sneered.

"Oh, her." Kane waved a dismissive hand. "I'm sure he'll find other women along the way. He'll know that she'll be waitin' for him when he gets back."

"That egotistical wolf really riles me." Storm gritted her teeth. "He really thinks he's something. I hope he gets his someday."

"I don't know, Sis," Kane said cheerfully, "he can have most any woman around here."

"There's one he can't have," Storm retorted with a snap of her teeth.

"Only because the damn fool is afraid to ask, for some reason," Kane said to himself.

A silence grew between them, and Kane was about ready to go to bed when Storm spoke.

"I've been thinking: I'm going on the trail with you."

"Like hell you are!" Kane sent her a glowering, no-nonsense look. "I'll have no time to look after you, especially on the way back when we're trailin' a bunch of cattle."

"What are you talking about?" Storm swung her feet to the floor. "I won't need looking after. I'm no greenhorn. I can ride as well as you can, and can almost shoot as well as you too.

"Please, Kane," she said, changing her tactic to pleading, "it's been so long since I've camped out, slept under the stars. You know how I love doing that. You've let me go on cattle drives before."

"Yes, but only on short drives to Fort Reno. This is gonna be a long haul. You'd get bored and then start whinin'."

"I would not, Kane Roemer." Storm's eyes flashed with the insult. "You've never heard me whine about anything in your life." Tears glimmered in her eyes. "You just don't want me along. You're afraid I might be a bother to you. Maybe you'll want to visit some women with Wade."

"Now, Storm, that's not true," Kane denied hurriedly, affected as usual by her tears. Ever since she was a little girl he had turned to mush when she cried. With an angry jerk of his shoulders at his weakness, he grouched, "If it means that much to you, I reckon you can come along."

Storm's tears ceased. She had learned a long time ago what her tears did to her brother. "Thank you, Kane." She knuckled her wet eyes. "After being cooped up in crowded, dirty Cheyenne for so long two weeks out in the fresh air and sunshine will be like heaven to me."

Kane didn't think to say that she could get all the fresh air and sunshine she wanted simply by riding the range at home. He was too thankful to see her smiling again.

He wondered what Wade would have to say about her coming with them as they yawned their way to bed.

Wade had plenty to say when he learned that Storm was accompanying them the night before they were to leave. Two weeks of Storm's almost constant presence would drive him crazy. It would be next to impossible for him to keep his hands off her.

"It's out of the question," he railed at Kane. "You said yourself that she's been sick. She won't be able to keep up with us on the trail. And what about the cowhands moonin' over her? There'll be fights breakin' out all the time."

"I'm sure we can keep the men in line," Kane pacified, "and it's not that Storm was physically sick; she was just worn out from teachin'. Bein' outdoors for such a long stretch will be good for her."

Wry humor twisted his lips as Kane added, "Do you want to tell her that she can't go?"

"I'd rather tell a wolf to roll over and play dead," Wade growled as he stamped away, his broad shoulders stiff.

Chapter Five

Dawn was just breaking when Storm stepped out onto the back porch, a cup of coffee in one hand, her packed saddlebag in the other. She laid the bag at her feet on the floor, then leaned against a supporting pole, sipping at the hot liquid. As she breathed in the freshness of the morning air the light went out in the bunkhouse and a half dozen cowhands spilled through the door.

Kane was already down at the corral adjacent to the barn, talking to old Jeb, and down on the river road she could make out the shape of a horse and rider galloping toward the house. Wade.

She breathed an unhappy sigh. Wade didn't want her to make the trip with them. He hadn't said so to her face, but she had overheard remarks he had made to Kane.

"Them cowpunchers aren't goin' to be worth spit," he'd said, "hangin' 'round her all the time, neglectin' their duties." . . . "She's gonna be whinin' and complainin' before we're half-way there." . . . "Some of the men won't like havin' to be careful not to cuss around her." . . . "What if they want to pick up a woman along the way?" . . . "And why does she want old Jeb to come along, jawin' night and day?"

Kane had mostly let him gripe away, answering with grunts and monosyllables. Both knew that despite all the reasons why she shouldn't go, Storm would be going with them.

When she had ridden over to Becky's to postpone their visit to their parents' graves her friend had laughed at Wade's arguments against her going on the drive.

"He just doesn't trust himself to be around you," she had said. "He wants you in the worst way, Storm, but he knows that to sleep in your bed he'd have to marry you first. I've been thinking that maybe he's marriage shy because his mother went off and left his dad."

Storm remembered what Kane had said about Wade being in love once. He had been ready to chance marriage then.

She shook her head. "You're wrong, Becky. He has no interest in me other than as Kane's sister."

Storm pulled her attention back to Wade as he rode past the house, looking straight ahead, as though he didn't see her standing in plain view on the porch. She watched him ride up to the corral, where the horses were plunging, huddling, dodging the loops tossed at their heads.

In the whirling dust kicked up by the trampling hooves the six cowboys trying to lasso mounts were barely discernible. Finally, each had roped himself an animal and saddled it. The remaing fifteen head would be brought along, too, as extra changes for the cowboys.

Storm's gaze ranged over these six men, taking in their garb. Each wore high-topped, high-heel boots, chaps, a broad-brimmed hat, and a big neckerchief tied around his throat. Their shirts and pants were wool, which absorbed body heat, making them more comfortable than cotton.

Once they'd acquired the herd, two of the cowboys would be "swing riders," their duty being to keep the cattle moving in the semblance of a line. Another couple would be "tail riders," who rode at the end of the line, keeping stragglers from dropping too far behind and protecting the rear from attack by Indians and rustlers. These two men were the best shots in the group. The other two riders, along with Kane and Wade, would ride along the sides, keeping the cattle bunched.

"And according to Wade," Storm muttered, "Jeb and I will just get in the way."

The sun, now peeking over the eastern rim, brought full daylight. As the men rode out, the grub wagon and extra horses following behind them, Storm placed her empty cup on the porch railing. She picked up her saddlebag and walked down to the corral, where Jeb had Beauty saddled and waiting for her.

"That long-legged Magallen has got somethin' stuck in his craw this mornin'," Jeb said as he boosted Storm into the saddle. "Ain't been a decent word come out of his mouth since he got here. I said to him, 'A fine mornin', ain't it, Wade?' You think he answered me? No, by damn. Just gave me a go-to-hell look and started gripin' at one of the men about somethin'. Kane, he just ducked his head and grinned, real tickled-like. I guess he knows what's botherin' the long drink of water."

"Don't pay any attention to the ornery coyote," Storm said, settling herself in the saddle and picking up the reins. "He's probably got a headache from drinking too much red-eye last night."

"I wouldn't doubt it for a dad-blamed minute," Jeb muttered as he climbed onto his own mount. "He sure is partial to the grain."

They nudged their mounts and cantered up to where Kane and Wade were leading. "Mornin', Sis." Kane gave Storm an affectionate smile. "You're lookin' all peppy and full of vinegar."

"Thank you, Kane. I'm feeling real good. And how are you this morning, Wade?" She looked across Kane to the stony-faced man whose back was ramrod straight.

He mumbled an inaudible answer and Storm gave him an impish grin.

"What's that you say, Josie had a headache last night and sent you home?"

When Wade made no response, only looked straight ahead, an angry tic in his cheek, Storm said to Kane, "You'd better have a talk with ol' Josie, warn her that she'd better bring her stuff up to snuff or she's going to lose her man."

"You think so?" Kane said, his twinkling eyes betraying the seriousness in his voice. "But what if she's really worn out? After all, she's thirty-two years old and has been Wade's . . . er . . . friend since she was around thirteen."

"And don't forget all the other men she's been friends with," Storm added, then gave a long, exaggerated sigh. "Poor ol' thing, she probably does have a lot of headaches these days."

"You reckon?"

"I reckon."

"I reckon you're both full of it," Wade growled and, jabbing a heel into the stallion, he galloped off, Storm's pealing laughter and Jeb's loud guffaw following him.

Every muscle in Storm's body was tight and sore when they made night camp just before sundown. It had been a long time since she'd spent an entire day in the saddle. Since starting out this morning they had stopped only once, while Cookie set out a cold lunch. It was all she could do not to limp as she and Jeb led their mounts to a lesser branch of the Platte to quench their thirst. She sensed that Wade was watching her, looking for just such a sign that the trip was too much for her.

As the horses snuffled the water, Jeb said, "Go over there in the bushes and do whatever you have to. I'll keep watch."

Storm grinned as she walked away, knowing that the old man would do whatever he had to do in her absence. By the time they led the horses back to camp, unsaddled them, wiped them down with handfuls of grass, and then hobbled them nearby, Cookie was calling out, "Come and get it."

As the first supper was eaten on the trek, Storm managed to smile brightly and answer that she was just fine when Kane asked about her welfare. She gave strict attention to her tin plate of stew and skillet-fried bread, pretending not to see the sardonic look on Wade's face at her answer. He knew how her muscles throbbed, that her legs and back were one big pain.

And damn him, he's glad, she thought. *It's probably griping him no end that he was wrong in claiming that the cowboys would fight over me.* But other than long, lingering looks, no one had approached or spoken a word to her. And not once had she complained or whined.

As for Jeb, Wade had been right about his jawing. The old fellow did talk all the time, but everyone was used to his running off at the mouth and paid him no attention. Just now, for instance, he was telling a long-winded story about Indian battles while no one listened. The men were all busy talking to each other.

But she loved the old white-haired man, who had worked at the ranch since she could remember. It was he who had taught her to ride, to sit straight in the saddle, that she was never to abuse a mount, to always take proper care of it, that the animal was a friend.

It was also from him that she had learned to swear, shocking her mother but amusing her father.

The evening meal was over and everyone sat around the campfire sipping coffee, the men smoking hand-rolled cigarettes. When Cookie finished clearing away the supper dishes and stowing them in the covered wagon he brought out a harmonica and put it to his lips. The strains of "My Old Kentucky Home" wafted on the night air, lonesome though comforting.

But when a wolf bayed at the moon, Cookie laughed and blew a more rollicking tune. As "Camptown Races" rang out, the youngest cowboy in the group rose and approached Storm.

"Care to dance, Miss Storm?" he asked shyly.

Storm was about to refuse. Her legs hurt so, she didn't think they could take very much hopping and jumping around. Then she saw Wade's eagle eyes watching her, and she knew she would accept the invitation if it killed her.

And kill her it nearly did. She found that after she had finished the dance with the kid the other cowhands were lined up for their own turn. She was ready to drop, to let Wade have his laugh, when Kane took pity on her after she had danced with the third man.

"Time to hit the blankets, men," he said as he stood and picked up his bedroll.

Storm's tortured leg muscles were screaming with pain as she made her way to the small tent Jeb had set up while she was being whirled around in the arms of an enthusiastic cowboy. She removed her boots, then her shirt and riding skirt, and stretched out on the bedroll. She was sure sleep would elude her. How could she sleep when she hurt so?

"Are you all settled in, Sis?" Kane asked from outside.

"Yes, Kane, I'm fine," Storm lied.

"I'll see you in the mornin' then."

It grew quiet after everyone had sought their bedrolls, only an occasional yowl coming from a wolf and Cookie's snoring breaking the night silence. Storm had turned and twisted several times, trying to find a comfortable position, when her tent flap was lifted.

"Stormie," Jeb whispered, "sit up and pull your undershirt off your back. I brought you some liniment to rub on your sore muscles. It works real good on them."

Storm pulled up her camisole and held it at her shoulders. Kneeling behind her, Jeb moved his callused, gnarled fingers over her back with the gentleness of a mother, kneading the liniment into her flesh. She felt the muscles beginning to relax, the pain easing away.

"You can take care of your legs yourself," he whispered after a while, tugging her camisole back down over her back.

"Thank you, Jeb," she whispered and kissed his wrinkled cheek.

Storm hadn't been the only one still awake in camp. Wade, too, was still staring up at the starlit sky when Jeb crawled into Storm's tent. The low-burning campfire flashed on the bottle in his hand, and Wade grinned. Where Storm was concerned the old fellow was like a mother hen with one chick.

He envied Jeb's right to enter Storm's tent in the middle of the night, to touch her bare skin. It didn't mean a thing to the old man, whereas it would be heaven for him to do the same thing.

He laid an arm across his eyes. He was treating Storm shamefully, but he had to keep her angry at him, make her keep her distance. He wouldn't be responsible for his actions if she came too close.

He sighed. It was going to be a long trip, and a hard one. The hardest he had ever taken.

Storm soon adjusted to the hard life of the cowboys.

By five o'clock each morning the men were roused out of bed by the cook beating on a pot with a long-handled spoon. In the early grayness of a new day they rolled up their blankets, tossed them into the chuckwagon, and saddled their mounts. They stood around the fire then, drinking strong coffee as they waited for breakfast to be ready. By the time they hit the trail again the rising sun was clearing away the mists hanging in low spots.

On the sixth day out they topped a grassy, rolling hill and looked down on a large farm. Kane's eyes went immediately to an adjacent field, where hundreds of shorthorn cattle browsed.

"This is it." His eyes sparkled as Storm drew rein beside him. "Keep your fingers crossed that I can strike a deal with Sam Benson." He turned to Jeb and said, "Tell the others to wait here while I talk to the farmer. I'll find out where we can camp and where to put the horses."

Storm rode with Kane and Wade down to the large farmhouse. She and Wade remained mounted while Kane slid to the ground, then knocked on the front door.

It opened, and a pretty young girl of about eighteen smiled at Kane as she greeted him.

Storm glanced at Wade to see his reaction to the shapely female and wanted to put her fist between his ogling eyes. When he whispered, "Whew, look at those curves," she wanted to smash him in the mouth. There was no doubt in her mind that before they departed the farm he would be inviting the girl to take evening walks with him. If the farmer was wise, he'd lock his daughter up for the duration of their stay.

She saw the girl nod, then call over her shoulder, "Here's that man you've been waiting for, Pa."

Storm

A portly, genial-faced man in bib overalls stepped out onto the porch. "Glad to meet you, Mr. Roemer." He looked over to where Storm and Wade waited and said, "You folks step down and come on into the house. We were just gettin' ready to sit down for lunch."

"We wouldn't want to put you out," Kane said. "Besides, I have seven men and a cook waitin' up there on the hill, plus a small herd of horses. I was wonderin' where we could set up camp and keep the mounts until we're ready to start back."

The farmer smiled. "I bet the young lady would like to take a nice hot bath and eat a meal at a table for a change. Come on, miss, get down and come on inside. You, too, mister." He grinned at Wade.

When Storm stepped up on the porch and Kane introduced her she was very conscious of her dusty face and clothes compared to the clean, rosy-cheeked young woman, who gave her a friendly smile. When Benson said, "This is my daughter, Aggie," Kane and Storm nodded and smiled at the girl. But Wade took her hand in his, his white teeth flashing in a wide smile as he said softly, "It's very nice meeting you, Aggie."

Aggie blushed with pleasure and invited them to step inside. When Wade would have stepped past Storm she brought her boot heel down on his toe as hard as she could, then sailed past him. She heard his grunt of pain and knew a great satisfaction.

Bess Benson was just as pleasant as her husband and daughter. After introductions were made she said to her daughter, "Get clean towels for Mr. Roemer and Mr. Magallen and show them to the back porch, where they can wash up. And you, honey," she looked at Storm, "come with me. I'll show you the room that will be yours while you're here."

As she spoke, the plump Mrs. Benson, somewhere in her midforties, took a teakettle of water off the stove. Storm followed her into a room that was sparsely furnished but was very clean and neat.

"You can wash up well enough here until after lunch; then we'll fill a tub and you can have a good soak," she said, pouring warm water into a plain white basin with a washcloth and a bar of soap beside it. "I always keep this room ready for when my niece comes to visit," she explained. "Come into the kitchen when you've finished and we'll eat."

Storm washed her face and hands, took a comb from her pocket, and pulled it through her curls. She then hurriedly brushed the dust off her clothes as best as she could. It would be impolite to keep the Bensons from their noon meal longer than necessary.

As she walked into the Benson kitchen, Storm could hear Kane and Wade talking to Aggie out on the back porch. She couldn't make out all the words, but she could tell, from the timbre of Wade's voice and the way the young woman was laughing in a breathless way, that Wade had turned on his charm. She wanted to tell the mother, who was dishing up potatoes and corn, to watch her daughter, not to leave her alone with the handsome man.

The farmer's wife was a marvelous cook, but Storm could have been chewing a piece of old leather for all she tasted what went into her mouth. Wade and Aggie sat across from her, giving each other long looks. Aggie's face glowed from Wade's sweet talk. Not once did he make eye contact with Storm; it was as if she wasn't even there.

At last the meal was over, and the three men went off to talk business in the pasture where the shorthorns grazed. Storm offered to help with the dishes, but Mrs. Benson shook her head. "I promised you a warm, soaky bath and you shall have it. Do you have a clean change of clothes?"

Storm said she had one last change of clean underclothing in her saddlebag, and she would like to wash a few articles before they started the trip back home.

"Aggie," Mrs. Benson ordered, "go down to the barn and fetch back Storm's bag. I'll drag the tub into the kitchen and get the bath ready while you're gone."

Within 15 minutes Storm was sitting in the wooden tub, scrubbing the dust and grime from her body and hair, while Aggie and Bess talked to her as they washed the dishes. The mother wanted to know about ranch life and the daughter was full of questions about Wade.

Storm answered all the questions about living on a ranch, but she pretended little knowledge of Wade. She wanted to warn the girl to stay away from him but knew it would be useless advice.

Feeling human again with a clean body and clean clothes next to her skin, Storm let her hair dry in the warm air as she washed the clothes she had used on the trail. When they were on the line and drying she went to the room given to her and stretched out on the bed. She just wanted to rest a few minutes, she told herself.

It was near dusk when Aggie shook her awake, announcing that supper was ready. She couldn't believe she had slept away the entire afternoon.

Everyone but Mrs. Benson was at the table when she walked into the kitchen. As she sat down next to Kane, she could tell from the pleased look on his face that he had struck a deal with their host. She ordered herself to ignore Wade and Aggie and to enjoy her meal.

She did enjoy the fried chicken, for she had caught Wade darting a fast glance at her. Maybe he was making up to Aggie just to make her jealous.

When supper was over, however, Storm wasn't so sure that Wade was using the girl to torment her. He had announced as he pushed away from the table that he was going to go check on the men; then he asked Aggie if she would like to come along with him.

"Can I, Ma?" There was a pleading quality in the three words.

"I guess so, but don't stay out in the night air too long."

Storm wanted to cry out, "Don't let her go, you foolish woman. Can't you see he's the worst kind of womanizer?"

Storm kept her mouth shut and her eyes lowered, knowing that it was jealousy that made her want to speak so. She wouldn't have cared a bit if it was some other man who was going to walk with Aggie in the moonlight.

She was surprised and delighted when Aggie returned to the house before she and Mrs. Benson had finished washing and drying the dishes. Only a few minutes had passed; there hadn't been time for even a *quick* tumble. Still, there was a glow on Aggie's face. She had, no doubt, been kissed.

The three men had remained outside on the porch, talking cattle and drinking the farmer's hard cider. Storm sat in the kitchen with Bess and Aggie, talking of mundane things, as strangers are apt to do. Aggie joined in the conversation, but it was clear from the way her eyes kept wandering to the door that she would rather be on the porch with the men . . . with Wade, Storm amended.

An hour later, to Storm's relief, everyone was ready to retire. Kane wanted to get an early start in the morning, and farmers retired early anyhow. Wade and Kane thanked Bess for her hospitality, and after Kane told Storm good night and Wade said something to Aggie that made her blush and giggle, they went to join the men camped on the hill. Storm said her good nights and sought her bed also.

As she lay on the soft, comfortable feather mattress, the distant sound of restless, bawling cattle drifted through the open window. She imagined they were the 200 Kane had purchased from Mr. Benson, and were unused to being penned in a corral.

Once she thought she heard Wade's rich laughter drifting from the hill and grew sad. He never laughed with her. He never did anything with her. Why was it, she wondered, that sometimes he seemed to hate her? What had she ever done to have made him treat her like a leper?

Her cheeks were wet when she fell asleep.

The sun was just coming up when Storm entered the Benson kitchen the next morning. The aroma of frying bacon and brewing coffee filled the air. Bess Benson, cracking eggs into a skillet of hot grease, looked up and smiled at her.

"Sit down, Storm. The men are washing up and will be in directly."

Kane was the first to enter the kitchen, and there was a stranger behind him. Storm's eyes widened a bit. Here was a man whose good looks were the equal of Wade's.

He was three or four years older than Wade, she thought, and he looked as if he had seen some hard living. His handsome face was weather-beaten, and there was a lot of gray at the temples of his brown hair. Yet there was a leashed power about him that would attract any woman. She wondered what Becky would think of this tall, splendid specimen of manhood.

"Rafe," Kane said, coming to stand behind her, "I want you to meet my sister, Storm. Storm, this is Rafe Jeffery. He'll be ridin' back to the ranch with us. He's an expert on the care of the shorthorn and will help me get them settled in."

"Well, now," Rafe Jeffery drawled softly, taking the hand Storm held out to him. "I'm looking forward to this trip suddenly. It's not every day a man has the pleasure of riding with a beautiful woman."

Storm blushed at his compliment and murmured, "Thank you." She became flustered when she glanced up and saw Wade glowering at her from the door. What had she done now? she wondered.

Everyone was in high spirits as they sat at the table; everyone except Wade. The scowl he had directed at Storm upon entering the kitchen had darkened even more when Rafe took the chair next to her. He ignored Aggie, who hurried to sit beside him. Storm felt a stirring of pity for the girl, for she looked as bewildered as she felt. The poor thing was probably wondering what had happened to the man who had lavished such attention on her only last night.

In a short time good-byes were said, and the men trailed out of the kitchen. Storm thanked Bess and Aggie for being so nice to her, and followed the men to where the shorthorns were penned. Soon Jeb and the cowboys came galloping down the hill. They waited until Kane swung wide the large gate of the corral; then they rode among the cattle, herding them through the opening. Wild-eyed and nervous, the stocky, short-legged animals rushed for what they thought was freedom. But they were hemmed in by whistling, yelling cowboys and popping lariats, and soon they were forced into a long line, headed back east.

The cowboys discovered that the new breed of cattle were much easier to handle than the wild longhorns. Also, because they didn't have a wide spread of horns, the men didn't have to worry about getting a leg ripped open if they had to ride among them.

Kane didn't rush the animals. He had forked over a good amount of hard cash for them and he wanted them in good condition when they arrived at the ranch.

Storm was enjoying the trip home. Her body was used to the long hours in the saddle now, and her conversation wasn't limited to old Jeb as she rode along. Most of the time Rafe rode beside her. His droll humor caused her laughter to peal out often, making Kane smile at the sound, and Wade glower.

The cowboys cast sideways looks at him, with knowing grins on their faces. Wade had given them the word before they started the trip that they were to stay away from Storm. It tickled them that he couldn't do anything about the new man who spent most of his time with Miss Roemer.

A pattern was set. Cookie was up as soon as the breaking dawn gave him enough light to see to build a fire and get breakfast started. By then the cattle were up and browsing, and the night riders were coming in. As usual, everyone stood around drinking coffee until Cookie told them to grab a plate and line up.

The morning meal was quickly eaten, and then the herd was started forward again. The days passed uneventfully, with no mishaps to hamper their steady eastward progress. They were a day and a night from home when the smoothness of their journey was broken.

The air was hot and still when the chuck wagon rolled to a halt, and reins were drawn for night camp. As Cookie hurriedly prepared supper, black, sullen-looking clouds gathered overhead, and lightning flashed occasionally.

"You men saddle fresh horses," Kane said to the cowboys. "It looks like we might get a storm, and I don't know how these critters will react to it."

The storm broke just after the meal had been eaten. The night became inky black, and lightning flashed across the sky. Thunder seemed to jar the earth. The rain came then, in wind-lashed sheets. The shorthorns, like longhorns, became nervous and milled about, bawling their unease. Everyone knew they would spook any minute and explode into a stampede.

Although it was the weather that had the cattle on edge, it was a loud sneeze from one of the cowboys that started them running in a frenzy. The men, already in the saddle, waiting for such a happening, immediately raced after them, trying to keep them strung out in a line as they headed toward the Platte, less than a mile away.

In this downpour there could be flood waters running full and swift. If the cattle reached the river, they could be swept downstream and scatter. Inevitably, many would drown.

Storm raced blindly through the darkness with the others, praying that Beauty wouldn't stumble and fall. If that happened, they would both be cut to pieces by hundreds of sharp hooves.

The terrified cattle would not be turned. They hit the Platte in a wild-eyed, bawling mass. The water was high and bore against them as they struggled to stay on their feet, pushing toward the opposite shore. Storm, along with the other riders, splashed in behind them. Only when the lightning flashed could she see anything in the black void that pressed around them.

Once Beauty slipped, her nose plunging underwater. But she quickly gained a foothold, and Storm's breath whooshed out in relief. Suddenly a dim blackness ahead made her heart leap: The bank was only yards away.

But even as Storm drew that breath, they were hit by a fierce rush of water, and Beauty was swept off her feet. Horse and rider went whirling down the river.

Wade wasn't far behind Storm when she and Beauty were swept away by the river. When a flash of lightning showed her blonde head it was as though someone had slammed his heart with a hammer. He'd had no idea she was with them. Holding his breath, he snatched the coiled rope from the saddlehorn and sent a loop snaking out in the direction in which he'd seen Storm.

It came back empty.

Frantic, he called her name again and again, but no answer came back to him. He knew that it was doubtful he could have heard her, even if she had called out. The noise of the bellowing cattle and the whoops and yells of the riders were deafening.

Wade's stallion, Renegade, snorted and lunged toward the bank, but Wade held him back, heading him downstream. He kept close to the shore, trying desperately to see through the gloom. Maybe the mare would make it to land, he told himself. If Storm held on to the animal's tail as she had been taught to do in such an occurrence, she would make it to shore also. But what if she had been hit by a piece of driftwood? he worried.

"Dear God," he was praying when a bright flash of lightning lit up the area, and he saw the mare standing on the bank, her head hanging and her sides heaving. At her feet lay a slender body, facedown. His heart pounding against his ribs, Wade urged the tired stallion toward shore.

He was out of the saddle before Renegade cleared the water. In two hurried strides he was hunkering down beside Storm, turning her over and smoothing the hair off her pale face. He felt for a pulse in her limp wrist.

He found it almost immediately, strong and steady. At his groan of thanksgiving, Storm's lashes fluttered, then her lids opened. She whispered Wade's name and he grabbed her up, his lips seeking hers. Her arms went around his shoulders as he kissed her with trembling desperation, as if she might be snatched away from him.

"I thought I had lost you forever," he rasped against her mouth, then stiffened, raising his head. From close by, his name and Storm's were being called in anxious tones. He recognized Kane's deep baritone and old Jeb's cracked voice.

"Over here," he yelled, laying Storm back on the ground. In a matter of seconds Kane and Jeb were splashing ashore, Kane asking, "Is she all right?" as he ran to his sister.

"I'm fine, Kane." Storm's voice was scratchy from the riverwater she had swallowed. "Only very tired."

Kane pulled Storm into an upright position, and as he felt her body for any broken bones, old Jeb awkwardly stroked the back of her soaked head with his gnarled hands.

"I didn't know you were out there, Stormie," he said, "otherwise I'd have kept an eye on you."

"Nobody knew you were foolish enough to ride with us." Kane was angry, now that his worry for her was over. "Why in the hell didn't you stay with Cookie in the chuck wagon?"

"I wanted to help," Storm cried, tears glimmering in her eyes. "And I did help, until the current became too strong and pulled Beauty under."

"We'll discuss it later," Kane said and stood up, Storm in his arms. "Right now I want you to get into some dry clothes and stay in your tent until this rain stops."

As he seated her astride his stallion, Storm saw Jeb grab up Beauty's reins, ready to follow them. She looked around for Wade but saw no sign of him or his mount. With a soft little sigh, she laid her head on Kane's shoulder. She still tingled from Wade's kiss.

The cattle were worn out from their run and their fight against the pull of the raging water. They were still nervous as the storm continued, but they now stood huddled in a group, too tired to run anymore.

Everyone was thankful when they found that Cookie had managed to drive the chuck wagon across the river and set up a new camp, and that he had a pot of coffee brewing: They would not have to cross the angry, muddy river again tonight. Not only was the chuck wagon on this side, but, by some miracle, the extra horses had followed the wagon.

Storm's tent had also been set up, and a lit lantern sat inside it. Kane helped her slide to the ground, saying, "Me and Rafe are goin' over to the herd to see if we lost any of them during the crossin'. Wade's already over there, checkin' them out."

So that's where he went, Storm thought as she lifted the tent flap and crawled inside. By the time she stripped off her dripping clothes and changed into dry underclothing, the rain had slowed to a drizzle and the thunder was dying away. As she was drifting off to sleep she heard Kane telling Cookie that two shorthorns had been swept away and one had been trampled to death.

"You can butcher that one," he said. "Steak will taste real good for breakfast in the mornin'."

Chapter Six

The aroma of frying steaks awakened Storm.
She started to turn over on her back and
groaned. Not only did it feel like her arms
had been pulled out of their sockets, but every
bone in her body hurt.

She remembered hanging onto Beauty's tail
as they were swept down the river and she
shivered. She had had a close call with death.
Her lips curved softly. How frightened Wade
had been. She remembered his kiss and grew
warm in her lower regions. That kiss had told
her that he loved her.

"Rise and shine, Stormie," old Jeb called
from outside the tent, breaking into her dreamy
thoughts of Wade. "Cookie's dishin' out the
steaks. You'd better get out here before the
hogs eat them all up."

Storm smiled, and in the gloom of the tent she sat up and felt for the clothes she had laid out the night before.

The cowboys had already eaten and were getting the cattle on the move when Storm stepped out of her shelter. Wade was just getting his steak and potatoes, while Kane and Rafe still stood in line. As she stepped behind Kane and Rafe, Wade took his plate and sat down on a large rock. She waited for him to smile at her, to speak. But with only a cool nod in her direction, he began to cut into his meat.

Storm's high spirits plummeted to her feet. Had she imagined Wade's kiss last night, his concern for her? Had she been hit on the head with something while she was in the water?

She shook her head. That kiss had been real. And it hadn't been a brotherly one.

When Kane and Rafe asked about her health she managed to smile and say brightly that she was feeling fine. How could she say that once again she had dared to dream, and again that dream had been shattered? Tears burned behind her eyes. If Wade Magallen ever dared to kiss her again, she'd slap him silly.

And though it was the last thing she wanted to do, Storm chattered away with Kane and Rafe, giving the impression that she didn't have a care in the world.

It amused Rafe to see the big, sour-faced man sitting on his rock, darting them black looks every time Storm's tickled laughter rang out. He gazed thoughtfully into his coffee, a devilish idea forming in his mind. Magallen was crazy about his friend's sister, but for some reason he liked to play games with her.

In the past days he had gotten to know Storm Roemer, to know that she was a fine young woman who didn't deserve such treatment. He scraped his plate clean, drank the rest of his coffee, and took the empty utensils back to the chuck wagon. It was time Magallen was taken down a peg or two, and he was just the man who could do it.

It was a couple of hours before dusk when the new cattle were driven onto Roemer range. The cowboys herded them past the ranch house and on out to an area a few miles from where the longhorns grazed. Kane wanted no mixed breeding, nor was it known what attitude the ornery longhorns might take toward the newcomers. One swing of a long, pointed horn could rip open the belly of the shorter animals.

Storm, along with Wade, Rafe, and her brother, cantered up to the barn. As Juan gathered up the reins of the four horses and led them to the wooden trough for a drink of water, Kane said, "Grab your saddlebag, Rafe, and bring it on up to the house."

When Rafe went to fetch the bag Wade, a dark frown on his face, said in a surly tone, "You gonna let him sleep in the house?"

"Why, sure." Kane looked at him in surprise. "I've hired him to stay on for a few months, but he's not a ranch hand. I don't expect him to sleep in the bunkhouse."

"I don't think it's wise to do that. He's got his eye on Storm, you know. Sweet-talks her all the time."

Kane hid an amused grin. "Do you reckon?" He thought a moment, then shook his head. "Naw, Rafe's an honorable man. If he cares for Storm, he won't try anything with her. Besides, he'll be sleepin' in my room, in the bunk you use when you stay overnight sometimes."

They had reached the porch now, and nothing more was said as greetings were exchanged with Maria, who had stepped outside. The housekeeper flashed appreciative eyes at the tall stranger and, to Wade's irritation, greeted him warmly. She looked at Wade then and said, "I'll have supper ready in about an hour. You'll be joining us, won't you, Wade?"

Wade shook his head and answered gruffly, "Thank you, Maria, but I'd better get home, see how Pa's been gettin' along while I was gone." He slid Storm a quick look from under lowered lids, and without further words he stepped off the porch and mounted the stallion.

"There goes a man of few words." Rafe laughed as Wade galloped away.

"Well, not usually," Maria said. "He's got a burr under his tail about something."

Rafe managed to keep a straight face. He knew what had put the sticker under Magallen's tail, and he hoped it was pricking him real good.

An hour later, as Storm, Kane, and Rafe sat on the front porch, the sound of thudding hooves down on the river road floated to them.

Rafe peered through the near darkness. "That's Magallen's stallion, isn't it?"

"Yes." Kane nodded. "I expect he's goin' to visit his friend Josie Sales. He hasn't seen her for a couple of weeks."

Rafe sensed the slender body next to his grow still and thought Wade Magallen was the biggest fool he'd ever seen in his life.

"He might be going to work," Storm said in a small voice, near tears.

"What kind of work does he do at night?" Rafe looked at her.

"His dad owns a saloon in Laramie called the Longhorn," Kane answered for Storm. "When Wade's not trailin' a herd of cattle he takes care of the bar at night."

A comfortable silence grew between the three as they sat in the hush of the coming night. A warm, sweet scent came from the rose bed, and a light breeze stirred the big cottonwood that provided welcome shade in the daytime.

As Kane and Rafe talked, soft-voiced, occasionally punctuating remarks with laughter, the bellowing of the shorthorns drifted faintly on the night air.

Kane looked up at the sky and said, "The moon is full tonight; a perfect time to go out and round up some of the wily longhorns when they come out of the thickets to feed and water."

"Mind if I come with you? I've only seen the wild brutes in pictures."

"Sure, but be careful of their horns. The damn things can kill a man."

"See you tomorrow, Storm," Rafe said, ruffling her hair as he followed Kane off the porch.

Storm sat a while longer on the porch, trying not to think of Wade and Josie together, what they might be doing. She prayed that he was in the saloon and not in Josie's bed.

"Stop thinking about him!" she finally ordered herself. "You only go around in circles. Think about something else for a change."

Storm forced herself to think about tomorrow, how she would pass the day. Before she went to bed she had decided that she and Becky would go visit their parents' graves.

"How was your trip?" Becky asked as she snipped flowers from their beds and stuck them into a jar of water. "Did Wade warm up to you any?"

Storm gave her a startled look. "I don't know what you mean."

"Come on, Storm, of course you do. He was real hateful to you that day when he dropped in. He didn't say a decent word to you."

"Oh, I'd forgotten that," Storm lied. "He didn't say anything mean to me. He mostly ignored me." She wondered if she should mention Wade's hungry kiss, then decided against it. Becky was a romantic in some ways and would probably read too much into that kiss.

Becky dropped the subject and stood up. "These will look real pretty placed in front of the tombstone."

Only one large monument had been erected to mark the four graves. The girls had wanted it that way. The parents had been close friends in life, and so it would be in death.

"Kane has kept the graves nice and neat all this time," Becky remarked, picking up the fruit jar. "Every spring he paints the picket fence he built around the graves."

Becky didn't want to linger on the loss of her parents, so she asked, "What did Maria pack us for lunch?"

"I'm not sure, but I think it's fried chicken," Storm answered as they reached the spot where their mounts were waiting.

"Good. I love Maria's fried chicken."

As the horses clomped along at a walk to hold the jar of flowers steady, Storm said, "We have a guest staying with us for a while."

"Anyone I know? Man or woman?"

"No, you wouldn't know him. He came back with us on the trail. He's an expert on Kane's new breed of cattle."

"Is he young? Is he good-looking?"

"He's handsome beyond belief," Storm answered, a smile taking away the seriousness of her claim. "I think he's around thirty-five or so. I want you to meet him; you'll like him."

"No thanks, Storm. I'm not interested in meeting any men." After a moment of silence

Becky asked hopefully, "Are you interested in him? Is there a romance building between the two of you?"

"No. Only a close friendship."

Becky frowned her disappointment and no more was said between them until they reached the grave site.

After placing the flowers before the tombstone and pulling the few weeds that had dared to raise their heads, Storm called Becky's attention to the changing weather. "I don't like those dark clouds that are gathering. I think we should forget about eating lunch and head for home."

"I expect so," Becky agreed after a glance at the sky. "I'm going to miss Maria's chicken, though." She had a sad little-girl look on her small face.

Storm laughed and said, "Take the chicken home with you. We'll probably have the same thing for supper."

They hurriedly mounted and kicked the horses into a gallop. Storm arrived at the ranch house just before the big drops of rain began to splatter in the dust. She hoped Becky had made it home in time too.

The friendly rapport that had sprung up between Storm and Rafe remained just that. They enjoyed each other's company, and were seen together all the time, riding the range, shopping, and lunching in Laramie. It wasn't surprising that gossip spread throughout the area. Maria called Storm's attention to what was being said, but the girl only laughed, not at all interested in what her neighbors said or thought.

Rafe kept her mind off Wade—at least in the daytime. At night, when she lay in bed, it was a different story. Rafe was not with her when Wade invaded her dreams, held her in his arms, made wild love to her.

Like most of Storm's neighbors, Wade was unaware that only friendship existed between her and Rafe. Wade's nights were also spent in fitful sleep and restless dreams.

It was after one such night that he literally bumped into Storm on Laramie's main street.

He was on his way to the saloon to talk to his father when, midway there, he was hailed from behind. He turned around and waited for a neighboring rancher to catch up with him. "If you're goin' to your dad's place, I'll walk along with you," the man said. Wade nodded, and when he turned around to resume walking, his broad shoulder caught Storm straight on. Only Rafe's quick action kept her from falling to her kees.

"Watch it, Magallen." Rafe's cool warning sliced through the tension in the air, his arm going protectively around Storm's shoulders. When his hand slid possessively down her arm, Wade's mouth became a thin, hard line. He took a threatening step toward Rafe, a wildness in his eyes, but Storm gasped and stepped between them. Rafe only worsened the taut moment by drawing her back against his chest, his mocking gaze daring Wade to do anything about it.

Wade sneered, "You're doin' a little cradle-snatchin' there, aren't you, Jeffery?"

He's spoiling for a fight, Storm thought uneasily and wondered why.

It was soon obvious that he had picked on the right man. Rafe smiled down at Storm and drawled, "Maybe I am, but they're so adaptable to a man's ways when you get them young."

Wade lunged forward, and as Storm was squeezed between the two large bodies, she squealed, "Stop it, you two! In case you've forgotten, we're standing in the middle of town and everyone is watching us."

Both men stepped away from her, and she straightened her shirt with angry jerks of her fingers. Then, linking her arm with Rafe's, she snapped, "Come on, Rafe, let's go have our lunch."

As Wade watched them walk away, the rancher spoke, bringing him out of his tortured thoughts. "Storm Roemer sure is a little beauty, huh? Looks like maybe there's a romance buddin' between her and the stranger." When he received no response he gave Wade a sidelong glance and said, "He does seem a little old for her, though."

When Wade only walked on silently, the rancher needled him. "I've heard that some women like older men; figure they're more experienced in the love department, if you know what I mean. It's easy to see that one has had plenty of experience in that line."

Wade's hands clenched into fists. He was torn between punching his neighbor and going after Jeffery to wipe the smug smile off his face.

He did neither. After mumbling a vague good-bye to the man he crossed the street and limped away. He'd go see Josie instead of going to the saloon. He was in no mood to listen to a bunch of drunks talking some nonsense or other.

He hadn't seen Josie since his return from the trail drive and he didn't know what kind of reception he'd receive. She would be angry, he knew, for she had sent a couple of notes to the saloon, inviting him to lunch or supper, whichever he wanted. He hadn't gotten around to letting her know.

As Wade had expected, Josie received him coolly. After she ignored him for a few minutes he put his hat back on his head and walked toward the door.

"Where are you goin'?" Josie rushed after him, grabbing his arm.

"I'm gonna go where my company will be appreciated."

"Oh, Wade, you know I appreciate your company." She pulled him around until his body was pressed against hers. "It's just that you hurt my feelin's, never answerin' my notes, not comin' around. . . ." Her voice trailed off as she slid a hand down the front of his trousers and stroked the bulge of his manhood. "I've been afraid that you've been seein' someone else."

She tugged him toward the door that separated her living quarters from her small dress shop. The door was no sooner closed than she was pulling his shirt out of his trousers and unbuttoning his fly. Her eager fingers slipped inside and pulled him free. She began to squeeze and massage him. Her stroking hand became almost frantic as his long length lay limp in her palm.

Josie looked up at Wade, her eyes questioning. Wade looked away, embarrassed. The same thing had happened to him with the girl, Aggie.

"I guess he wants to be coaxed a bit," Josie murmured and, dropping to her knees, she kissed the flaccid flesh, then took it into her mouth.

Long minutes passed as she nibbled and fondled him. Nothing happened. Every time Wade felt a stirring in his loins, Storm's face would appear before him, and the momentary desire slipped away.

Finally, Josie sat back on her heels, her face flushed angrily. "Who have you been seeing? Who has been drainin' you dry?" Her green eyes glittered. "Which one, the little Roemer princess or her whorin' friend?"

"Watch your tongue, Josie," Wade said furiously as he tucked himself back into his underwear and buttoned his trousers. "I watched those girls grow up and I'd never touch them in that way."

"Maybe that's the way you feel," Josie said, jerking to her feet, "but Miss Storm Roemer

116

doesn't have the same sentiments. She'd spread her legs for you in a minute. And so would Becky Hadler if you had her price."

Wade knew he had to get away from the foul-speaking woman before he did her real harm. And Josie knew she had said too much when, without another word, he opened the door and slammed it behind him.

Out on the sidewalk, Wade muttered, "I need a drink. Several of them," and headed for his father's saloon again.

As Rafe boosted Storm onto the mare's back, she asked, "Would you mind if we skipped lunch? I've lost my appetite."

"Of course not, honey," Rafe answered, mounting beside her. "I'm not very hungry either after our run-in with that wild man."

They rode down the street in silence until they came to the end of town. Rafe looked at Storm's tear-streaked face and said softly, "I knew he was the one who put that sadness in your eyes. You love that big dumb buffalo very much, don't you?"

At first Storm was going to deny it hotly, but she had learned already that Rafe Jeffery was a hard man to fool. She silently nodded her head.

There was another stretch of silence as they clomped along, then Rafe said, "There's something here that don't make a lick of sense to me. It's as plain as a wart on a toad that the man is hog wild about you, but he doesn't do a thing about it. Could it be that he thinks you're too young for him?"

Storm gave a bitter laugh. "You couldn't be more mistaken. Other than that I'm Kane's sister, he doesn't care a wit for me. And as for my age, he goes around with women younger than me."

"You're wrong, Storm. It eats him alive every time you even talk to another man. He's gonna lose control one of these days and jump on me with both feet."

"Well, you do egg him on; pretending that there's a great romance between us. He probably thinks you're out to seduce his friend's young sister."

"Your bein' Kane's sister has nothin' to do with it. He's thinkin' only of himself. And that's why I keep raggin' him. I'm gonna keep on until I force his hand. One day he's gonna come right out and say how much he cares for you."

"You're wasting your time, Rafe. He'll never do it."

Laramie lay some distance behind them when Storm said, "I've been wanting to introduce you to my friend Becky. Shall we go visit her?"

"Sounds good. I've been hopin' I'd get to meet this friend I overheard you and Maria arguin' about. Does she have a bad reputation or somethin'?"

Storm stiffened and rode along in silence for a moment. Then, giving Rafe a level look, she said clearly, "I guess you could call her a whore."

At Rafe's low whistle, she jumped to Becky's defense. "She's not like the ones you see in saloons or bawdy houses. She only sees three men in Cheyenne . . . very wealthy ones. Becky and I grew up together, and she's had a lot of bad luck since her parents died. She's good and kind and never hurt anyone in her entire life.

"And she loves animals," she added lamely, darting a look at Rafe that dared him to laugh.

There was no amusement on Rafe's face. "You're a loyal young woman, Storm Roemer," he said. "I'm lookin' forward to meetin' this friend of yours that you champion so fiercely."

The look Storm flashed him had suspicion in it. "Hey, now," he scolded, reading her correctly, "not as a future customer."

"Sorry, Rafe," Storm said, embarrassed. "Her house is just around that bend in the road up ahead."

Chapter Seven

"This sure doesn't look like the home of a whore," Rafe said as they drew rein in front of Becky's house, his surprised gaze going over the neat white farmhouse, the flower beds.

"Rafe!" Storm warned as they swung to the ground.

"I know." Rafe grinned. "Wealthy men friends, right?"

"Right. And if Becky's home surprises you, wait until you see her," Storm said as she stepped up on the porch and rapped on the door.

Becky answered Storm's knock almost immediately, and Rafe stared down at the curly-haired, barefoot girl and wondered who she was. His lips curved in disapproval. Did this Becky person have teenage girls working for her? Did she take them into Cheyenne to help her entertain her *men friends?*

His mouth hung slightly open when Storm said, "Becky, I want you to meet a new friend of mine. Rafe Jeffery, meet Becky Hadler."

The petite woman lifted clear blue eyes to the bemused dark ones studying her so intently. Pushing the black curls off her forehead, she said quietly, "I'm pleased to meet you, Rafe."

Rafe's voice was a deep, warm sound when he answered, "No more pleased than I am, Becky."

Watching the pair, Storm felt suddenly very unnecessary. She took a step back, her heel coming down on a kitten's tail. Its ear-splitting yowl made all three jump, pulling Rafe and Becky's gaze apart.

Becky gave a flustered laugh, then said, "Come on in. I've just taken a pie out of the oven. We'll have some with coffee."

"It's apple, I hope," Rafe said, close behind Becky, admiring the swing of her hips.

"You saw my apple tree, didn't you?" Becky sent him a sparkling smile over her shoulder.

"Don't get your hopes too high, Rafe," Storm teased as they stepped into the kitchen. "You've never tasted this lady's cooking before."

Becky and Storm mingled their laughter as each silently remembered Becky's past attempts at the culinary arts. "I'll have you know, Storm Roemer, that I've improved over the years. Why don't you get down the cups and pie plates while I go put on some shoes."

"Well?" Storm looked at Rafe as soon as Becky left them. "What do you think of her? Isn't she something?"

"She is that," Rafe answered, still looking at the door through which Becky had disappeared.

"Look, Rafe," Storm said with a snap to her voice, "don't go getting any ideas. Don't go treating her like . . ."

"Like a man friend," he teased, then grew serious. "Don't worry, Storm; I'll treat your friend with respect."

Becky returned to the kitchen and set about putting a pot of coffee on the stove, then slicing the still-warm apple pie. "While the coffee brews, come out to the shed and see my animals." She smiled at Rafe, making his heartbeat quicken.

"Becky's studying to become a veterinarian," Storm said proudly.

"You are?" Rafe looked surprised. "I've never heard of a woman bein' an animal doctor before."

"I've always wanted to be one," Becky said as she swung open the wide door of the shed.

"I see the doe is gone," Storm said as they stepped inside.

"Yes. I turned her loose last week, but she's still hanging around. I put water out for her."

"But you've still got this ornery bobcat," Storm said as the animal hissed at her.

Becky laughed. "Would you believe he let me scratch behind his ear yesterday, and he only snarled at me one time? I'll be setting him free next week sometime."

"And the birds?"

"They're fine. They've got their feathers now. I had to put a chicken crate over them to keep the cat from getting to them."

Becky walked to the far corner of the shed. "Here is what I wanted to show you. My latest guest." She stepped to one side, and Rafe stared with admiration at a beautiful, sleek-lined mare.

The animal's glossy hide shone like polished bronze and her tail and flowing mane were creamy white in color. Her delicately formed head and proudly arched neck spoke clearly of her breeding. She was probably a conquest of the rogue stallion that had been spotted in the area.

The handsome beast had most likely sired at least one foal on her. Rafe imagined the magnificent foals his pure bloods could get on her.

"How did you come by her?" Storm asked quietly, trying not to further frighten the mare. "She's beautiful."

"She got tangled up in some barbed-wire fence Timmy's father strung around a patch of corn. She was streaming blood from several deep cuts when Timmy brought me to her. It took us an hour to get a rope around her neck, and then free her from the wire. I don't think we'd have ever got her here to the shed if Timmy's father hadn't come along with his old plow horse. She followed him right in."

"How come you've got her head snubbed so close to the post?" Rafe asked. "Is she a biter?"

"No, she's never offered to bite or kick me. She seems to be a sweet-tempered little animal. She's only scared. I have her tied short so she can't twist her neck and lick the salve off her cuts. You can't see them. They're all on her other side."

"She's a fine piece of horseflesh. A purebred, I think."

"That's what I think too," Storm said. "Do you know much about horses?"

"A bit. I was raised with them, worked with them until my father died."

"I love horses," Becky put in. "They're my favorite kind of animal."

Rafe scanned the interior of the shed. "This building looks sturdy enough, but the door needs some bracing and new hinges. That wild stallion would have no problem breaking it down. I'll come by and fix it for you one day this week."

Becky looked at him, all the friendliness gone from her eyes. "That won't be necessary," she said coolly. "Timmy's father is taking care of it tomorrow."

Rafe swore silently at himself. He had moved too fast. He knew what she was thinking, and nothing could be farther from the truth. He only wanted to help her, not bed her. . . . That wasn't quite true, he amended. He couldn't think of anything that would please him more than to take this petite woman to bed and make love to her all night.

But there were other things about Becky Hadler that drew him to her, and he wanted to explore them. It could turn out that once he got to know her he would only feel affection for her, as he did for Storm.

He didn't make a big issue out of Becky's refusal of his help. He gave her a genial smile and said, "That's good. He can probably do it better than me anyway. I'm not much of a carpenter."

Becky's face pinkened. Had she jumped to the wrong conclusion about Storm's friend? Maybe he had only meant to help her. Well, she told herself, she'd know what he'd had in mind if he came knocking on her door some night.

As she turned to Storm and asked brightly, "Shall we go have that pie and coffee?" she was wishing with all her heart that this handsome stranger wouldn't come to her house with lust on his mind. For the first time in her life she was attracted to a man in more than a physical way.

Rafe complimented Becky on her pie, saying it was the best he'd ever eaten. She smiled her thanks; then he said, "Your backyard reminds me of my mom's yard when I was growing up. She was a great one for flowers. Her favorites were roses. She had a big bed of them right off the front porch. In the evenin's when we'd sit out there the smell of them was almost overpowerin'."

"Is your mother still living?" Becky asked.

"No. She's been gone about ten years now. Dad went first, then Mom a couple of years later."

Becky made a soft sound, then said, "I guess the three of us are orphans, then."

Rafe grinned. "Old ones, but I guess we are orphans. But from what Kane told me, I got to know my parents longer than you two did yours."

Storm and Becky nodded, and a small silence settled over the table as both young women remembered their parents. When Becky's hound with pups began to bark they came back to the present.

"Kane mentioned that you're mostly a horse trainer, Rafe," Storm said.

"I used to be. My dad was the best trainer in Oregon. I was around eight years old when he began teaching me how to train and handle them."

"But you don't train them anymore." Becky frowned at him. "How come?"

Rafe gazed out the window. "I don't know. I guess the horses reminded me too much of Dad. Besides, someone had to run the farm. Trainin' horses is a full-time job, so I sold them. When Mom died I rented out the farm and went to work for Mr. Benson."

He looked back at Becky. "About five years ago, though, I began to get the urge to get back into trainin'. I saved my money and invested it in young, pure-blood stallions. I now have four handsome fellows. My sister and her husband are living on the old homeplace now, where I keep the stallions. When I've saved enough to purchase two or three mares I'm going back into business."

Becky's shining eyes told him that she approved.

Storm, who had been quiet during Becky and Rafe's conversation, now asked the question both girls wondered about. "Have you ever been married, Rafe?" Her hand went immediately to her mouth. "I'm sorry; I shouldn't have asked you that. It's none of my business."

"Hey, don't fuss it, Storm." Rafe laughed at her embarrassment. "It's no secret. I've never been married."

"I see," Storm said weakly, not about to ask any more questions about his private life.

Rafe glanced at Becky, then looked down at his coffee cup. "I've just not met the right woman yet, I guess. It's not that I'm picky; it's just that I've never clicked with one."

Storm gave him a teasing smile. "Time's running out, you know. If you want to be a papa someday, you'd better start paying more attention to the women you meet. Maybe you're using that 'clicking' business as an excuse. Maybe deep down you don't want to give up your freedom."

"Like Wade Magallen?" Rafe asked with a grin. "That one shuns marriage like a cagey old wolf walkin' a wide circle around a baited trap."

Becky raised a questioning brow at Rafe's caustic tone. "They don't like each other," Storm explained with a little smile. "Kane says they're like two mean roosters, each determined to be the main cock amongst a flock of hens."

"Not me," Rafe denied. "That man took one look at me and became hostile."

Becky took a sip of coffee, then asked, "When you met Wade did he know you were coming home with Kane?"

"I expect he did. Kane had that understanding with my boss before he came to the farm. He probably mentioned it to Magallen."

"That explains it then," Becky exclaimed in amusement. "He probably figured you'd be a farmer, no threat to him. You see, Rafe, there's only one hen around here that Wade wants to be cock to, and that's Storm. You're a threat to his . . . cockdom?" She grinned at her choice of words; then she and Storm burst into peals of laughter, and Rafe's deep guffaws joined them.

When they settled down Storm said sternly, "Becky, you know that's not true."

"Maybe," was all Becky would say.

Storm didn't want to stay on the subject of Wade. Noting that the sun had swung well westward, she said it was time she and Rafe were getting home.

Becky walked with them to where their mounts were tethered, and as Rafe boosted Storm onto the mare, she said, "Timmy isn't feeling well—too many green apples, his mother says—so I was wondering if you'd ride over

128

and feed and water my animals while I'm gone this weekend."

"Sure," Storm answered, then grinned down at her friend. "Those meadowlarks can feed themselves now, can't they?"

"I knew you didn't like those babies." Becky thumped her on the knee with a laugh. "But they eat by themselves now. I keep a can of seed beside their crate. Just give them half a cupful every time you come over."

"I'll see you next week then," Storm said, and nudged Beauty into motion.

"Thanks for the pie and coffee, Becky," Rafe said as his mount followed the mare. He smiled at her, but some of the warmth had gone out of his eyes and voice.

Becky gazed after him, bitterness in her eyes. If only things were different.

Storm and Rafe had ridden about half a mile when Rafe asked, "Where is Becky goin' this weekend?"

"She . . . well, she ah . . . she's going to visit some friends in Cheyenne," Storm finally got out.

"I see," Rafe said dully. "Men friends, I take it."

Storm made no answer, and Rafe was strangely silent the rest of the way home.

Chapter Eight

Wade awakened early. He turned his head carefully and peered through the window at the gray smudge of light. His nose wrinkled in a grimace of distaste. Mingling with the heavy silence was the odor of sour whiskey and sweat-stained clothes.

Damn boar's nest, he thought, rubbing his throbbing temples. He swallowed a couple of times, trying to bring some saliva to his cotton-dry mouth. His eyes fell on the almost-empty whiskey bottle on the bedside table. God, had he drunk that much last night?

He raised his right hand and peered through the gloom at the broken skin on the knuckles: the result of hauling off and striking the bed-room wall before hitting the bottle to blunt his gnawing thoughts of Storm.

Dear God, why did she have to come back? He stared unseeing at the ceiling. Her absence the last four years had dulled his ache for her, although a day never passed that he hadn't thought of her, wondering how she was, wondering about the men in her life. That thought had always tied knots in his gut, and now it was ten times worse, seeing her with Jeffery all the time.

As the sky pinkened and objects took shape in his room, Wade heard the bed creak in the room next to his, then heard his father stamp on his boots and make his way to the kitchen.

He and Pa hadn't crossed paths for a couple of days, he thought, listening to Jake open the firebox of the big range, then chucking wood into it. In a moment the smell of burning pine wafted into his room, and soon he heard the clank and thump of the little hand pump splashing water into the coffeepot.

They were all familar sounds, sounds he'd heard since he was nine years old.

Wade continued to lie in bed until Jake finished washing up at the dry sink, water splashing all over the place as he rinsed the soap off his face. When he heard the splat of water tossed out the door and onto the ground, he sat up and swung his feet to the floor. Wade's leg began to pain him as he rummaged in a dresser drawer for clean underclothes and a shirt. When he withdrew them the drawer was left empty. He frowned. Either he'd have to buy some new ones or wash out a few.

Jake stood in the kitchen door, his back to Wade as he sipped a cup of coffee and gazed at the rising sun. It struck Wade that his father was no longer a young man. The once-black hair now had more gray than ebony, and the once-muscular body seemed lost in his long red summer underwear. A great welling of love and regret for this gentle man swept over him.

"'Mornin', Pa," Wade said quietly. "Admirin' the sun?"

"Yeah." Jake gave an embarrassed laugh. "Each mornin' it's different as it rises. I think it's the most beautiful sight in the world when it peeks over the mountain and strikes the Platte, turning it red for a minute."

Wade came and stood beside Jake. "I like to watch the sunsets. They're a wondrous sight too."

Jake nodded. "All of Wyoming is a wondrous sight." A hint of sadness colored his voice when he added, "I guess there are some who would disagree."

Wade knew the elder Magallen was thinking of his wife. Nella's leaving them had always been a closed subject. Wade had learned early on that it was painful for his father to talk about it.

He stepped aside as Jake turned back into the kitchen, asking, "You feel like havin' bacon and eggs for breakfast?"

"Sounds good. I can't remember if I had supper last night, but my stomach is tellin' me I didn't."

"You did," Jake grouched, "out of a bottle." As he placed thick slices of bacon into a frying pan, he added, "You ought to slow down on your drinkin', Son. Whiskey never did solve any problems. Only makes them worse. Keeps a man from thinkin' straight."

Wade wanted to answer that he knew that, that he didn't want to think straight; that he'd go crazy if he did. He said no more as he stood in the doorway, and Jake, not the sort to nag, let it go.

Later, as they sat eating breakfast, Jake asked, "Will you be workin' tonight? Jones said he won't be able to come in. His wife is ailin'."

"I'll be there," Wade said. "I should be able to work all next week. Sometime after that Kane and I are takin' a hundred or so cattle to Fort Laramie. We shouldn't be gone longer than three or four days."

They finished the meal in silence; then Jake was slapping his hat on his head and leaving for Laramie and his saloon.

Wade rolled a cigarette and refilled his coffeecup. Feeling more human now, he sat at the table, gazing out the window, watching the rising sun burn away the mists that hung over the river.

His smoke finished, he was on the point of rising and clearing the table when through the open door he saw Josie Sales's two-seater carriage turn into the driveway. "Dammit," he grated, "I should have known she'd be out here as soon as the sun came up."

133

He had foolishly thought, hoped, that after their run-in yesterday he would be rid of her. What would it take, he wondered, to get her off his back once and for all?

Wade sat on at the table, not offering to go outside and help Josie from the carriage. There was an angry flush to her cheeks as she walked toward the house, for she had seen him sitting at the table, watching her.

None of her irritation sounded in her voice when she stepped up on the porch and said sweetly, "Good mornin', Wade."

"'Mornin', Josie. What brings you out here at sunrise? You plannin' on doin' some fishin'?" His eyes scanned her green satin dress, its low-cut neckline unsuited for daywear . . . unless you were a whore. Which she was, more or less, Wade thought.

"Don't tease, Wade," Josie pouted, taking the chair in which Jake had sat. "You know why I'm here. I couldn't leave things the way they were when we parted yesterday."

She put her hand on Wade's. "I'm sorry for what I said about Storm and Becky. It was just that I couldn't . . . you know . . . get you aroused, and I knew you had been seein' some other woman. I just accused the first one I could think of. I didn't mean it."

The hell you didn't, you vicious bitch. Wade eased his hand out from under hers.

"Anyway, I hear that the handsome stranger Kane brought back home is quite taken

134

with Storm, that there's a hot romance goin' on between them. A couple of women in my shop yesterday were sayin' they wouldn't be surprised to get a wedding invite before long."

It was all Wade could do not to grab Josie by the neck and push the words back down her throat. Though it nearly killed him, he managed to say calmly, "They just might."

Josie rose, her intention to sit on Wade's lap, to try again to make him desire her. The pleased smile that had sprung to her lips at his casual answer faded. Wade had stood up also.

"You'd better be gettin' back to town and get your shop open," he said. "I've got a lot of work to do too."

They stepped out onto the porch just as Storm cantered past the cabin. She flashed them a glance, and then, head held high, looked straight ahead.

"I wonder where she's goin'?" Josie said, her hostility toward the younger woman not quite hidden. "Off to see her little whore friend, I imagine. I'm surprised big brother allows that."

"Storm and Becky have been friends since they were children, and Storm is a loyal person," Wade said stiffly, thinking that Josie Sales would know nothing of that.

Josie's eyes glittered like polished glass for a split second before she lowered her lids, hiding her hatred for Storm Roemer from

Wade. "Her loyalty will ruin her reputation if she's not careful," she said, unable to keep some of the dislike out of her voice. "People will start talkin' about her."

"They'd better be careful what they say. The Roemers are well-liked around here. Too loose a tongue can land a person in plenty of trouble."

Josie saw the angry threat in Wade's gray eyes and realized too late that she had let her tongue get away from her. "I'm sure nothing too harsh will be said about her," she said hurriedly. "I, for one, wouldn't listen to such gossip."

Like hell you wouldn't, Wade thought, and urged her down the stairs.

When Storm arrived at Becky's house and went to the shed to tend the animals she found young Timmy there. He looked up from tossing hay to the mare and gave her a wide smile.

"Hello, Miss Roemer. I started feelin' better and came on over to care for Becky's patients." He gave the mare a gentle pat on the rump. "They're all used to me."

"I'm glad you're feeling better, Timmy. I like animals well enough, but I'm not as fond of them as you and Becky are. Outside of dogs, cats, and horses, I'm a little nervous around them."

"Yeah, most girls are," Timmy agreed, a male smugness in his voice. "But not Becky," he said, admiration in his tone this time. "She

ain't afraid of any animal . . . 'ceptin' snakes."
He grinned.

Storm talked a while longer to the young man, then told him good-bye after he promised he would see to Becky's patients until she returned. She swung onto Beauty's back and started for home, still in the doldrums. Her mood hadn't been the best when she started out, and it had worsened when she saw Wade and Josie standing on the porch. There was no doubt in her mind that Josie had spent the night with Wade. She tried to tell herself that she didn't care how many women he brought home with him. But she cared; she cared dreadfully.

All was quiet at the Magallen cabin as she rode past. Josie's carriage was gone now, and Wade had probably gone back to bed for a much-needed rest.

She felt a bleak emptiness as she rode on.

To Storm's surprise, Kane was home when she arrived. "What are you doing home at this time of day, and where is Rafe?" she asked, sitting down beside him on the leather couch.

"Rafe is still in Laramie, sittin' in on a poker game, and I came home early to spend some time with my scrawny sister."

"I feel very honored." Storm gave his hair a yank.

"You should. It isn't every day I waste my time this way."

"Oh, I know that. Kane Roemer's time is more valuable than money."

"Yes, it is, but I'm still ready to expend some of it on my ungrateful sister. I had a great idea when I was ridin' home."

"You mean you can still get those?" Storm looked significantly at the gray sprinkled in his hair.

"You've got a real smart tongue today, don't you?" Kane reached over and caught her hand, then bent her thumb back until she squealed. "You're not to poke fun at your elders, missy."

He smirked approval and released her hand when she cried, "I take it back. You're absolutely brilliant."

"And don't you forget it." The grin tugging at his lips belied the stern look he had turned on her.

He crossed his long legs at the ankles and clasped his hands behind his head in a movement that said he wouldn't broach the subject of his idea again.

Storm waited a full minute, until curiosity made her say, "So, what is this wonderful thought that managed to pierce your thick skull?"

Kane made as though to capture her hand again, and she hurriedly sat on it. He laughed, then said, "Before Wade and I leave on our cattle drive from Fort Laramie I'm gonna throw a big party. We'll invite all our friends and neighbors. It will be a welcome-home party for you."

"That's a wonderful idea, Kane!" Storm's eyes lit up. "I'll get to see all my old friends, find out who married whom, how many children they have. When will you have it?"

"A week from Saturday, I think."

But as Storm listened to her brother make his plans out loud, deciding what kind of food would be served, that there would be no hard liquor served—he didn't want any fights breaking out—her enthusiasm began to wane.

Her dearest friend of all wouldn't be at her party. She couldn't dare invite Becky. It wasn't fair. In all probability Wade would bring Josie to the party, an old worn-out whore who had slept with every man in a 50-mile radius, and she would be welcome. But Becky—honest, generous to a fault, who had never harmed anyone in her life—was ostracized for doing the same thing Josie did. Just because she took money for doing it made it shameful.

Storm's resentment sounded in her voice when she muttered, "I expect Wade will bring ol' string bean Josie."

"Most likely." Kane gave her a curious look. "Why are you frownin'? You look as if you'd like to do harm to someone."

"I would. I'd like to pound Wade Magallen's soft head into a pulp. How can he lower himself to be seen in public with the likes of that woman? He must know what she is."

"Why, little sister," Kane drawled, amusement twitching his lips, "of course Wade knows what she is. Why do you think he goes out with her? He squires her around for the same reason all the other men around here do."

The picture of Wade in bed with Josie snapped Storm's control. In pain and anger she grabbed up a small pillow and whacked Kane across the chest with it. "You men make me sick," she grated out. "You only think of one thing."

She jumped to her feet and, glaring down at him, said, "I don't want Josie at my party. You tell Wade that."

Tears pricked the backs of Storm's eyes as she fled up the stairs. Kane shook his head sadly when her bedroom door slammed shut.

Chapter Nine

Even before Storm opened her eyes she knew
that the day was hot and humid. Her nape and
the undersides of her breasts were damp with
perspiration. She lay on her back, the sheet
kicked to the floor. She debated two questions:
Should she go visit Becky and ask how it had
gone with her *men friends* over the weekend, or
ride into Laramie and buy something for her
party?

Downstairs in the kitchen she could hear
Kane and Wade discussing the cattle drive they
would start at the end of the week. She wondered where Rafe was. He and Wade avoided
each other like the plague. He was probably
down at the stables doing what he liked best:
currying Kane's pampered mares.

Storm continued to lie in bed, waiting for

Wade to leave. She might hit him if she saw him. The sight of Josie at his place was still fresh in her mind.

She didn't have long to wait before she heard the two men leave the kitchen and walk outside. When the big black stallion's hoofbeats faded away she rose and walked to the window, her attention drawn to the stables. Rafe was coming from the barn, riding his mount and leading Kane's. When Kane had swung into the saddle and they had ridden off in the direction in which the shorthorns grazed, she turned back into the room. After slipping on a cotton robe she opened a dresser drawer and took out clean underclothing. Taking a shirt and riding skirt from the wardrobe, she folded them over her arm. She picked up a towel and bar of soap from the washstand and headed downstairs. The last storm had filled the big holding tank with soft rainwater, and she was going to have a shower.

She tiptoed past Maria in the kitchen, her Indian moccasins making no sound. Maria didn't like her using the apparatus hooked up to the tank unless Kane was within shouting distance. But Maria fretted about everything.

As she opened the door to the shoulder-high wooden cubicle, Storm grinned. Jeb was in the stables, loudly singing in his off-key, cracked voice. She folded her clothes over the top of the stall, then pulled the rope that released a shower of water over her. When she felt that her hair was throughly wet she turned loose the rope and worked up a thick lather in her blonde hair with the rose-scented soap. Throwing the thick rope of hair over her shoulder, she started with her face and then soaped the rest of her body. She tugged on the rope again, holding it, letting the sun-warmed water flow over her until all traces of lather were rinsed from her hair.

She had just finished toweling her hair and had started on her body when she heard thundering hooves and the high, trumpeting whistle of a stallion. She peered over the enclosure toward the stables, wondering what had set off one of Kane's horses.

Her eyes widened in surprise and alarm. The rogue stallion had entered the area near the barn and was trying to climb over the corral to get to her mare. Beauty was in heat.

What should she do? she wondered frantically. Should she yell at him, try to drive him away? But if she did, would he come at her? This structure wasn't very strong.

Storm fumbled into her clothes, everything clinging to her still-damp skin. She swore furiously as she struggled to get her arms into her shirtsleeves. If she could slip to the house without drawing the brute's attention, she could take Kane's rifle off the wall and shoot over his head, scare him away.

She was easing the flimsy door open, holding her breath when it creaked. Then the barn door flew open and Jeb stood there, a rifle at his shoulder. The firearm cracked, and bullets kicked up dust at the stallion's feet. He gave an angry clarion call and raced off across the plains, his tail held high, his great hooves sending clods of dirt and grass flying.

Jeb saw her standing, the door in her hand, frozen in place, and came up to her. "That wild bastard is gettin' braver and braver. Comes right up to the barn now. Kane had better shoot the devil before he kills one of us."

"Do you think he would attack a human?"

"He sure as hell would if a person stood in the way of what he wanted."

"I guess he should be put down, but it would be a shame. He's such a handsome animal."

"He is that," Jeb agreed as they watched the stallion until he disappeared over a rise. "The fact is, though, that besides bein' dangerous, he's stolen six of Kane's mares in the past two years."

Noticing then that Storm wore her riding skirt, Jeb said, "If you intend to go ridin', don't take the mare. He can smell her for miles. I'll saddle my roan for you."

"Thank you, Jeb. I'm riding into Laramie. Would you bring Red up to the house when you've got him ready?"

In her room again, Storm took some money from the top drawer of the dresser, shoved it into her back pocket, put on her hat, and went downstairs to the kitchen.

Maria looked up from the dry sink, where she was cleaning vegetables for a pot of soup. "My, don't you look fresh and pretty," she said. "I like

your hair curling loose around your shoulders."
Storm smiled her thanks, then Maria added, "If
you're going into town, there're a few things I'd
like for you to pick up for me."

"Sure," Storm answered, pouring herself a
cup of coffee while Maria wrote out her list.
When Jeb arrived with his roan Storm told
Maria she wouldn't be gone long and left the
house.

As the big horse cantered along the dusty
road to Laramie, Storm found her thoughts
going back, back to when she used to tag along
behind Kane and Wade every chance she got.
Often, aggravated by his young sister's presence, Kane would shoo her away with cutting
remarks. But almost always her handsome idol
would brush aside the hurtful words and with
a tolerant smile, say, "Let her be, Kane. She's
not botherin' us."

And sometimes, to her delight, the black-
haired, gray-eyed boy would pick her up and
set her on his shoulders, giving her short legs
a rest. Thrilled to the soul of her tiny being,
Storm's chubby hands would pat his curly
head. He'd look up at her, a crooked smile
on his lips as he gave her a slow wink.
She'd throw her arms around his head then,
her heart hammering as she squeezed him
tightly.

It had been a very sad time for her when Wade
and Kane reached adolescence and became
physically aware of the big girls; how nice
they smelled, how soft their curves were. Gone,

then, were the rides on sturdy shoulders, gone the tender teasing.

Through the next years she had seen Wade only fleetingly, times when he would ride up to the ranch, a giggling girl sharing his horse. Kane would have his mount saddled, waiting to tear off with him.

Laramie suddenly loomed ahead, and Storm thankfully left off her reminiscing. She pulled the roan to a walk as they rode down the dusty, rutted street, reining him in when they came to Henderson's Mercantile. She would pick up Maria's items there.

She swung out of the saddle and was looping the reins over a hitching post when a sharp finger was poked into her back. Storm jerked her head over her shoulder and looked into Becky's smiling face.

"Becky. What are you doing in town so early?"

"I have to pick up some food for my animals. You wouldn't believe how much those critters eat."

In the excitement of seeing her old friend, Storm said, "Let's go to the café down the street and have a cup of coffee while you tell me about your trip to Cheyenne. Sometimes I miss it a little."

When hesitation and uncertainty jumped into the brown eyes gazing back at her Storm remembered that her friend had a bad name now, and that association with Becky could tar her with the same brush. She paused only a heartbeat before taking Becky's arm and steering her down the street. She'd take the consequences, whatever they might be.

Storm was very conscious of the looks directed at them as she and Becky entered the café. Some were curious, while others were condemning. As she and Becky made their way to a table in the back of the room, she knew that tongues would wag at supper tables tonight.

Let them talk, she thought rebelliously as they sat down. She said brightly, "So. Tell me everything."

"Everything?" Becky grinned, raising an eyebrow.

"Well, not everything." Storm's face reddened. "You know what I mean."

Becky laughed softly. "Don't be embarrassed, Storm. I know it's hard for you to accept what your childhood friend does for a living. But keep in mind that I don't walk the streets pandering."

"I know." Storm nodded. "I'll get used to it."

"It might interest you to know that one of my customers asked me to marry him."

"Really, Becky?" Storm sat forward, her eyes sparkling with excitement.

"Yep," Becky answered, amused at Storm's happy surprise. She added, "And he's very wealthy too."

"Oh, Becky, I'm so happy for you," Storm began, then paused at the lack of enthusiasm on the small woman's face.

Her own elation died at Becky's next remark. "Don't get carried away, Storm. I'm not going to marry him."

The happy glow gone from her face, Storm said weakly, "I see."

"No, Storm, you don't see," Becky said earnestly. "The man is fifty years old, twenty-eight years older than me. Now how long do you think he could keep up with a passionate woman like me? Possibly five years, and then what? You know what the end result would be."

At Storm's puzzled frown, Becky sighed impatiently. "I'd start cheating on him, and I'd hate myself for it." After a slight pause Becky said softly, "When I marry, and I will someday, it will be a young man, a man I love."

"That's the way it should be," Storm said at the end of a long sigh. "I imagine that marriage without love could be hell."

Becky nodded. "I saw that in many of the homes I lived in."

They both looked up when a middle-aged, disapproving waitress reluctantly approached their table. She gave Becky a cold look, then turned one on Storm that wasn't much warmer.

"We're only having coffee." Storm gave the woman her warmest smile but wasn't surprised when it wasn't returned. She and Becky looked at each other and shrugged with shared laughter as they watched the woman's ample hips sway away as she fetched their drinks.

"She must have had a cup of vinegar with her breakfast this morning." Becky giggled.

"Or a crab apple," Storm added.

They were still trying to smother their laughter when their coffee was slapped in front of them, the dark liquid splashing over into the saucers. They ignored the woman's rudeness and when she walked away they continued to talk.

"What did you think of Rafe?" Storm asked. "Isn't he nice?"

"And handsome too. Is he becoming special to you?"

"Only as a friend." Storm grinned mischievously. "I think he was quite taken with you."

Becky stared into her coffee. "I suppose he'll be showing up at the house some night," she said, her eyes bleak, her voice bitter.

Storm laid her hand on the small one clenched on the table. "Not for the reason you're thinking, Becky. If he does come to see you, it will be to court you."

"Oh, sure." Becky snorted. "He'll want me to go into Laramie to have supper with him in the hotel dining room. He'll be real proud to let everyone see him with the infamous Becky Hadler." She looked up at Storm. "You're a romantic dreamer if you think that, Storm."

"Would you go with him if he asked you?"

"I would not. He's too nice a man to have people snickering behind his back."

"Rafe wouldn't mind what a few narrow-minded people might say. He's not that way.

He's a very special sort of man."

"Well, I'd care, so let's talk about something else. For instance, I saw Wade in Cheyenne. He was with a woman I've never seen before."

"Oh?" Storm placed the cup from which she had been about to take a sip back in its saucer. "Describe her. Maybe I know her."

"Well," Becky said thoughtfully, "from what I could tell from my room in the hotel she was kind of pretty in a quiet sort of way. She was dressed very somber, her hair done up in a roll at her nape. She wasn't too tall, very slender, almost thin. What I noticed most about her was that her face looked drawn, tired and sad. Wade was awfully solicitous of her, holding her arm as they walked along."

Becky paused. "Come to think of it, Wade looked down in the mouth too . . . like something was bothering him real bad."

The breath drained from Storm's lungs. She didn't know the woman, but she knew who she was: Wade's old love. She was back in his life, but for some reason they were keeping their relationship secret. Why? Could it be that Kane was mistaken about the mysterious woman having never married? Maybe she had wed and was now sorry that she had.

"She doesn't sound like Wade's usual kind of woman," Storm finally said, her voice only a thread of sound.

"That's true, but if Wade ever becomes serious about a woman, she won't be the kind he's used to running with." When Storm nodded her head in agreement Becky said, "Let's get out of here. I'm beginning to feel scorched from all the looks we've been getting."

Storm placed the price of the coffees on the table and, their heads held high, she and Becky walked outside. They paused for a moment, making plans to see each other one day the next week. When they parted Becky went down the street to the feed store, while Storm went up the street toward the end of town where the Mexicans lived and did most of their buying. There was a shop there that she had often visited with Maria. They sold beautiful, bright-colored skirts and blouses: the perfect barbecue ensemble.

"Senorita Storm," she was greeted warmly when Storm stepped inside the cool shop, its walls covered with skirts, dresses, blouses, shawls, and wide-brimmed straw hats. "Maria told us you had come home. She is very happy about it."

"I am happy about it, too, Senora Lopez." Storm smiled at the short, plump woman. "I'm looking for a skirt and blouse, and I remembered the beautiful ones you sell."

"*Sí*, and I have just what will look lovely on you." Senora Lopez beamed at Storm.

When she left the shop half an hour later Storm carried a package containing a beautiful outfit, plus a pair of Mexican sandals. Returning to the place where she had tethered Jeb's roan, she fastened the package to the back of the saddle, then went into the mercantile to purchase Maria's items.

As Storm rode out of town, she passed Josie's dress shop, and shot a fast glance through the large window. Startled, she looked again. A few feet into the room, Josie stood in an amorous embrace with a man who was not Wade Magallen.

What would the big man think about that if he knew? Her lips curled as she rode out of town. It would certainly take a big chunk out of his manly pride if he were to know that Josie had gone to the arms of another man only hours after spending the night with him. Storm would give anything if she could twit him about it.

And as for that, what would Josie Sales have to say if she knew about Wade's woman in Cheyenne?

What a pair they are, Storm thought, lifting the roan into a canter.

Chapter Ten

The screen door slapped shut behind Storm as she left the kitchen and headed for four long tables placed end-to-end beneath the two large cottonwoods at the end of the yard. She carried a stack of tin plates in the crook of her arm and pieces of flatware in her hands.

Maria's nephew, Juan, came behind her, four checkered tablecloths folded over his arm and four sets of salt and pepper shakers cupped in his palm.

With swift, deft movements, Storm smoothed the cloths over the tables, two belonging to the ranch, the other two borrowed from a neighbor. She placed the tins, knives, and forks on an end table where the women guests would place theirs as they arrived. It was the custom that at a large event, the ranch wives brought along whatever they had in the way of serving utensils. Outside of a restaurant, nobody owned fifty or more plates and their accompaniments.

Everything in place, Storm sniffed at the tangy aroma of barbecue sauce floating in the air. She glanced over to see that Kane was stirring a bubbling mixture in a large iron pot on the fire. Amusement twitched her lips. Her brother wore a look of exasperation and helplessness as he watched the two cowboys who had volunteered to help him. It was plain the two were out of their element as they moved awkwardly about, getting into each other's way as they tended the great slabs of short ribs and steaks that were cooking over a trench of glowing coals.

Turning her back on them and walking away before she laughed out loud and embarrassed the young men, she glanced up at the misty-colored sky. The days were growing shorter as autumn approached, and already dusk was settling in. Even now a full, nearly white moon hung above. When darkness came it would be a bright yellow, lighting up the area as though it were daylight. However, Kane had hung lanterns from the trees where the moonlight wouldn't be able to penetrate the leaves.

It's a fine night for my party, Storm thought as she hurried back to the house to change her clothes and ready herself to greet her guests, who would be arriving in fifteen or twenty minutes.

She had bathed earlier, so all she had to do

now was slip into her Mexican outfit. It took but a few minutes to pull the blouse over her head and step into the full skirt. She stood in front of the dresser mirror then, wondering how to wear her hair. Should she leave it hanging free? She would look older if she fashioned it into a chignon at her nape.

In the end she simply pulled the brush through the soft curls and then left them alone. She didn't want to have to worry about her hair escaping from a fancy roll.

She gave her attention to her attire next. The skirt, very full and with a wide ruffle at the hem, was white, with bright red poppies scattered over it. The blouse, tucked into the skirt's tiny waistband, was also white, with a wide ruffle around the neck that matched the design of the skirt.

She played with the neckline a moment, pulling it down over her shoulders, then arranging it in a more decorous position. She studied her reflection in the mirror. The Mexican women looked very beautiful wearing theirs down around their shoulders, as the garment was meant to be worn.

"And whether Kane likes it or not, that is the way I'm going to wear mine," she muttered. "I am no longer a young girl to be dictated to."

So saying, Storm tugged the ruffle back down over her shoulders, to a point where a slight hint of cleavage showed. Then, with a last pat to her hair, she left the room, the full skirt swirling around her knees, her slim feet moving gracefully in the new sandals.

Kane and Rafe had also taken the time to change their clothes. When Storm joined them she smiled and said, "My goodness, I don't know which of you is the more handsome." Both were dressed in tight twills that were shoved into shiny boots, soft woolen shirts open at the throat, and sleeves rolled up past their elbows.

"Well now, you're a pretty sight." Rafe looked at her in appreciation. "It won't be hard to decide who the prettiest girl is at the party tonight."

"Thank you, kind sir." Storm smiled, linking her arms with both men and directing their steps toward the door. Kane looked down at her neckline and frowned but made no remark about it.

It seemed to Storm that everyone came at once. There was a steady line of wagons, light carriages, and riders turning onto the gravel road leading to the ranch house. She had one surprise, but a very pleasant one. Josie Sales arrived alone in her light two-seater carriage.

Rafe stayed by her side as she walked about, greeting old friends and neighbors, happy to be with old acquaintances again. The old sense of belonging was returning. While living in Cheyenne, Storm had never quite captured that feeling. When her new friends talked of past events and happy times shared she had felt left out, a stranger.

Only one thing marred Storm's contentment. The party was over an hour old and Wade hadn't put in an appearance yet. Wasn't he coming? Had he forgotten the party?

Trying to keep her anxiety from showing as she moved about, her gaze went often to the gravel road, looking for a big black stallion to come galloping up to the house, praying that another horse wouldn't be running alongside him.

Another half hour passed before Storm's watch was rewarded. She felt a jolt to her heart when she saw the shadowy shape of the black horse and its rider.

"He's alone," she whispered, trying to keep her mind on what was being said by the small group of which she was a part.

The gay voices faded to nothingness when Wade swung out of the saddle and walked toward the group. Storm's eyes moved over the lean body, taking in the soft white shirt, the black close-fitting twills that rode low, molding the shape of his manhood and making it easy to discern as he came closer.

A desire to stroke her palm over the slight bulge gripped Storm; to make it stir, come alive. When she lifted her eyes to Wade their eyes met and clung, blatant desire in them. They were oblivious to everyone around them as they sent their silent message to each other. They both gave a startled jerk when suddenly Josie Sales's shrill voice shattered the moment so precious to Storm.

"Wade!" The redhead pounced like a cat, wrapping long fingers around Wade's arm. "I thought you would never get here."

A shadow of annoyance swept across Wade's face, and his voice was cool when he said, "I don't remember tellin' you I would be here."

"You didn't have to tell me, silly man." Josie pretended not to see the irritated drawn eyebrows. "Kane would have your hide if you missed the little princess's welcome-home party."

Josie's voice was loud and carrying, and Storm sensed the curious looks sent their way. Two desires ran through her at the same time: one, to tackle Josie, bring her to the ground, and beat her senseless; the other, to dash into the house and stay there until the party was over.

She did neither. To run was not her way, and a catfight was demeaning. She stiffened her spine, inhaled deeply, and pulled a welcoming smile to her lips. "Hello, Wade," she said. "I'm glad you could be here."

"It's good to have you back, Storm," Wade said softly, pulling his arm from Josie's clutching fingers and taking Storm's slender hand in his.

"Thank you, Wade." Storm's words came breathlessly, shyness coming over her.

"Yes, welcome home, Storm." Josie remembered her manners, then disregarded them as she jostled Storm aside and looped her arm in Wade's again.

She is still attractive in a brittle kind of

way, Storm thought as she studied Josie, but her birthdays are beginning to show. At the moment her features, which had coarsened with age, were drawn into a pouty crossness that gave away her displeasure at the way the man at her side had greeted the younger woman.

Understanding the woman's jealousy—she had experienced the emotion herself over Wade Magallen—Storm pasted a smile on her face and said pleasantly, "How are you, Josie? It's nice seeing you again."

Hostility poured from the hard green eyes that swept over Storm, not missing the flawless skin, the firm young breasts. Instead of answering in the same tone with which she had been greeted, she ignored Storm's welcome and said nastily, "Well, well, the little princess all grown up."

Pity for the older woman deserted Storm. If that was the way Josie wanted it, that was the way she would get it. "We all have birthdays, Josie." Storm deliberately let her gaze linger on the fine lines around her enemy's eyes.

Josie's face turned a mottled red at feminine snickers and a choked laugh that Storm was sure came from Wade. She waited for Josie's retaliation, but when it came it was in an unexpected way.

Pretending not to have heard the pointed remark, Josie tipped her face up to Wade, her thin lips twisted in a poor facsimile of an amused smile, and said, "Remember what a pain in the neck she was to you and Kane, always underfoot, always pesterin' you? Remember how the two of you were always chasin' her away?"

Fighting back the desire to slap the thin, angular face, Storm slid Wade an uncertain glance, wondering if he would agree with the wretched woman.

Her heart leapt. He was eyeing Josie with dark disapproval. When his gray eyes shifted back to her he said quietly, "Only a fool would chase her away today." Storm flinched at the pure hatred Josie's glittering eyes shot at her.

How the furious woman might have reacted to Wade's remark wasn't to be known. Rafe had come up beside Storm, and now he slid a possessive arm around her waist. Holding her against his side, he said smoothly, "Truer words were never spoken, Magallen, and I'm no fool."

Oh, Rafe, Storm cried inwardly, I wish you hadn't said that.

A fiddle and a banjo sent their music out into the night air and couples jumped up on the wooden platform some of the ranch hands had thrown together, the loosely nailed boards bouncing with the thumping of hopping and stomping feet. Wade gave Storm a cold look and, taking Josie's hand, said, "Come on, let's dance."

An emptiness inside her, Storm watched Wade swing Josie in among the dancers. When

Rafe said, "Come on, honey, let's join them," she went woodenly into his arms.

As they two-stepped with the others, Rafe drew Storm closer and whispered in her ear, "Loosen up, Storm; smile. Make that big buffalo think you're havin' the time of your life. I want to get a real rise out of him tonight. I want us to get him so jealous, he'll damn near choke on it."

Storm looked at the couples drifting around them, her eyes falling on Wade and Josie. Josie wore a smug look as she held her thin body as close to Wade's as she could without crawling inside him.

And Wade didn't seem to mind as they circled the floor.

"Where's your pride?" a voice whispered inside her. "Get that hangdog look off your face and enjoy your party. When did that longlegged wolf ever give you any joy?"

Storm knew she had given herself good advice and, relaxing in Rafe's arms, she laughed as brightly and stomped her feet as loudly as anyone else.

Three more tunes followed with barely a pause between. Then Kane was calling out, "Grab your partners and get ready for a hoedown." Storm's eyes sparkled. She loved the foot-stomping, twirling, and spinning of the old-time dance.

With a wide smile, Rafe reached for Storm; then a heavily veined hand grabbed her wrist.

"Sorry, Rafe," a gravelly voice said, "but

Storm always dances the first hoedown with me."

Rafe grinned as Storm threw her arms around the gray-haired man. "Uncle Jake," she cried. "I didn't know you were here."

"I just rode in." Wade's father returned her hug. "I was late gettin' away from the saloon. A couple of drunks got into a ruckus, and it took a while to put them out on the street."

Storm leaned back in the wiry arms and smiled up at a face brown and wrinkled from all kinds of weather. "You're looking good, Uncle Jake," she said, remembering how kind this elder Magallen had always been to her, especially after the loss of her parents. Once a week he would leave his saloon in the hands of his bartender and they would climb into his rowboat and go fishing on the Platte. Storm never caught many fish, but her pain was relieved by Jake's comforting presence.

While two sets were being formed, Storm and Jake caught up on the events of the past four years. Neither had mentioned Wade when with whoops and yells the dance began. Jake whirled Storm away, her skirt flying high, exposing flashing long legs and a glimpse of thigh.

Storm's complete enjoyment of the moment radiated and touched those around her, making them smile. And the man who had previously watched the vibrant figure with angry fire in his eyes was now as captivated as the rest. Wade's leg had started paining him too much for the rollicking dance.

The hard-eyed woman at his side looked on, her rage and hatred barely concealed. By the time each man had swung his partner home and the music makers had broken for a rest, Josie Sales was trembling with her dark emotions.

Matters weren't improved when Wade wordlessly left Josie and began making his way toward the couples leaving the dance floor. She called out to him, but after one backward glance Wade ignored her.

Josie had distracted Wade's attention enough, however, to make him lose sight of the blonde head. His eyes searched the crowd but only found his father. When he couldn't see Rafe around either Wade muttered, "Damn," and struck off to his left, wearing an angry scowl.

Rafe had been waiting for Storm, and when she joined him, her face flushed from the rousing dance, he said, "Let's find a place where you can sit down and catch your breath."

Taking Storm's arm, Rafe led her down the shadowed path that led to her mother's rose garden. The full moon revealed every sweet-scented blossom, and Rafe paused to snap a bright-red bud and hand it to Storm. "It's just like you, Storm. Sweet and innocent, and yet somehow wild."

"Thank you, Rafe." Storm took the rose from him and lifted her arm to stick it in her hair behind her ear. Rafe lifted a hand to help her weave it through her curls; then a rough voice brought them both swinging around.

"Kane wants you back at the party, Storm." Wade stood glaring at them.

Storm glared back, her eyes hardening obstinately at the undisguised order in the flat statement. Her resentment hissed in her voice as she snapped, "You can tell my brother that I'll return when I please."

"You heard her, Magallen." Rafe's jaw thrust forward. "She's not a little girl to be ordered around."

"Stay out of this, Jeffery." Wade's tone and body suggested violence as he finally acknowledged Rafe's presence. He grabbed Storm's wrist and tugged. "Come on, let's go."

Rage enveloped Storm as she was pulled along. "I'll go when I'm ready," she repeated, tugging to free her hand. "And you're hurting me, you big ape."

"Damn you, Magallen, turn her loose." Rafe clamped his fingers on Wade's shoulder and spun him around.

Wade stiffened and put Storm aside. With a movement so swift it was hard to follow, his fist shot out, connecting with Rafe's chin. The horse trainer swayed a moment, then went down on his knees. As he knelt, his head wagging, Storm gave a small cry and started toward him.

"Stay where you are," Wade ordered, grabbing her arm and holding her, paying no attention to her struggling or the angry insults she shouted at him.

Rafe hid a satisfied grin. His plan had succeeded better than he had hoped. Magallen had reacted violently. There was no doubt in his mind now that the man was crazy about Storm. But why did he try to hide it? Rafe rubbed his sore chin and staggered to his feet. "You win this time, Magallen," he said in frosty tones. "I won't fight over Storm like she was a bone between two hungry dogs. I'll see you later, honey." He smiled at Storm, and then disappeared up the path.

"You big bully!" She hammered her fists against the broad chest that kept her from running after Rafe. "You had no right to hit him."

Wade made no response, only let her batter him until Rafe's footsteps faded away. Then he grasped her wrists and held them to her side. "Why the anger, little girl?" His gray eyes bored into her. "Are you upset that you didn't get any lovin'?" Before she could respond he jerked her into the shadowed darkness of a tree, growling, "You don't have to go to Jeffery to get your thrills."

Storm opened her mouth to deny that she was looking for thrills, or anything else from Rafe, when the words were pushed back by firm lips covering her mouth. She tried to keep her body stiff, to ignore the tongue that seductively traced her lips, begging for entrance.

She was partially successful until Wade tugged the wide ruffle of her blouse down past her bare breasts and stroked them with caressing fingers. Pride and determination were overridden, and a moan of pleasure issued from her throat. She lifted a hand to his dark head and moved her trembling fingers through his thick hair.

She blinked in bewilderment when Wade tore his lips away and pulled her bodice back into place. His words were like a knife slash as he sneered, "Do you think that will hold you for a while?"

She stumbled slightly as he took her arm and hustled her up the path and into the light, where the dancing had resumed. Without another word he released her and stalked away. A minute later she heard the sound of hard, galloping hooves and knew that they belonged to Wade's black stallion. She felt empty, all the joy of her party gone.

Storm's spirits were raised a little when she scanned the crowd and saw Josie, a disappointed frown creasing the woman's forehead. At least Wade hadn't taken *her* with him.

Kane was calling out, then, that it was time to eat, and everyone was crowding around the long tables. Rafe appeared at Storm's side, and together they fell into line behind the others.

"Well, Storm," Rafe spoke in a low voice, his eyes twinkling, "the rooster bared his talons tonight, didn't he? He was blind with jealousy."

"Jealousy had nothing to do with it, Rafe," Storm said, her voice wistful. "Kane sent him after me and he was determined that I return with him."

Rafe gave her a skeptical look. "And what did Kane want you for?"

Storm was baffled. "I don't know. He saw me when I came back to the party, but he only smiled and waved at me." Resentment grew in her voice. "He probably thought it wasn't proper for me to go off and leave my party."

Rafe only shook his head. Storm Roemer was dense beyond words. He filled a plate for her and heaped his own. Then they joined a group of Storm's friends, who were watching Josie, betting on which of the two men she was talking to would take her home from the party.

"Maybe they'll draw straws," the man next to Rafe said.

Laughter greeted his remark, and someone else said, "Yeah, draw straws who goes to bed with her first." Another peal of laughter rang out.

On a more serious note, one of the women said, "I heard that Wade has dropped her, and she's like a crazy woman, trying to get back his attention."

As her friends continued to discuss Josie, amid laughter and crude remarks, Storm couldn't help feeling a little pity for her. What would the woman do when it became common knowledge that Wade and an old love were back together again?

She'll be hurt, just like I've been, she answered her own question.

Another hour passed, the longest Storm had ever experienced. Her lips ached from the false smile that stretched them, and her throat was sore from the forced laughter she pushed through it. At long last the party was breaking up and she and Kane were saying good-bye to their last guest.

Before the last sound of galloping hooves and creaking wagon wheels had died away in the darkness, Storm confronted her brother with her hands on her hips.

"What was the idea of sending Wade after me," she demanded, "ordering me back to the party as if I was ten years old?"

"What are you talking about?" Kane looked at her as though she had lost her mind. "I didn't send him after you. I hardly had time to speak to him, I was so busy. I saw him when he left, though, lookin' like a wounded grizzly bear. Did you two have words?"

"Who could have words with that one?" Storm snorted. "He issues orders, then closes his ears to any argument."

"Yeah, that's Wade, all right." Kane turned his head to hide his pleased look, thinking that one of these days his stubborn friend would have to give in to his love for Storm and ask her to marry him. Otherwise the idiot was going to drive himself crazy.

After a long, loud yawn, Kane said, "I'm dead tired. Let's go to bed. We can clean up this mess tomorrow." He looked up at his window. "I see Rafe has already turned in."

The frown between Storm's eyes deepened as she followed her brother into the house and up the stairs to the bedrooms. What kind of game was Wade playing, she asked herself, the big brother on one hand, the jealous lover on the other?

That had been no brotherly kiss he had given her, she thought as she drifted off to sleep.

Did she dare hope?

Chapter Eleven

It was a beautiful cool morning when Storm joined Kane and Rafe at the breakfast table. They were into the first week of October, and the sun striking through the window wasn't as strong as it had been a month before. Fall had arrived.

"Who's going riding with me this morning?" Her glance took in both men as she reached for a platter of fried eggs.

"I wish we both could, honey," Kane said, "but we're gonna be busy all day, roundin' up the cattle me and Wade are drivin' to the fort."

Storm shrugged. "I'll go alone," she said, then added in a mock hurt tone, "I happen to like my own company."

Rafe grinned, and Kane reached over and gave her hair a yank. "No one has ever had a doubt how set you are on yourself."

When the two men had finished eating and were leaving the table Rafe leaned down and whispered to Storm, "If you should happen to see Becky, say hello to her for me."

"I'll not be seeing her today," she whispered back. "Why don't you go tell her in person?"

Storm had one foot in a stirrup and was ready to swing onto the mare's back when she heard the sound of a horse approaching. Her heart lurched when she recognized Wade's big stallion coming up the ranch road. But it felt like it stopped beating when she saw that Wade wasn't alone. Perched behind him, her arms wrapped around his waist, sat an uneasy Josie, bouncing with each pound of the hooves.

When Wade had awakened at sunrise the same thought he had gone to sleep with returned: He had erred badly at Storm's party. His jealousy of the horse trainer had blinded him to proper behavior. But seeing the man so close to Storm in the moonlight, his hands in her hair, had driven all clear thought from his head. He only knew that he wanted more space between them, and so he had blurted out his lie.

With a long drawn-out sigh, he sat up in bed. To worsen matters, he had lost control and kissed and caressed Storm. What would she make of that? Either she would feel insulted or she would take it for what it was: the action of a jealous man.

Wade reached for his trousers. He didn't have to guess what importance she would place on his action. He knew that she returned the love he had for her. It showed in so many different ways: the way her eyes would light up when she saw him, the hurt that showed there every time she saw him with Josie or he deliberately ignored her.

Wade realized as he buttoned up his shirt that Rafe Jeffery was becoming important to Storm, that the handsome older man could very well make her fall in love with him. How he could bear that he didn't know. It would tear him apart to see her married to him . . . to any man.

But that was wrong, selfish of him. His golden-haired girl deserved to have a good man, children, a home of her own. He should be happy for her if that came about.

Right now, though, he must hurt Storm once again, make her think that his kiss had meant nothing to him. He would pick up Josie and ride to the Roemer ranch on the pretext of borrowing one of their horses for Josie to ride. Storm was bound to see them together.

Storm's lips firmed in a straight line when Wade and Josie dismounted and walked toward her. She thought of the talk at her party: that Wade no longer had anything to do with the woman who had her arm looped tightly with Wade's. It certainly didn't look that way today.

He has a nerve bringing Josie Sales here, she raged silently. He knows we don't get along, yet he deliberately shoves her under my nose. Well, Storm wasn't going to hang around and swap insults with the other woman.

She had just thrown a leg over the saddle when Wade called her name, and angry impatience underlined the word. She dropped back to the ground and, looking over her shoulder, said stiffly, "Kane isn't here. He'll be gone all day."

"I'm not lookin' for Kane, you bitter little weed." Wade freed his arm from Josie and reached Storm's side in long strides. His hard eyes raked over her. "I was hoping I could borrow a mount for Josie. Are you ridin' alone?"

Storm flashed him a look of pure dislike. "Yes, I am."

Wade was silent for a moment. His eyes had honed in on her full breasts, thrusting against her soft cotton shirt, and had lingered. She blinked in confusion when he lifted his eyes to her face and said, "Josie and I are goin' ridin' too. We might as well ride together."

Storm glanced at Josie, and from the alarmed denial that flashed in her eyes Storm knew that no such plan had been discussed between them.

Well, by God, she was just as opposed to the idea. Damn Wade's hide; he didn't even ask if they'd be welcome to ride with her. He just announced that they were going to.

"Just a cotton-picking minute, Wade Magallen." She stormed after Wade as he disappeared into the barn, her boot heels kicking up dust. "I don't want company today. I want to ride alone."

"Why?" Wade wheeled around, his voice harsh as his big body almost collided with her. "Are you meetin' Jeffery down by the river? That used to be a favorite place of yours to go swimmin'."

Storm thought for a moment that anger had nearly blinded her; Wade's face appeared to her through a thin veil. Then Josie, who had hurried after them, giggled, and in a lightning-quick change, Storm smiled sweetly. She stepped closer to Wade and said in her friendliest manner, "Why don't you go to hell, Wade Magallen?"

Wade stared down at her, his expression saying that he knew she wasn't finished with him yet. As he waited for her next barrage, she swung back a foot, then brought the hard toe of her boot up against his shin. When he let out a yelp of pain and grabbed his lower leg Josie's shrill voice yelled, "You little bitch, you could have chipped a bone."

Her hands on her hips, Storm shot back, "I could have done worse than chip a bone, Josie. I could have kicked higher, ruined him for you. Why don't you give thanks for small mercies?"

While Josie spluttered angrily, Storm growled in Wade's direction, "Come on, let's go choose a mount for your lady friend."

Despite his pain, amusement sparked in Wade's eyes as he limped along behind Storm.

Josie didn't know how lucky she was that she hadn't been attacked too.

His eyes followed every provocative twitch of the shapely little derriere three steps ahead of him, making them suddenly glaze over with desire. He looked down and saw that he had an arousal that threatened to bust the buttons containing it. He jammed his hands in his pockets as Storm stopped in front of a stall two doors away from Kane's favorite mount.

Rubbing the nose of the gentle-eyed mare, Storm said, "I think Missy will suit Josie. She's a very well-behaved little animal." When she turned to leave Wade put a hand on her arm, holding her back.

"Were you tempted to ruin me back there?" he asked, his voice gentle.

Confused by his tone and the intensity of the gray eyes watching her, a half smile curved Storm's lips. "It would have served you right if I had."

He lifted a hand and stroked his finger down her cheek. "But what if *you* wanted me someday? Wouldn't you regret that I'd be unable to send you soaring to heaven?"

Storm caught her breath. Was Wade hinting that someday there might be a future for them? She lifted her face to him, then went cold. Bright mockery gazed back at her. He had only been amusing himself, playing with her emotions.

Thankful for the gloom in the stables, which hid her hurt, her humiliation, she masked it all with a twist of her lips as she said, "I strongly doubt the occasion will ever arise. Josie Sales's leftovers would never interest me."

She walked away, Wade's angry, sucked-in breath a balm to the wound he had dealt her.

Outside, Josie sulked in the shade of a cottonwood tree. Storm ignored the black look directed at her and concentrated on hiding a grin as she imagined the woman trying to keep astride a running horse all on her own. She was no horsewoman, and it would be interesting to see if she could hang on when the mounts were kicked into a hard gallop.

Storm pretended to fuss with her saddle, to adjust the stirrups, wondering where Jeb had taken himself off to. It would be useless to try to talk to Josie in a friendly manner. The woman was furious and in no mood to suffer the sharp edge of her tongue.

She flinched when Josie spoke behind her, her voice sharp with resentment. "Storm, you're not a little girl anymore. Don't you think you're a little chesty not to wear a camisole?"

An exasperated sigh whistled through Storm's teeth. She whipped around to confront the woman she disliked so intensely. The bright rays of the sun relentlessly revealed the lines around Josie's thin lips, the crow's-feet around her eyes, the fear in their green depths. She began to understand: Josie was approaching 35, and a young woman of 22 was a fearful threat to her.

But for as long as she could remember Josie had never missed a chance to take verbal slings at her. She pushed back her pity and, running a contemptuous glance over Josie's no longer firm breasts, Storm retorted, "I haven't gone without a camisole since I was thirteen. Maybe you've forgotten that I matured at an early age. At least that's when you started riding me."

Josie's angry gasp came only a fraction before a smothered, choking sound. When had Wade come up to them? Storm wondered, flags of red burning her cheeks. He would know that, indirectly, he was the cause of this little set-to. And damn his arrogant hide, what pleasure that would give him.

But when she looked over her shoulder at Wade only anger showed on his handsome face. "Are you at Josie again?" His voice cut into the tight silence. "I thought by now you'd have learned to control that temper of yours, Storm."

Storm bristled at the unjust chastisement. "I didn't start it," she began. "Josie . . ."

Her protest died away as Josie touched Wade's arm and said sweetly, "Don't yell at the child, Wade. You know how she is. Anyway," she pouted, "I'm wiltin' in this heat. Let's get this ride over with so we can get on to more pleasant things."

Storm turned away at the hungry look Josie gave Wade. Catching up Beauty's reins and grabbing the pommel, Storm swung onto the mare's back. Before Wade and Josie could mount she dug in her heels and sent the horse racing across the plains. She didn't look back at Wade's concerned shout.

The whipping wind freed the scalding tears that burned her eyes and sent them rolling down her cheeks. She could still see the intimacy in the look Josie had given Wade.

It took a minute for her to hear the fast beat of hooves coming up behind her. She didn't have to look back to know it was the black stallion that was gaining on her.

Wade overtook Storm and rode along beside her until they were hidden by a rise in the ground. She threw him a scathing look as he grabbed the mare's reins and pulled her up. She blanched then at the rage burning in his eyes.

"You little fool," he grated out. "What have I told you about racing a horse across gopher-hole–infested range? It's a miracle Beauty didn't put her foot in one and break both your necks."

"I was watching for them." Storm swiped at her wet cheeks. "What about Renegade? He could have stepped into a hole just as well."

Wade ignored her blustering response, tenderness welling up in him as he gazed at her tear-smeared face. "Would it make you feel better if you told me what Josie said to you?" he asked softly.

Angry resentment stiffened Storm's back. He was treating her like a child again. Where did she hurt? How had she hurt herself? She wondered if he would offer to kiss her next to make her feel better.

Staring straight ahead, her face closed and stony, Storm muttered, "It was nothing important. Like Josie said, you know me."

Wade was silent for a moment; then he asked, "Do you really want to ride alone today?"

Storm nodded. "I really do."

"Ride along then. I was wrong to foist our company on you." He released the mare's reins, and Storm wordlessly nudged her with a heel and cantered away. Wade gazed after her for a moment; then, with a ragged sigh, he turned the stallion around and rode back to join Josie, just topping the rise.

When Storm was sure Wade was out of sight she reined Beauty toward the ranch house. The desire for a long, leisurely ride had deserted her.

As Storm rode into the barnyard, a highly agitated Maria came bolting out of the house and ran toward her. "What's wrong, Maria?" she called, bringing Beauty to a rearing halt.

"Where's Wade?" the housekeeper puffed, holding her plump side.

"He's out riding with Josie. Why?"

"It's Jake. He slipped in the saloon and fell. The Mexican kid who rode in looking for Wade thinks his leg is broken. He's in Doc Wright's office now."

"Poor Jake," Storm exclaimed, wheeling Beauty around. "I'll go fetch Wade."

The little mare was running flat out when Storm spotted Wade and Josie emerging from the fringe of a pine grove. She stood up in the stirrups and, whipping off her hat, waved it wildly. When Wade pulled away from Josie, rapidly putting distance between them, she eased back into the saddle.

"What's wrong, Storm?" Wade sawed on the reins, looking anxiously at her worried face.

When she repeated what Maria had said he made no response other than to go pale. Wordlessly, they lifted their mounts in a hard gallop, leaving Josie far behind.

When they came to the ranch buildings Storm reined in, but Wade rode on toward Laramie. As Storm swung off Beauty and handed her over to Jeb, she said, "Have one of the hands ride over to the Magallen place, hitch up the two-seater, and drive that bitch home."

Chapter Twelve

Night had fallen, the lamps had been lit, and Maria was putting supper on the table when Wade rode in. When he walked into the kitchen Storm noted the strain around his mouth, the remaining traces of anxiety. He looks beat, she thought as he took a seat across from her.

He removed his hat and placed it on the floor before he answered the silent questions directed at him.

"Pa does have a broken leg." He took the platter of fried chicken Kane passed to him. "Just below the knee."

Maria clicked her tongue in sympathy, and Wade said harshly, "If he hadn't been carryin' that case of whiskey, he'd have seen the puddle on the floor."

Storm's eyes widened when he shot her an

accusatory look and added, "I should have been there, doin' that for him."

While Storm tried to make sense of the censuring look, Kane said impatiently, "That's stupid reasonin', Wade, and you know it. What about when you're gone for a couple of weeks at a time, drivin' a herd of cattle somewhere? And even if you'd been there at the time, you know damn well Jake would have still carried that whiskey."

"Yeah, I guess you're right. Pa's a proud old rooster. But somehow I've got to convince him to leave the heavy work to someone else."

"I don't suppose he's home yet," Maria said. "I could send him over some supper."

"No, he's still in Laramie. Doc doesn't want his splints disturbed for twelve hours or so, so he's keepin' Pa in that room in back of his office overnight. I'll take a wagon in tomorrow and bring him home."

Storm was wondering when Wade was going to ask about Josie—how she had gotten home—when Kane said, "I guess it will be a while before he can get around."

"A month at least, Doc said. At Pa's age the bones are pretty brittle and take longer to heal. Not like when I was ten and fell out of a tree and broke my leg. Seems like I was as good as new in a couple of weeks." He paused to grin crookedly. "Pa won't be completely helpless, though. He'll have crutches to help him get to the privy and back."

Kane laughed and remarked, "Jake would

crawl to the outhouse before he'd use a chamber pot."

They all smiled at that; then Wade looked at Kane and said soberly, "I expect Pa's accident has put paid to my going with you on the cattle drive. I could hire someone to stay with him, but you know how he is about havin' strangers around. He'd never allow it."

Storm saw the disappointment that washed over her brother's face and stared thoughtfully into her coffee. When there was a lull in the conversation she looked at Wade.

"I'm not a stranger to Jake. He and I are completely at ease with each other. I'll look after him."

Kane's eyes lit up at her offer, but a frown creased Wade's forehead. "You wouldn't be able to handle him," he said coolly. "He'd sweet-talk you into lettin' him hobble around on his crutches before Kane and I were out of sight."

Storm looked down at her plate to hide the pain of Wade's rejection. He didn't want anything from her; not her love, not her body, not even her help. Suddenly she was caught up in a fury that surprised herself as well as everyone else at the table as she yelled for the second time that day, "Go to hell, Wade Magallen."

Pushing away her plate, she jerked to her feet. "We all know the reason you don't want to go with Kane, and Jake has nothing to do with it. You don't want to leave your precious Josie for such a long period of time."

She ran out of the kitchen, headed for the stairs, with Wade's rich baritone roaring after her. "Dammit, Storm, that's not true."

The slamming of her bedroom door was Wade's only answer. "Ah, hell," he said, "I've hurt her feelin's."

Several minutes later Storm heard his stallion galloping away. She stared up at the ceiling, wishing she hadn't brought Josie's name into her fiery outburst. She had wanted to say "your woman in Cheyenne," but didn't know if Becky would want her repeating what she had told her. A fresh batch of tears flooded her eyes.

They were still red and swollen when Kane entered her room an hour later and sat down on the edge of her bed. When she didn't acknowledge his presence he gave her hair a tug. "You have no reason to be mad at me, you know." He waited a minute, and when she still didn't look at him or make a response he continued in a reasonable tone, "As for that, you have no cause to be mad at Wade either. He truly thinks that Jake wouldn't listen to you."

Kane stood up and stretched his lean body. "But he's willin' to give it a try." He grinned down at Storm's startled face, his announcement making her eyes snap open. "He's gonna make Jake swear an oath that he'll behave himself with you. Otherwise he'll threaten to leave Jake with a stranger."

"Jake and I will get along fine, Kane; you'll see."

"You'd better." Kane walked to the door. "Wade will have a strip of your hide if you let Jake talk you into doin' somethin' he shouldn't."

As Storm blew out the lamp, she told herself that she would tie Jake into bed if necessary.

Storm stepped out on the back porch and sniffed the air. The morning was clean and crisp, the rising sun scattering the mists that hung over low spots. Her gaze drifted to the river road, where Wade's stallion should be appearing at any minute. He and Kane wanted to get an early start on the cattle drive.

She was up early to fix breakfast because Maria had spent the night with her sister, who had just given birth to her sixth child.

Storm swung her gaze to the bunkhouse and the cookshack next to it. Smoke rose from the cookshack chimney, and the lamp light inside it showed the dim figure of Cookie moving about, making breakfast for the cowhands who would help drive the cattle to Fort Laramie. Even as she watched, six young men emerged from the bunkhouse, yawning and rubbing their eyes as they stumbled their way to the bench that held several basins, soap and towels, and a pail of water. A cowboy's life was a hard one, she thought, but she knew they wouldn't change it for any other.

Storm heard the stallion before she saw him. Tightening the belt of her robe, she stepped back into the kitchen. She opened the range's firebox and shoved another stick of wood into it, then peeped into the oven to check on the sourdough biscuits baking inside. "Almost done," she whispered with satisfaction. "They look almost as good as Maria's."

She was slicing bacon off a big slab when Wade rode into the yard. She watched through the window as he swung out of the saddle and tethered his horse. When he walked toward the porch the unconscious roll of his hips stirred a warmth in her lower body, and her eyes lingered on the spot where his chaps molded his sex, a spasm of desire rippling through her.

"Stop it!" she told herself crossly, and carried the strips of bacon to the stove.

The meat was beginning to sizzle when Wade walked into the kitchen, followed by Kane, who had just arrived after saddling his mount. Taking his usual seat at the table, Wade grinned crookedly at Kane as the tall rancher poured them both a cup of coffee.

"Do you think it's safe to eat breakfast this mornin'?" His voice held a worried tone.

His eyes reflecting his friend's humor, Kane said, "All I can say is, I hope the cook has improved in the kitchen department. I remember some of the messes she used to cook up for us."

Wade nodded in agreement. "And we couldn't say a word about it. We had to sit there and choke it down while Maria stood in the doorway glaring at us, darin' us to say a word."

Kane exaggerated a sigh. "It's a wonder she didn't stunt our growth."

The teasing went on as Storm continued making breakfast, not letting on that she even heard the pair at the table. But when she slammed heaping plates of eggs, bacon, and fried potatoes in front of them her eyes were flashing dangerously. When she went back to the stove to fetch more coffee Wade looked at Kane and winked.

"I must say her kitchen *manners* have changed. Remember the sunny smile and lilting voice that used to accompany her gastronomical delights?"

"Wade Magallen." Storm stood over the grinning man, the steaming coffeepot in her hand. "Do you want this in a cup or in your lap?"

"God! Never his lap!" Kane exclaimed in pretend horror. "Think of all the women he'd disappoint in the future. Pour it over his head."

"I think that's what she's got in mind," Wade muttered, eyeing Storm warily.

"What I have in mind is to shut you two up," Storm snapped, splashing the hot liquid into Wade's cup and making him quickly move his hand to safety.

Wade gave her a hurt look, although his lips twitched in amusement. "You've got a mean streak in you, Storm."

Storm made no response, only picked up her own cup of coffee and carried it over to the window. She sipped the steaming liquid carefully, pulling her lips away from the hot rim as she listened to Kane and Wade discuss their trip. Almost immediately they were standing up, ready to leave.

Kane walked over to her and squeezed her shoulder affectionately. "Take care of yourself while I'm gone, Sis. Rafe will be checking in on you and Jake. And don't go ridin' near the rogue's territory."

"I'll hardly be doing any riding," Storm said. "I'll be taking care of Jake, remember?"

"Right." Kane gently cuffed her on the chin; then with a lift of his hand he left the kitchen.

Left alone with Wade, Storm waited for him to make some cutting remark about Rafe stopping in. But he surprised her. He only said, "Don't let Pa give you a hard time"; then he was gone. She soon heard the clattering of the cowboys' mounts coming from the stables and ran to the window to wave as they swept by the house. Everyone but Wade waved back. He didn't even look her way.

"To hell with him," she muttered, and hurried to put the kitchen in order. Jake mustn't be left alone too long.

It took Storm less than fifteen minutes to pack her saddlebag with two dresses and four changes of underclothing. Before she buckled the bag's strap she tossed in a bar of her scented soap. When she had changed into a riding skirt and shirt she carried the bag down to the kitchen and picked up a haversack that was leaning in a corner. Inside it were rags, lye soap, and vinegar, which Maria had put together.

"I'm sure you won't find anything of that nature in that pigsty of Jake's," she had explained.

At the barn she saw that Jeb had Beauty saddled and waiting for her. She smiled her thanks. As he gave her a boost into the saddle, he said, "Give Jake my best."

"I will," Storm answered, nudging Beauty to head out. "I'll see you in four or five days," she called as the mare broke into a smart canter.

The sun was an hour high when Beauty rounded the curve in the road and the Magallen cabin appeared, a building built of logs with a shake roof. Like the Roemers' house it had four rooms, with a window in each one, and a wide porch that extended across its width. The front of the building faced the Platte and the back windows looked out on a stand of lodgepole pines that sheltered the small barn where Jake and Wade stabled their mounts. Other than a tall, narrow outhouse and a small corral, that was the extent of the Magallens' holdings.

Storm rode Beauty up to the corral and swung to the needle-strewn ground. She removed the saddlebag and sack of cleaning material and set them to one side before tugging off the saddle and hanging it on the corral fence. Then, removing the bridle and bit, she sent the mare into the pole enclosure.

A meadowlark burst into song as she stepped up on the wide porch and pushed open the screen door.

Maria's description of the house hadn't prepared her for the moment when she stepped inside, and she came to an abrupt halt. Storm stood and stared in wondering dismay at the disorder in the big room. Her nose twitching at the odor of dust, sweaty clothes, and stale whiskey, she muttered, "Good Lord, I'll have to work flat out all day just to scrape the surface."

Had it been like this when she was a youngster, running in and out of Wade's home? she wondered, unloading her arms onto a leather couch whose cushions were half covered with dirty trousers and shirts. Most likely, she decided. Kids never noticed dirt and clutter.

"Is that you, Storm?" Jake's querulous question came from the back of the cabin.

"Yes, it's me, Jake," Storm called back brightly, and she began making her way through debris of every kind. "How are you feeling?" She finally entered his bedroom, assailed by the same stale air and disorder.

"I feel like hell," Jake grumbled, a woeful expression on his thin face. "And I'm goin' loco in this damned dungeon."

"I'm not surprised," Storm agreed, looking at the begrimed window that kept the sun's rays from shining into the room. She walked across the floor and jerked up the sash. "You need some light and fresh air in here. The first thing I'm going to do is wash all the windows and let the sun in so it doesn't look like you're living in a cave."

When she turned around she was surprised to

see a look of embarrassment on Jake's face. "I figured if the windows were dirty, the mess wouldn't be so noticeable," he muttered.

"Well, dammit, Jake, you don't have to live this way," Storm said bluntly, gathering up the newspapers that were scattered all over the floor. "You can certainly afford to hire some woman to come in once in a while and clean up the place." Her arms full, she added, "And the pair of you could pick up after yourselves a little."

"Yeah, I know. Wade calls the place a boar's nest. But the thing is, we don't want no stranger comin' in and nosin' around. Every month or so we go over the place and shovel out the worst part."

"Well," Storm said, "I don't give a hoot how you and Wade live when I'm not here, but by golly, for the next few days this place is going to be whipped into a fit habitation for human beings."

"Sure, honey." Jake hurried to pacify her. "Do whatever you want to the place. You're the boss."

The elder Magallen looked so apologetic, so helpless, Storm couldn't help smiling at him. "Good," she said. "I'll start by changing your bedclothes. But first, have you had breakfast?"

Jake nodded. "Wade made me some bacon and eggs before he left. Most likely there's still coffee in the pot if you want a cup."

"I will a little later," Storm said and left the room.

191

When she had searched everywhere she could think of and could find only one clean towel, Storm knew that the first thing to do was start washing clothes, bed linens, towels, and such.

Storm walked out onto the back porch and was staggered at the mountain of dirty clothes waiting to be washed. My goodness, she thought, this is at least two months' of dirty laundry. She rolled up her sleeves, stepped off the porch, and walked behind the cabin.

As at most ranch homes, two wooden tubs sat on a low workbench, a scrub board in one of them. There was an iron kettle a yard or so away, its three legs straddling a pile of gray ashes. Storm would heat the water for washing in it, then boil the clothes in it later.

Squatting in front of the huge kettle, she raked away the ashes and charred ends of burned wood, then gathered a pile of dry wood chips from a plentiful supply where, over the years, firewood had been chopped. She went back into the cabin and returned a minute later, a newspaper and several matches in her hand. In a short time she had a fire roaring under the kettle and the first pail of water poured into it.

After several more pails followed, filling the vessel almost to its rim, she went back to the porch and started sorting through the dirty clothes. There were so many trousers and shirts of Wade's, she imagined that when he ran out of clean ones he went out and bought new ones instead of taking the time to do the washing.

She shook her head. There was no under-standing men.

Storm carried an armload of sheets, pillow-cases, and underwear out to the backyard and tossed them into one of the tubs, then tested the water in the kettle. It was just the right temperature for her hands.

Close to an hour had passed by the time Storm had a load of white clothes drying on the line strung between two trees. The sun shone straight overhead when she wrung the rinse water from the last shirt.

Her hands on her waist, she stretched her tired back, then entered the kitchen through the back door. Jake must be wanting his lunch by now, she thought. She had looked in on him twice, and both times he had been sleep-ing.

She looked around the kitchen and sighed. How was she ever going to prepare a meal in this mess? There wasn't a clean pan or skil-let to be seen, and with the amount of plates, cups, and flatware piled in the dry sink and cluttering the table, it seemed there was noth-ing clean to eat off. She had planned to clean the kitchen last, but she would have to tackle it next; otherwise she wouldn't be able to make them supper.

In the larder, off the kitchen, she found a sugar-cured ham, a loaf of sourdough bread, and a tin of peaches. It was clear the Magallen men didn't eat at home very often. Tomorrow she would ride over to Becky's and ask her to go into Laramie and pick up some supplies for them.

Some 20 minutes later a fresh pot of coffee had been brewed and Storm was carrying a plate of ham sandwiches into Jake's room. "That sure looks good." Jake smiled, awake now, and scooted up until his back rested against the headboard.

"Thank you, sir." Storm smiled back and placed the plate on his bony knees.

Storm sat down on the edge of the bed, being careful not to jostle Jake's leg, and the ham and bread were eaten with hearty appetite. When the plates were empty Storm took them back to the kitchen and returned with two cups of coffee.

"I found a tin of peaches in the larder," she said, placing the cups on the table beside the bed. "Would you like some?"

"No thanks, honey. I'm pretty full for now."

As they sipped their coffee, they fell to reminiscing, talking of the days when she and Kane and Becky and Wade were growing up, the happy days spent on the river, the pleasant times spent at the Roemer ranch.

"I owed your ma so much," Jake said, a sadness coming into his voice. "She had a big influence on Wade, growing up motherless as he did. Any tenderness in my son is thanks to Ruth Roemer. He was awful bitter there for a while, what with Nella goin' off and leavin' us."

Storm thought about that nine-year-old boy, picturing him bravely hiding his hurt at being deserted by his mother, maybe blaming himself for the desertion. She remembered her mother saying once that Wade's older brother, Ben, whom Nella had taken with her, was a weakly child, that he seldom played with the other children, and that perhaps that was why Nella took him with her.

Without thinking, Storm asked, "Why did Nella leave, Jake?"

Jake didn't seem to mind her question. He leaned his head back and stared at the raftered ceiling. "Nella came from Chicago, Illinois, and she loved the society there. She couldn't get used to the loneliness on the river, and my bein' away so much, just gettin' the saloon started and all. I guess she missed her family and friends too much. Anyway, one day she packed up her duds and went back to Chicago. I ain't heard from her since."

Storm caught herself in time before asking why Nella had left Wade behind.

"I think I'll hobble out to the privy." Jake broke the silence that had fallen between them. He threw back the sheet and revealed that the right leg of his underwear had been cut off at the knee to accommodate his splint.

"Should you, Jake?" Storm frowned, standing up.

"Yes, I damn well should," Jake barked. "I ain't about havin' you bring me the chamber pot."

"Well, do be careful," she said as he sat up and lifted his leg over the edge of the bed. When he slowly stood up she picked up the crutches from the floor and handed them to him, one at a time. He settled them under his armpits, then swung himself into the kitchen and on out the back door.

"I'll change his bed while he's gone," Storm thought out loud. She wasn't surprised to find that Jake's sheets weren't soiled. She had discovered a contradiction in how the two men lived. Amid the dirt and neglect, that which pertained to their personal hygiene rivaled the care she took of her own.

For example, on the narrow shelf fastened beneath a good-sized mirror hanging on the wall in the kitchen, she had found two clean combs resting there, no hair clinging to them, along with two spotless straight razors and two shaving mugs. Even the mirror had no dried soapy spots splattered on it. Not at all the way Kane left theirs at home after he had finished washing up and shaving. Her brother was spoiled, she decided. He knew that Maria would clean up after him.

Storm had finished changing the bed and was folding back the freshly laundered sheet when Jake returned. She helped him lie back down, then settled a pillow under his leg. "Now," she said, grinning down at him, "yon kitchen awaits me."

"You're gonna wear yourself out," Jake worried. "Why don't you leave it until tomorrow?"

Storm didn't want to embarrass her old friend by saying that if he wanted some supper tonight, she'd better get the kitchen cleaned up. She said instead, "It won't take long."

But later, as she stepped into a wooden tub of water and sat down in it, she wryly remembered it had taken most of the afternoon to wash the chinaware, pots and pans, and skillets. Then had come scrubbing the table and range, and finally sweeping out an accumulation of dirt and mud that must have lain on the floor for at least a month.

She had never been so glad to see Maria as she was when the woman walked into the cabin carrying a pot of stew. Even if she had been up to cooking the evening meal, Storm had no idea what she would have cooked.

"My goodness, Storm, you've scrubbed the kitchen within an inch of its life," Maria exclaimed. "I haven't seen it look like this since Jake's wife left him."

Storm's face flushed with pleasure at Maria's praise. "I'm flat beat out from cleaning," she said. "And I can't thank you enough for bringing over our supper."

"I figured there wouldn't be anything in the house for you to cook. As soon as I got home I put the stew on."

"How is your sister and her new baby?"

"They're both doing fine. She finally has a little girl, and the whole family is just crazy about her."

While Storm was wondering if she would

ever have the passel of children she wanted, Maria said she was going to have a few words with Jake and take him his stew, then she must get home before dark.

Storm finished her bath and, after drying off with one of the towels she had washed that day, she slipped into one of Wade's shirts, which also smelled of soap and sunshine. She dragged the tub of bathwater out onto the porch and tipped it to let the water run into the yard. Then she ate her own stew and cleaned the bowls that Maria had brought into the kitchen before she left.

She tiptoed into Jake's room and found him sound asleep. She turned down his lamp, then went to Wade's room, blowing out the lamp in the other room as she passed through it. She slipped between the sheets, breathed in Wade's scent from the pillow, and fell instantly into a deep, dreamless sleep.

As Storm lay sleeping, Rafe rode down the river road, wondering if he was making a mistake, calling on Becky Hadler alone. Maybe he should have waited until he had seen her a few more times with Storm, given her the time to know him better.

But the little, curly-haired woman had fascinated him as soon as he laid eyes on her. She was so small, so delicate-looking, with a sadness in her eyes that even her laughter didn't quite hide. He'd had an instant desire to protect her, to make that little-girl-lost look in her eyes disappear. Her past didn't bother him a wit. It couldn't compare with the life he'd lived, the women he'd bedded, his drunken sprees. Compared to him, Becky was an angel. She was the first woman he had ever felt anything for, other than lust.

He grinned wryly as his horse stepped along. He had lusted for Becky, all right. When she and Storm weren't looking his eyes had stripped away her clothing, seeing in his mind her firm, round breasts, her tiny waist, her rounded hips that could nestle and hold him as he made long, slow love to her. He had been hard put to keep hidden the arousal that had jumped to the fore.

But he had a deeper feeling for this woman. She was one female who wouldn't bore him to death after a couple of hours of her company. She didn't giggle, act coy, give him flirtatious looks. She met a man's gaze straight on, clear and honest. She talked of important things, things that a man wanted to talk about.

Rafe slowed his mount, growing nervous as Becky's house grew near. What would a young thing like Becky see in an old, worn-out horse trainer approaching his fortieth birthday? he asked himself.

After Becky had eaten her supper and fed her animals she and the hound, Trey, walked around to the front porch. Night had fallen about an hour before she sat down on the top step, the dog flopping down beside her.

Idly scratching behind his ear, she looked up at the sky, glittering with a million stars. Was there a night sky anywhere else in the universe as beautiful as a Wyoming one? she wondered, doubting it.

Tree frogs began to peep their evening song, and an owl flew across the yard looking for its supper. "I should be happy and content," Becky thought out loud. "I have everything I always dreamed of having.

"But you lost respect while getting them," her conscience whispered. "And it's getting harder and harder for you to make that trip to Cheyenne every Friday. It's time you took stock of yourself, my girl.

"And do what with myself? Sit out here alone, devote myself to animals the rest of my life?"

Becky left off her depressing monologue when the hound gave a low growl, her hackles raised, her nose pointing in the direction of the Magallen place. Becky raised her head and listened, then heard hoofbeats.

Her body went still. Who would be traveling the river road at this hour? Kane and Wade were trailing a herd of cattle somewhere, and Storm wouldn't be riding at night . . . unless something was wrong. But if that was the case, she'd be riding the mare. This horse was unfamiliar.

Becky's eyes narrowed in suspicion. With Kane away from the ranch, was one of his cowboys coming for a forbidden visit? She knew he had warned them away from *courting* her, told him that if any man made a trip out to her house he would be fired. So far no one had bothered her.

She laid a quieting hand on the hound's head and sat quietly. Maybe whoever it was wasn't coming to visit her at all. It could be someone going to visit the Hayes family. Then the rider rode out of a patch of lodgepole pine and into the moonlight.

Sharp disappointment gripped Becky when she recognized Rafe Jeffery. She had thought he was different, had thought of him many times since meeting him. But as she had said to Storm, here he was and probably randy as hell. Wouldn't he be surprised when she sent him on his way?

She watched Rafe dismount, trail the reins over the mount's head, and then walk up the path toward her. She called no greeting to him, no welcome. He stood before her, smiling crookedly.

"I was hopin' you were still up," he said as he sat down on the other side of the dog, who looked at him suspiciously, then thumped the floor with her tail.

"And why was that?" Becky asked, her voice cool.

"It's lonesome over at the Roemers." He stretched out his long legs, crossing them at the ankles. "As you probably know, Kane is on a cattle drive, and Storm is takin' care of Jake. And this afternoon Maria took off to visit her sister. 'Course there's Jeb, but that old man could jaw you to death."

Becky couldn't help the tickled giggle that escaped her. Jeb could talk the ears off a person.

"So," Rafe continued, "I said to myself, why not go over to Becky's and gab with her for a while?"

When Becky made no response, only waited for him to say why he had really come calling, he sniffed the air and said, "I don't know of any nicer smell than that of freshly cut grass. I bet you trimmed your yard today."

"Yes. Just this afternoon."

There was a short silence, and then, "What's your hound's name?"

"Trey."

"Trey?" Rafe laughed. "Isn't this dog a bitch?"

"She is. I named her after a dog I had when I was a kid."

Well, Rafe thought with a small smile, I got a few more words out of her this time. He understood her wariness of him, though and, leaning back on his elbows, he looked up at the sky. "You know, your skies are almost as pretty as Oregon ones."

"What are you saying?" Becky flared, giving him a hostile look. "There are no lovelier skies in the world than Wyoming has."

"You think so?" Rafe sat up. "Have you ever

been to Oregon, sat of an evenin' watchin' the moon rise over the tops of towering pines, seen the stars come out one at a time like a shy lady until finally the whole world is lit up by their light? That is a sight unequaled by anything else in the world."

Becky gave him a startled look. Beneath the hard-looking surface of Rafe Jeffery, there was a romantic. The way he described his home made her want to see it.

"It does sound nice," she said, "but I'd have to see it and decide for myself."

"Maybe some day you will," Rafe said quietly. "I'd love to have you come visit me and my state, meet my sister and her family. You could stay with her if you don't mind a bunch of noisy younguns runnin' about."

"Oh, I doubt I'll ever get up that way."

"You never know; you might. It's an open invitation if you should ever decide you'd like to compare skies." He laughed softly.

Becky loosened up, relaxed, as Rafe kept his seat, the dog between them. His voice had a soothing quality as he spoke of his sister and her husband, and the nieces and nephews. There was a deep fondness in the words he used to describe the youngsters. What a good father he would make.

"You like children, don't you?" she asked.

"Yes, I do," he answered; then he grinned. "I also like old people and animals."

"Especially horses." Becky gave him a teasing smile. "What animal is your next choice?"

"The wolf."

"The wolf? Why the lobo?"

"They're brave, they kill clean, and they mate for life. Besides the horse, I think they're the most handsome animal there is."

They fell to discussing animals in general, Becky speaking of her plans to be a veterinarian, Rafe talking about the horse ranch he hoped to have someday.

They both looked startled when the clock inside the house struck ten times. They had been talking close to three hours. Rafe stood up. "Boy, time got away from us, didn't it? I'd better get started back to the ranch." He lingered a moment, gazing down at Becky's upturned face. "I enjoyed talking with you Becky. You reckon I could ride over again some evening?"

"I reckon." Becky smiled. "Trey and I sit out here for a while most evenings."

Rafe had hoped she might invite him over for supper, or at least offer him a piece of pie and a cup of coffee. But he was thankful for small mercies. At least she hadn't objected to sitting on the porch visiting with him. It wasn't going to be easy getting her to trust him, to win her over. Her experience with men hadn't been the best, he imagined.

"I'll say good night, then."

"Good night, Rafe. I enjoyed your visit." Becky watched him walk away, climb onto his palomino, and ride away with a wave of his hand.

Storm

For the first time since moving to the small house she felt lonesome. Rafe was the kind of man she had always dreamed of falling in love with someday. Did she dare hope?

Chapter Thirteen

Storm stood at the dry sink, washing dishes. She had served steak and all the trimmings to Jake for supper. Becky hadn't been home when she'd ridden over to ask her to go shopping for her. She had left a note and her list of meat and staples on Becky's table, and the kid who worked at the mercantile had delivered her order later in the afternoon.

An unconscious smile curved Storm's lips. In the two days since her arrival at the Magallen home every room in the cabin had been thoroughly scrubbed and polished. Wade wouldn't know the place when he returned.

It was a couple of hours to dusk when Storm rinsed the last pot and placed it in the drainer. She spilled the basin of water into the sink, wrung out the dishrag, and then dried her hands on the towel hanging on the wall. Then she poured the remains of the coffee into a cup and carried it out onto the porch. She would relax for a few minutes before having some hands of poker with Jake. He enjoyed their games, claiming she had card sense: that she watched the cards and remembered which ones had been played.

Storm sipped the coffee, her thoughts turning to Wade. What was he doing right now? Would he be spending the night with some woman he'd picked up somewhere?

Before she could linger on that unwelcome thought, a horse trotted down the river road and turned onto the Magallens' gravel road. She put down the coffee cup beside her and peered at horse and rider, then swore under her breath.

"What's that bitch doing here?" she muttered as Josie Sales swung awkwardly from the saddle.

As Josie walked toward her, Storm stood up, her eyes skimming over the thin body in the fawn-colored riding skirt and brown silk shirt. She was suddenly acutely aware of the limp, dirt-stained dress she had worn all day while she scrubbed away at the cabin. She glanced down at Josie's highly polished boots and then at her own bare toes, and tried to curl them into the floorboards.

The slight lifting of Miss Sales's lips as she stepped onto the porch told Storm that she looked as bedraggled as she felt. "Wade isn't here," she blurted out. "He'll be gone for the rest of the week."

Amusement twisted the older woman's lips as she sneered, "I'm well aware of that, Princess. Wade asked me to stop by and check on his father while he was gone; make sure he's being well taken care of."

Hurt surprise drained the color from Storm's face. This was the worst insult Wade had given her yet: his lack of trust. Could he honestly think that this cat-faced woman would be more caring toward his father than she would?

Her squared shoulders sagged a bit as she remembered his reluctance to go off and leave Jake in her care. He had only agreed because he was going to ask this bitch to keep an eye on her. Storm's pain was so intense, anger could not penetrate it. When Josie walked into the cabin she silently followed her.

"My, you've been a busy little beaver, haven't you, Princess?" Josie's sharp voice rasped against Storm's ears as she stood surveying the room. "I must thank you, dear. I had no idea the place could look this good. I won't have to do as much changing of things as I had imagined."

She lifted her left hand to smooth the back of her hair, and Storm swallowed convulsively. A diamond ring glittered on the third finger. Stunned, Storm sat down, and after a gloating look at her Josie walked into Jake's bedroom.

With Josie's shrill voice and Jake's mumbling baritone only hitting the edge of her awareness, Storm sat in numb silence. How could Wade ever consider marrying that awful woman? Couldn't he see that she had no depth to her, that she would probably never give him any children? And what about the woman in Cheyenne? Storm had thought that if he ever married anyone it would be her, his old love.

She was so deep in her misery, Storm wasn't aware that Josie had returned until she heard the rasp of a match. She looked up and watched her light the big kerosene lamp sitting on the small table at the end of the sofa. When it burned brightly Josie went to the window and fingered the thin material of the drapes.

"These will have to go, of course," she said, as though to herself. "They must be as old as the cabin." She sent her gaze over the rest of the room and gave a small shudder. "Everything in here is much too masculine. A woman . . . a wife could never be comfortable with it."

Suddenly Storm couldn't listen another moment to the imperious tone and words. She jumped to her feet and, her breasts heaving and her eyes flashing, she pratically yelled, "You're forgetting one thing, Josie Sales. This house belongs to Jake, and he likes it just the way it is. He'll never agree to changing so much as a lamp."

Wheeling around to face Storm, her own anger leaving the sharp planes of her face almost ugly, Josie's lips pulled back in a sneer. "My, my, but you're upset, Princess," she said. "Why should you care what goes on in the Magallen household?" When Storm only glared back at her Josie taunted, "Are you living in the delusion that you'll be mistress here someday?"

The woman came so near to the truth, Storm could only stare at her.

Josie's hateful laugh slithered like a snake in the large room. "Don't look so surprised. I know all about your little crush on Wade. He and I have a lot of laughs about it."

When Storm would have interrupted her hotly Josie raised her voice, talking over her. "So you can forget your little tricks, like pretending to lose control of your horse so Wade would come after you."

"That's not true," Storm cried out. "I never pretended to . . ." But again Josie wasn't listening to her. It was as though she had lost control, couldn't stop the venom from pouring out.

"Why don't you grow up, Storm Roemer," she said scathingly, "find a man nearer your own age? Wade is too old for you. He knows it if you don't. You're an embarrassment to him, always makin' those cow eyes at him and followin' him around. He can't tell you off like he'd like to because of his friendship with Kane. So why don't you let up on the poor fellow?"

Her tirade at an end, Josie flashed her ring once more, then stalked out of the room, the screen door slapping behind her.

Storm had no sense of time passing as she sat in anguished silence. The refrain, "Grow up, Storm, you embarrass Wade," beat at her brain. Was Josie right? Had her feelings for Wade shown all this time? Did she embarrass him? Had she been too blind to see it all these years?

Jake's gruff voice jarred her out of her soul-searching. "Are we gonna play poker, Storm?"

Forcing a cheerful note to her voice, she called back, "I'll be right there."

But as she dealt the cards a little later, the forced smile on her lips died. She glanced at Jake and caught the question in his eyes. She hadn't fooled him for a minute. "I guess you heard me and Josie going at it." She smiled weakly.

"I can't say that the two of you was keepin' your voices down." Jake grinned, picking up his cards. He looked at Storm's bowed head. "Look, honey, don't put any importance on what that one said. She's been after Wade for a long time and she'll say and do anything to get him."

"It looks like she's finally going to get him," Storm said, despair in her eyes. "She's wearing his ring."

"Until Wade tells me different I'm not puttin' any stock in that either." Jake reached over and patted her hand. "When my son marries it will be someone sweet and fresh, not a worn-out whore."

Yes, Storm thought, a woman like the one in Cheyenne.

When Storm lost four hands in a row Jake took pity on her; he knew her mind wasn't on the game. "Let's call it a night after this hand, honey," he said kindly. "I'm gettin' sleepy."

Storm gathered up the cards and leaned over to kiss Jake's cheek. "Thanks for trying to cheer me up, Jake. I'll be fine."

When she slid into bed soon after she hung on to Jake's comforting words even though she didn't believe them. And when she drifted into a restless sleep she dreamed of the ring on Josie's finger and of Wade holding the arm of the unknown woman.

The sun shone so brightly it made the sky look faded as Storm guided Beauty down the rutted road to Becky's house. She ignored the coyote that skulked in the brush, the little prairie dog that sat up and watched her for a moment before darting back into his hole.

Josie's visit last evening was still on her mind. She could still hear her hurtful words, her cruel accusations. But the worst of her thoughts were of the ring on the woman's finger.

Beauty came to a halt and Storm came back to the present. She looked around, then slid to the ground. Out of habit the mare had turned into Becky's yard, coming to a stop at the hitching post.

"You are so smart," Storm said affectionately as she bent over and loosened the saddle cinches.

"Do you always talk to Beauty?" Becky called,

coming around from the back of the house.

"I suppose you never talk to that hound that follows your every footstep." Storm reached down and patted the tail-wagging Trey's head.

"I admit that I do. It gets kinda lonesome out here sometimes, and I have to talk to someone or something. I'm picking apples; come and help me. I remember how those long legs of yours used to climb trees."

"And I can remember some of the switchings I got from Jeb because of it. He was always afraid that I would fall and break my neck."

Becky pointed to the half-filled basket of apples. "I've picked all I can reach. Timmy promised he'd be over later to get the ones on top, but like most males the little devil hasn't kept his word."

She grinned at Storm, expecting a like response. The amusement faded from her face as she noted the purple shadows under her friend's eyes, the droop to her mouth.

"You know," Becky said brightly, "I'm tired of picking these blasted things." She shoved a toe at the basket. "The coffeepot is still hot and almost full. Let's go have a cup or two and gab for a while.

"How is Jake coming along?" Becky asked after pouring coffee and placing a platter of sugar cookies on the table. "I've been meaning to come visit him. Is he behaving himself for you?"

"Oh, yes." Storm helped herself to a cookie and nibbled on it. "He's doing real well,

although he still has a lot of discomfort. I
imagine the bone is beginning to knit."

"Wade and Kane should be coming home
any day now, shouldn't they?"

Storm nodded. "I look for them tomorrow
sometime. It can't be soon enough for me."

"Why so?" Becky asked, a little surprised. "Is
it too lonesome out there on the river?"

"No," Storm said weakly, and then she burst
into tears.

"Oh, Storm, I knew something was bothering
you." Becky rose and came quickly to her
friend's side. "What's wrong, honey?" She put
her arms around the shaking shoulders.

In a rush of words Storm sobbed out the
story of Josie's visit, and that she wore Wade's
ring. "Can you imagine, he's going to marry
that awful . . . creature."

"No, I can't, and I don't believe it for a minute." Becky sat down next to Storm and pulled
her coffee cup to her. "I think that bitch straight-
out lied. I can't see Wade Magallen marrying the
town whore."

"You can't help who you love, Becky." Storm
wiped her eyes with the back of her hand. "Look
at me, for instance. God knows I don't want to
love Wade, but I do. I can't seem to help myself
no matter what common sense tells me."

Storm smiled shakily. "Enough about me.
What have you been up to?"

"Oh, nothing much; taking care of my animals mostly. I released the bobcat yesterday.
The kittens and puppies are weaned." She

grinned at Storm. "Would you care to take one with you when you leave? They're darling little animals."

"Maybe I'll take one of the pups after I go home."

Becky poured them another cup of coffee. When she sat down she said shyly, "I had a visitor the other night."

"Oh? You seem pleased about it. Anybody I know?"

"Yes." Becky made a big deal out of spooning sugar into her coffee. "It was Rafe."

"Did he behave himself, Becky?" Storm asked tightly, leaning forward to look into Becky's eyes. "If he didn't, he's going to . . ."

"He was a perfect gentleman," Becky interrupted. "We sat on the porch the whole time he was here." She laughed softly. "With Trey stretched out between us."

"And?"

"He asked if he could come visit again."

"And you said . . ."

Becky shrugged, trying to look indifferent. "I said that I usually sat on the porch in the evenings."

"My, my, that must have sounded real enthusiastic to him." Storm smiled wryly. "Aren't you afraid you sounded too eager?" she teased.

"I don't want him getting any wrong ideas," Becky answered defensively. "How do I know what he's got on his mind? How do I know he's not like all men, looking for the same thing? Maybe he's just approaching me in a different manner, acting real respectful-like in the beginning."

"Becky, I've told you Rafe isn't like that," Storm said seriously. "Don't you think it's possible he's attracted to you, likes your company?"

Becky shrugged again. "Time will tell, won't it? In the meantime I'm not getting my hopes up that there are still some decent men in the world."

"There aren't many, are there . . . decent men in the world," Storm said, and she pushed her empty cup away and stood up. "And speaking of decent men, I'd better get back to Jake and make him some lunch."

"Tell Jake I'll be over to see him before the week's out." Becky followed Storm outside and waited on the porch, waving as Storm put the mare to a canter.

Chapter Fourteen

The supper dishes were washed and the kitchen in order when Storm shrugged into a lightweight jacket of Wade's. Jake was reading the daily newspaper out of Cheyenne, and while he was occupied she was going to take a walk along the river before sunset.

There was a serpentine beauty to the Platte as it turned and twisted and then disappeared from view. So smooth and flowing in the summertime, Storm thought, walking slowly, but ice-encrusted in the winter, allowing only a faint murmur of running water in some places.

She came to a sheltering patch of lodgepole pine and breathed deep of rotting logs and shiny needles. This had always been her favorite spot along the river. Here she had sat on Beauty's back and dreamed of Wade; tingling, romantic dreams. Here she had shed bitter tears over him.

She picked up a stone and absently skipped it across the water. All that was a thing of the past. Tears and dreams of Wade Magallen were definitely behind her now. As she had ironed clothes, and then baked a supply of bread and pies, she had thought bitterly of the wasted years, her battle to get over Wade, her infatuation that blinded her to the fact that to Wade she was only his best friend's sister.

"One last night," she told herself, turning around and retracing her steps to the cabin. "Wade will be home tomorrow and I can leave here. I can finally get down to some really living, an existence he will have no part in."

Storm arrived at the cabin and stood outside for a moment, listening to the night sounds, the murmur of the river, an owl giving an occasional hoot, the lonely sound of a whippoorwill, the croaking of frogs on the riverbank. Regret shadowed her eyes. She would miss this part of the evening . . . and Jake. She would miss their fierce poker games, their friendly bantering.

Because she would never come here again.

"You look tired, honey," Jake said, gentle concern in his voice as he looked up and saw Storm standing in his doorway.

"I am, a little." She smiled at him, aware that he was upset at the bruised look in her eyes. "If you don't mind, I'll pass up our game tonight and maybe read awhile."

"Sure, you go right ahead. I'm gonna finish readin' the paper and turn in myself."

"I'll see you in the morning then." Storm smiled and walked into Wade's room.

A few minutes later she had sponge-bathed in Wade's plain white basin and pulled a skimpy sleeveless gown over her head. She walked into the comfortable family room, lit a lamp, and settled into a chair, swinging her legs over one arm and resting her back on the other. She opened the book she had brought from home and began to read.

The love story held her interest and the pages fell away, along with the moving hands on the clock. At length she hit a long passage of boring description, and the book began to lose its pull. Unaware, she sank deeper and deeper into the soft confines of the chair, her lids drooping. Her body relaxed and her breasts rose and fell gently in sleep.

She didn't hear the outside door open quietly, nor did she hear the indrawn breath of the tall man who stepped inside and with cat-silent feet moved across the floor and squatted down beside her chair. His firm lips, which customarily held amused cynicism at the world, softened as he lifted a fall of blonde hair and drew it caressingly through his fingers.

Wade's gaze dropped to the partially revealed breasts thrusting against the softness of the gown, and his loins contracted tensely. When desire shuddered through his body he rose stiffly, stood a moment massaging his right leg, and then limped over to the fireplace and took a bottle of whiskey and a glass off the mantel. The leg had been giving him hell the past few days, and sometimes a good belt of mash liquor helped a bit.

Storm came slowly awake to the sound of a cork popping, and the splash of liquid. She pushed herself upright and asked in a sleep-husky voice, "Wade?"

"In the flesh," he drawled, stepping into the glow of the lamp and sitting down on the sofa across from her.

Storm's heart gave a joyful leap: He was home. Then her brain, cleared of its fuzziness, remembered Josie's visit. "You're home early," she said in a carefully controlled voice. She swung her feet to the floor, then blushed and tugged at the gown that struck her midthigh.

"Did the trip go well?" she asked, still tugging at the garment that refused to cover any more leg.

Wade rested an ankle on a knee, amused at her effort to stretch her gown. "We didn't have a speck of trouble," he answered after tossing off half his drink. "That's why we're home half a day early."

You probably rode your horse half to death in your hurry to get back to Josie, Storm thought, her lips curling.

Wade saw the grimace and raised a questioning brow at her. When Storm only looked away he let his gaze drift around the room. A look, almost of wonder, came over him. "I never knew the room could look like this," he said, as though to himself. "Maybe when Ma . . ." He stopped abruptly and raised the glass to his lips again.

Storm pretended not to see his discomfort and stood up. "I want to get back to sleep. Do you want the bed or the sofa?"

Wade's hand shot out and grasped her wrist. "What's wrong, Storm? What happened while I was gone?"

Storm stared at his tense features, then shot out bluntly, "Why did you send Josie Sales out here to check on me, to see if I was taking proper care of Jake?"

"What!" The astonishment that leapt into Wade's gray eyes was proof enough that Josie had lied. "I never told her to check up on you, Storm." His flashing eyes added more evidence. "She said that maybe she would ride out and visit Pa, and I said fine. I swear to you, Storm, that's all that was said."

Storm's heart pounded, the blood seemingly singing through her veins. Josie had out-and-out lied about everything. Her heartbeat slowed. That fact didn't change anything between her and Wade. If he had hurried home, it was to see the other woman. Wade didn't have any more feelings for Josie than he did for herself.

"I believe you, Wade," she said, then added in a small voice, "I think I'll take the bed, if you don't mind. I'll get you a blanket and a . . ."

221

Her words trailed off. Wade's eyes were fastened on her breasts, which were outlined clearly beneath the thin material. She felt her nipples harden, and when his eyes leapt to her face she knew he was aware of their condition.

He cleared his throat and asked, "How has Pa been? Has he been behavin' himself?"

Storm nodded. "He's been very good. He's stayed in bed most of the time."

"What about you?" Wade studied her through narrow lids. "Have you been good?"

"What do you mean?" Storm frowned.

"I mean, has Rafe Jeffery been hangin' round?"

"And what if he has?" Storm raised her chin defiantly. "I don't see that it's any business of yours if he has."

She shrank back when Wade jumped to his feet, his fingers biting into her shoulders. "It's my business if he caused you to neglect Pa."

His words were like a slap in the face. When rage and resentment twisted Storm's features Wade released her and stepped back. "I think you did send Josie to spy on me," she hissed. "Well, I'm pretty damn sure Jake will tell you he's been well taken care of."

Her eyes shimmering with tears, she made for the bedroom before they spilled over.

Wade's fingers closed over her wrists just as she got to the door. "Ah, honey, I've hurt you," he murmured contritely, turning her into his arms and pushing her head down on his shoulder. "Don't you know I hate hurting you?"

But you hurt me all the time, Storm wanted to cry out through the tears that were soaking his shirtfront. Instead, she quavered, "You insulted me, sending Josie here to check on Jake."

"Storm, I told you I didn't send Josie over here." Wade's words were muffled in her hair. "I never thought for a minute that you wouldn't take good care of Pa. I don't know why I said that about Jeffery."

As his deep voice soothed her, his hands stroked up and down her back. It felt so good, even if it was the same way he used to calm her tears, her hurts, when she was a child.

Suddenly Storm's body grew still. Wade's caressing hands had slid along her sides and now cupped the soft curves of her small rear end. Her body rippled with sensuous delight when he pulled her into him, her hips fitting snugly into the well of his. She felt his throbbing masculinity against her thigh, and when she slowly rubbed against it he groaned deep in his throat.

Storm pushed the thought of Josie and the woman in Cheyenne to the back of her mind as she was faced with the utter hopelessness of her rejecting Wade if he should want her. God help her, she still loved him desperately.

Forgotten were the resolutions she had made as her arms swept up to encircle his neck. She leaned into him and he shuddered.

"God, Storm," he moaned, slipping the gown over her head. She sighed as he stroked a hand over her tight stomach, then up her narrow rib cage. And while she held her breath, waiting, his palms finally settled over her passion-filled breasts.

Her breath became labored as his fingers gently tweaked her pink nipples into jutting firmness. When his mouth, hot with need, covered one and suckled urgently, she gasped her delight and pressed his head more closely to her.

Lost in a mindless bliss, she whimpered protestingly when Wade pulled away from her. Avoiding her glazed eyes, he said hoarsely, "It's time for all little girls to be in bed."

She stared up at the resolute set of his jaw and wondered dazedly why Wade was holding back; he was just as aroused as she.

Storm pushed herself back into Wade's arms, determined that whatever was his trouble concerning her, it was going to end this night. She could no longer ride the emotional seesaw he had her on.

Her fingers slid open a button on his shirt, then another and another, until she could slide a hand inside and stroke his broad chest. "I don't want to go to bed," she whispered huskily. She raised her head and kissed his throat. "Not alone."

Wade's pulse raced against her lips and his muscles corded beneath her caressing fingers. Storm peeped through her lashes at his face; it was taut with desire. His voice passionately thick, he whispered, "If I go in there with you,

Storm, you know what will happen. I won't be able to stop at kisses."

Storm breathed a little sigh and, pressing closer to him, murmured, "I certainly hope not, darling."

With a low cry of defeat, Wade swept her into his arms and carried her into his room. Kicking the door shut, he laid her on the bed and stretched out beside her. His lips, warm and moist, fastened on hers as his palms roamed feverishly over her silky body. When his tongue parted her swollen lips and stroked inside her mouth Storm's fingers flew to his shirt, almost tearing off the rest of the buttons in her frenzy to feel his flesh against hers.

His breathing ragged, Wade lifted his head and helped her to slide the shirt off his arms and shoulders. His body tightened when she raised up on her elbows and slowly, tantalizingly, dragged her hardened nipples across his hair-covered chest.

"Oh, God," Wade moaned, lying on his back and pulling Storm on top of him, "you're drivin' me crazy." He grasped her small waist and, lifting her a few inches away, whispered, "Let them move all over me."

Storm braced a palm on either side of his tanned, muscular body and began her seduction.

Her long hair falling forward, dragging against Wade in the wake of her breasts, Storm let her hardened nipples rest on his chest a moment before burning a fiery path across his midriff, his flat, taut stomach. When the waistband of his twills hindered further progress he rolled over, bringing her slenderness beneath him. And as if to thank them for giving him such pleasure, he lowered his head and suckled first one breast and then the other.

Moaning his name, her pulses beating a riotous tattoo, Storm's fingers tugged at the buttons confining the length of his erection.

In a daze with the passion he had withheld from Storm for so long, Wade stood up, kicked off his boots, and stripped off his trousers.

Storm's eyes roamed hungrily over his beautiful masculine body, desire darkening her eyes. Her trembling fingers shyly reached out and stroked the throbbing hardness. Mesmerized, Wade watched her slender fingers move on him, realizing a dream of many years.

He came down on the bed, and as he smoothed the damp hair off her forehead, he said shakily, "I want you desperately, Storm, but seeing you lying there, so slender and delicate, I'm afraid I'll hurt you."

"You won't darling," she whispered, lifting her arms to him.

There was doubt in Wade's eyes, though, as he tenderly parted her thighs and positioned himself between them. And for all the exquisite care he took when penetrating the thin barrier that protected the gift that had always waited for him, her cry of pain would have rung through the house had he not caught it in his mouth.

"Should I stop, honey?" he whispered, holding his body perfectly still.

Storm shook her head and wrapped her arms around his waist, urging him on.

Hating himself for the pain he was causing her but unable to stop, Wade continued his entry. Storm bit her lips, holding back her cries as Wade moved deeper and deeper into her body.

Storm was telling herself that she was willing to suffer any pain in order to bring pleasure to this man who she loved with every breath in her body when suddenly the pain was gone, leaving her with a sense of sensual delight.

Slowly, at first, she began to move, to respond. Feeling her hips reach to meet his, Wade relaxed his caution a little and began a slow, rhythmic thrusting.

The spiraling passion that built inside Storm was almost as painful in its way as the breaking of the protecting membrane had been. Lost in the rapture of Wade's working hips, she was unprepared for the body-weakening explosion that sent her straining into his large, shuddering frame.

Wade moaned her name, and she felt the flow of his spent desire, warm and soothing to her stretched and torn femininity. A moment later his head, wet with sweat, lay in the curve of her throat and shoulder, his breathing harsh in her ear. She gently stroked his shoulders when he whispered, "I've always known that someday I'd have you in my bed."

Storm paused in the slow stroking of her palm. Was that regret in Wade's voice? Was he thinking of his sweetheart in Cheyenne, feeling guilty that he had made love to another woman?

No! she denied firmly. It's me he loves. His every action tonight showed it.

She resumed the movement of her hand and she said softly, "I have always hoped that you would."

Wade chuckled and started to lift himself from her. She shook her head and wrapped her legs around his waist. "You feel good here."

"But I'll crush you, honey." Wade smiled tenderly, smoothing the tangled hair off her damp brow. "You're so small, so fragile."

Storm slid the tip of her tongue across her top lip and murmured wickedly, "I think you forgot that a few minutes ago." When Wade's eyes turned the color of slate she bucked her hips at him and said suggestively, "Maybe if you concentrate real hard, you'll think of something that will take part of your weight off me."

Her action, and the throb in her voice, brought Wade swelling inside her. "You're out to break my back, aren't you?" he said huskily, lifting the top half of his body away from her.

"Yes." Storm sighed, her pulses throbbing as Wade slid his hands under her small rear and lifted it several inches off the bed. "Wade," she whispered, the single word becoming a litany on her lips as he held her hips steady and began to slowly stroke inside her.

A pinkish gray light showed outside the window when Wade and Storm had at last sated their driving need of each other. Storm squirmed her derriere into the nest of his drawn-up knees and fell instantly into an exhausted sleep, a smile on her face.

Wade loved her.

His arms wrapped around Storm's sleeping form, savoring the feel of her soft, curled body, Wade stared bleakly at the open window. He had finally done the unforgivable. He had lost control and done what he had known he shouldn't for the past six years. And if that weren't enough, he had given Storm hope where there was none.

Storm stirred in her sleep and snuggled closer in his arms. Dear God, what if he had gotten her with child? "Please, Lord," he whispered, "don't let it be so. I promise I'll never touch her again."

He carefully withdrew his arms from around the warm body, gently kissed a flushed cheek, and then slid out of bed. He pulled on his trousers and shrugged into his shirt, leaving it unbuttoned, and picked up the boots lying next to a pair of dainty house slippers. He took one last lingering look at the woman he had loved through the night, then quietly left the room.

The bright rays of the morning sun striking her in the face awakened Storm. She stretched lazily, winced slightly at the soreness of her body, then turned to Wade. Her lips pouted in disappointment: He was already up. Her hand moved caressingly over his pillow, coming to rest in the indentation made by his head.

A dreamy smile curved her lips as she remembered the incredible depth of their lovemaking. If she had needed proof of Wade's love for her, it had certainly been demonstrated last night. His every action, every murmured endearment had said it clearly.

A warm sensation formed in her lower body. What heaven it was going to be, knowing his lovemaking every night. A smile curved her lips as she stretched languorously. They'd probably kill each other, once they were married.

Leaning up on an elbow, Storm listened for sounds of activity in the cabin. All was quiet. Maybe Wade was taking a dip in the river. She heard the clock strike and gasped. Surely it wasn't ten o'clock. Jake must be starving.

Leaving the bed, she hurriedly washed up at the white basin and got dressed. Close to half an hour later she bounced into Jake's room, her eyes sparkling.

"I'm sorry to be so late with your breakfast, Jake." She placed a platter of ham and eggs and fried bread on his lap. "I'm afraid I overslept."

Jake looked at her radiant face. "You and Wade must have sat up late gabbing," he said.

"You know that he's home, then?" Storm tried to speak in a normal voice, but some of her happiness came through.

"Yes, I spoke to him earlier this morning." Jake avoided her eyes.

"I expect he's hungry too. I'll go find him, see how many eggs he wants for breakfast."

Jake was suddenly making a big thing of stirring his coffee, and Storm knew with an icy sureness that something was wrong. She also knew that she wasn't brave enough to hear what it was.

She made a motion to leave the room, and Jake croaked out, "He's not here, honey."

An almost paralyzing dread sliced through Storm. She clenched her hands to stop their trembling as she lifted shadowed eyes to Jake. "Oh? Do you know where he's gone?"

Jake stared down at his breakfast, and it seemed an eternity before he said in a cracked voice, "He took off real early. Said he was goin' to see that Sales woman."

Storm tried to speak, but her lips wouldn't move. She felt so used, so foolish. Wade had gone straight from her arms to Josie's. What she had thought was so wonderful, so special, meant no more to Wade than any of his other women ever mattered to him. Making love to her hadn't held any special significance for him.

As from a distance she heard Jake ask concernedly, "Are you all right, Storm?"

Storm forced her lips to part, her tongue to move. "I'm fine," she managed to say calmly. "I think I'll get my things together now and go on home." She turned toward the door, then paused when Jake spoke.

"Me and Wade can't thank you enough for comin' over here and takin' care of me. I'm gonna miss the sunshine you brought into this house, and I'm not talkin' about clean windows."

"I'll come by and visit you," Storm choked out her lie, knowing that she would never again set foot in the Magallen cabin. "In the meantime," she smiled at Jake, "take care of yourself."

You do the same, honey, Jake thought sadly, watching the brave, heartbroken young woman leave him. If he could get his hands on his son right now, he'd pound lumps all over him.

In Wade's room, keeping her eyes off the bed and its rumpled covers, Storm gathered up her belongings and shoved them into the saddlebag any old way. She must leave before Wade returned. She felt such a hatred for him that only doing him harm could placate her.

As Storm rode away, her eyes blurred with the tears she had held back, a pair of gray eyes, full of remorse and tenderness, watched her.

After Wade had turned his stallion into the pasture back of the barn, well out of sight, he had climbed to the barn's loft and stretched out on a pile of hay. Guilt rode him as he stared up at the rafters. He had lied to his father, saying that he was going to see Josie, knowing that he would tell Storm. It had been a cowardly thing to do, leaving his dirty work for Pa to do.

But he would have rather faced down a gunman than tell Storm to forget the night they had spent together, that she shouldn't put any importance on it. He couldn't have borne the stricken look that would have come into her lovely eyes.

When the little mare cantered out of sight Wade laid back down, hating himself, hating the world.

Chapter Fifteen

Five weeks had passed since Storm's hurried departure from the Magallen home. Gloom hung over her like a black cloud as she automatically followed the routine of household chores, answering mostly in monosyllables when Kane or Maria tried to engage her in conversation. Many times the housekeeper searched her face, trying to discern the reason for her moodiness. But her expression revealed nothing of the misery inside her.

It was when she was alone, astride Beauty, as she was today, that Storm allowed her pain and disillusionment to show. It was the little mare that felt and heard the shuddering sobs, the muttered words.

She held the mare at a leisurely walk as she rode toward Laramie. Maria had asked her to do some last-minute shopping for their Thanks-giving dinner the following day.

It wouldn't be a very festive occasion, she thought. Probably just the family, Rafe, and, of course, old Jeb. They weren't sure yet if Jake could make it, and Kane had said a couple of days ago that Wade was spending the holiday in Cheyenne.

Storm's lips turned down at the corners. He would no doubt be spending it with the woman with whom Becky had seen him.

Her mind was still on the unknown woman, wondering if she was Wade's old love, when she rode into Laramie. The first person she saw was Wade, walking down the street toward her. She pretended not to see him as she reined Beauty in at the mercantile and slid to the ground. She hurriedly flipped the reins over the hitching post and was about to enter the store when Wade grabbed her arm. She tried to jerk free only to have his grip tighten.

"Stop it," Wade growled. "I want to have a word with you."

From the corners of her eyes Storm saw three of her neighbors watching them. She stopped her struggling and snapped, "Well, what is it you want to say? I'm in a hurry."

"Damn you, woman," Wade's voice rasped harshly. His hand lifted as though to touch her face, then dropped back to his side. "I only wanted to know if you were all right. That nothing's . . ." his eyes dropped significantly to her stomach . . . "there that shouldn't be."

Storm blinked in surprise. It hadn't occurred to her that there could be consequences from that wild night of lovemaking. Thank God she was still as regular as clockwork.

She toyed with the idea of making Wade sweat a bit, to say, "Yes, I am carrying your baby," but that would be so childish.

Sliding him a taunting look, she said, "Who knows? I do know, though, that nothing of yours is in there."

It was hard to keep her features calm as Wade's face paled, then twisted furiously. For a split second she was sure he was going to strike her.

As Wade struggled to give voice to his rage, Storm wheeled and walked into the mercantile. "Chew on that and see if you like its taste, Wade Magallen," she whispered over the tears that rose and threatened to choke her.

Wade watched her twist away, his fists clenching and unclenching. He stood for a minute, trying to decide whether he was glad or sorry that Storm wasn't carrying his child. There had been a time when he would have shouted his happiness that Storm was going to make him a daddy.

His eyes grew bleak. That had been a long time ago. Now he had no reason to shout with happiness. The worst possible thing that could have happened to Storm was for her to be carrying his child.

He stood a moment longer, then walked on to accomplish what he had ridden into town to do. He had never thanked Storm for taking care of his father, and for some time he had wanted to buy her a gift, but he hadn't known how she might react to it. He didn't want to give her hope again, but he longed to give her something. Something personal that would last through the years, so that when she was an old lady she could look at it and think fondly of him. Midway down the block he pushed open the door to the only jewelry shop in Laramie. He stood at a glass-topped counter, studying the gems that sparkled under the strong rays of the sun that poured through a window.

When Wade left the store some 20 minutes later he was in possession of a delicate gold chain, a perfect emerald suspended from its center. As he walked back up the street he noted that Storm's mare was gone, and he stopped at a small diner and had two cups of coffee, giving her time to get home.

When close to an hour had passed Wade left the eatery and headed out of town, going in the direction of the Roemer ranch. She'll probably hit me with something before I can give her the necklace, he thought ruefully, remembering how furious she had been with him. He pushed from his mind what she had hinted at just before leaving him on the sidewalk; he couldn't bear thinking that Jeffery had made love to her.

To Wade's disappointment, only Kane and Maria were home to greet him when he arrived at the ranch house. When he asked for Storm, Kane said, as he motioned him to sit down, "She hasn't come home yet. She went into Laramie, and if she happened to run into Rafe they won't be home until suppertime."

Kane poured them each a glass of whiskey and, handing Wade his, asked, "Where have you been keeping yourself lately? I haven't seen you in weeks. Your women never used to keep you away from your oldest friend."

Avoiding Kane's teasing eyes, Wade said that extra work at the saloon had kept him busy. He wasn't about to say that shame and a relentless desire for his friend's sister had kept him away. "I have to work at the saloon every day now with Pa laid up."

"How is Jake comin' along?" Kane asked. "I've been meanin' to ride out and visit him, but somethin' always comes up."

"Pa's comin' along fine. Doc let him throw away his crutches today. He can go back to work in a couple of weeks."

Wade finished half his drink, and then, stirring uneasily, asked gruffly, "How long is that horse trainer stayin' with you?"

Kane glanced at Wade's moody face and smiled inwardly. So, my friend, he thought, you're a little jealous, are you? His face expressionless, he answered smoothly, "I can't say for sure. I'd like for him to stay permanently, though. The man is an expert with shorthorns and horses. But I couldn't afford him, even if he agreed to stay on. Men of his caliber draw hefty wages."

Wade's fingers strayed to the breast pocket where the little white box lay. "Why don't you have Storm ask him to stay?" he asked tightly. "He'd probably work for nothin' if she wanted him to stay."

Kane turned his face away to hide the amusement twitching his lips. "They do get on well," he said slowly, as though the idea had just occurred to him. "I wonder if they might get married." He turned his face back to Wade, his eyebrows pulled together in a pretend frown. "Of course, that would mean Rafe would become a partner. Storm owns half the ranch, you know."

"Dammit to hell, man, are you crazy?" Wade was on his feet, a nerve ticking in his cheek. "He's old enough to be Storm's father."

Kane gave him an unconcerned shrug. "Storm needs an older man to look after her, tame her down a bit. A man her own age could never handle her. She'd walk all over him."

Pain and fury on his face, Wade reached into his breast pocket, then shoved the mangled white box into Kane's hand. "I've got to go. Give this to Storm when she comes in. It's a little something for takin' care of Pa while we were on the trail."

Kane took Storm's gift, then followed his friend's rigidly held body outside. When Wade sent the stallion lunging away in a spray of gravel a wide, pleased grin touched Kane's face. "You big dunderhead," he said as he turned and went back into the house, "when are you going to give in and marry her yourself?"

Kane was mistaken about Storm and Rafe being together. Rafe had been involved in a poker game at the Stag since noon, and Storm had decided to stop by and visit Becky for a while. Her friend always managed to raise her spirits. And God knew they needed raising, she thought as she arrived at the small farmhouse.

The spicy aroma of pumpkin pie greeted Storm as she entered the Hadler kitchen. "I had a feeling you'd come by today." Becky walked in from the parlor, smiling. "That's why I baked the pie that's cooling on the table."

"I just bet." Storm returned the smile, taking off her jacket and hanging it on the back of a chair. "I bet I wouldn't be wrong in thinking that you are also hoping that a certain horse trainer might stop by."

She knew she was right when Becky blushed a bright pink but made no response. "Come on, 'fess up," she teased. "Rafe's been disappearing in the evenings a couple of times a week, and he's not gone long enough to ride into Laramie and back."

"All right, he does stop by once in a while," Becky admitted as she busied herself cutting the pie.

"Do the two of you still sit out on the porch?" Storm continued to rag the small woman. "It's pretty cool these evenings. I hope you invite him in for a cup of coffee."

"Yes, I do." Becky glared at Storm. "But that's all I invite him in for. We're friends, that's all."

"Of course. I never thought otherwise," Storm said innocently, hiding a grin. When she realized that Rafe was a tender subject with Becky she asked, "Did you go into Cheyenne over the weekend?"

"Yes, I did," Becky answered shortly, placing a wedge of pie before Storm, then taking the chair across from her. At Storm's disappointed look, she added, "I went to tell my friends that I wouldn't be seeing them anymore."

"Oh, Becky, I'm so glad." Storm reached across the table and squeezed Becky's hand.

"So am I, actually." Becky picked up her coffee, cupping a palm around it. "Since I . . . ah . . . want to devote all my time to becoming a veterinarian . . ." Her voice trailed off.

"And maybe spending more time with a certain handsome horse trainer?" Storm grinned hopefully.

"Maybe." Becky blushed. She set her cup down and looked earnestly at Storm. "Rafe wants me to meet his sister and her family. Do you think I should, or am I setting myself up for a big disappointment?"

"Becky, Rafe is thirty-eight years old. He's beyond the age of playing games, going to such lengths to get you into his bed. If that were all he had in mind, he'd have seduced you long ago."

"You really think so, Storm? That's what I've been telling myself."

"You've been telling yourself right." After a short pause Storm said, "Rafe's the fellow you've been waiting for, isn't he?"

"Yes, he is. I guess that's why I'm so scared nothing will come of it."

"Well, you just stop being scared. Before you know it you'll be Mrs. Rafe Jeffery."

Radiant-faced, Becky smiled at Storm. A moment later, however, she grew sober. "I saw Wade again when I was in Cheyenne. He was with that same woman. This time there was a young girl, around twelve years old, with them." When Storm gave her a startled look Becky reached for her hand and said gently, "The girl looked just like Wade, honey."

Storm had thought she'd reached the depths of despair where Wade was concerned, but she knew differently now. Without her really realizing it, in the back of her mind she had had the hope that someday Wade would tire of carousing and ask her to marry him.

That hope died now in the Hadler kitchen. Wade had a daughter, and if he married anyone it would be the child's mother.

She pushed back her chair and stood up. "I'd better be getting home," she said, her face stony as she shrugged into her jacket. "Maria may be waiting for some of the things I picked up for her."

As Becky followed Storm outside, she wanted to put her arms around her friend to console her. But the stiffly held body told her that Storm's hurt was too deep, too painful for mere words. She could only stand by and watch the slender woman swing onto the mare's back and ride away.

Storm rode in a numb state, giving the reins over to the mount, too blinded by tears to guide her. "I really don't care anymore," she sobbed. "I'm worn out from wondering and waiting. I only regret the wasted years of mooning over him."

She swiped a hand across her wet cheeks, ordering herself not to shed another tear over Wade Magallen as long as she lived.

Her eyes dry now, Storm noted that the sky had grown overcast. She lifted Beauty into a gallop, hoping to get home before the weather grew wet. But even as the thought hit her she saw the sheets of falling rain bearing down from the mountain like a moving wall. She urged Beauty on, trying to outrun the deluge, but within seconds she was enveloped in a cold slash of rain.

Kane stood in the open door of the barn as she came tearing up the drive. He stepped aside and she rode inside. With a wide smile on his face, her brother lifted her from the saddle.

"I see you still don't have enough sense to come in out of the rain." He laughed and pushed her face against his broad chest.

"Stop it, Kane!" Storm struggled, her words muffled in his shirt.

Norah Hess

"Stop what?" Devilish amusement glittered in Kane's eyes. "Stop giving you a brotherly hug?"

Storm began to struggle in earnest when her nose was flattened against the firm chest. This was an old trick her brother had pulled on her many times.

Her small fists struck out, landing wherever they could. She felt the long, lean body shaking with silent laughter and drew a foot back to deliver a healthy kick to his shin.

Kane released her, then nimbly stepped back, and she drew in long breaths of air. "You idiot!" she yelled. "You're going to smother me one of these days, doing that."

"Naw, baby sister, I know just when you're ready to draw that last breath." He rumpled her hair. "Maria's got supper ready and I'm starved." He looked out across the plains where the rain was still coming down. "I wonder what's keepin' Rafe."

"I expect he's still in town," Storm said, but privately she thought he was with Becky by now.

Kane was eager to talk about the shorthorns as they sat eating the evening meal. So far the new herd seemed quite content in their new environment. Of course, the real test was to see how they survived the harsh winters.

After receiving vague and absentminded responses from Storm and Maria he gave up with a snort. "Some people can't take wet

244

weather," he muttered, attacking his steak with vicious slices of his knife.

They were about to leave the table when Kane fished a small white box from his shirt pocket and handed it to Storm.

"Wade dropped this off for you. Said it was a thank you for takin' care of Jake while we were gone." He watched Storm's face closely as she took the box from him. "Go ahead and open it," he urged. "Let's see how much he appreciates you."

"Precious little, I'm sure." Storm's lips curled. She tossed the gift onto Maria's worktable and stood up.

"Women," Kane growled and, rising, he left the kitchen.

Although Storm's eyes drifted often to the white square box as she gathered up the dirty dishes, it wasn't until she said good night to Maria that she picked it up and climbed the stairs to her room.

Still, she restrained her eagerness, washing up and getting into her gown first. Then she sat on the edge of the bed and took up the box, lifting its lid.

The lamplight sparked lights off the green gem, and she gasped at its beauty and obvious worth. She gently picked it up by its delicate chain and let the stone rest in her palm. An almost hysterical fit of laughter overtook her. At least Wade hadn't held her virginity cheaply. This little trinket had set him back quite a bit.

She stroked the emerald a few times, then laid it back in its box. Pulling open the drawer of her small bedside table, she muttered as she blew out the light, "It's only conscience payment."

Storm scooted down under the sheet, and in seconds the tears she had promised herself would never fall again swam in her eyes. One end of her pillow was soaked when she finally fell asleep.

The sky was overcast and a cold wind was blowing down from the mountains when Rafe walked out of the Stag, $30 richer than when he had sat in on the poker game.

He looked up at the gray, lowering clouds and frowned; he'd never make it back to the ranch before the rains came. But a smile gleamed in his eyes as he mounted the palomino. If he pushed Sunny, he could make it to Becky's before the skies opened up. She might even give him supper.

Becky closed the shed door and hurried toward the house, the hound at her heels. It was going to start raining any time now, and there were some windows to be closed. She shivered when a blast of cold wind blew against her, and added mentally that some fires needed to be started as well.

She had a fire going in the cookstove in just a few minutes, and ten minutes later a roaring fire in the fireplace was sending heat out into the cozy room.

Storm

Becky was back in the kitchen, washing her hands and wondering what to make for her supper, when she saw the palomino galloping up the road from Laramie.

Her pulses raced. Rafe! She looked down at the worn trousers Timmy had outgrown and given to her. The knees were baggy and mudstained from crawling along in the dirt, pulling up her crop of turnips. And my shirt looks worse, she thought; one elbow out and a top button missing. She glanced in the mirror over the sink and made a woeful face. The damp air had turned her hair into tight curls all over her head.

"My God, I look like a street waif," she muttered, her hand freezing on her comb as Rafe knocked on the door. "Damn," she said, "why did he have to come in the daytime?" She stubbed her bare toe on a chair as she hurried to let him in.

Rafe stood smiling down at her, an eyebrow raised. "Is your mama home, little girl?"

"No, she's not," Becky answered just as seriously, but her eyes twinkled also.

"That's a shame," Rafe said. "It's gonna rain any minute and I thought she might let me stay with her until it passed."

"Well, I don't know. She's awfully particular who she lets in. Are your intentions honorable? Is it only a roof over your head that you're looking for?"

Rafe looked deep into Becky's eyes. "If that's all I can have, I'll gladly take it."

Becky realized that the conversation was becoming too serious and all levity left her. "If you don't hurry and put your stallion in the shed, you're both going to get wet."

"Yes, ma'am." Rafe tipped his hat. "I'm goin' right now."

"How does steak for supper sound?" she called after him.

"Sounds real good."

Becky closed the door and hurried to her room to change her clothes. When Rafe returned just before the rain began to fall she was standing at the sink peeling potatoes. She wore a blue gingham dress, the bodice shaping her firm breasts, and soft black slippers. Her hair was still a riot of curls, which in Rafe's eyes made her look adorable.

She looked up and smiled at him. "Pour yourself a cup of coffee. Supper won't be long."

Rafe had meant to sit at the table, sip his coffee, and talk to Becky as she worked. But as she moved from sink to stove to the cupboard for dishes, her curvaceous little body was setting his loins on fire. It was all he could do not to pull her into his lap and kiss her silly while his hands roamed over her curves.

Finally he knew that if he sat there much longer he would do exactly that. He would spoil any chance he had of earning her trust, her willingness to make love with him eventually. He had known from the beginning that she was wary of men, had little faith in them.

He stood up, his coffee in his hand. "I'm goin' out on the back porch and watch the rain," he said, his voice thick.

Becky, placing two steaks in a hot skillet, looked up and smiled at him. "I like to watch the rain too." When he stepped through the door she breathed a sigh of relief. Rafe's presence had been driving her to distraction. The last thing in the world she wanted to do was cook a meal. She wanted to be in her big bed, in Rafe's arms.

I have never felt this way about a man before, she thought, turning the steaks to cook on the other side. She had never yearned for a male body to lie next to her own, to hold her through the night. It was true she had enjoyed the encounters with the man who had introduced her to the act of lovemaking, but there had been no love in it. It was over and soon forgotten.

Her hand stilled as she lifted the meat from the skillet. She loved Rafe Jeffery.

"Get that thought out of your mind, woman," she muttered. "Certainly a man like Rafe won't return such sentiments." When she called Rafe in to eat supper some of the warmth had left her voice.

Rafe noticed her changed demeanor right away. Gone was the sparkle in her eyes, the ready smile. What had happened in the short time between his leaving the kitchen and then returning?

Midway through the meal he pushed away from the table, walking around it to draw a surprised Becky from her chair. "Becky, what's goin' on?" He held her by both elbows.

"I don't know what you're talking about." She played with the buttons on his shirt, refusing to look at him.

"Yes, you do. What made you decide you didn't like me anymore? What did I do? Do you want me to leave?"

"Oh, Rafe, none of that is true," she denied hurriedly. "I . . . it's . . ." Her words faltered and stopped.

"It's what?" Rafe cajoled huskily, tipping her chin and gazing into her eyes.

"I know you want to go to bed with me, and I'm afraid that afterward I'll lose your friendship; you won't come visit me anymore."

Rafe gently stroked her cheek. "You wouldn't like losing all that?" he asked gently.

"I would hate it." Becky leaned toward him unconsciously.

"What if the friendship I had for you has turned into love? What if I wanted to see you all the time?"

"Is that true?" Doubt and hope warred in Becky's dark eyes.

"That I love you is the truest thing I've ever said."

Becky gave a small, glad cry at the sincerity in Rafe's voice and flung her arms around his neck. Rafe caught her to him, his head descending to hers.

The kiss he planted on her lips was hot and hungry, and he held it as he swept her into his arms and carried her into the bedroom. He stood her on her feet, and together they hurried out of their clothes, each hungrily eyeing the other's body with longing. When the last article of clothing pooled around their feet, and Rafe's boots lay next to her small pair of slippers, he took Becky in his arms, and together they tumbled onto the bed.

Becky grew nervous now. What should she do? With the other men she had known she was expected to make the first move, all the moves. Now, with everything within her longing to caress Rafe's body, to rain kisses on his throat and across his chest, she was afraid to. What would he think if she did all those things? Would he think it was a whore's trick? Would it remind him of the many men she had been with? Would it drive him away in disgust?

In her uncertainty her body grew still and rigid, waiting.

When Rafe stroked a hand down her throat and came to her breasts, cupping one, she clenched her hands and held her breath.

She was at a fever pitch after he lowered his head and stroked his tongue across a hardened nipple, then gently nibbled it with his teeth. God, how long could she bear it? She bit her lip, trying to hold back her moan of pleasure.

Finally, after Rafe had suckled both breasts until the nipples were pebble hard and swollen, his caressing hand coming closer and closer to the moist core of her, he raised his head and gazed down at her.

"For God's sake, Becky," he whispered hoarsely, "touch me; let me feel your lips against my flesh."

Having been given his permission, so to speak, Rafe received the attentions of a lover well versed in the art of pleasing a man. So heady was the feel of her tongue caressing him, her knowing hands touching special spots on his body, he embarrassed himself by reaching a climax almost at once. Never in his life had such a thing happened to him.

Becky's skilled fingers soon had him hard again, and he hastened to climb between her legs, hoping as he plunged inside her that he could control himself long enough for her to receive satisfaction.

After the penetration, Becky controlled the lovemaking. When his breathing quickened and his thrusts became a little stronger she stroked his back and relaxed the hold the walls of her femininity had on his maleness. His penis slowed its action until it was stroking in slow rhythm inside her.

Becky brought Rafe to a peak of ecstacy only to calm him back down. And then it came to a point when it was beyond either one of them to hold on any longer. With a deep, hoarse growl, Rafe grabbed Becky's hips and lifted them high to receive the full force of his swollen, aching organ.

Storm

The bed shook and creaked from the hard rising and falling bodies; then the room rang with the roar of the conquering male and the satisfied peal of the female.

His sweaty head tucked under Becky's chin, Rafe fought to catch his breath. He'd had many women, but all of them put together couldn't compare with this delicate little woman lying beneath him, also fighting to regain her breath.

When he could finally move Rafe rolled over on his back, bringing Becky with him. He stroked the damp curls off her forehead.

"How soon will you marry me, Becky?"

Several seconds passed before Becky raised her head and gazed down at him. "Do you mean it?"

"With all my heart."

"Well then, what about tomorrow?" Her eyes twinkled. Rafe gave a glad laugh. He hadn't been at all sure that Becky would want marriage, especially to an old worn-out horse trainer.

"I'd like that fine," he answered, "except I'd kinda like to get married in Oregon. . . . You know, have my sister and her family see me get the ring put through my nose."

Becky's happy laughter rang out. "I can just see you with a ring in your nose." She grew quiet for a moment, and then she said, "It will be so nice, belonging to a family again."

Chapter Sixteen

Storm's spirits lifted a bit as the sun pierced the gray, leaden sky, offering hope that the weather would improve. Yesterday, Thankgiving day, it had half rained, half snowed.

Matching my mood exactly, she thought, gazing out of Becky's kitchen window at the dead flower beds, their brown, brittle stalks beaten into the mud. She shivered; winter would soon be here in earnest, and Wyoming winters were so fierce.

She turned her head back to watch Becky cutting an apple pie and filling two mugs with coffee. Becky was in her robe, and the curls at her nape were damp. "Did you just take a bath?" she asked as Becky placed the pie and coffee on the table and then sat down.

"Yep." Becky grinned at her. "Don't I smell good?"

Storm leaned forward and sniffed, then sat back. "The pie smells better."

"Why, you little . . ." Becky grabbed Storm's pie plate and held it out of her reach. "That's my most expensive soap you just turned your nose up at."

"I'm sorry, so sorry. I was only joking," Storm begged, lunging for the tasty sweet.

"Well, if you really mean it." Becky pretended great reluctance. "You do look sort of weedy, like you need nourishment."

There was a moment's silence as the girls took their first few bites of pie; then Becky laid her fork down.

"Storm, Rafe has asked me to marry him."

Storm's head jerked up and she put her fork down also. "Oh, Becky, you did say yes, didn't you?"

"Relax, Storm." Becky laughed softly. "Of course I said yes. Do you think I'd let a man like Rafe get away from me?"

Storm jumped up, ran around the table, and hugged her smiling friend. "I am so happy for you, Becky. You couldn't find a nicer man to marry in a million years."

"Thank you, Storm. I still can't believe that something good is finally happening to me."

"Well, it is, and you deserve it," Storm said as she returned to her seat. "When is the big event going to take place?"

"Sometime after the new year. We're going to be married at his farm. Rafe wants his sister to see us get married . . . put the ring through his nose, he calls it."

"Are you looking forward to meeting his sister?"

"I'm a little nervous about it." Becky pushed her pie around on the plate. "I want her to like me. She and Rafe are awfully close."

"She'll love you, honey, just like Rafe does," Storm said earnestly, then reached over and ruffled the woman's black curls. "He'll hit her if she doesn't," she joked.

"Rafe really does love me, doesn't he, Storm?"

"Yes, you silly goose, he really does. In fact, he's goofy about you. But you know," Storm said thoughtfully, her lids lowered, "I've been wondering what happened to that *young* man you told me you were going to marry someday." She lifted guileless eyes to Becky. "Surely you don't think Rafe is some callow youth."

"Storm Roemer, I swear I'm going to choke the life out of you one of these days." The sparkle in Becky's eyes took away the threat of her words. "I know now that I was talking nonsense that day," she said soberly. "My entire way of thinking has changed since meeting Rafe. I have discovered so many things that until recently I had never experienced. I have learned the joy of sharing my thoughts with Rafe, listening to his, doing small things together. For instance, handing him the hammer and nails when he fixed the roof on my shed, or having a rousing argument about politics."

Becky's eyes grew dreamy as she confessed

smugly, "None of it would mean a thing, though, if excitement was missing in the bed department."

A twinge of envy stirred through Storm. She had known that heady sensation once, but she doubted she ever would again.

She stood up and reached for her jacket. She could do without listening to further words about the joy of lovemaking. "I'd better get on home. I promised Maria I'd do some ironing this afternoon."

Becky watched Storm ride away, praying that someday her friend would find the happiness she was experiencing.

As Storm rode up to the ranch house, she knew that something out of the ordinary had happened. All the hands were down at the corral, and old Jeb, in the center of them, was wringing his bony hands and practically jumping up and down on his spindly legs. His toothless mouth was working, but she was too far away to hear what he was saying.

The kitchen door slammed and Storm turned her head to see Maria hurrying toward her, a look of anxiety on her face. A chill ran down her spine.

"What's going on, Maria?" she called. "Where's Kane?"

"Oh, honey, he's probably in Laramie in the infirmary by now. That rogue stallion jumped the fence and got to his prize mares. When Kane went after him the devil bit him on the

257

thigh. Two of the hands loaded him onto the buckboard and left for town an hour ago."

Maria was still talking as Storm wheeled the mare and took off down the ranch road, stone and gravel flying into the dead weeds edging the narrow track. When she reached Laramie she had shortened the distance between the ranch and town by fifteen minutes. Bringing Beauty to a plunging halt in front of the four-room hospital, she tossed the reins over the fence surrounding the building and burst into the small receiving room.

"Where's Kane?" Storm took the arm of a white-uniformed nurse and shook it.

"Settle down, Miss Roemer," she was told. "He's being settled in a room."

"Is he all right? Was he badly bitten?"

"Bad enough." The nurse spoke calmly, leading Storm out of the room. "Dr. White put thirteen stitches in his thigh muscles to hold together the tear."

The nurse stopped in front of a closed door at the end of a short hall. "He's fine and in no danger," she added as she pushed open the door. "He's in some pain, but Doc will give him laudanum for it. He'll settle down then and sleep for a while."

The nurse stepped into a white-walled room and called cheerily, "You have a visitor, Mr. Roemer, and she looks worse than you do."

Kane, propped up against pillows, held out his arms, and Storm flew across the room and threw herself into them. "Ah, honey." He stroked her pale hair. "I knew you'd be scared. Look how you're tremblin'."

Storm pulled away and searched Kane's face. He was pale under his deep tan, and his jaw was clenched and taut. A sympathetic smile touched her lips as she smoothed the hair away from his eyes. "You're in pain, aren't you?"

"But not for long," Dr. Wright's voice spoke from the doorway. He held a glass half filled with liquid. "Go wait out in the hall for me, Storm," he said, "while I take a look at Kane's bandages, see if his wound has stopped bleeding. I'll be with you in about ten minutes."

The doctor joined Storm in less than the time promised. His face was tired as he leaned against the wall and explained the extent of the damage done to Kane's leg. He ended with, "If he behaves himself and lets the leg heal properly, he'll be as good as new in a month or so. It will be up to you and Maria to see that he follows orders."

"When can he come home? He's going to hate it here."

The doctor smiled knowingly. "I want to keep him here at least a couple of days, keep an eye on his stitches, make sure no infection sets in."

When Storm reentered Kane's room he was watching the door. "I'm goin' home tomorrow," he greeted her, a threatening note in his voice despite the wide smile on his face.

"Oh really." Storm took up the thinly veiled challenge. "That's a grand assumption on your part." She pulled up a chair and sat down. "Doc just told me that *maybe* you can come home day after tomorrow, and only then if you promise to behave yourself."

Kane gave a scornful grunt, and Storm slid a suspicious look at his disgruntled expression.

Pretending not to know that he planned on going home the next day, Storm said, "I suppose you still don't want that stallion put down."

"No, I don't. I only want to get back the five mares he stole from me."

Storm took his clothes off the hook where they had been hung. She folded them over her arm and said grimly, "You're not going home tomorrow, Kane Roemer."

"What in the hell do you mean?" Kane growled, a tinge of alarm in his demand.

Storm smiled at him sweetly. "I'm taking your clothes home."

"You'd better damn well have them back tomorrow if you know what's good for you."

"I don't know what's good for me, but I know what's good for you, brother dear." She paused at the door, her eyes dancing. "A couple of days of complete rest, and I'm not going to stand here arguing."

With a lift of her chin she pushed the door open and left, Kane's outraged threats following her.

The cowhands were waiting for her when Storm rode a tired Beauty up to the corral. "How is he, Stormie?" Jeb rushed up to take the mare when Storm dismounted.

The others gathered round as she told of the stitches required and what the doctor had told her. "He's in pain, but he's going to be all right."

"We're goin' after the mares tomorrow," one of the hands said. "Tell Kane that when you see him."

Storm nodded, and Jeb said, "And put a bullet in that renegade's head. He's stole his . . ."

"No," Storm interrupted. "Kane still doesn't want him killed. He gave me strict orders about that. Sometimes I think he'd like to capture that devil and tame him."

Storm left the men muttering among themselves. She was greeted with the aroma of baking cookies when she opened the kitchen door and stepped inside. She smiled. Maria always baked when she was upset.

"Oh dear," the housekeeper exclaimed, her eyes going straight to the articles of clothing lying across Storm's arm. "Kane must have lost a lot of blood." She took the trousers and held them up, shaking her head at the red-black stain covering most of the right leg.

"Yes, he did," Storm said, "but thanks to his good health, Dr. Wright said that with a lot of red meat and your good cooking he'll soon recover it."

"He'll certainly get a lot of that." Maria pulled a chair away from the table. "Now sit down and eat your supper. I don't know where Rafe has taken himself off to, so we won't wait for him. Half the time he's not here for supper anymore."

Storm made no reply as she dug into the plate of stew Maria had placed in front of her. She knew where Rafe was, and she knew what he'd be eating for supper once he got around to it. She had smelled the beef roasting in Becky's oven.

During the meal Storm was occupied with an idea she had, and she answered Maria's chatter in monosyllables. The housekeeper grew tired of her brief answers, and supper was finished in silence.

An hour later, after a long soak in the wooden tub in the kitchen, Storm crawled into bed. "I'll have to be on my toes in the morning," she muttered, already half asleep. "Every hand is going to be against my riding with them to rescue the mares tomorrow."

The sky in the east was turning pink when Storm awakened. She lay a moment in that transition from sleep to awareness, her brain fumbling for the importance of this particular day.

"The hunt for the mares!" she whispered, and she slid out of the cozy warmth of her bed. She flinched when the cold air wafting through the window brushed against her body. She hurriedly lowered the window sash, then quietly filled the washbasin with water from the matching pitcher. When she had washed her face and hands and run a comb through her hair she carefully crossed the floor to the wardrobe and took out some clothes.

Dressed in riding skirt, flannel shirt, and heavy jacket, and carrying her boots, Storm slipped down the stairs, making sure she didn't step on the fifth step, which always creaked. She didn't need Maria coming out of her room to investigate the noise it would make.

Safely downstairs, she pulled on her boots, took her broad-brimmed hat from the coatrack, and slapped it on her head, pushing the blonde mane of hair up into its crown.

The back door made no noise as Storm eased it open and stepped outside. She stood a moment, her eyes trying to pierce the early dawn to better see the vague outline of the hands gathered at the corral. They talked among themselves as they saddled their mounts, their voices drifting to her on the cold, still air.

Now, she thought nervously, bracing her shoulders, the trick was to get to the stables and saddle a horse.

Keeping in the shadows, she gained the long barn. Congratulating herself for not being spotted, she chose a horse whose long legs promised speed. It took but a minute to saddle him, then swing into the saddle. She drew a long breath, lifted the reins, and rode the animal outside.

Old Jeb, of course, was the first one to spot her. His thin leathery face working spasmodically, he shouted, "Stormie, what in the blue blazes are you doin' out here at this ungodly hour, and mounted besides?"

Storm reined in a few feet from the old man and, her eyes flashing defiance, she shouted back, "I'm going with you."

Jeb's battered hat hit the dirt while six male voices chorused together, "You can't come with us, Miss Storm."

Storm's only response was to lift her head obstinately and stare straight ahead. All her life Kane had been doing for her. At last she had the opportunity to repay him in a small measure. She was going to help bring in his mares, and no one was going to stop her.

"Stormie, you know dad-burn well that Kane wouldn't let you go on this hunt," Jeb half threatened, half pleaded. When she only pulled her jacket tighter against the morning chill, the old man scrambled onto his mount, mumbling, "I wish Wade was here. He'd soon haul you off that mare."

Storm discreetly stayed several yards behind the others, knowing how they disapproved of her accompanying them. She let her gaze drift over the terrain as the distance was eaten up in a long, easy lope. In unsheltered places frost shone on the grass, and she thought that it would be easy to track the herd through its icy whiteness. But getting back their own from the rogue would be something else again.

The sun had risen fully when they came to the foothills of the mountain, the wild stallion's home ground. They had climbed for about ten minutes when Jeb fell back and rode alongside her.

"See that ridge up there?" He pointed a crooked finger at a high structure of stone and stunted pine. "I want you stationed there. I just remembered your keen eyesight; you'll have a better view than the rest of us when we start combin' the canyons." His eyes dropped to the gun holstered at her waist. "If you spot them, let off a couple of shots . . . up in the air."

Storm stared after the thin back swaying on the big roan and made a face. "You old coot," she grouched, "as if I'd shoot straight on." She turned the mount toward the ridge, not convinced that Jeb was sending her there with any thought that it was strategically a good spot. "Most likly to keep me out of the way." Her lips turned down at the corners.

Storm followed the slant of the ridge until she came to a break in the rock formation. She gazed down into the valley, thinking it was nearly impassable. However, there was a heavily trodden trail leading around boulders and large rocks. And by the clean, sharp hoof prints, it had been recently used. She shifted her eyes to gaze unfettered by trees, at a small, level, grassy patch about five acres square, the sun glinting off a narrow stream of water cutting across it.

"So, you rogue devil," she whispered, "this is where you hide out." She pulled the mount in and waited.

About five minutes had passed when Storm

heard the light, quick clatter of hooves. With a leap of her heart she stood up in the stirrups, and from her vantage point, she saw the herd winding their way along the narrow trail. She counted them as they passed beneath her. Besides their own five beauties, there were ten other mares, mostly blacks, and a couple of bays and two buckskins.

Not bad, she thought, looking over the animals critically before they rounded a bend that took them from sight. But they showed a lot of in-breeding, she tacked on.

Her mount nervously tossed his head, clearly affected by the scent of the wild herd. Storm was wondering why the wild stallion wasn't with the mares when she heard a slower, heavier plod of hooves: The rogue was coming.

Admiration grew in her eyes as from behind a large boulder a pure white stallion appeared. He is magnificent, she thought. No wonder Kane is reluctant to have him shot.

She was close enough to see the pride and fire in the animal's dark, intelligent eyes when he paused and gave a wild snort, his expression looking uncertain.

Has he scented me? Storm wondered, switching her gaze back to the grassy plot where the mares were now grazing. While she debated letting off a couple of shots at once, or waiting until the stallion joined the mares, a volley of shots exploded from three different directions.

The men had spotted the herd.

The stallion's fine head jerked up, his nostrils flaring. He stood a moment; then, bunching his muscles, he sprang away, racing to avert danger.

He was only yards away from his harem when he was met by yelling riders and popping ropes. Without a break in his gallop, the horse raced straight toward the men, making their mounts whistle their fright and scatter out of his way. He headed straight for the five ranch mares, who had stayed together. Storm gave a startled gasp when the stallion gave a piercing blast. His eyes black fire, he raced among them, nipping their flanks and shoulders, trying to break up the knot they had formed.

"You're a smart devil," Storm whispered in admiration, "but today you are going to lose the battle." As he had worked to keep his new mares, the cowhands were moving in on the others. Squealing his fury, the big white animal whirled and circled his orginal herd, then drove them back up the narrow way they had so recently traveled.

But just before he disappeared out of sight he stopped, staring after the five mares the cowboys were driving home. He gave a shrill whistle, as though announcing that eventually the mares would be his.

Her body weary from the rough mountain riding, Storm trailed after Jeb and the men, the dust hanging in the air smarting her eyes and throat. Reaching the corral, she turned her mount over to one of the cowhands and walked toward the house to face Maria's wrath.

But when she entered the kitchen the house-keeper only gave her a stern look and said, "Foolish girl, wash up and I'll fix you something to eat."

"Thank you, Maria." Storm kissed her smooth, plump cheek, grateful for the offer of food but more grateful not to have the kindly woman harangue her.

"Kane will be happy to have his pets back," Maria said a short time later as Storm ate hot biscuits and sausage gravy. "I'm going in with you when you visit him, just to see his handsome face light up when you tell him."

"You'll see another look on his handsome face when I tell him he's not coming home tomorrow," Storm said with a grin as she gazed out the window, watching the five mares being groomed. Their hides, which had once glistened from daily currying, were now rough with cuts and scratches. Thankfully, none had been in season, and none would be dropping the rogue's offspring months from now.

It was shortly after noon when Storm and Maria rode into Laramie and drew rein in front of the hospital. "Oh drat," Maria exclaimed as she dismounted and took a small package from her saddlebag, "some of the cowhands are already here. I can just hear that loose-mouthed Jeb blabbing everything to Kane."

Storm felt the same annoyance as she swung to the ground. Kane would be like a wounded bear when he learned he wouldn't be coming home today, and he would be twice as angry with her because she had insisted on riding with Jeb and the men.

They could hear the male voices and laughter when they stepped into the hall. "I hope the nurse throws them all out," Storm muttered just before she opened the door to Kane's room.

Kane was sitting up in bed, his damaged thigh outside the covers, cushioned with a pillow. Gratitude shone in his eyes as the men, all talking at once, told him of their raid on the stallion, how they had rescued the mares. It was several seconds before he saw the two women standing just inside the door, the older one wearing a disapproving look, the young one looking uncertainly at him.

"Maria!" he exclaimed, then ignored his sister when a fast glance showed him she carried no suitcase. After a quick bear hug and a smacking kiss on Maria's cheek, he unwrapped the package she handed him and sniffed loudly. "Beef sandwiches! I knew *you* wouldn't let me down." He slid Storm an accusing look.

Storm made no response, only smiled her thanks to the cowboy who quickly rose and offered her his chair.

When a seat was brought forward for Maria the housekeeper sat down, then directed a glower at Jeb, leaning against the wall. "You just had to rush over here and snitch on Storm, didn't you?"

Ready to bite into his sandwich, Kane put it back down and shot Storm a sharp look. "Were you with the men on the hunt?"

"I was just about to tell you that, Kane." Jeb's reedy voice broke in before Storm could answer. "I told her to go back to the house, but she wouldn't mind me. She was bound and determined to go along. I had a mind to take a switch to her."

There was total silence in the room for a moment; then the men threw back their heads and roared with laughter. Storm's face went brick red with embarrassment. She jerked her hat off the floor and stamped out of the room, ignoring Kane's demand that she come back.

Maria jumped to her feet and, snapping furiously, "You stupid old goat," at a suddenly confused Jeb, she hurried after Storm.

Neither woman spoke on the way home, nor immediately after reaching the house. Storm went straight to her room and was lying across the bed when Maria knocked, then entered. She sat down next to Storm and said quietly, "Don't be upset at that old fool. Sometimes I think he's getting a little senile. We have no idea how old he is; he probably doesn't know himself. Kane said he could remember Jeb saying he worked here as a young man for your grandfather. The old fellow looks on you and Kane as family, and he thinks you're still a child who needs to be told what to do."

Maria's well-intended words released a torrent of tears from Storm. She turned her head into her arm and sobbed, "That's what everyone thinks. Jeb, Kane, and . . ."

"And Wade," Maria finished for her. "Especially Wade."

"Oh, Maria." Storm turned over on her back and flung an arm across her eyes. "You know everything, don't you?"

"Well, not everything," Maria said, her dark eyes twinkling, "but I've known you were infatuated with him since you were a kid."

Storm dropped her arm to her side and gazed up at Maria, her eyes mirroring a startled thought. "Infatuated? Is it possible I've been fooling myself all these years?"

"It's possible." Maria nodded. "I always thought it was too bad you didn't give any of the young men who came around a chance to get to know you. You were always too busy wondering what Wade was doing, where he was, and with whom. It's too bad you lost the opportunity to discover your true feelings for Wade."

Maria watched confusion flit across Storm's face. "The four years you were gone brought a lot of changes in Wade. He drinks too much, has too many women, and rides that stallion of his into the ground. He's as wild as that rogue stallion you and the men chased yesterday."

When Storm leaned up on an elbow Maria teased, "Now tell the truth; you wouldn't like to take on a wild stallion and try to tame him, would you?"

"Don't you like Wade anymore?" Storm

271

ignored Maria's question.

"Of course I still like Wade." Maria's eyes snapped indignantly. "Next to you and Kane, he's my favorite person. I just don't think he's the man for you."

"Not for me," Storm spoke to the ceiling after Maria had gone. "I was too stupid to realize that years ago. But Maria is mistaken about it being only infatuation I felt for Wade. I loved him with my whole being."

Chapter Seventeen

It was early afternoon when Storm and Rafe drove into Laramie, Rafe handling the reins of a pair of horses pulling the light buckboard. Jeb had made a bed of hay in back of the high seat, and Maria had folded several blankets over it so Kane would be comfortable on his ride home.

"I hope he's in a better frame of mind than he was last night when I stopped by to visit him," Rafe said a little later as he swung Storm to the street. "He was like a grizzly bear with a bee sting on his snout."

He took Storm's arm and helped her onto the wooden sidewalk. "He was making dire threats at you." Rafe laughed.

"I'm afraid I'm not his favorite person right now." Storm smiled thinly.

As they entered the hospital and walked down the hall, the middle-aged nurse stepped from Kane's room. The frazzled look she bore relaxed in relief.

"I hope you've come to fetch Kane home, Miss Roemer," she said. "He's about to drive me crazy. He's been up since before dawn, thumping around on his crutches, keeping the other patients awake. They've been threatening to lynch him."

Rafe grinned and held out the small valise for the nurse to see. "We've brought his duds. We'll have him out of here just as fast as we can."

"That's the best news I've heard all year," the woman grumped as she walked down the hall.

Rafe received a hearty welcome when they walked into Kane's room, but Storm only got a grunt to her cheery greeting. She had expected as much and merely shrugged her shoulders as she walked over to the window, turning her back as Rafe helped Kane into his clothes, her brother asking a dozen questions about the ranch and his shorthorns.

For heaven's sake, Storm thought impatiently, you've only been gone for two days. How much could happen in so short a time?

"All set, Storm?" Rafe asked after a few minutes. "Let's get this wild man out of here."

Once they were out of town and headed toward the ranch, Kane became almost boyish in his enthusiasm. With a broad smile on his face, his head swiveled from side to side as he took in the plains, the distant mountains.

Storm smiled in understanding and forgave her brother for being angry with her. The past two days must have been terrible for him, cooped up in one small room and mostly in bed. He was too energetic to be idle for so long.

The horses had drawn the buckboard within a couple of miles of the ranch house when from down the rutted road Storm saw Wade's black stallion galloping toward them. Her heart began to pound as the distance between them shortened. She hadn't seen him in over two weeks and he looked so good to her.

"Easy, Storm," Rafe said in a low voice when Wade met them and turned the stallion in a circle to ride alongside the buckboard. He gave Rafe a curt nod, spoke Storm's name in a flat, expressionless voice, and then turned his attention to Kane, a warm smile on his face.

"I've been in Cheyenne," he said, "and just learned of your run-in with the rogue. Did he do you any permanent damage?"

"Naw, I'll be fine in a month or so. I'm gonna have one hell of a scar, though. That devil took a good chunk out of me."

"You'd better have that animal put down before he kills somebody."

"We'll see," Kane answered, then switched the subject to Cheyenne. "Did you meet any agents looking for cattle?"

Storm didn't know what Wade answered; she was deep in misery, knowing that Wade had spent more time with his old love than he had with any agents.

She wondered about the new lines etched around Wade's mouth. Weren't things going well with him and the woman? Did she have a husband she wouldn't leave?

Whatever the problem was, Wade didn't look very happy as they approached the ranch house.

Old Jeb came hurrying from the stables to help Kane slide off the buckboard, garrulous as ever, getting in the way more than helping. Maria stood in the kitchen doorway, beaming as Kane swung along on his crutches and called out, "What's for supper, Maria? I'm starvin'."

"Your favorite food: steak," Maria answered, then cautioned Jeb to get out of the way so Kane could enter the kitchen.

Storm gave a short, sour laugh and said to Rafe, "You'd think the prodigal son has returned. I wonder if Maria had a steer butchered."

Rafe gave a hearty laugh at her remark, causing Wade to turn his head and give him a cold look before following Kane inside.

"There, how's that, Kane?" Old Jeb's bones creaked as he straightened up from shoving a pillow under Kane's heavily bandaged leg, stretched across a footstool.

"Just fine, Jeb. Now if you'll just pour me a couple of fingers of whiskey, I'll be in dandy shape."

"Save your energy, Jeb," Storm said from her stand beside the fireplace, watching her brother being settled in. "You won't find any liquor in the house."

"Why in the hell not?" Kane glared at her, his eyebrows rising like thunder clouds. "Did you have a big party while I was gone and drink up all my whiskey?"

"No. Nobody's been around, Kane." Jeb tried to soothe Kane. "I'd have knowed. Maybe . . ."

"Shut up, Jeb," Kane yelled. "Let me hear her excuses."

Storm tried to check her rising temper. She suspected Kane was probably in pain, or at the very least uncomfortable. Still, that was no reason for him to hurt the old man's feelings.

"There's no liquor in the house," she snapped, "because Dr. Wright said you shouldn't drink while you're taking the medicine he prescribed. Alcohol would weaken its effectiveness."

"Dammit, Storm, I don't plan on gettin' rip-roarin' drunk. I don't see how one small drink is gonna harm anything."

"Look, you spoiled jackass," she snapped, "stop acting like you're ten years old. Do you want to lose that leg to infection?"

The way the handsome face paled, Storm hoped Kane had finally realized the seriousness of his wound. But he continued to grumble, looking to Jeb for sympathy. When he quickly received it, Storm threw up her hands in disgust.

What a pain her brother was going to be these next few weeks.

When Kane turned to Wade and started talking cattle Storm sat down next to Rafe on the leather sofa. He smiled at her and picked up her hand. "What did you get up to today while I was gone?"

"Nothing much." Storm scooted a little closer to Rafe, sliding a look at Wade. He seemed to be listening to every word Kane said, even answering a question put to him, but nevertheless he was alert to every word and action between her and Rafe.

Rafe hadn't missed Wade's close attention to them either. With a devilish gleam in his eyes he leaned closer to Storm and said in loverlike tones, "Let's take a walk before supper."

Storm hid the twinkle in her eyes as she stood up. Rafe really enjoyed baiting Wade.

She was taking her jacket from the clothesrack when Wade said gruffly, "Kane, don't you think Maria could use some help in the kitchen?"

As Kane looked at Wade, a little baffled, Storm said sweetly as she shrugged into the warm garment, "How nice of you to think about that. I'm sure Maria will welcome your help."

While Kane almost bit through his lip to keep from laughing, Storm took Rafe's arm, smothering her own laughter at the anger in Wade's eyes.

When the door closed behind the pair Kane glanced at his friend but didn't speak. One wrong word and the big man would explode. They sat in silence, even Jeb knowing to keep his mouth shut.

Kane gave a startled jerk when Wade asked abruptly, "Did you give Storm my gift?"

"Of course I did." Kane frowned at him.

"Well . . . what did she say?"

"She didn't say anything. Just kind of curled her lip . . . like this." Kane quivered his upper lip in an exaggerated sneer, then bit the inside of his mouth not to laugh at the riled look that came over his friend's face. "What did you give her?" he asked finally. "She never did say."

"Nothin' much," Wade answered stiffly. "Just a little ol' necklace." There was silence again; then Wade asked hesitantly, "You haven't seen her wearin' a chain with a . . . green . . . green lump on it?"

Kane rubbed his chin thoughtfully. "A green lump?" After a moment he shook his head. "No, Wade. I haven't seen any lumps on Storm's throat, green or otherwise."

He met his friend's suspicious look with a perfectly straight face. Wade growled, "You long drink of water, I'm wonderin' if you're findin' a little amusement at my expense."

"Who? Me?" Kane blinked innocent eyes. "I'd never."

"Bull," Wade grunted and stalked over to the window. "It's gettin' ready to rain any minute. Don't you think that . . ."

"They've got sense enough to come in out of the rain, Wade," Kane cut him off.

"Yeah, like going into the barn," Wade muttered to himself, then the next minute hurried back to his chair. "They're comin' in now."

"See, I told you I didn't raise no dumb sister."

Storm and Rafe came into the big room, briskly rubbing their hands together as they hurried to the fire. "I think it will snow tonight," Rafe said.

"I thought you were going to help Maria." Storm looked at Wade, her palms held to the fire. "I notice the table isn't set yet."

Wade's eyes glinted at her, but he didn't respond to her sly remark. She straightened up and said with a long sigh, "I guess I'll have to do it myself. Never let it be said that I'm lazy." She glanced at Wade, but his lowered lids hid what he was thinking. However, she felt the heat of his eyes on her back as she left the room.

Maria called them to supper shortly, and Storm held her breath when it appeared that Wade and Rafe were heading for the same place at the table. If Rafe took Wade's chair there would be a ruckus.

At the last moment Rafe took the chair next to Kane's. Storm looked at her brother and shook her head at the way he was demolishing his steak. Her gaze went to Jeb, sitting to his right, and smiled to herself. He was gumming his meat as rapidly as Kane was chewing his.

Kane and Rafe discussed the shorthorns, wondering if it would snow and how well the short-legged cattle would tolerate it. Wade and

Maria talked quietly about Jake, Maria asking how he was coming along, and Wade answering that he was doing fine, that he was going to return to work in a week.

Storm entered neither conversation. She only wanted to go to her room and stop pretending that Wade no longer meant anything to her.

Finally the dessert, a peach cobbler, was eaten and everyone was leaving the table. When Kane started to swing away on his crutches Maria said, "Until you can get up and down the stairs, Kane, I've swapped rooms with you. I switched our clothes and things today."

"Thanks, Maria. I've been wonderin' how I was goin' to navigate those stairs."

When the housekeeper began to clear the table Storm took her arm and steered her from the kitchen, saying, "Go sit down and rest. I'll do the dishes."

Storm worked swiftly and deftly, and within half an hour the kitchen was in its usual immaculate state. She longed for a long, leisurely soak in hot, soapy water, but that would have to wait until the house settled down for the night.

Removing the towel she had tied around her waist, Storm rolled down her sleeves and walked into the big room. "Good night, everyone." Her eyes swept the room, taking them in. "I'm going to bed."

"You mean you aren't goin' to stay up with me for a while?" Rafe rose and walked with her to the foot of the stairs.

Her eyes shimmering with silent laughter, Storm answered sweetly, "Not tonight, honey. I'm really tired. But tomorrow night . . ." She let the words trail in a significant manner, in a tone full of promise.

They both swung around when the outside door slammed with a strength that left it shuddering. Rafe grinned in satisfaction. "Boy, that is one angry rooster." While Maria and Jeb stared at the door in bewilderment, Kane gazed into the fire, a knowing grin on his face.

Ol' Wade was getting near the end of his rope.

It was nearing ten o'clock when Kane and Maria retired and Rafe left, apparently to sleep in the bunkhouse, since Maria now occupied the bedroom upstairs. But Storm knew better. If she went outside and stood on the porch and listened, she'd hear the palomino's hooves pounding down the river road, heading for Becky's place.

She wondered when that pair was going to tell everyone their news as she picked up her robe from the foot of the bed. Becky was the one who wanted their approaching marriage kept secret. If he had his way, Rafe would shout it to the world.

The kitchen was still warm when Storm slipped quietly down the stairs and took down the wooden tub that always hung behind the stove. She took the large teakettle off the stove and emptied its hot water into the tub, then tempered it with cold water from the hand pump. She tossed in a bar of rose-scented soap and a washcloth, pulled the gown over her head, and stepped into the water.

As she lathered the cloth and began her bath, she could hear Kane snoring in Maria's room, off the kitchen. He usually didn't snore, so he must have taken a little laudanum before retiring. He would probably sleep through the night.

Storm didn't linger in her bath. The fire had gone out in the stove and the room was cooling off. She could see frost on the windowpanes.

Standing up, she reached for the towel she had draped over a chair. Her skin was satin smooth as she rubbed it dry. But gooseflesh was popping out all over her body, and she shrugged into her favorite fleecy robe, appreciating its warmth as she made her way to the other room.

The lamp that was always left burning during the night gave the room a relaxing coziness. She settled down on the sofa and stretched her bare feet to the low-burning fire, wide awake.

She was hoping she wasn't going to have one of those restless nights, where Wade came to tease her in her dreams, when the scrape and flare of a match made her turn her head and peer into a darkened corner.

"Rafe?" she squeaked.

"No, it's not Rafe," came a cool, sardonic reply. "Were you expecting him to sneak back and keep you company?"

"Damn you, Wade Magallen!" Storm kept her angry voice down. "You scared me half to death.

What are you doing here? I thought you went home."

"So I came back. I thought *I'd* keep you company for a change," he taunted softly.

"I don't want your company," Storm whispered hoarsely as Wade rose from his chair and came to stand over her.

"Why not?" He studied her from heavy-lidded eyes. "I can be just as entertainin' as Jeffery. Maybe even better," he added softly, slowly running his gaze over her body, clearly defined beneath the soft material. She jumped when he grated out, "What's that?" His eyes were fastened on a spot where the robe had parted at her knees.

Storm jerked the robe together. "It's nothing; only a bruise I got helping Jeb curry one of Kane's mares."

"And you've got one down here." Wade knelt and took her ankle, straightening out her leg.

"It's nothing," Storm repeated, struggling to free her foot as a familiar fire licked through her veins at his touch.

Cupping her ankle in his palms, Wade slowly slid them up her calf, stopping at her knees, where she gripped the robe together. "I don't like to see marks on this lovely flesh." He leaned forward and kissed the blue mark.

"You've put your marks on my *lovely flesh*." Storm hardly knew what she was saying, her pulse was racing so hard from the touch of his lips.

"Ah, but those were different." Wade's hands slipped past her knees. "Those were love marks."

"What do you think you're doing?" Storm cried, trying to remove the caressing hands that stroked up her legs.

"You know what I'm doin', Storm," Wade whispered huskily, his eyes dark with desire, his hands on her thighs now, gently pressing them apart.

"No, I don't, and I wish you would stop."

"I can't stop, Storm," Wade moaned, regret in his voice. "It's been too long since the last time." He pulled her robe apart, and her nerveless hands allowed it. But when he bent his head and kissed the soft flesh behind her knee she gasped.

"Don't do that, Wade. I don't want you to."

"Yes, you do," Wade said softly, his lips moving up her leg, at the same time easing her down on the sofa.

When he pulled open her robe, revealing her bare body to his hot gaze, she cried brokenly, "No, I don't want . . ." Her sentence was never finished as Wade's mouth slid hotly up the inside of one thigh, then concentrated on one spot.

Her fingers dug into his shoulders, and his name was a constant murmur on her lips as his tongue took possession of her.

She thought she could bear it no longer when Wade raised his head and gazed into her desire-filled eyes. With a possessive hand on each breast, he demanded harshly, "Have Jeffery's hands ever been here?"

Storm could only gaze back at him and shake her head mutely. His head dipped down then, and the warmth of his mouth moved over her breasts, his lips and teeth gently tugging at the tender pink nipples. When they stood hard and puckered he lifted a breast in his palm and suckled it until liquid fire raced through her blood.

"Oh God, Wade," Storm moaned, "I need you."

In fluid movements Wade rose and tore off his clothes. He stood a moment, naked, gazing down at her in uncompromising manhood, every line of his perfect body saying that she was his. Storm moved her bent legs a little wider, silently conceding that, yes, she belonged to him.

Wade read the movement and threw himself down beside her. Storm went into his arms and his mouth came down to cover hers. Her arms came up around his shoulders, and his hot and hungry kiss deepened, his tongue slipping between her lips, wrapping itself around Storm's.

With a low, throaty moan, Storm began moving her hands over his back, kneading and stroking. Then Wade took her hand and guided it down his flat stomach. When it came to his rock-hard maleness he curved her fingers around it.

"Ah, yes, honey," he moaned when her fingers gently tightened around him and she began to slowly stroke her hand up and down. "Oh, Storm," he whispered, and rolled over on his back, giving himself into her hands.

And Storm, loving this power over him, grew brave. She leaned over him and, with quick little kisses, worked her way across his broad chest, down his flat stomach, and then down farther to where the core of him pulsated in her hand.

She lingered there a teasing moment, making Wade's body tighten as he waited, daring to hope that her lips would replace her hand. He moved his fingers urgently through her hair, but she swerved her mouth to lick the hollows of his slim hips.

"Little coward," he growled in amusement, removing her caressing hand and pushing her back on the sofa.

Storm tried to hold his gaze as he pulled her legs apart and knelt between them. But the raw desire in the slate-gray eyes made her blush and lower her lids.

"My shy baby," he whispered huskily and, lifting her hips slightly, he slid smoothly inside her, his moan of pleasure smothered in her hair. "It's been so long," he whispered. "Every night I lie in bed aching for you."

Storm wanted to ask, "Why have you stayed away from me, then?" but she was beyond speech as he held her hips firmly and began to slowly stroke inside her.

She clung to his shoulders, eagerly accepting the smooth slide of him, straining not to miss one word of his whispered commands. Storm did as he coaxed, bracing her feet on the sofa and reaching for every thrust that brought their hips grinding together.

Their bodies gleamed with perspiration when a long time later they shuddered together, convulsed in a mind-shattering climax. Together, they floated in a dreamlike world as their breathing returned to normal.

Storm smiled at Wade as he lifted his head from her shoulder and gently smoothed the damp hair away from her face. "You're the best," he whispered softly, then carefully withdrew from her.

Storm stared at him blankly. Is that all he's going to say to me? she cried silently, watching him draw on the clothes he'd torn off in such a hurry.

Her skin crawled in self-loathing when he joked, "I'd better get out of here in case Kane wakes up. He'd tear a strip off me if he knew what we've been up to."

Without another word he pulled on his boots and left, taking his jacket as he passed through the door. Storm lay where she was, furious. Wade had used her again.

As Wade sent the stallion racing through the night, a hard-driving snow lashed at his face. He wasn't aware of it; he was too busy mentally lashing himself. The last thing he'd had on his mind when he returned to the Roemer ranch had been seducing Storm. He'd meant only to

288

return the two pots Pa had asked him to give to Maria. He had noticed they were still tied to his saddle when he was halfway home.

But, as usual, he had lost all control when Storm had entered the room, smelling so sweet and looking so damn beautiful. He shook his head. Every time he was around her he either made an ass of himself or took her to bed.

A savage curse escaped him as he thundered through the night. Again he hadn't protected her against his seed. Just like a rutting bull, he had spilled himself inside her.

The big black turned off the river road and galloped up to the small barn behind the Magallen cabin. As Wade dragged the saddle off the horse, he wondered how much whiskey it would take to send him into oblivion tonight.

Chapter Eighteen

The wintry sunshine strove to pierce the grayness of the leaden sky, and a bitter cold wind whipped down from the mountains. Winter had once again settled over Wyoming. Heavy snow blanketed the plains and valleys throughout the winter. It was two weeks until Christmas, and already there was ten inches of the white stuff on the ground, with drifts as high as two feet.

Storm paused and leaned on the shovel, her breath making small clouds of vapor on the cold air. She watched Jeb drag open the ice-encrusted gate to the corral and tramp through the snow to break up the ice in the water trough. He would turn Kane's mares out now for a couple of hours of fresh air and sunshine.

Storm

With a resigned sigh, she gripped the shovel handle with both hands and took up where she had left off. For over an hour she had been clearing new snow from the path leading to the outhouse and the barn. The shovel-wide lane was beginning to look like a tunnel with the snow banks shoulder high on either side.

Ordinarily Kane kept the paths clear, old Jeb's rheumatism making it too painful for him to shovel, but these days her brother could do nothing but grumble and grouch, driving everyone around him crazy. And Rafe wasn't around much these days. Most of the time he was with Becky.

Storm's smile was a mixture of happiness and sorrow. She was happy for Becky; it was time her little friend had something good happen to her. But she would miss her dreadfully when Rafe took her away.

But then, Storm wouldn't be around here either after the holidays, she reminded herself. During that long black night after Wade left her as though she had been one of his one-night flings, she had reached a firm decision: She was returning to Cheyenne. She would go back to teaching, but she would pace herself so that she wouldn't become ill again. She was convinced at last that there was no future for her here. She couldn't go on piling up wasted years.

At last the paths were clear, and Storm looked up at the gray sky, hoping it wouldn't snow again for at least a couple of days.

Carrying the shovel over her shoulder, she walked to the house, leaned it against the wall, and scraped the snow off her feet before entering the kitchen.

She was pulling off her boots on the rug placed for that purpose when Maria turned from the stove and said angrily, "He's driving me crazy."

"What's he done now?" Storm asked wearily, knowing without asking who *he* was: Kane, of course. He'd been driving everybody loco. In fairness, though, she imagined he was going a little crazy himself, cooped up in the house so long.

"He's trying to tell me how to cook now. After doing nothing but handle cattle all his life suddenly he's a cook," Maria complained, highly agitated. "He claims my chili is too bland so he up and adds more red pepper to it. Now it's not fit to eat. It'll burn the lining out of your mouth and singe the hair off your head."

Storm had taken off her jacket during Maria's long, angry tirade and now walked over to the stove. She dipped a spoon into the pot of red-brown liquid at the back of the stove and cautiously sipped it.

"God," she gasped, wheezing. She rushed to the sink to pump herself a glass of water.

"What did I tell you?" Maria stood, hands on hips. "You've got to talk to him, Storm."

Storm sighed and replaced the lid on the pot. "I'm not up to arguing with him right now, Maria, but he's not going to get away with ruining our supper. Serve him *his* chili in the biggest bowl you have and make us a big, juicy steak."

"Good idea!" Maria gave a satisfied nod of her head. "Now sit down and have a cup of coffee and a piece of pie. You deserve it, after all that shoveling."

Storm had just chased the last bite of apple around her plate when she heard the scraping of boots outside. The door opened, and Jeb stepped inside.

"Don't step off that rug," Maria ordered. "I just scrubbed the floor."

"I got no intention of steppin' on your blasted floor," the old man grouched, then looked at Storm. "Stormie, today is a good time to go get our Christmas tree. The snow is frozen and the horses won't get bogged down."

It was on the tip of Storm's tongue to turn the old man down. The last thing she felt like doing was wading through the snow searching for that perfect tree. The *perfect tree* had been a project of Jeb's since she could remember.

It took the sound of something falling and Kane's disgruntled swearing to change her mind. She felt less like being around her brother than hunting for a Christmas tree.

She smiled at the old man. "Let me finish my coffee."

"It's just plain contrariness on your part, Stormie." Jeb kicked angrily at a snowdrift.

"I'm tellin' you, the best trees are farther down the valley."

"Jeb, I'm not being stubborn," Storm argued back, beating her gloved hands together, trying to keep the blood flowing to her fingers. "We've been tramping around for over an hour and I'm tired and half frozen. That tree over there is perfect. If we get one any larger, we won't be able to get it home."

"What are you talkin' about? My horse could drag one twice that size to the house."

"Probably, but would it fit in the house? Our ceilings aren't ten feet high, you know." She handed the ax to Jeb and, grumbling to himself, he stalked after her.

Jeb had chopped the four-inch bole in half when Storm felt a queer tightness between her shoulder blades. Someone was watching them. She spun around, then gasped, "Jeb! Look!"

Jeb glanced up, following the direction of her gaze. "The rogue!" he swore under his breath.

The wild stallion stood about 20 yards away, his coat shaggy now, but still as pure white as the snow in which he stood.

The sharp wind blew against him, lifting his long tail and mane in streaming banners. It was too far away to see his eyes, but Storm knew they were shooting red rage. She and Jeb had wandered into his territory and he now stood between them and their mounts, tied several yards away.

"What are we going to do, Jeb?" Storm's voice quivered.

Jeb's rheumy gaze quickly measured the distance to their horses. They could never make it if the wild one came after them. His eyes feverishly scanned the landscape, looking for anything they could climb to safety. There was nothing; only smooth, rolling, snow-covered plains, broken occasionally by a tree that was smaller than the one that still held the ax.

He jerked the double blade free and, hefting it in his hands, said in a voice not much steadier than Storm's, "If he comes after us, I can hold him off long enough for you to dash to the mounts."

"But what about you?" Storm whispered fiercely. "I'm not going to leave you to face that brute alone."

"Listen, you mule-headed child," the old man swung on her, his wrinkled face working spasmodically, "you do what I tell you. If that stallion charges us, you get your runty ass on your mount."

The young woman and the old man stood silently in the trampled snow, bodies stiff, challenging each other, though not a word was spoken between them. Even the wind died down, making the moment more profound.

And then in the silence, from behind a small knoll, there came the faint snarls of a wolf pack. Jeb's head swiveled in the direction of the yapping wolves and the shrill, terrified neighing of horses. His peering gaze swung to the stallion and he grunted a sound of relief. The wild one now faced the small hill, his head held high, vapor snorting from his flaring nostrils.

"Stormie," Jeb's voice was uneven, "I think maybe our bacon is saved. Them wolves are after his harem. He's got no interest in us now."

Storm could only nod, her limbs as weak as water. They watched the stallion lunging laboriously through the snow, snorting and blasting his displeasure. He stood highlighted against the sky for a moment, as though observing his enemy or planning his battle maneuvers. Then, rearing up and pawing at the sky, he gave a shrill scream and disappeared down the sloping incline.

"Isn't it unusual for him to come so far down the valley?" Storm looked at Jeb, breathing a little easier. "I thought he stayed closer to the mountains."

"He's lookin' for somethin' to eat. If you look down there where he was standin', you'll see patches where he's pawed through the snow to get to the grass buried beneath it. He's a smart devil. He remembers it growin' there last summer."

Jeb prepared to finish chopping down the tree. Then he paused when from over the rise there drifted a mingling of outraged screams, long yowls, and painful yelps.

"Let's get a move on, Stormie." Jeb brought the ax down with a hard whack. "Once that hellion drives the wolves away he might come back lookin' for us."

Darkness was at hand, and a lamp glimmered cheerily in the kitchen window when Storm and Jeb rode into the barnyard.

"Go on up to the house and get warm, Stormie," Jeb said as they dismounted. "I'll drag the tree into the barn to thaw out until we set it up on Saturday."

So, Storm thought, grinning to herself, hurrying up the cleared path to the back door, now he's decided when the tree will go up.

A cold blast of air followed her into the kitchen, and Maria yelled, "Shut the door. My bread will fall."

"Sorry." Storm's gaze went to the worktable, where three cloth-covered mounds sat in a row. She knew from the delicious aroma drifting through the kitchen that there were others baking in the oven.

Her mouth watered as she stripped off her wet gloves and placed them near the fire to dry. As she removed the shawl from her head and shrugged out of her jacket, she watched Maria turning three steaks in a large skillet.

"Storm," that busy person said, almost peevishly, "will you take those wet woolens out of my kitchen? They're smelling it up."

"Are you out of sorts, Maria?" Storm moved to stand beside the frowning housekeeper.

"No, Storm." Maria shook her head. "Just busy. That brother of yours tasted his chili, then sweetly announced that he had decided he would have a steak with us. I wish you'd have been here to lay the law down to him.

297

He always gets around me, and that makes me mad as all get out."

Storm patted Maria's shoulder. "You've always spoiled him. I guess it's too late to stop now."

The steaks had been eaten and the coffee poured when Jeb opened the door and stepped inside the kitchen. Before Maria could order him to do it he jerked off his boots and sat down at the table. He looked longingly at the steaming cups of coffee, and with a grin Storm rose and poured him a cup.

"Did Stormie tell you we had a brush with that wild stallion when we was gettin' the tree today?" Jeb asked, helping himself to sugar.

Kane looked at Storm, then glowered at the old man. "Why in the hell did you go into his territory?" he demanded.

"Don't go blaming Jeb," Storm snapped indignantly. "We weren't more than three miles from the house, well away from where he usually ranges."

"Kane, when are you going to do something about that animal?" Maria frowned her question. "Are you going to wait until he's killed someone? He's going to be coming closer and closer to the house as winter continues and his mares get hungry. I wouldn't put it past him to batter down the door to the grain shed."

"I know." Kane ran agitated fingers through his hair. "But I look at him and he's so fierce and proud, I can't give the order to have a bullet fired into that fine head." He looked over at Jeb. "How serious was this thing today?" he asked. "Did the stallion charge you?"

"I think the only reason he didn't was because he was distracted by a pack of wolves worrying his mares." Storm shivered, remembering the threatening stance of the handsome white horse. "Jeb's ax wouldn't have been much protection, I'm afraid."

"Where in the hell was your rifle?" Kane shot the question at the old man.

"On his mount," Storm barked back, her tone saying that she wouldn't have Jeb found fault with. "That devil was the last thing we expected to find so close to home."

"That's right, by doggie." Jeb sent Storm a look of thanks. "We never expected to see *him*."

"Well," Kane said, shoving away from the table, "tell the men that from now on whenever they ride out they're to make sure they have their rifles with them."

"I take it the white is reprieved, then," Storm said.

"I want to study on it a little longer," Kane answered. Picking up his crutches, he swung out of the kitchen.

"I hope he doesn't study too long." Maria slammed a pot onto the stove, then groaned when a loaf of rising bread lost its plumpness and slowly flattened out into a shapeless mass.

Storm and Jeb scrambled from the table and hurried after Kane, a string of Spanish epithets following them. Then, just before they stepped into the other room, Jeb stopped Storm with his hand on her arm. She looked at him questioningly. Refusing to look her in the eye, he whispered, "I've been thinkin', Stormie, why don't you and Maria go over to Becky's for a visit tomorrow afternoon? Kinda let Kane have the house to himself for a couple of hours?"

"But . . ."

"So he can relax, and such."

"He's relaxed around me and Maria." Storm frowned at the old man.

An angry, determined light grew in Jeb's eyes. "Dad-burn it, Stormie, can't you do anything without arguin' about it first?"

It finally dawned on Storm what Jeb was asking of her: get herself and Maria out of the house for a while so that Kane could have a woman come to the house . . . to his bed.

For a moment she was staggered. She had always known, of course, that her brother wasn't a monk, that there had been many women in his life. But her brain had always balked at imagining him in bed with one, arms and legs entangled, making love.

Jeb hurriedly shifted his eyes away from her when she blazed beet red. "I can't ask Maria to go with me to Becky's," she said after a moment. "She doesn't know . . ."

"That you ride over to see Becky at least three times a week? Was that what you was gonna say?" Jeb broke in.

"Well, yes . . ."

"Sometimes you're downright dumb, Stormie. Me and her and Kane has knowed all the time that you picked right up with your old friend."

"But why didn't you say something? Forbid me to see her?"

"I guess we figured it was no use. And when you didn't go sashayin' all over town with Becky we figured there was no harm done."

When Storm returned to the kitchen and nervously asked Maria if she would like to accompany her on a visit to Becky's the next day, the woman agreed right away, adding, "I haven't been over to see the girl since it snowed."

Chapter Nineteen

Storm felt a headache coming on as she leaned against a glass-topped counter displaying gaudy glass beads, pins, and earbobs. She frowned at Jeb, who was closely studying every piece on the bed of dusty sateen. Her feet hurt from following the grizzle-haired man around for half the day while he did his Christmas shopping.

She shifted her wool-lined jacket from one arm to the other and parted the scarf that clung damply to her throat.

"Jeb," she groused, "aren't you about finished? I'm hungry, my throat is dry, and I'm dead tired."

"Dammit, Stormie, stop your whinin'." A brown, wizened face glared at her. "If you'd help me pick out Maria's trinket here, I'd be all through with my shoppin'."

Storm

Storm sighed and moved down the counter to stand beside him. She had forgotten that before she went to Cheyenne to teach school, it was she who had always accompanied Jeb on his shopping jaunts, and that the final selections had always been left up to her, except for her own gift, which was chosen by Jeb himself.

Who had gone through this misery while she was away? she wondered, running her gaze over the baubles Jeb was giving such close attention to. Certainly not Kane. Her brother did well to do his own gift-buying. She decided that most likely Maria had been stuck with the chore.

And had Jeb, as usual, bought Kane a silver buckle and Maria a "trinket"? Her lips curved softly as she thought of the dresser drawer in her room crammed with the scarfs she had always found under the tree every Christmas morning.

"Maria would like those hoop earbobs," she suggested, pointing at the gold-plated circles. She repressed an amused smile at how rapidly the old cowhand made up his mind. He must be as tired as she was.

With the small package in her handbag and the rest of Jeb's purchases already strapped on his horse, they left Hagger's Emporium and joined the throng on the sidewalk.

"Whew! I'm glad that's over." Jeb pushed along with everyone else, giving jab for jab with his bony elbow. "Now we'll go to Buck's and have a corn beef and a glass of beer."

"I wouldn't set foot in that smelly place." Storm rejected Jeb's pronouncement with a stubborn jut to her jaw. "We'll go to the Cattlemens and have a steak."

"Stormie." Jeb balked in the middle of the sidewalk, unmindful of the frowning people who were forced to walk around them. "I can't go in there. I ain't never been in a high-falutin' place like that."

"Then it's high time you try it." Storm gripped his thin arm and marched him down the wooden walk. When they stood in front of the heavy, dark wood door Jeb pulled back, an almost wild look in his faded eyes.

"Stormie, you forgot somethin'. I ain't got no teeth. I can't chew steak."

"I've seen you gum through a steak in five minutes. Now come on, you old fraud, you're going to like it in here."

"Damn you, Stormie." Jeb's arthritic hand tried to pry the young fingers off his arm. "I'm gonna tell Kane how you've been talkin' to me today."

"Go ahead." Storm scowled down at her old friend. "If he yells at me, I'll just go out and shoot his wild stallion."

Biting her lips not to laugh, Storm wondered how much wider Jeb's eyes would become. He opened his mouth, and while she waited to hear what he would have to say about her threat, two neighboring ranchers came up behind them. With loud greetings and back slapping, she and Jeb were swept into the private club.

"How are we supposed to see what we're eatin' in this dark?" Jeb grumbled, fumbling along behind Storm and stepping on her heels, while the hard brim of his hat, clutched in his hand, jabbed her in the back. "It beats me why some people like to sit in the dark when they eat. I like to know what I put in my mouth."

"I'm going to put my fist in it if you don't shut up," Storm hissed as he pushed her into the waiter, who was leading them to a table in the center of the dining room. "Just relax; you'll be able to see in a minute."

Storm took the chair pulled out for her and Jeb sat down opposite her. When menus were handed to them Storm peeked over the top of hers and felt a pang of guilt when she saw Jeb holding his upside down. She had forgotten that the old fellow didn't know how to read. She shouldn't have forced him to come in here; he looked so uncomfortable.

But I couldn't have gone with him to Buck's, she defended herself. It might have surprised Jeb, but the saloon at the end of town was a favorite place of whores.

And speaking of such, Storm thought, seeing Josie Sales enter the room, here comes Wade's favorite one.

Her eyes narrowed as the woman spotted them and started winding her way among the tables toward their table. Without asking permission, she pulled out a chair and plopped down in it. "Well, Princess," she sneered, "what brings you to town?"

"Not to see you, that's for sure," Storm answered pointedly.

Jeb snickered, and Josie shot him a dirty look before saying to Storm, "So, how's your love life, Princess?"

"Why are you so interested in my love life?" Storm asked, inwardly shrinking from the naked hatred that sparked in the green eyes studying her.

When with a scraping of her chair Josie moved closer to her, Storm caught the scent of whiskey. She had been drinking. Storm knew trouble was coming when Josie grabbed at her wrist, missed, and knocked over a glass of water instead.

"You little bitch," Josie slurred through thin lips, "you've managed somehow to wheedle Wade away from me. But don't feel too secure about keeping him."

Her eyes skimmed scornfully over the younger woman's tender curves. "He likes to love his women hard. He'll soon grow tired of acting the gentleman in your bed and come back to me."

So, Josie, Storm thought, you haven't learned about the woman in Cheyenne. She lifted her gaze to the thin, irate features and drawled, "I can't believe that Wade ever made hard love to you, Josie. He'd have been sliced to ribbons if he got too close to those bony hips of yours."

Jeb's shrill cackle rang out and Josie turned on him, her eyes glaring furiously at the laughing, toothless mouth. "Shut up, you useless old bag of bones!" she cried.

"Don't you talk to him like that, you old whore!" Storm jerked to the edge of her seat, a hand clenched on either side of the menu, lying forgotten on the table.

"I'll speak any way I like, Magallen's *new* whore." And before the open-mouthed stares of the diners about them, Josie's palm slapped smartly across Storm's cheek.

Storm blinked her surprise for a split second; then, without conscious thought, she shot out her fist, catching Josie's nose straight on. Josie's chair went over backward, taking her with it. And while she lay tangled in chair legs and the tablecloth she had pulled down with her, Storm jerked the staring Jeb off his seat.

"Come on," she gritted, "let's go to Buck's. They let anything in here these days."

Admiring looks and laughing comments followed Storm as she marched past the bar, Jeb almost running to keep up with her long-legged stride.

Unable to restrain his relief at leaving the fancy place, he rattled on in his cracked voice. "I told you, Stormie, I told you right off that we should go to Buck's. They're friendly there. Won't nobody bother you. Buck will whack them 'cross the head, does anybody bother you."

An hour later, sitting on a stool at Buck's saloon, Storm was blinking at the double rows of bottles displayed behind the burly owner of the establishment.

She weaved a bit on her seat. For a woman who seldom had more than a glass of wine during an evening, she had rashly drunk three whiskies in the last 60 minutes. They had hit her empty stomach and gone straight to her head.

"Ready for another drink, Stormie?" the question came from a pair of garish red lips.

"Sure thing, Meg." Storm's nose twitched at the cheap perfume reeking from the whore's satin blouse, undone to the third button.

"Havin' a good time, Stormie girl?" Jeb slurred from his stool next to Storm, having trouble with his speech as well as his vision.

"Sure am, Jeb."

"I told you that you would, didn't I?" He turned slowly and carefully to the bartender. "Another beer and a couple of whiskies over here, Buck," he called.

Buck came and leaned on the bar in front of them. "Jeb, Stormie," he said, "I been wonderin' if you two will be able to ride home tonight."

"Tonight?" Storm blinked at the big man. "We're not riding anywhere tonight."

"Well, you're going home, aren't you?"

"Of course, silly Buck." Storm grinned lopsidedly. "As much as we like your place, me and old Jeb here can't stay until dark. Brother Kane would have our hides, huh, Jeb?" She swatted her companion on the back, and he clutched the bar not to slide off his seat.

Buck looked up at the fly-speckled clock over the bar, then back at the unlikely couple. "Maybe you two haven't noticed, but it's night now. Nine o'clock, in fact."

"Ah, go on." Storm slapped playfully at the beefy arms folded on the bar. Then, peering through the dirt-streaked window, she exclaimed, "I'll be dammed, Buck, you're right."

She giggled and leaned a shoulder against Jeb's skinny one. "Do you think we can outrun ol' Kane?"

Jeb leaned back and stared at her like an owl. "Hell, Stormie, I don't think I can walk, let alone run. But while he's poundin' on me, you can scoot upstairs and lock your door."

Meg, Storm's new friend, slung an arm around her shoulders. "You're dreamin', Jeb." She laughed. "Right now Stormie couldn't crawl up a flight of stairs."

Storm reared back. "You wanna make a bet on how firm I am on my feet?" she demanded, sliding off her stool.

While Buck spoke to one of his customers at the end of the bar, another customer took a knife from his pocket and, with the point of the sharp blade, scratched a line down the middle of the floor. Twenty minutes later, when Wade strode into the saloon, six patrons, led by Storm, were still trying to prove their sobriety by walking the drawn line.

Storm didn't see the stony-faced man until he brushed past her and lifted Jeb onto his back. She narrowed her eyes and reached a tentative hand to Jeb's limp body, slung across a wide shoulder. Then, even in her fuzzy state, she knew the man before he growled from the corner of his mouth, "Get your coat and reticule and be ready to leave when I come back."

"Like hell, Almighty Magallen!" she shouted. But the back supporting Jeb's gray, wagging head had disappeared through the door and into the night.

Meg grabbed Storm's jacket off the wall, knocking down three other shapeless, dirt-stained ones in her haste. "Come on, Stormie, be a good girl now," she coaxed, forcing squirming hands through the sleeves. "Magallen is really mad. He'll peel your hide if you're not ready when he comes back."

The young whore scooped up bills and coins off the bar and crammed it all into Storm's bag. "Now," she said, "hold still while I button you up."

The friendly Meg was just closing the last button when Wade stalked back into the bar. He closed the door and stood a moment, gazing at the slender figure that stood unsteadily in the unevenly fastened jacket and stared belligerently at him. Everyone stepped, or staggered, aside, making a path for him as he bore down on the woman whose stance dared him to touch her.

Only the bartender saw the flicker of amusement that twitched his chiseled lips.

"Say goodbye to your friends, Storm," Wade said, his voice soft and persuasive. "It's time to go home."

"I wouldn't go across the street with you, you alley-prowling tomcat," Storm yelled, and swung her bag at him.

Wade easily ducked under the wild swing. Grabbing Storm around the knees, he scooped her up and put her over his shoulder in the same manner in which he had handled Jeb. Delivering a smart smack to her derriere, clearly outlined in her riding skirt, he nodded at the bartender on his way out. "Thanks, Buck."

The cold air hit Storm, and her flaying fists were stilled almost immediately. Wade slid her off his shoulder and onto the seat of the carriage he had hired at the livery when the man Buck had sent told him Storm and Jeb were at his place. Her brain had given in to the whiskey; she was as out of it as old Jeb, snoring away in the back.

Wade snorted when he climbed in beside her and picked up the reins. "I wonder if I dare light a cigarette in here. The fumes are apt to blow us up."

He turned his lean body and looked moodily at the blonde head tucked down away from him. He cupped the firm little chin and tenderly turned her so that she rested more comfortably against the cushioned seat. He brushed the tumbled hair from her face, freeing a few strands that were caught between her slightly parted lips.

"Oh, baby." He sighed raggedly. "What have I done to you? Pray God you're strong enough to accept what comes later." With hopeless despair in his eyes, he drew Storm across the seat until her head rested on his shoulder. With the reins in one hand and his arm firmly around the slender body, he drove out of town and on toward the ranch.

Chapter Twenty

The rented carriage had carried Wade and his two sleeping companions a couple of miles from Laramie when he saw a group of riders coming toward them.

"Damn," he grunted, knowing immediately who they were; cowhands from the Roemer ranch, out looking for Storm and Jeb. He had hoped to get the pair home unnoticed, but all along common sense had told him that Kane would be out of his mind with worry and would have the men out looking for his sister and the old man.

He pulled the horse in when the riders swept up to them. "You men are pushin' them mounts awfully hard, aren't you?" He grinned, speaking casually. "Big Lil's girls aren't goin' anywhere. They'll be right there where you left them the last time."

313

"We ain't lookin' for Big Lil's girls tonight," one of the men said, his eyes falling on Storm, leaning into Wade, and old Jeb, snoring in the back. "We're out lookin' for them. The boss is half out of his mind with worry."

"I'm sorry to hear that." Wade put regret in his voice. "I had a little Christmas party for a few friends in that big room in back of Pa's saloon. I guess time got away from us."

He looked over his shoulder at Jeb. "As you can see, the old fellow celebrated a little too much. There was nothing I could do but put their mounts up at the livery and hire this carriage to get him home."

The cowboys looked at each other, then grinned, as though reaching a decision together. "Since we're only a couple of miles from town," one of the men said, looking at Wade, "we might as well ride on in and say howdy to Big Lil."

Wade nodded with a grin and whipped up the horse, hoping the men hadn't noticed that Storm was as drunk as Jeb.

As he drove into the barnyard an hour later he could see the dark figure of Maria at the kitchen window, her hands cupped around her face, peering into the darkness. He halloed for the cook as he tried to get Storm to sit up straight. But when Hank Cleaver stepped from the cookshack her head was still on his shoulder.

"Take the old man into the bunkhouse and put him to bed, will you, Hank? He got carried away with the holiday spirit, I'm afraid," Wade managed to joke.

Again Jeb was thrown across a shoulder, but this time he was grumbling as he was carried into the bunkhouse. With a sigh, Wade snapped the reins on the horse's rump, and the carriage rolled toward the house.

Maria flung open the door as Wade stepped up on the porch. "Oh, my God, what has happened to her?" she exclaimed, stepping aside so that he could enter the kitchen with his burden. Kane was just coming into the kitchen, his crutches coming down hard on the floor as he swung along, asking the same question.

This time Wade didn't try to hide the truth. With the whiskey fumes coming off Storm, it would be futile even to try. At any rate, Kane had the right to know that his sister had spent several hours in the roughest saloon in Laramie.

"I don't know why," he answered, "but she and Jeb went to Buck's and tied one on."

"Buck's place?" Maria cried in disbelief.

"You mean she's drunk?" Kane leaned over and sniffed Storm's breath, then grimaced.

"She's gettin' heavy." Wade shifted the slender body in his arms. "Shall I take her upstairs to her room?"

"Yes, bring her along," Maria said, leading the way up the stairs.

When Wade leaned over the bed to put Storm down her arms clung around his neck. "Don't leave me, Wade," she begged softly. "We'll make . . ."

Wade gently laid his fingers over her lips, cutting off the rest of her words. When her arms fell to her sides he straightened up, saying, "She's gonna be sicker than a dog tomorrow."

An irate Kane waited in the kitchen. To Wade's surprise, most of his friend's anger was directed at him. "What have you done to her now? What made her drink herself senseless?"

"Hell, man, I didn't do anything to her," Wade shouted back. "I didn't even know she was in town until Buck sent a man to Pa's to fetch me."

Kane's shoulders slumped as he sat down at the table. "I'm sorry, Wade. A man can't help who he loves." He looked up at Wade. "Thanks for bringin' her home."

There was so much Wade wanted to say, to explain; that he loved Storm with every beat of his heart, but that it was impossible for him to marry her. "I'm sorry, Kane," he said quietly, and left his friend staring down at his clasped hands.

A way off in the distance a wolf was howling as Wade pulled up behind his barn. He hopped to the ground, unhitched the horse, and turned it into the small building. Closing the door and dropping the heavy bar in place, he limped to the cabin.

Tonight Wade had reached the very depths

of despair. Kane had been right, accusing him of causing Storm's drinking. He had led her on, made love to her, and then cruelly ignored her. Self-hate gripped him. How would she take the next blow he was to deliver to her?

Wade stepped quietly into the cabin, not wanting to wake his father, and went straight to his bedroom. There, he bent over and eased open the bottom drawer of his dresser. Reaching into a corner, his fingers felt for a folded blue silk scarf that Storm had worn as a girl. From beneath it he brought out a letter: the letter he had received a little over four years ago.

He returned to the big room, turned up the lamp, and sat down to read again the letter that had turned his life upside down.

His fingers shook slightly as Wade withdrew the two sheets of paper and began to read the letter from a brother he hadn't seen since their mother left with him nineteen years before.

Dear Wade,

No doubt you will be stunned hearing from me after all these years. But two things have happened recently that I think you should know about.

Our mother passed away a month ago. It was a heart attack. The last words she spoke were, "My poor little Wade." I think you should know that she loved you dearly, and that a day never passed that she didn't mention you.

I'm afraid that my second reason for writing you will be equally distressing. However, it is very important that you know about it.

About a year ago I learned that I am ill. Chronic progressive hereditary chorea, the doctors call it. If you aren't already aware of this disease, it strikes a man in his late twenties or early thirties. The affliction, according to my doctor, combines progressive unsoundness of mind with bizarre involuntary movements and odd postures.

I have reached the stage where each month I lose more and more control over my limbs. Dementia will soon follow, and that is why I'm writing to you now, while I can still think clearly.

Although the condition is hereditary, cases do occur where a generation escapes this affliction. It would appear that Pa is one of the lucky ones. I am only thankful that I don't have a son to pass it on to.

I would like to see you, Wade, after all these years, and have you meet my wife and daughter. Amy is ten years old and looks like you and our mother. Her eyes and expression are exactly like yours and Ma's.

Do what you think best about telling Pa. I have missed him all these years, his kind and caring ways. On second thought, perhaps you shouldn't tell him. He would only feel a terrible guilt.

Waiting to see you, your brother, Ben.

Wade gazed unseeingly into the fire, grieving, as he had so many times, for the mother he had adored, still at a loss as to why she had left him behind. Yet again he asked himself why she had taken only her elder son with her—the brother he had both loved and scorned.

Wade had always ridiculed Ben's sissified ways, always hanging around the cabin, his nose usually stuck in a book. Nevertheless, he had always fought the weaker boy's battles for him, even though Wade was three years younger.

Wade's slim fingers closed into fists. A few years from now his strength would be no greater than Ben's. His throbbing thigh was just the first sign of the deterioration to come.

A ragged sigh escaped Wade. He wondered how his brother was tonight. Ben no longer recognized him when he visited the hospital in Cheyenne. The disease had progressed exactly as he had explained four years before. First Ben had lost control of his muscles; then his mind had begun to slip.

Wade's mind went back to the evening four years ago when he had received the letter. He had taken a coach to Cheyenne the following day, then boarded the Union Pacific for Chicago, and the hospital where Ben had been a patient for three months.

It had been a joyous reunion despite the bitter reality that had brought them together. Ben's illness wasn't visible yet; pain hadn't yet etched deep lines on his face. He had looked quite healthy.

As youngsters growing up, he and Ben had

never looked alike. He had taken after Ma, while Ben looked like neither of his parents.

Wade's face softened. Ben's daughter, ten years old then, resembled him closely. His sister-in-law, Jane, had remarked on it when they met. "A person can see right away that the three of you are related," she'd said.

Jane was one of the nicest women Wade had ever met. There was a sweetness, a gentleness about her when she sat beside Ben, either holding his hand or stroking his forehead. She was attractive in a quiet way, her blue eyes wide and her blonde hair pulled back in a soft chignon at her nape. She wasn't the kind of woman Wade was drawn to, but she was the perfect mate for Ben, who was quiet and reserved.

Ben had worked in a bank since he was nineteen, Wade learned. He'd never made a great deal of money, but he and his little family had been happy in their four-room apartment, upstairs over a grocery store. Their mother had lived with Ben and Jane, working in the grocery store.

Sharp resentment had shot through Wade on hearing this. Why had he been denied the chance to live with her all those years?

Ben must have seen the pain in his eyes, for he had changed the subject at once.

They had visited for a couple of hours, catching up on each other's lives. Wade had told Ben about his leg. His brother had looked sad but unsurprised. He said quietly that his pain had started in his arm.

Wade left then, promising to return in the evening. On his way out of the hospital he had stopped a nurse and asked if he could speak with Ben Magallen's doctor. The young woman gave him a wide smile, then led him to the doctor's office.

He and the gray-haired, tired-looking man of middle age had discussed Ben's illness, but Wade had learned no more than what Ben's letter had already told him. Before he left he asked if it would be all right to move his brother to Cheyenne.

"I see no reason why not," he was told, "as long as there's a doctor there to attend Mr. Magallen."

So the move had been made. Wade had rented a small house for Ben and his family within walking distance to St. John's Hospital.

A year and a half later Ben had been moved to the hospital itself.

Pain flickered in Wade's eyes as he remembered the day he had taken Ben to St. John's. Little Amy, her gray eyes swollen with tears, had clung to her father's wasted body, squeezing him fiercely as she told him good-bye.

It was that same day, after Ben had been settled and Jane had gone home, that his brother had asked him to look after his family when he was gone.

"They have no one else, Wade," he had said, his eyes pleading. It went without saying that he would look after Jane and Amy.

Poor Ben, Wade thought now; even then clear

321

thinking was beginning to leave him. He hadn't remembered that the day would come when Wade, too, would be incapacitated by the same disease that was daily eating away at him.

Wade stood up, took a bottle of whiskey and a glass from the mantel, and went back to his chair. Any day now Ben would pass away. And as painful as it would be, it would be a blessed relief for him *and* for Jane. For, in a real sense, Ben had left them over a year ago. Only the shell of the once intelligent man now remained.

Chapter Twenty-one

If only my head would stop pounding, Storm wailed silently as she pulled a brush through her hair. How much had she drunk last night, for heaven's sake? More than enough, for she couldn't even remember coming home. She vaguely recalled Wade carrying her into the house.

Certainly Maria and Kane remembered her arrival; she had heard all about it when she came down to breakfast. The pair had ranted and raved at her, taking turns telling her how she had disgraced the Roemer name; drinking and chumming with a whore; brawling with Josie Sales in the Cattlemens. Kane had declared that he'd never be able to show his face in there again.

Finally the pair had run out of breath, but

before she could ask where they had gotten all their information Kane had swung out of the room and Maria had stamped off to make up the beds.

What was Wade thinking about her today? she wondered; then a self-derisive smile stirred her lips. He probably wasn't thinking anything about her one way or the other.

Her head still feeling as if drums were beating inside it, Storm went quietly down the stairs, carrying her jacket. As she stood in the kitchen, she could hear Maria moving about in her room—Kane's for the time being. She glanced into the big room and could see Kane's long legs stretched out to the fire.

Her hand was on the doorknob, ready to step outside, when he called to her. "Where are you goin'?"

"Down to the bunkhouse to see how Jeb feels."

"He's all right. Maria checked on him earlier this mornin'. She got the whole story of your little escapade. Please come in here. I want to talk to you."

"Kane, I don't feel like having you yell at me anymore."

"I'm not gonna yell. I just want to talk to you."

Storm sighed and walked into the other room. She took a chair across from Kane.

Slouched in his own chair, Kane studied his sister, concern in his eyes. Where had the bright, laughing girl gone, the one who

324

always had such enthusiasm? She's lost weight, he thought, worried. Her face was almost gaunt, and she had purple shadows under her eyes.

When Storm looked up at him, waiting, he said, "Do you want to tell me about it, Sis? I'm a good listener, remember?"

"You mean about last night? I thought Jeb told Maria all about it."

"You know that's not what I'm talkin' about. I'm askin' you about Wade. You still love him, don't you?"

Storm opened her mouth to vehemently deny that she could love a man who treated her so cruelly. But the words never came. Instead, she burst into tears.

Kane swore and held out his arms. "Come here, honey," he invited softly, and Storm threw herself onto his lap. With her face buried in his shoulder, Kane stroked her blonde head as deep sobs racked her slender body, wishing he could do his friend bodily harm.

When Storm quietened, with only an occasional hiccup escaping her lips, Kane said gently but decisively, "You must forget Wade, Sis. It appears he's not for you. You're a sensible, clearheaded young woman, and it's not like you to beat a dead horse."

He tipped up her wet face and, gazing into her sad eyes, said, "So he doesn't love you the way you want him to; it's not the end of the world."

Storm sat up and wiped her eyes on the tail

of Kane's flannel shirt. "It looks that way to me," she said on a sigh.

Kane hugged her close. "In time you'll know it's not, honey. You're so young; there's plenty of time for that right man to come along."

Storm slid off his knee. "We'll see," she said. "I think I'll saddle Beauty and take a ride. Maybe that will clear my head."

Kane nodded. "You do that."

The clouds in the north were increasing in size and becoming darker in color as Storm guided Beauty down the frozen, rutted river road. "It's going to snow again, and before nightfall," she thought out loud as she turned the mount onto Becky's gravel drive.

She swung out of the saddle and flipped the reins over the hitching post. As she started toward the house she was nearly knocked down by four youngsters, who burst around the corner of the house, chasing Becky's pet gander. She watched the children and the animal disappear around the house, then shifted her amused gaze to the porch, where Becky stood, a mixture of anger and helplessness on her face.

When a man and a woman came from inside the house and stood beside her, Becky waved and called, "Go on in, Storm. I'll be with you in a minute."

Storm's heart sank. The couple must be interested in buying Becky's house. In the kitchen she shrugged off her jacket, poured a cup of coffee, and sat down at the table.

Storm

Everything was happening so fast, Storm thought as she stared into her coffee. Her whole world seemed to be crumbling. She had finally accepted that she would never have Wade, and she would soon be losing Becky.

"But I mustn't be selfish," she told herself just before Becky burst into the kitchen, her dark eyes sparkling. When she cried out that the couple wanted her house Storm kept her despondency hidden.

Becky picked up the coffeepot on her way to sit down. "The deal should be closed in around three weeks, which will give me and Rafe time to settle things for leaving for Oregon."

"Becky, I'm so happy for you," Storm said sincerely. "I'm going to miss you something awful, though."

"I'm going to miss you too." Becky's face grew sober. "We waited so long to get together again; then, like a puff of wind, I'm off again."

"But under entirely different circumstances this time." Storm squeezed the small hand lying on the table.

"Yes, thank God," Becky said soberly; then, on a happier note, she added, "Rafe and I are catching the coach to Cheyenne tomorrow. We'll be staying overnight. Would you mind riding out and feeding my gander and Trey?"

"Sure. Why are you going to Cheyenne? Are you going there to celebrate the coming nuptials?" Storm teased.

"Oh, we celebrate that every night." Becky grinned.

"I figured as much." Storm laughed. "Rafe looks worn out these days, and it's not from working with the shorthorns."

Becky grinned, then said, "We're going to do some Christmas shopping. I want to get something real nice for his sister and her family."

"I'll be going into Cheyenne, too, in the near future," Storm said.

"To shop?"

"No; to see about getting my old teaching job back."

The look that came over Becky's face clearly said she disapproved of Storm's decision. Then, after a moment, she said quietly, "Maybe that's a good idea. I don't like to think that you might continue pulling stunts like you did last night."

Storm looked at Becky, her eyes wide in surprise. "You know about that already?"

Becky nodded. "Timmy told me and Rafe this morning. Seems his father was in Buck's last night."

Storm's headache returned. "I guess everybody in the county knows about it," she said weakly.

"I wouldn't worry about it, Storm. Your friends will think it's funny, and who cares what anyone else thinks?"

"Did Timmy's father know about my brawl with Josie?"

"Yep." Becky's grin widened. "You really gave her what for, didn't you? I hear she has two black eyes."

"Oh, my God; if Kane hears about that, he'll lock me in my room for a month. And no telling what he'll do to poor ol' Jeb."

"I wonder what Wade thinks about it all."

"I don't know, and I don't care."

Wade wasn't thinking of Storm at all at the moment. He was in Cheyenne, standing in front of St. John's Hospital, situated between Twenty-third and Twenty-fourth, Evans and House. He gazed up at the dim light shining in a top window.

A long sigh shuddered through him. He felt certain he wouldn't be passing through the big double doors too many more times.

Would he find his brother the same as he had last week? Certainly Ben wouldn't be any better. With a ragged sigh, Wade mounted the steps and pushed open the door. A nurse looked up from her desk in the small waiting room and gave him a warm smile. She and Wade had become well-acquainted during the many times he had visited Ben.

After greeting her he asked, "Do you have Ben's bill ready, Martha?"

The nurse nodded and, opening a drawer in her desk, brought out a sheet of paper.

Wade glanced over the itemized bill and noticed a new medication had been added to the list. "How is my brother doing? Is he showing any improvement?" he asked hopefully.

"He's about the same," Martha answered gently. "Maybe a little worse. His wife and daughter are with him now."

He laid the money on the desk, then walked down a narrow hall and entered his brother's room.

Wade received a tired smile from Jane, but an exuberant one from his niece. The now fourteen-year-old came to meet him, squeezing him tightly around the waist. "It's so good to see you, Uncle Wade. It seems like ages since you were here last week."

"I know, honey." Wade hugged her back. "But I can't come more often."

"I understand." Amy released him and stepped back. "Ma explained about keeping Dad's illness from Grandpa Jake."

Wade stroked a hand over the shiny hair that so resembled his own, then walked over to the bed and looked down at his brother. The pale, twisted body lay so still, the eyes closed in the pain-wracked face.

"He's sleeping," Jane said, adding, "The doctor just gave him some laudanum."

Wade sat down in the chair his niece had just vacated and took the sleeping man's thin hand in his own. A gnawing pain began in his leg, and in his mind Wade saw himself lying in Ben's place in the near future.

After about ten minutes Jane touched Wade's shoulder and said quietly, "Let's go to the house and I'll make us some supper."

While Jane bustled around in the kitchen, putting their meal together, Amy entertained

Wade with stories of her school, telling him of a Thanksgiving play she had been in and how she dearly loved her teacher.

Jane interrupted her after a while to announce that supper was ready.

As they ate the pork chops, mashed potatoes, and canned tomatoes, Jane put up a cheery front. But Wade saw the misery and suffering in her face and eyes and was more sure than ever that he had made the right decision about Storm. He had hurt her, he knew, but she would hurt worse if she had to go through what Jane was experiencing now.

When the meal was over Amy went into the bedroom and Wade dried the dishes for Jane. When the kitchen had been tidied up Jane took off her apron and led the way into the sparsely furnished parlor. While Wade settled himself on the worn sofa Jane brought out a glass and a bottle of whiskey she kept purposely for him. Placing it on a table beside him, she sat down in an equally worn chair. Wade helped himself to the bottle, filling the glass. "Time is runnin' out for Ben, isn't it?" he said quietly.

"The doctor says around Christmas," Jane answered bleakly.

"Do you have any plans for . . . later?"

Jane shrugged wearily. "Go back to Chicago, I guess. Get a job, pull my life back together."

Wade set the glass down and, clearing his voice nervously, said, "You have another alternative." At Jane's questioning look he drew a deep breath and said, "You could marry me."

When Jane made a protesting sound he held up his hand. "Let me finish. It wouldn't be a real marriage, only one that would provide for you and Amy while I'm alive. And Amy would be my heir." After a short pause he added, "I don't want Ben's daughter ever to want for anything."

"Oh, Wade." A tear slipped down Jane's cheek. "What a wonderful brother you have been to Ben. It's tragic that the two of you were separated all those years."

"Did Ma ever mention to you why she left Pa?"

"Not exactly, but I put together from remarks she made that it was too lonesome for her in your place on the river, having no nearby neighbors. She had always lived in a big city with lots of friends. I guess she missed them and the bustling activity of people all around."

It grew quiet. Wade wished he could get up the courage to ask if his mother had ever said why he had been left behind. But he knew he wouldn't ask; the answer might twist him inside.

Dropping the subject of his mother's leaving, he said, "You haven't given me an answer about marryin' me."

Jane stood up and went to stare out the small window, looking in the direction of the hospital where her husband lay dying. Until Wade had brought it up she hadn't given any thought to what she would do once Ben was gone.

She wondered about it now. It didn't seem

right to accept Wade's generous offer, but would she be able to provide a home for Amy? She had never worked outside her home in her life.

When she returned to her chair a few minutes later Wade said, "If you're thinkin' that you'd be lonesome out on the river, it wouldn't be for too long a time. I'll be swappin' places with Ben in the not-too-distant future."

"Oh, Wade, don't say that." Tears came to Jane's eyes.

"I'm sorry. I didn't mean to make you cry." Wade came and hunkered down beside her.

"It's all right." Jane gave Wade a watery smile. "I get weepy very easily these days." She pulled a handkerchief from her sleeve and wiped her eyes. "Let me think about your offer tonight and I'll give you an answer tomorrow."

Wade left the small house shortly after that, to go to the Dyer Hotel. It had recently been built, and he was looking forward to a good long soak in a tub of hot water. The fancy hotel even had a newfangled water closet.

He was passing another hotel when familiar laughter made him pause. He turned his head and his body stiffened. Stepping out onto the boardwalk, arm in arm and smiling at each other, were Rafe and Becky. Rage engulfed him. He'd had that horse trainer pegged right from the start; he was a womanizer.

If he never did anything more in his lifetime, Wade told himself, he'd see to it that Storm didn't marry the bastard who was already cheating on her. If he had to, he'd challenge him and shoot him.

Becky saw Wade first and came to an abrupt halt, blushing guiltily at Wade's cold, level gaze. Rafe became aware of his presence when, his voice a cold, chilling sound, Wade said, "You little bitch, how could you do this to your best friend?"

Becky lifted her chin in defiance. "We are taking nothing away from Storm."

"That's right." Rafe stepped forward. "The thing is . . ."

Becky hurriedly interrupted Rafe, afraid he was about to say that the two of them were getting married. She didn't want that fact known yet. It would set too many tongues to wagging. Her voice was cold and accusing when she said, "You have a hell of a nerve finding fault with me and Rafe. What about the times you've played fast and loose with Storm? What about the woman we saw you with a few hours back? And the little girl who is the spitting image of you? How is Storm going to feel when she hears about those two?"

Cold dislike shone from her eyes when Becky said, "What Rafe and I are doing is only a fraction of what you've done to her." She gave Rafe's arm a tug. "Let's go. I'm sure we're keeping him from his lady friend."

Wade watched them walk away, arms linked, their footsteps snapping crisply on the frozen snow. Every word Becky had said was true. Time after time he had hurt Storm cruelly, and the worst hurt was still to come if Jane agreed to marry him.

The next afternoon, as Jane and Amy waited with Wade for the coach that would take him back to Laramie, Jane said in a quiet voice that her daughter couldn't hear, "I accept your offer of marriage, Wade, and I thank you very much."

Chapter Twenty-two

White mist curled ghostlike over the Platte as Storm guided Beauty down the river road. She shivered and pulled up the collar of her sheep-lined jacket to ward off the saturating dampness.

The setting sun dipped below the horizon and night was closing in. Storm lifted the reins slightly, urging the mare to walk a little faster, but not to break into a trot. Though she was quite late getting to Becky's and her pets, the road was much too rough to try for speed.

The dark bulk of the Magallen cabin appeared up ahead, a glimmering light shining from the kitchen window. Storm wondered if that room had reverted back to its original disorder: dirty dishes, pots and pans stacked in the dry sink, the stove and floor grease-splattered.

Storm

As Beauty clipped past the cabin and barn, a fast glance revealed Wade's stallion, saddled and hitched to the porch. Was he coming or going? she wondered, then answered her own question: she didn't care one way or the other. She had worked hard at keeping him out of her thoughts and was making a little headway in that attempt: He had only entered her mind twice today.

The long yowl of a wolf on the winter air made Storm sigh her relief when Becky's house came into view before her. She'd make sure she got out here before dark tomorrow. She was late today because she had gotten caught up in trimming the Christmas tree with Jeb. Thankfully, Becky would be home day after tomorrow; that gander of hers was a mean thing. Instead of eating the food she put out for him, he attacked her. She had three big bruises on her legs where he had nipped her.

Riding Beauty to the back of the house, Storm slipped from the saddle and looped the reins over the porch railing. She walked as quietly as she could to the shed and eased open the door. She reached inside and picked up the can of cracked corn, lifted off its lid, and hurriedly scattered some on the floor. Then she slammed the door closed just in time as the big white goose came honking toward her.

Storm's feet crunched through the snow as she walked up to Beauty and took a package of table scraps off the saddle. She pushed open the back door and made her way in the semidarkness to the lamp, sitting in the center of a table. Removing the chimney, she struck the match she had taken from her pocket and touched it to the wick. The kitchen was bathed in a warm light, spotlessly clean except for the two coffee cups turned upside down in the sink. Trey, her tail wagging a greeting, came from her nest of blankets behind the stove. Storm rubbed her head, scratched her ears, and talked to her for a moment before she emptied the chunks of meat into her bowl.

While the hound gulped down her supper, Storm checked through the rest of the house and found it in the same condition it had been when she had left it yesterday. She was coming from the bedroom, carrying the lamp, when she suddenly knew she wasn't alone in the house.

Storm broke out in gooseflesh, a shiver of fear running down her spine. As she stood paralyzed in her tracks, she could only think that no one knew she was here. While she was visualizing anything from a mountain lion to a saddle tramp, a familiar, gravelly voice spoke from the shadows.

"Did I frighten you, Storm?"

"You idiot!" Storm cried furiously, glaring into Wade's gray eyes. "You scared the life out of me. Why didn't you call out? What are you doing here anyway?"

"I saw you ride past the cabin and figured you were comin' here to feed Becky's animals. I thought I'd stop by and say hello."

Relieved of the fear and tension that had gripped her, Storm wanted to laugh, to swear. Instead, she burst into tears.

Uttering soothing sounds, Wade took the lamp from her, placed it on a table, and wrapped her in his arms. She sobbed and shivered, and Wade unbuttoned her jacket, and then his own. He pressed her against the warmth of his body, and without conscious thought Storm arched her slenderness into him.

A soft gasp escaped Wade; then his hands were stroking her back, her waist. When she pressed closer to him still his hands moved down to her hips. They stroked there a moment; then he was gripping them, holding them steady as he slowly and suggestively bucked himself against her. She picked up his rhythm, meeting each thrust of the hard manhood pressing against the material of his trousers.

When he raised a hand to gently lift her chin she closed her eyes, waiting for his kiss. His hot, passionate mouth came down and moved over hers, and thrill after thrill shook her body.

She tried to remind herself that she was finished with this man, that he would never use her again, but it was useless.

When Wade slid the jacket off her shoulders and laid her on Becky's couch, stopping him was the last thing on her mind. He sat down beside her and unbuttoned her shirt, and she sighed in anticipation as his trembling fingers freed her straining, aching breasts.

Bending his head and holding a heavy breast in each hand, his tongue licked each rosy-tipped nipple into a turgid point before pulling one into his mouth and sucking it.

Her pulse pounding, her body an agony of need, Storm reached out a hand and stroked his confined hardness. Without moving his mouth, Wade undid his trousers and pulled himself free. Her fingers closed around him and moved, the way he had taught her. He groaned his pleasure and her lips tilted in a smile as his breathing became short and harsh.

His hands were at the waistband of her riding skirt then, and she raised her hips so that he could remove the garment from her. Her drawers came next, and then he was crawling between her legs. There followed the brush of the woolen trousers, then the smooth slide of his thick, long hardness. For a moment they lay united, hipbone to hipbone, then he arched over her and, lifting her hips so that she could feel every inch of him, his body rose and fell, driving deep inside her.

Wade's thrusts were slow and regulated, dragging out the time of the eruption of their passion. He had never thought to have the chance to make love to Storm again, and he must make the most of it, no matter that he would hate himself later.

Finally his needs would be put off no longer. He raised up on his knees, lifting Storm's hips with him and, keeping his eyes on her face, pumped fast and hard inside her.

They called each other's name in unison as the floodgates opened, sweeping them into their own private world of released passion.

His head thrown back, Wade continued to hold their position, his masculinity jerking and throbbing while Storm flexed and unflexed around him.

He came down on Storm then, his head buried in her shoulder. As his breathing slowed and his heartbeat stopped racing, cold reality swept over him. He was a first-rate bastard who should be shot. How could he have made love to Storm again knowing that soon he would be marrying Jane? Although he wouldn't be sleeping with his wife, he meant to be true to her. She was too fine a woman to have people gossip about her randy husband.

Wade was of two minds, each warring with the other. He wished Storm would marry Rafe Jeffery, but he didn't know if he could bear it if she did.

With a long sigh he lifted Storm off himself. It was time to grit his teeth and hurt her again.

Standing up and buttoning his trousers, he said coolly, "You'd better be gettin' home. Kane will be worried about you. And as for that," he added, "Josie will have a strip off my hide for being so late."

He heard Storm's little gasp of pain but hardened his heart to it. He dared not do otherwise. "I'll wish you a merry Christmas now," he said, walking to the kitchen. "I'll be in Cheyenne then."

Storm didn't hear the back door click shut. She lay staring blindly at the ceiling, aware of nothing outside herself, only the fierce aching in her very soul.

Becky's clock struck eight and Storm's numb brain told her she must get home. She sat up, an emptiness in her eyes as she buttoned her shirt and slipped on her jacket. She left the house and walked to where Beauty was tied. She stood at the little mount's head, gazing out into the darkness. As soon as Becky returned, she was going to Cheyenne also. Not to celebrate, as Wade would most likely do, but to make arrangements to move back there permanently.

She swung into the saddle and tugged gently on the reins, and Beauty moved out. As the little mare picked her careful way down the road, Storm remembered old Jeb saying once that things were always easier to accept in the daytime. She doubted he was right. Ground-up pride would be just as hurtful tomorrow as it was right now.

To Storm's relief, when she walked into the Roemer kitchen half an hour later Maria accepted her explanation that she had been in the barn the last two hours, talking to Jeb and grooming her mare.

She forced herself to yawn, and Maria said, "Why don't you go on up to bed?"

"I think I will," Storm answered, wondering if she would ever sleep again.

But the trauma of the past hours had drained her of energy, left her exhausted. She had barely pulled the covers up around her shoulders when the blessed balm of sleep settled over her.

Chapter Twenty-three

A roaring fire in the big fireplace sent warmth through the living room as Wade stood at the window watching the steady fall of snow. It had started sometime during the night and now a new ten inches covered the ground.

His attention was caught by a rider going down the river road. A slight smile tugged at his lips. Young Timmy Hayes, astride his father's old plow horse, was dragging home a Christmas tree.

Wade's smile widened a bit. The kid was a tough little customer, but Becky's gander scared him witless; that was the reason Storm had to feed him and the hound while Becky was in Cheyenne . . . her and that bastard Jeffery.

How was Storm this morning? he wondered, remembering with a pang how hurt and disbelief had grown in her eyes when he had cruelly announced that he had to hurry to Josie.

"It's a damn sure thing I'll go to hell when I pass out of this world," he thought out loud.

He wiped away a patch of moisture his breath had left on the windowpane, watching his father come scuffing through the snow from the direction of the barn. What had he forgotten at the house before riding into Laramie and opening up the saloon?

Jake opened the door wide enough to stick his head in the room. "Man alive," he said through the scarf wrapped around his face. "A blue norther must have blown in."

He took a crumpled envelope from his jacket pocket and held it out to Wade. "Here," he said. "This came in on the coach yesterday afternoon and I forgot to give it to you." He grinned. "Looks like a woman's handwriting. You got a new filly in Cheyenne?"

"Maybe," he managed to say lightly. "How do you feel about havin' a daughter-in-law?"

"Well, all right, I guess." Jake's grin faded. He was hard put not to say that he had always hoped that someday Wade would marry Storm. "Is she a nice, respectable girl?"

"She's a woman, Pa, and very respectable. You'll like her."

"Good," Jake said, and quietly closed the door behind him.

Wade ripped open the envelope as soon as the door was closed. The letter inside was short, only a note.

Come at once. Ben is sinking fast.

Wade felt as though he was moving in slow motion as he packed a change of clothing in his saddlebag, all the time praying that he would get to the hospital in time. If only Pa had given him Jane's letter yesterday, he could have caught the afternoon coach. Now he would have to ride Renegade through deep snow that would increase the time it would take him to reach Cheyenne.

He took the time to write a note to Jake: *Pa, I have gone to Cheyenne. Don't know exactly when I'll return. Wade.*

Propping the note against the lamp where Jake was sure to find it, Wade pulled on his heavy sheepskin jacket and slapped his hat on his head, pulling it low on his forehead. He opened the door, the cold, bitter snow beating against him as he made his way to the barn.

As Wade had expected, the trip was slow due to the deep snow. There were some places in the road where the snow had drifted so high he had been forced to dismount and break a path through it with his body, pulling the stallion along behind him. He didn't stop to eat or make camp for the night. He paused only occasionally to let Renegade drink at a stream.

Both he and the stallion were dead tired when he rode into Cheyenne the following morning.

Wade rode straight to Newman's livery stable, and after giving the teenager there orders to rub the stallion down and give him a nose bag of oats, he stopped at the nearest diner and gulped down two cups of coffee to keep him going.

Wade stood in front of St. John's, oblivious to the biting wind that cut through a man like a sharp knife. He dreaded entering the hospital, dreaded telling his brother good-bye.

Then, firming his lips and gathering his courage, he went up the steps and pushed open the wide door. As he walked down the hall toward Ben's room, Martha left her desk and hurried after him.

"Wade," she said gently, "your brother isn't in his room. He passed away around four o'clock this morning." While he stared at the nurse blankly, she said, "His wife had his body taken to the funeral home next door."

Wade shook his head as though to dislodge the nurse's words. All along he had thought to arrive in time to hold his brother's hand one last time, to gently squeeze his fingers, to feel them respond.

"Was his death easy?"

"Very easy. Father Kelly from St. Mary's gave him the last rites and he slipped away in his sleep."

Surprise flickered in Wade's eyes. He hadn't known that Ben was Catholic. He and Pa were Methodist—not that they went to church all that often. Pa went once in a while, but Wade himself hadn't been in a church in years.

He sensed that Martha was waiting and he

turned back toward the door. "I'll be back to settle Ben's bill," he said. "Right now I'll go see Jane and Amy, and then make arrangements for the funeral."

Walking alongside him, Martha said, "Didn't you know, Wade? Mrs. Magallen is having Ben's body shipped back to Chicago. She wants him buried beside his mother."

"I see." Wade nodded, unable to say anything more. He guessed Jane was doing the right thing. She and Amy would no doubt return to Chicago once he was gone.

Martha patted him on the back as he opened the door and stepped out onto the street. Pulling his hat down and his collar up, he started walking toward the little house he had rented for Jane. How upset they must be.

Jane opened the door to Wade's knock, her eyes red and swollen. As she went into his arms, young Amy came flying from her room to be clasped against his chest also. When they had calmed down a bit he led them to the worn sofa and sat down with them.

Holding their hands, he said, "I'm sorry I couldn't get here in time. I was late gettin' your note; then a hellish blizzard had caused snowdrifts across the road in many places." He waited a minute, then asked, "Do you feel like talkin' about it, Jane?"

Jane dried her eyes with a crumpled handkerchief. "There's not much to tell, really. He just slipped away. I was holding his hand and didn't realize he was gone until Martha came in and told me his suffering was over."

"As hard as it is, I guess we should be glad it's all over for him."

"I know." Jane stared down at her hands, clasped in her lap. "It's ourselves we're grieving for, the loss of him."

After a long silence, broken only by Amy's quiet sobbing, Wade said, "Martha tells me that you're havin' Ben's body shipped back to Chicago."

"Yes; it's what Ben wanted. There are two empty lots next to Mother Nella."

"Will you be goin' too?" he asked.

"No. I'll say my good-bye to him here. I sent a wire to my uncle. He'll take care of things on that end."

"When?"

"Tomorrow afternoon." Jane's voice broke. "After we've said good-bye to Ben."

Then Jane asked softly, "Will you tell your father about Ben now . . . and about Mother Nella's passing?"

Wade stood up and walked to the window, staring down at the people moving along the boardwalk, stepping gingerly so as not to slip on patches of ice; seeing yet not seeing the carriages, wagons, and riders maneuvering for space on the rutted, frozen street.

He refused to let his gaze travel in the direction of the funeral home, where Ben was probably being laid out right at that moment.

His back still to Jane, he said, "Pa has a right

to know. I just don't know how to tell him; what to tell him. I can't bring myself to tell him the truth about Ben's death. I don't know how to explain that I've been seeing Ben all this time; that he had a fourteen-year-old daughter. Sometimes I think I'll go out of mind with all that's goin' on inside me."

"When the time comes, you'll think of the right thing to say," Jane said quietly.

Wade turned from the window and sat back down. "I guess you're right."

"When will you tell your father?"

"I'll go home in three or four days and tell Pa. I'll explain that you and Amy have taken Ben back to Chicago but that you'll be returning to spend some time with us. After that we'll just take it as it comes."

Jane nodded; then, with a tired smile, she said, "You look exhausted, Wade. Why don't you go to your hotel and get some sleep? I know Amy and I are worn out."

Wade picked up his hat from the floor and took his jacket from the chair on which he had tossed it. "I am beat," he admitted, preparing to leave. "What time do you want to go to the funeral home tomorrow?"

"Sometime around noon."

Wade nodded and bent over to kiss his niece on the head; then Jane quietly closed the door behind him.

Wade's steps were heavy as he made his way to the Dyer Hotel. Ben was gone, and now he had to hurt Storm one last time.

Storm

"You rested up, old fellow?" Wade spoke softly to the stallion as he slipped the bridle over the proud head. "The ride back won't be so bad, now that the storm is over," he continued, tossing the hand-tooled saddle onto the broad back. "We'll be in no hurry this time around."

Leading the big black outside, Wade slipped a foot into the stirrup and swung into the saddle. With a touch of the reins, Renegade moved out.

Midway down the street, the coach was pulled up near the train station, preparing to pull out for Laramie. Wade frowned. Becky and Jeffery were waiting to board it. They look very loverlike, Wade thought, his frown deepening as Becky slipped her hand in Rafe's and smiled up at him. He swore under his breath when Rafe bent his head and dropped a light kiss on Becky's lips.

Rage boiled inside Wade. Storm must not marry that bastard. He would make her life a misery, chasing skirts every chance he got. Wade intended to have a talk with Kane to let him know what a skunk his new friend was.

When Renegade came abreast of the couple Becky looked up at Wade. He scowled at Rafe when he kept his arm around Becky's waist.

"I'd like a word with you, young lady." He reined the stallion. "Privately."

"Anything you have to say to me you can say in front of Rafe," Becky shot back at him.

351

Rafe narrowed his gaze on Wade. He saw the pain and grief in the man's eyes, and pity stirred inside him. For some reason the big man was hurting. He removed his arm. "Let him have his say." He smiled at Becky and moved some distance away from them.

"Well, what is it you want to say?" Becky glared at Wade, her hands on her hips. "The coach is going to pull out any minute."

"I want to talk about the woman you saw me with. It's not the way it looks, and I'd appreciate it if you didn't mention seeing us to anyone for a while yet. In a week or so everyone will hear all about it."

Becky studied his ravaged face, anger curling inside her. "You're going to hurt Storm real good this time, aren't you?"

Wade couldn't meet Becky's eyes, and his silence confirmed her charge. Several seconds passed before she said, "Because I once liked and respected you, Wade, I'll bend to your wish."

"Thank you, Becky." Wade finally looked up at her. "Do you think Jeffery will keep quiet?"

"He'll do whatever I tell him."

"You're gonna hurt her just as badly as I have," Wade grated out, angry again.

"No." Becky shook her head. "No one can hurt Storm like you can." She turned her back, and after a moment Wade lifted the reins and the stallion moved out.

* * *

Wade arrived in Laramie an hour before the coach. He stopped at the saloon to let Jake know he was back, then rode on out to the river. After feeding and watering Renegade he walked into the cabin, went straight to his room, and threw himself on the bed. He was exhausted in body and mind. He was still sleeping when Jake shook him awake around dusk. Wade sat up, his mouth watering. "Is that steak you're fryin', Pa?"

"Yeah. I thought you looked a little peaked when you stopped in at the saloon, and I decided that what you needed was a good meal under your belt."

"I won't argue with that." Wade rubbed the sleep from his eyes. "I'm damned near starved."

As Wade washed his whisker-stubbled face at the dry sink in the kitchen, Jake asked, "How was your stay in Cheyenne?"

Wade knew his father was curious about the letter he'd received and his hurried trip to Cheyenne. But he knew Jake wouldn't come right out and ask him about it.

"If it's all right with you, Pa, I'll tell you all about it after we've eaten." Wade sat down at the table and forked a big steak onto his plate, then helped himself to raw fries.

They had pushed back their plates and were having coffee when Wade spoke.

"That letter you brought to me, Pa, was from Ben's wife."

"Ben's wife?" Jake looked stunned.

"Yes." Wade nodded, then proceeded to tell his father of Ben's death. He left out the nature of Ben's illness, not wanting his father to suffer over the thought that he had passed the fatal disease on to his son.

Jake shook his head sorrowfully. "I'd have liked to have seen Ben. He was a real nice lad. Always quietlike, never had much to say. Kind of studious, read a lot." His lips tilted in a soft smile. "Your ma liked to read too."

Now came the really hard part, Wade thought, rising and walking to the window. "I have more bad news, Pa. Ma passed away around five years ago. A heart attack."

He heard Jake's soft gasp of pain and knew he had been cut to the quick. He continued to stare blindly into the gloomy twilight, giving the man behind him time to come to grips with his grief. When Jake asked, "Did she die instantly?" he sat back down.

"Yes, she did, Pa. In her sleep."

Jake nodded, his eyes wet. "That's good," he said.

"I've invited Ben's wife, Jane, and his daughter, Amy, to come visit us. You'll love Amy. She's the spittin' image of Ma."

Jake's face brightened a bit. "What's his wife like?"

"She's a very nice woman. Pretty in a quiet sort of way. The sort that Ben would marry."

"It's too bad they couldn't be here for Christmas."

Wade gave Jake a startled look. "When is Christmas?"

Jake laughed softly. "A couple of days away. We're invited to the Roemers' for dinner, as usual."

Wade made no response to the remark, but he had no intention of eating the holiday meal with their neighbors. He didn't have the nerve to face Storm after what he had done to her and what he was going to do to her next.

"Did Ben leave his wife well fixed?" Jake asked. "Does she have relatives in Chicago who will look after her and young Amy?"

"To answer your first question, no, I'm afraid all Ben left Jane were fond memories. From what I could gather from a few words Jane dropped, they'd always led a frugal life. Ben worked in a bank, and the pay he brought home was small, I imagine."

"What will Jane do then, do you reckon?"

Wade wondered if now was the time to tell Jake his plan to marry Jane, or if he should wait until she had been with them for a while.

He decided to wait and said, "I thought maybe she and Amy could stay with us until they got used to Ben being gone; then we can figure out somethin'. Jane has an uncle in Chicago, but I doubt he could help her. I think he's up in years."

Jake shook his head. "No, I wouldn't like

someone else takin' care of Nella's grand-daughter. We'll see to the girl's welfare."

Jake's eyes were tear bright when he asked, "You said she looks like your ma?"

"Spittin' image." Wade grinned, pleased. "She looks like me too. She could pass for my daughter."

A growing excitement passed over Jake's features. "It will feel good, havin' a young person around the cabin again. Her friends runnin' in and out, just like it was when you were a kid."

All the more, Pa, after I'm gone, Wade thought.

"I can't wait for her to meet our friends," Jake said. "Won't they be surprised."

A picture of Storm passed before Wade, and he found himself saying, "Let's not mention Jane and Amy until they're here."

Jake looked at him, a little surprised, but nodded his head, wondering at the bleakness that had settled over his son's face.

Wade stood up. "I'll change my clothes and shave, then get on to the saloon."

The night was cold and still as Wade rode toward Laramie, the billions of brilliant stars reflecting on the snow, making it almost as bright as day. His thoughts were on the man back in the cabin, making plans for his grand-daughter. Why, he wondered, had Pa taken the death of his eldest son so lightly? Had the passing years dulled his memory of Ben?

He had wept for his Nella, though. Time

hadn't faded his memory of her.

Wade could understand that. A man never forgot the woman he loved. He, himself, would go to his grave remembering and loving Storm.

Chapter Twenty-four

Storm gazed pensively into the crackling fire. Christmas had come and gone in much the same fashion as Thanksgiving had, their only guests being Jake and old Jeb. Jake had explained that Wade was running the saloon, giving their fill-in bartender the day off to spend with his family.

Her lips curled. Pete Jones couldn't care less if he spent Christmas day with his Indian wife and two half-breed sons. Wade had only used that as an excuse not to have dinner with them. A fact of which she was glad, she assured herself. If she never laid eyes on him again it would be soon enough.

Storm glanced over at her brother, his face serene as he leafed through his latest newspaper. He had been so exuberant Christmas day, she had wanted to hit him. His new herd of shorthorns had survived the blizzard remarkably well. They had been smart enough to get into the lee of the mountain, where the wind didn't hit so fierce and the dry grass had been swept clear of snow. They would do very well in Wyoming.

With a bored sigh Storm stood up and walked over to the window to stare outside. The pale sun gave little cheer and no warmth as it slanted through the leafless cottonwoods. In mere hours, it seemed, it would be replaced by the moon, chill and remote, dead as the white world on which it shone. Behind her she heard Maria enter the room, heard the creak of the chair as the housekeeper lowered her weight onto it.

"I sure am tired of these cold, gloomy days," Maria said to Kane, receiving a mumbled answer from him.

Storm suddenly felt like the walls were moving in on her. She had to get away for a while. In reckless bravado, she said, "Maria, let's go visit Becky."

She turned around to see Kane's head shoot up. "What do you mean, go visit Becky?" He snorted his indignation.

"I mean just what I said," Storm answered just as sharply. "Visit Becky."

"You're loco if you think I'm gonna allow you to associate with her. I thought I made myself clear on that when you first came home."

"You did." Storm returned to her chair and

glared at him. "And I didn't pay any attention to it. I've been seeing her all along, with you none the wiser. You choose your friends and I choose mine. Becky is worth more than all your friends put together."

"My friends don't have bad reputations," Kane thundered.

"What about Wade? I suppose his reputation is as white as that snow out there."

"I know there's some talk about his drinkin' and woman chasin', but he's . . ."

"A man and that excuses anything he does," Storm cut in. She jerked to her feet. "You might as well know that I have kept up my friendship with Becky and that I intend to as long as she's around."

Storm looked at Maria, her eyes snapping. "Are you coming with me or not?"

Maria slapped her hands on her knees as if in decision. "Yes, I believe I will." She heaved herself up.

Kane stood up, his crutches making an angry thumping sound as he left the room.

Storm and Maria grinned at each other; then, bundled up to their noses, they went to the barn and saddled their mounts.

They didn't talk as the horses picked their way along the rutted river road. Their voices would have been too muffled to be understood through the scarfs tied around their mouths.

When they passed the Magallen cabin Storm glanced at it, noting that smoke was coming out of the chimney. Evidently Wade was at home, she thought. Probably sleeping off a drunken spree. She had overheard a couple of cowhands saying that Magallen was putting away more whiskey than usual. She told herself that she didn't care if he drank himself to death.

But her mind knew that she lied as Beauty followed Maria's mount to Becky's hitching post at the edge of the yard.

"Becky, where are you?" Storm called as she and Maria stepped into the Hadler kitchen and paused to remove their boots.

"We're in here in the parlor," Becky called back. "Come on in by the fire."

Leading the way, Maria came to an abrupt halt in the doorway, causing Storm to bump into her. "Rafe!" she exclaimed. "What are you doing here?"

Storm looked over her shoulder, a tickled grin twisting her lips. Rafe was stretched out comfortably on the sofa, his head in Becky's lap. Her grin turned into a wide smile when Becky jumped to her feet so fast his head came down on the sofa's wooden arm with a loud thump. He sat up, rubbing his head and smiling ruefully.

"Well, Maria, I didn't come here to get my brains whacked." He grabbed Becky's wrist and pulled her back down beside him. Putting his arm around her waist, he said, "I'm here to court Becky."

"You'd better be courting her," Maria snapped. "I don't want you playing fast and loose with her."

361

"He's not, Maria." Storm pushed the irate woman into the room. "They're getting married soon."

"Getting married?" Maria gaped as she divested herself of jacket, hat, and scarf. "It's pretty sudden, isn't it? Shouldn't you get to know each other a little better?"

"We know each other well enough, Maria." Becky patted a spot beside her, inviting Maria to sit down. "We've been *courtin'* since late summer."

"And you kept it a secret all this time? How come?"

"That's how Becky wanted it," Rafe answered. "I wanted to tell the whole world that finally I had found a woman to love."

"Well, I'm just so pleased for both of you." Maria beamed at them. "Will you be living here in Becky's place?"

"No." Rafe shook his head. "I'm takin' Becky back home to Oregon with me. I'm going to start up my horse trainin' business again."

"Tell me about the farmhouse where you'll be living," Storm asked, smiling at Becky.

"I love it. It's huge, has four bedrooms." Becky's face pinkened as Rafe added, "I want them filled with sons and daughters as soon as possible."

"I'm so happy for you, Becky," Storm said, "but I'm going to miss you dreadfully."

"And I'm going to miss you, too, Storm," Becky said after a short pause. "Why don't you come to Oregon with us? It's beautiful country and full of handsome men. You could make a new life for yourself."

Storm smiled. "You make it sound enticing, but after the first of the year I'm going back to Cheyenne, get back to teaching again."

"You are?" Maria exclaimed, surprised. "This is the first I've heard about it. Does Kane know?"

"No. I'm waiting until after the holidays to tell him. And I dread it. He's going to raise quite a ruckus."

"And rightly so. You got sick, teaching before," Maria pointed out.

Becky narrowed her eyes. "You don't look too well now. Were you ill while I was away? You've got such dark circles under your eyes, you look like a little raccoon."

"Well, thank you very much, friend," Storm said dryly. "I'm going to miss your compliments, too, when you're gone. I had a fierce headache all day yesterday and part of the night," Storm lied.

Becky nodded her understanding, then asked, "How's your grumpy brother? On the mend, I hope."

"Grumpier than ever," Maria answered the question. "Now that he can't get down to the stables and play with his pets, he's driving us crazy."

"I can understand that," Rafe said. "Kane has a real love for horses."

"I wish he'd love some woman half as well," Storm said.

"He will someday," Becky said as she stood up. "Let's go into the kitchen and have some cookies and coffee."

Gathered around the table, the four talked of sundry things: the weather, that Timmy Hayes was taking Becky's gander when she left, but that she was taking Trey with her, that she had a lot of packing to do. Rafe spoke of the horses he intended to breed, and Maria told of the latest baby her sister had birthed. Storm had little to add.

Time passed swiftly, and the sun was edging toward the west when Maria said she and Storm must be getting home.

Just before they stepped out into the cold air, Maria said, "We'll expect you two at our New Year's Eve party. Oh, and maybe you'll come over that morning and help us get the food together, Becky. We could sure use an extra pair of hands."

"I'll be happy to help out, Maria." Becky kissed the cheek turned up to her.

With the approaching sunset the air had grown colder, and the two women set their mounts at a canter, eager to reach the comfort of the warm house.

They were within sight of the barn when the whistle of a wild stallion split the cold, clear air. Storm looked over her shoulder and caught her breath. Highlighted against the horizon stood the renegade, his proud head pointed in their direction.

"That blasted animal is getting braver and

braver," Maria exclaimed, kicking her mount into a gallop. "Kane has to do something about that beast before he kills someone."

Jeb met them at the barn door to take their mounts. "You ladies runnin' from the devil?" he joked.

"Yes," Maria puffed, clambering to the ground. "That white devil back there."

Jeb looked in the direction of her pointing finger, then shook his fist at the statue-still stallion. "Get out of here, you bastard!" he yelled. "Go on back to your harem."

The magnificent animal tossed his head defiantly, as though he understood what Jeb had said. Then, with a shrill, angry blast of his flaring nostrils, he reared up on his hind legs, pawed at the air, and then pivoted, bringing his hoofs down. He disappeared over a rise, kicking up clouds of snow.

"Come on, Storm; let's get to the house," Maria said, her teeth chattering.

The first person Storm saw when she walked into the house was Wade. He and Kane sat sprawled before the fire, a bottle and glass sitting on the table next to Wade. She gave him a frosty look as she took off her jacket and hurried to the fireplace.

"I hope you haven't been drinking, Kane." She held her cold hands up to the flames. "You know that whiskey and . . ."

"Medicine doesn't mix." Kane finished her sentence, his voice impatient.

"Right," Storm said and walked into the

kitchen. As she set to peeling potatoes for the evening meal, she could hear Maria and Wade talking and tried to shut out the sound of his voice. He had gall, showing his face here after insulting her in the worst possible way.

She heard Maria ask him if he would be taking supper with them, and she decided that if he said yes she would march in there and tell him he wouldn't be welcome . . . not by her, anyway.

But Wade said no; he had to get to the saloon.

She was listening for the closing of the front door, announcing his departure, when suddenly he spoke behind her.

"Storm, I'd like to speak to you for a minute."

"I can't imagine why." Storm continued to wield the paring knife.

"I want to tell you how sorry I am about what happened at Becky's house." He waited for her to turn around, to look at him. When she didn't he continued, "And I'm just as sorry that I can't explain everything to you. I can only beg you to forget it, but if you can't, please forgive me."

Storm dropped the knife with a clatter and spun around to face him. Her eyes a blue flame and her voice as cold as frost, she said stiffly, "I'm not sorry about what happened, Wade Magallen. That night was truly my awakening. I finally realized what kind of man you really are. You like hurting women, and for some reason you like hurting me more than all the others. So take your explanations away with you. I'm not interested in hearing them."

She wheeled around and left the kitchen, her bootheels clicking angrily on the floor. Maria, ready to enter the room, looked at Wade and thought she had never seen such misery in another person's eyes.

"I'll see you at the party, Maria." A ghost of a smile stirred his lips, and a few minutes later she heard him saying good-bye to Kane.

The evening meal was a quiet one, each of the three deep in private thoughts. It was later, after the supper dishes had been washed and put away, when Storm and Maria had joined Kane in the other room, that the housekeeper brought up Wade's name.

"Sometimes I think Wade is ill; his face looks so gaunt and haggard. He's lost some weight too."

"I noticed that also," Kane said. "Somethin' is worryin' his mind. Of course, he'd never talk about it. Sometimes he's too close-mouthed." He shot a fast glance at Storm before saying, "He did say somethin' that was kinda interestin', though. He wanted to know if he could bring a couple of guests to our party."

"Who?" Maria asked. "Anyone we know?"

"No, strangers to us. A woman and her young daughter. They're from Cheyenne. Seems they'll be visitin' Jake and Wade for a while."

Maria shot a fast look at Storm, whose face

had gone white. "Was that all he had to say about them?"

"Pretty much. He said the woman had lost her husband recently and needed a quiet place to live for a while."

"I just can't believe Jake would have a woman in his cabin, especially one he doesn't know. He won't even let one come in and clean up the place once in a while."

"Well, Wade is fetchin' her and her daughter there in a couple of days."

"I wonder who she is, and how Wade happened to meet her," Maria said. "I've never heard of him chasing a married woman before."

Storm wanted to jump to her feet and yell, "He chased her years ago when she was single." But Kane had sworn her to secrecy about Wade's lost love, so she sat quietly, all her resolutions to never again let Wade Magallen hurt her fading away. She hurt as she never had before. She had no doubt that the woman and her daughter were the same people Becky had seen with Wade in Cheyenne.

Almost in a stupor, she stood up, mumbled her good nights, and climbed the stairs to her room. Kane and Maria watched her go, shaking their heads at the bleakness in her eyes.

Chapter Twenty-five

The sap in the burning logs sputtered and the wind howled around the corners of the house. Another snowstorm had come out of the north.

Silent and detached, curled up in the warm woolen robe Maria had given her for Christmas, Storm stared into the leaping flames as the snow lashed against the window. How, she was wondering, could she bear meeting the woman Wade would bring to the party tomorrow night? She wished she could climb the stairs, crawl into bed, and stay there until it was time for her to return to Cheyenne.

She had received an answer to the letter she had written to the head of the school there, asking if she could return to her old post. There would, indeed, be a spot for her if she was sure she had regained her health.

369

Storm's lips twisted wryly. Her body was healthy enough, but her mind? That was something else. At the moment it was in a very weak condition.

"But I'll work on that," she muttered to herself. Actually, she felt almost relieved that she no longer had to play the guessing game: Wade loves me, he does not. She knew now that he had been drawn to her only in a physical sense; love had had nothing to do with his actions. The woman he loved, and would marry, would please him in every way, and he wouldn't waste another thought on his best friend's sister.

Storm's thoughts drifted back to the party that would take place tomorrow, the one the Roemers had thrown every year since she could remember.

Before she had moved to Cheyenne Storm had looked forward to the affair, the date always circled on her calendar. Weeks in advance she would start daydreaming: This time Wade would ask her to dance; he would discover that she had grown up.

Bitter amusement glittered in her eyes. Every year had been the same. The party would end and she would cry herself to sleep. As usual, Wade hadn't asked her to dance. He hadn't even noticed she was there.

The dim lights of Cheyenne came into view as the coach rattled along, the four horses pulling it battling the wind and snow. Wade straightened up from his slouched position and carefully stretched his throbbing leg. It hadn't appreciated the jolting it had received.

He was alone in the coach, for which he was thankful. He doubted he would have been able to keep up a conversation with a riding companion. There were too many thoughts running around in his mind. Foremost was his last encounter with Storm, when she had looked at him with such contempt. A look he had fully deserved.

His treatment of Storm had been unforgivable that last time they had made love. But he hadn't known what else to say when it was all over. He'd have rather cut out his tongue than pretend to her that Josie Sales was waiting for him. But he knew that he must kill that look of love that was shining in her eyes somehow. He didn't know if he had succeeded, but he knew he would never forget the deep hurt that had looked out at him from her gaze.

Did he really have to marry Jane? he asked himself. Did he have to give Storm that ultimate pain? Pa would see to his granddaughter's welfare, as well as her mother's, after he was gone.

When the coach rumbled into Cheyenne, bouncing and swaying in the deep ruts that were hidden by the new snow, another worry was added to Wade's mind: how to tell his sister-in-law that he had changed his mind about marrying her.

As he left the coach and battled his way against the snow that lashed at his face, Wade decided that he would say nothing to Jane about marriage for the time being.

"Uncle Wade, you look like a snowman," Amy exclaimed, laughing, as she opened the door to Wade's knock.

"I feel like one too." He laughed back, kissing the smooth, rosy cheek that was lifted to receive it. As she helped him off with his jacket, her mother came from the kitchen, smiling a welcome to Wade.

"Amy has been so anxious for you to arrive. She was afraid you wouldn't come because of the storm."

"It would take more than this little snow flurry to keep the coach from runnin'." Wade grinned at his niece, ruffling her hair. "You're gonna have to get used to our winters, I can see that."

"Oh, I will." Amy clung to his arm as he limped over to the potbellied stove to warm his hands.

Jane frowned in concern. "Your leg is bothering you a lot, isn't it, Wade?"

"Some." He dismissed it lightly. "Being cramped up in the coach didn't help it any."

"Maybe you should see Ben's doctor. He could give you something to help ease the pain a bit."

Wade shook his head. "I'm thinkin' about goin' to see the doc when I get home. I'll tell him I've been havin' some bad headaches." He looked down at Jane's pale face, the dark shadows under her eyes. "Did everything go all right with Ben? His body arrived safely in Chicago?"

"Yes. I received a wire from my uncle this morning." Her eyes glimmered with tears. "Ben was laid to rest this afternoon."

Wade drew her into his arms, then pulled Amy into the embrace too. He held them close as they sobbed against his chest. He had done the right thing in pushing Storm away. At least she would never have to suffer what these two were.

Jane pulled away first, wiping her eyes on a handkerchief she pulled from her pocket. She gave Wade a watery smile and said, "If you've warmed up, supper is waiting."

His arm still around his niece, Wade followed his sister-in-law into the kitchen.

Jane said little as they ate dinner, but Amy was full of questions about her grandfather, and where they would live. Was it really close to a river? Did Wade think the children at school would like her?

Finally Jane said, "That's enough, Amy. You're going to talk your uncle's ears off. Anyway, it's time you were in bed. We have to be up early in order to catch the coach."

When Amy said good night and went to her room Wade glanced at the two boxes and three suitcases placed in the corner of the room. That wasn't very much for a woman and a young girl, he thought. But he would rectify that soon enough, he promised himself.

His newfound relatives, especially Amy, would have the prettiest dresses in Laramie.

Jane broke in on Wade's thoughts. "How did your father take the news about Ben and Mother Nella?"

"He felt bad, of course, and was really broken up about Ma's death. I guess he never stopped lovin' her."

"I don't think she ever stopped loving him. She spoke of him often, and she never went out with any other man. I guess she just couldn't bear living so isolated. I guess your father was away most of the time, keeping his business going."

Wade made no response to Jane's last remark. He was still resentful that his mother had left him behind. He rose and pushed his chair up to the table. "Let me help you with the dishes; then I think I'll go to the hotel and soak in a tub of hot water for a while."

"No, Wade, you go on along," Jane said. "I'll do these few things. You look tired. Get a good night's sleep and we'll see you in the morning."

Amy was pratically jumping off her seat in excitement as the carriage Wade had rented whirred along. She hadn't stopped talking since they left Laramie, headed for home.

Wade hadn't stopped at the saloon when they arrived; there would be too many curious eyes watching when Pa first met his daughter-in-law and granddaughter. That meeting should take place in the privacy of their home, where possible tears wouldn't be seen.

He grinned to himself as he expertly handled the reins of the trim mare that was pulling them along. He wouldn't be surprised if Pa wasn't already at home, even though it was only a little past three o'clock. Besides being anxious to meet Amy, he would want to make sure the cabin was warm and the place neat. He had even had a woman come in and clean it up.

Jane was very quiet sitting beside him, and Wade asked in a teasing, though serious, voice, "Do you think it's gonna be too lonesome for you, Jane? You are, after all, a city person like my ma was."

"I don't think it's going to be at all lonesome for me, Wade. It's beautiful country, a wonderful place in which to heal."

They hit the river road, and Amy caught a glimpse of the Platte through the trees. Then Wade was turning the mare onto the short gravel road to the cabin.

"It's just as Ben always described," Jane said softly, gazing at the rustic building bathed in the setting sun. "He loved and missed it so much."

Wade felt a surge of sorrow for his brother. He, too, loved this old place, and he'd hate having to live anywhere else. He steered the mare up to the porch and pulled her in just as

Jake opened the door and stepped outside.

Jake's eyes went straight to Amy, and a mixture of joy and sadness came into them. Amy stood up, smiled at him, and an instant bond was formed between them.

"Grandpa!" she cried, "I've waited a long time to meet you."

"And all this time I didn't even know you existed." Jake moved stiffly down the steps, favoring the leg that had been broken. He held his arms out to his granddaughter and lifted her to the ground as she leaned forward. He hugged her tightly, then held her away from himself, his eyes scanning each feature of her beaming face.

"Ain't you a pretty little thing," he said huskily. "You look exactly like my Nella."

"And Uncle Wade, too, Grandpa," Amy pointed out.

"Yes, you do, honey; that's a fact," Jake agreed, and he hugged her again.

"Pa," Wade interrupted, "meet Ben's wife, Jane."

"Welcome to our home, Jane." Jake gave his daughter-in-law a gentle smile and lifted a hand to help her out of the carriage. "I was awfully sorry to hear about Ben. I know his death must have been an awful shock to you."

"It was," Jane said as he took her arm and led her onto the porch, Amy coming along behind them.

"I'll be in as soon as I've stabled the mare," Wade said, turning the carriage around.

Storm

As he unhitched the horse and gave it some oats, he thought that he hadn't ever seen his father so happy. It was like years had dropped off him.

Chapter Twenty-six

The snow had stopped, and the wind died down sometime during the night. The Roemer household awakened to a bright day, the sun's rays sparkling like diamonds on the frozen snow.

Maria had left her bed around six o'clock, and by seven the oven in the big black range was sending mouthwatering aromas throughout the house.

The mantel clock was striking eight when Storm came downstairs. Maria gave her an absentminded smile as she poured cake batter into two flour-dusted cake pans. "There's a stack of pancakes keeping warm on the back of the stove," she said.

Storm forked three pancakes onto a plate and poured herself a cup of coffee. As she placed butter and syrup on the table, she asked, "Is that lazy brother of mine up yet?"

"No, and I hope he stays in bed for a long time. I don't need him under my feet, telling me how to cook."

Storm agreed silently. Not knowing what to do with his time, Kane was becoming a real pest, sticking his nose into things that shouldn't concern him. Hopefully his splints would come off next week and he could at least hobble his way to the barn to visit his prize mares. Otherwise she, or Maria, might take a piece out of his other leg.

But I won't be here to see it, she reflected with a small sigh. Day after tomorrow she was catching the stage to Cheyenne. *And tomorrow I must tell Kane and Maria.*

And oh, how I dread that, she thought, rising and carrying her dirty plate and flatware to the sink. It would take all her willpower not to give in to Maria's crying and Kane's anger.

But for the sake of her sanity it had to be done. Storm's soft lips firmed as she went upstairs to make the beds.

She was dusting the furniture in the big room downstairs when she saw Becky and Rafe gallop up to the barn. Soon they were knocking the snow off their boots; then, their faces rosy, they stepped into the kitchen, bringing a rush of cold air with them.

"Boy, it's cold enough to freeze your you-know-what out there," Rafe said with a grin as he helped Becky out of her jacket.

"Well, come over here by the stove and get warmed up," Maria said, "and then I've got a pan of apples for you to start peeling, Becky."

Becky readily agreed, happy to be back with the Roemers again, working in the kitchen with Maria as she and Storm had done as girls.

"Where's Kane?" Rafe asked, hugging the side of the stove, knowing better than to get in Maria's way.

"He's still sleeping, thank God," Maria muttered.

"I think I'll go wake him up," Rafe said.

"Don't you dare!" Storm walked into the kitchen. "Let that pain in the neck stay right where he is. Maybe we'll be lucky and he'll sleep all day."

"But I want to tell him how close to the barn we saw the wild stallion."

"How close?" Storm and Maria asked in unison.

"A distance of only several yards. The arrogant devil took his time leaving, too, when he saw me and Becky ride up. It's like he knows Kane won't allow him to be shot."

"Do you suppose he's lonesome, and just wants some human companionship?" Storm asked.

"That one wantin' to be around people?" Rafe snorted derisively. "He'll kill anyone who's foolish enough to come close to him. He's hungry. This last storm has made it too hard for him to paw through the snow to get to the grass below."

"I can't help but feel sorry for him and his mares. Maybe we ought to bring some hay out to his territory," Becky said, her love of animals showing through.

"I'm sure Kane would agree to that." Storm nodded. "I think he'd do anything rather than have that devil put down."

"Agree to what?" Kane stepped into the kitchen, his hair tousled and blond whiskers shadowing his jaw.

"Me and Becky saw the white stallion on our way in," Rafe explained, and while Kane washed up at the dry sink, Maria complaining at the water he was splashing on the floor, he filled him in on Becky's suggestion.

Kane agreed it was a good idea to haul hay to the stallion; then, sitting down at the table, he ordered Storm to bring him his breakfast. She slapped a plate of pancakes in front of him, poured him some coffee, and then stood with arms crossed against her chest, glaring at him as he started to eat. When he saw Maria giving him the same dire looks he finished his breakfast in record time.

Sighs of relief feathered through feminine lips when Kane and Rafe left the kitchen. Maria put the girls at their chores—Becky peeling apples and Storm mixing up a large bowl of cookie batter—while she herself mopped up the water Kane had splashed all over the floor.

At one point Jeb came into the kitchen and dumped an armful of wood in the wood box in back of the range. When it looked like he was all set to talk for a while, Maria made shooing motions with her hands. "Go on, Jeb, get out of our way."

As Jeb reluctantly moved toward the door, eyeing the batch of sugar cookies Storm had taken from the oven, she grabbed up several and slipped them to him with a sly wink. He winked back, and now he wasn't too averse to leaving.

At high noon Maria remarked that they could stop long enough to eat a sandwich. "Which of you girls wants to take some lunch in to Rafe and Kane?" Maria and Storm grinned at each other when Becky said at once that she would.

When Maria handed Becky a platter of cold beef sandwiches she said sternly, though her eyes twinkled, "Don't lollygag in there with Rafe. We've still got a lot of work to do."

"Oh, Maria," Becky exclaimed, blushing a rosy pink.

Around four o'clock Becky rested her hands on the pan of apples and complained, "I don't think I can peel another one of these darned things. Don't you think ten pies are enough?"

"And I'm tired of dropping cookie batter onto cookie sheets," Storm added her plaints to Becky's. "We must have baked a thousand. I'll be seeing them in my sleep tonight."

The housekeeper looked up from the rolling pin she was wielding over a mound of dough and looked judiciously at the bowl of sliced fruit waiting to go into another pie. She nodded. "I guess this one last pie will do."

"Thank God for small mercies," Becky said. "I won't be able to look an apple in the eye for at least a year."

"I suppose you're all packed and ready to leave for Oregon," Maria said, her face and voice somber.

"We'll leave in the morning as soon as it's light," Becky answered in an equally grave tone.

"I'm going to miss visiting you, honey." Maria put an arm around Becky's shoulder and hugged her, "but I'm glad you found yourself a good man."

"We'll be back to visit, Maria. Rafe and Kane have become good friends, and they'll want to keep in touch. And yes, I have found myself a good man. And now I'm going to get that good man and get home to change."

Storm followed Becky into the other room and as Becky began bundling herself up for the cold ride home, she said, "You've been very quiet today, Storm. Are you dreading tonight?"

"Some. I'll be glad when it's over."

Rafe joined them then, and no more was said as he shrugged into his heavy jacket. They were leaving then, with Becky saying, "We'll see you later."

Wade sat in front of the fire, a glass of whiskey at his elbow, listening to his father and niece talking of the things they would do once spring arrived and the weather warmed up.

It seemed to him that the pair hadn't stopped talking since they laid eyes on each other. He was grateful, though, that they had hit it off so well. Young Amy would be a bulwark against the pain his father would suffer when he lost his second son.

He could hear Jane moving about in the kitchen, making them a light supper. They would be eating later at the Roemers' and Maria always put on quite a spread.

God, how he dreaded tonight. Wade leaned his head against the chair back and closed his eyes. How he'd get through it he had no idea. He didn't know if he could bear the sight of Storm and Jeffery together, laughing, giving each other intimate looks. He'd probably drink too much and make a fool of himself by inviting Jeffery outside and plowing into him with his fists.

Wade came out of his gloom when Jake told him for the second time that the grub was on the table.

At the same time the Magallens were eating the Roemers were having bowls of chili with Maria, enough to hold them until they ate with their friends and neighbors later in the evening.

And it would be a feast. In the front room was the picnic table Jeb and one of the hands had carried in and placed along the wall adjacent to the Christmas tree, which had been set up at the corner of the fireplace, almost groaning with the weight placed upon it. Every available space on it was filled with the fruit of

Maria's and Storm's and Becky's labor; three different kinds of cakes, apple and dried peach pies, platters of cookies, several loaves of bread that Maria had baked the day before, pots of butter and homemade jam. Keeping warm in the oven were a large sugar-cured ham and a ten-pound roast. Enough to feed an army, Kane had remarked.

"What are you wearing tonight, Storm?" Maria asked as she stacked the dirty bowls and gathered up the spoons.

"I don't know," Storm answered with little enthusiasm as she gazed out the window, watching the darkness of night settle in. "Probably my blue woolen."

As Maria worked the handle of the small pump attached to the dry sink, Kane said, under the noise of the splashing water, "I know you're dreading tonight, Sis, but draw on that Roemer courage and hold on."

"There's not much else I can do, is there?"

Kane shook his head. "No, there isn't. I'm afraid you're gonna have to get used to seein' Wade with that woman and young girl. Rafe was tellin' me earlier that the girl looks enough like Wade to be his daughter."

Storm lowered her lids to hide the pain in her eyes. "Becky told me the same thing. I imagine the woman is Wade's old love. The one you told me about."

Kane turned a startled face to her; he paused before he said, "No, I don't think so. It didn't sound like her from the way Rafe described her.

I guess there was another woman in Wade's life that none of us knew about."

"I imagine there are plenty of those," Storm said contemptuously as she rose. "I'm going up to my bedroom to sort through my dresses. Then I think I'll nap." As she walked past Kane she gave his shoulder an affectionate squeeze. "I'll be fine, Kane; don't worry about me. I'm not a little girl who is going to throw a temper tantrum because she can't have something she wants."

But later, stretched across her bed, Storm indulged in one last cry over the man she had loved so deeply, for so long.

When she had cried herself out Storm slid off the bed and opened the double doors to her wardrobe. Her eyes fell on the blue woolen dress, but she passed it up. She was in a reckless mood now, and she went through the dresses until she came to the one she sought, a bright red velvet. She had worn it several times in Cheyenne when she went to the theater and to parties. She knew it flattered her, and it would help bolster the courage Kane said she must have. She took the bar of scented soap from her washstand and went downstairs to take her turn at the wooden tub in the kitchen.

Chapter Twenty-seven

The clock downstairs struck eight as Storm carefully placed a hairpin in the last curl on top of her head. She turned her head slightly to the left, then to the right. Every hair was in place, the back pulled up smoothly to curl with the rest of her hair.

Storm nodded her satisfaction. The hairstyle made her look older, and showed to perfection her slender neck and throat, rising gracefully from her bared shoulders. She opened her jewelry box and felt a jab of pain when her eyes fell on Wade's emerald necklace, lying on top where she had tossed it in anger. For a moment she wished he was here so that she could hurl it in his face.

Storm reminded herself that it would be the action of a spoiled child and, pushing the gem aside, she dug to the bottom of the black lacquered box and brought out her mother's cameo on its velvet band and matching earbobs. When she had the three pieces in place, she gently pinched her cheeks to bring some color to them, then stood back from the mirror to get an overview of herself.

Regardless of all the reasons why she should look worse than at any time in her life, Storm knew she had never looked better as she left her room and descended the stairs.

Maria, Kane, and old Jeb waited for her in the front room. She stood in the doorway, unnoticed for a moment. Maria looked lovely in her bright Mexican-style dress, and Kane was very handsome in black twills and a blue checked shirt, although a little pale from being inside for so long.

Jeb had scrubbed himself up, shaved the whisker stubble off his face, and slicked back his gray hair. Storm smiled fondly; he looked almost respectable.

Sadness darkened Storm's eyes. How could she bear to tear herself away from these three people she loved so much?

She cleared her throat in an attention-getting gesture and sailed into the room.

"My, my, look at you. Ain't you somethin'." Kane smiled proudly at his sister, knowing that beneath the smile she had pasted on her face she was hurting inside.

"Yeah, you sure do look purty, Stormie," old Jeb agreed, equally proud but not seeing beneath the surface of her carefree smile.

"You're going to have all the bachelors fighting over you tonight," Maria teased.

"There aren't all that many bachelors left," Kane claimed. "She waited around until most of them were grabbed up." When he would have said more the sound of creaking wheels outside announced that the first of their guests had arrived and he closed his mouth.

Greetings were called out as their nearest neighbor and his wife knocked the snow from their boots and then hurried to the fireplace. Jeb, who had been given the job of acting in Kane's place, splashed whiskey into a glass importantly and handed it to the man warming his hands over the flames.

In another fifteen minutes all their friends and neighbors had arrived with the exception of the Magallens. There weren't as many guests as had been present at the barbeque; this party was by invitation only. Still, the big parlor was filled. While Jeb poured whiskey for the men, Storm and Becky kept the ladies supplied with sweet cider.

The women had looked askance at Becky when they first arrived, whispering among themselves. Then Storm had passed the word that her friend and Rafe Jeffery were getting married soon and would be making their home in Oregon. She and Becky had exchanged amused grins when their neighbors did a complete turnabout and chatted away with Becky, as though they hadn't snubbed her on the street a week earlier.

Everyone had settled down, the men on one side of the room, discussing cattle and the weather, and wondering what beef would bring on the market in the spring, while on the other side of the long room, near the kitchen, sat the women, complaining about the snow that kept their children from school and their husbands under their feet. It was at this point that the Magallens arrived.

At the sound of them stamping snow off their boots Maria hurried to open the door for them. Jake stepped into the room first, ushering before him a woman somewhere in her midthirties. Wade followed close behind, holding the hand of a shy young girl. The room grew quiet as everyone stared at Wade and the girl who stuck close to his side.

Kane called out a greeting then and, their shock broken, others did the same. The women, however, leaned toward each other, whispering.

Maria smiled at the latecomers, saying, "Let me have your jackets so you can get to the fire and thaw out." Storm couldn't pull her eyes away from the lovely young lady who looked so much like Wade.

The blood pounded in her ears, shutting out the sounds around her. All the rumors that had made the rounds were true. The proof stood at the other end of the room. Thirteen or fourteen years ago Wade had fathered a daughter on the sad-faced woman at Jake's side.

She saw Jake's mouth open and knew by the movement of his lips that he was speaking. From the surprise, and then the wide smiles on their guests' lips as they looked at the woman and youngster, there was no doubt in her mind that he was introducing his granddaughter and his future daughter-in-law.

Storm's gaze was caught and held by Wade, and her heart skipped a beat at the abject apology in his gray eyes. He might as well have said, "I'm sorry, but I love this woman and I'm going to marry her."

From the corner of her eye Storm saw Jake and his guests coming closer, pausing before each woman who smiled and shook hands with the slender woman. The roaring in her ears increased. I can't meet her yet, she cried inwardly. *I've got to get away for a while, be alone.*

She slipped into the kitchen, grabbed up Maria's worn jacket, and quietly opened the door and stepped outside.

Storm's feet crunched on the crusted snow, clearly visible in the light of the full moon, as the sound of activity in the house became muted. She shoved her hands into the deep pockets of the jacket, wondering if she would ever again feel what the people back there were feeling: happy and carefree.

Happy. She hadn't been completely happy in years. There had been a few times when she had almost grasped that elusive contentment. But . . . She shook her head; like a fallen leaf skipping before the wind, happiness always dodged away from her.

Storm walked without purpose but found herself in the barn, standing in front of Beauty's stall. The little mare stuck her head over the half door and nickered softly. Without conscious thought Storm lifted the board that kept her horse safely inside her stall and, fastening her fingers in the animal's mane, swung onto her back. She jabbed a heel into the firm flank, and Beauty bunched her muscles and sprang out of the stall, dashing into the stable yard.

Two men had seen Storm leave the kitchen. Both had seen the state she was in and after a few minutes each decided he had better follow her.

As Rafe left the house through the kitchen door, Wade slipped out through the front door. When they literally bumped into each other outside they stood for a moment, glaring like two fighting roosters.

"What are you doin' followin' Storm?" Rafe demanded. "Haven't you put her through enough hell? Do you want to twist the knife a little more?"

"Why are you followin' her?" Wade came back. "You don't care for her or you wouldn't be smellin' 'round a whore."

Furious, Rafe gave Wade's shoulder a shove that sent him stepping backward. "Be careful what you say, Magallen. That whore, as you call her, is goin' to be my wife."

Wade gaped at Rafe for a long moment before

he said, "The hell you say."

"That's right. You say one more word about Becky and I'll shove it down your throat."

"Hey, I'm sorry." Wade lifted apologetic hands. "Becky is the finest little woman who ever walked the earth." His eyes narrowed suspiciously on Rafe. "If it was Becky you cared for, why did you lead Storm on, let her think you cared for her?"

"What's it to you if I led her on?" Rafe prodded him. "You don't love her."

"The hell I don't!" Wade burst out. "She means everything in the world to me."

"Then why don't you tell her so? Stop this cat-and-mouse game you've been playin'."

A hopelessness came into Wade's eyes. "I wish to God I could."

"What's stoppin' you?" Rafe asked bluntly.

Wade shook his head. "I can't. . . ." His words froze in his throat as a horse and rider burst through the barn door. "Storm!" he shouted, recognizing the small figure on the mare's back.

Both men ran forward, grabbing for reins that weren't there. Beauty raced on, her thundering hooves tearing up splinters of ice from the frozen ground as she headed for the open plains.

As Rafe and Wade sprinted toward the barn to saddle their mounts, both saw the wild stallion, only yards away. "Oh, God," Rafe groaned, "he's going after the mare."

Bent over Beauty's neck, her hands full of

mane as she gave the animal its head, Storm felt hot tears run down her cheeks. She had known that it would hurt her dreadfully to see the woman and her daughter, but she hadn't known it would almost tear out her heart. The pain was so strong, she doubted she would ever be free of it.

It took the bone-chilling blast of the wild stallion to bring Storm out of the vacuum of despair that surrounded her and into a frightening reality. She had not heard the animal's hooves in the snow. Before she could kick Beauty into a full-out gallop the wild one was upon them. Storm didn't think to scream out her danger; she was too concerned with trying to dodge the powerful hooves that lunged at the little mare and the snapping teeth at her flanks as the determined rogue tried to turn her toward his other mares, waiting nearby.

Then, without any warning of what she was about to do, Beauty braced her forelegs, coming to an abrupt stop. As Storm went sailing over her head, one of the stallion's hooves caught her a glancing blow over her left ear. Storm hit the ground and lay still.

As she lay crumpled in the snow, swimming in and out of consciousness, she could feel anxious hands going over her body; then she faintly heard Wade saying, "She's alive, thank God."

She felt herself being lifted by strong arms, heard Rafe say in low, urgent tones, "Don't hold her so tight, Magallen, you're gonna break her ribs."

She was aware of being transferred to Rafe's arms; then Wade was taking her from him and settling her on a saddle, his arms around her. As he set the mount in motion, she heard a shot ring out and felt, rather than heard, Wade's grunt of satisfaction.

Rafe ejected the spent shell from his rifle. There was regret in his eyes when he looked at the fallen body of the wild stallion, some yards away. "I'm sorry, fellow," he said, "but you were becoming too dangerous."

Storm lapsed into unconsciousness on the ride back to the house. The next things she became aware of were warm air, shadowy figures, and anxious voices rising and falling. She felt herself being borne upward, then lowered gently to her bed. Again voices beat at her ears, one raspy and despairing, rising over the others. Then, clearly, she heard Doc snapping angrily, "Dammit, Wade, if you don't stop carrying on, I'm going to have you put out of here."

Storm thought she heard Rafe say, "Come on, Magallen, let's get out of Doc's way." Storm grabbed her head and moaned when there came a shifting of feet, grunts, curses, and the sound of falling objects. A glass of liquid was pressed to her lips and held there until she drank it. Soon she was floating above the pain in her head, above the muddle of voices.

Kane and Jeb waited anxiously for the doctor to come downstairs, as did their guests, who sat quietly, wondering why in the world Storm had decided to go for a ride at night with a house full of company.

Jake, knowing what had sent Storm out into the night, sat between his daughter-in-law and his granddaughter, anxiety written on his face. He prayed silently that the young woman upstairs wasn't seriously hurt.

And Jane's heart bled for Wade. He had never mentioned that he was deeply in love with someone. How much he had suffered these last few years!

Wade was the first to come downstairs, with Rafe not far behind. It was plain by the disarranged state of their clothing and the swelling of Wade's left eye, plus the red marks on Rafe's face, that the two had come to blows.

Rafe went straight into the kitchen, and Wade growled to his three relatives, who stared at him in open-mouthed surprise, "Let's go home."

Hurried good-byes were said by the Magallens; then the door closed behind them. Kane was reaching for his crutches, intending to talk to Rafe to find out what he knew, when the doctor and Becky came down the stairs.

"Well," the gray-haired doctor came straight to the point, "your sister is in shock right now, Kane, and has a slight concussion. When she fell she landed on her shoulder and dislocated it. I put it back in place and bound it up. I gave her a dose of laudanum and left the bottle with Maria. Storm will probably sleep for three or four hours."

"Is there anything we should do for her?" Kane asked.

"No, just keep her in bed for three or four days. Don't let her get upset or worried about anything for a while."

"We'll see to it, Doc," Kane assured him.

"And we're sure enough thankful you was here when it happened," old Jeb added, some color returning to his face.

Everyone left soon after. Storm's accident, which might so easily have been fatal, had dampened the high spirits of the celebration.

Becky and Rafe, the last to go, informed Kane that they would postpone their departure for Oregon for a few days. Then Kane and Jeb sat alone in front of the fire. "You want me to stay with you, Kane?" Jeb asked.

"No, but before you leave I want you to help me get upstairs. I want to sit with Storm for a while."

Chapter Twenty-eight

Storm's disconsolate gaze roamed the familar confines of her bedroom. Not since childhood measles and chicken pox had she spent such a long period of time in here. Dr. Jacob had said she could go downstairs tomorrow, but to stay off a horse for a couple of weeks.

Storm's eyes drifted to her dresser, where a gaudy scarf of bilious green was draped over one corner of the mirror. A soft smile curved her lips: It was a get-well gift from old Jeb. He must have picked this one out himself; neither Maria nor Becky would have helped him choose such an outrageous-looking thing. Storm grinned. She'd have to wear the thing a few times; otherwise the old fellow's feelings would be hurt.

Her gaze dropped to a bottle of fragrance

Becky had brought her, expensive stuff bought when she had plied her trade in Cheyenne. Becky and Rafe had gotten a late start to Oregon because of her run-in with the wild stallion, but they had left yesterday morning. She hoped Becky had remembered to send the wire to the supervisor at the school, announcing that Storm would be a couple of weeks late arriving.

Sitting next to Becky's gift was a box of candy from Jake. A sigh feathered through her lips. She had hurt the gentle man's feelings when he came to visit her and said, as he was leaving, that Jane and Amy planned to come to see her. The thought of spending time with those two was more than she could bear. She had answered that she wasn't up to seeing strangers yet.

Storm laid an arm across her eyes. She'd had several visitors, but Wade hadn't been one of them. She hadn't really expected him to come; in fact, she was glad he hadn't. Undoubtedly he would have brought the woman and her daughter with him.

Her thoughts went back to the night when she had been struck by the wild stallion. She must have been hallucinating when she thought it was Wade who had lifted her up out of the snowbank and later so gently laid her on her bed. It must have been Rafe, she concluded.

Storm wondered why no one had mentioned Wade's name to her these past three days. It was as if it was taboo, or else everyone had been ordered not to speak his name for fear of upsetting her.

Why was that? She frowned, scooting up in bed and gazing at the window, frosted over from the freezing temperature outside. Had Wade married the mother of his daughter or announced plans to do so? Was everyone afraid she would go into a decline when she was informed of it? She hoped not; she was made of stronger stuff than that. She wasn't a child to be mollycoddled. Still, it was the last thing she would want to hear. Pain flickered across her face.

The sound of feet on the stairs banished the despondency on Storm's face. She mustn't let her unhappiness show.

She had pulled a smile to her face when Maria entered the bedroom and placed a wooden tray across her lap. "It's snowing again," the house-keeper grumbled as she plumped the pillows behind Storm's back. "It started last night. Your brother is like a wild man, worrying if his shorthorns are all right. He wanted to send the old man out to check on them, but Jeb's rheumatism is acting up so he sent a couple of the cowhands to look them over instead. And though they reported that the cattle were doing fine, Kane thinks they didn't check them close enough."

Storm made no reply; she was too hungry to talk. When she removed the clean white dish towel from the tray Maria moved to stand at the foot of the bed. She smiled her approval as Storm's healthy appetite made short work of the bacon, eggs, and fried potatoes.

When Storm had cleaned her plate and wiped her mouth she asked, "What happened to my water pitcher and basin?"

"Oh, I've been meaning to tell you about that. It got broken when Rafe and Wade had their fight in here."

Storm lifted startled eyes. "What fight? When?"

"That night when the wild stallion attacked you. You wouldn't remember because you were unconscious most of the time."

Maria made herself comfortable on the edge of the bed. "Wade started it. Doc was trying to see to you and Wade was swearing and carrying on. He wouldn't budge an inch from the bed. Finally Doc ordered him out of the room, and Rafe, very nicely, tried to get him to leave. Wade turned on him like a madman, swearing at him, swinging at him.

"Rafe didn't want to hit him, but when the doctor got knocked against the bed and almost fell on top of you, he did. They fought all over the room, breaking your pitcher in the process. When you began to moan and hold your head at the racket they were making Wade left."

Her story finished, Maria rose, picked up the tray, and went out, leaving behind a very confused Storm.

It was around ten o'clock when Wade's big stallion turned into the Magallen drive, six new inches of snow covering it, and came to a stop at the barn, jets of vapor streaming from his nostrils.

Wade, his eyebrows white with the snow clinging to them and the ends of his collar-length hair dripping wet, climbed stiffly from the saddle and fumbled with cold fingers at the bar securing the door. When he dragged it open he led Renegade inside, put him in his stall, dragged off the saddle, and removed the bridle; then, before he left for the cabin, he smoothed a horse blanket over the animal.

It was early in the evening for him to be home from the saloon already, but because of the snow and cold few customers had stopped in. When only the town drunk and a lone cowboy remained in the place, nursing a glass of whiskey, he'd told them to go home; he was closing for the night.

As Wade stepped on the porch and reached for the doorknob, he hoped that Jane and Amy had retired. Or at least that Amy had. He loved the kid, but tonight he didn't want to listen to her chatter. His mood was too low, too dark, too bitter. He had nothing to look forward to, and he dared not look back.

The warmth of the big room hit him in the face as he stepped inside, making his cold cheeks tingle. Only the light from the fireplace lit the empty room. The door to his bedroom was closed, telling him that Jane and Amy were in bed. As he removed his jacket, hat, and boots, he could hear his father moving about in the other bedroom.

Wade poured himself a glass of whiskey from the bottle on the mantel, and with a weary sigh he dropped into a chair. Stretching his long legs to the fire and crossing his ankles, he sighed again. He was a tired, lonely man.

"You're home early, Son." Jake came quietly into the room. "Business slow?"

"Yeah." Wade nodded as Jake sat down next to him. "A man with any brains is gonna stay home tonight."

"I think it will stop snowin' by midnight. The clouds are clearing away," Jake said, also stretching his legs toward the fire.

"Yeah, I noticed."

"On my way home from the saloon I stopped at the Roemers' to see Storm again."

Wade lifted interested eyes. "How is she?"

"She's comin' along fine. Doc's lettin' her get up tommorow." Jake watched Wade from the corner of his eye as he said, "Maria complained to me that you haven't been over to visit Storm. Is there any special reason that you haven't?"

"No . . . I've been busy with Jane and Amy."

There was a short silence; then Jake said, "Young Amy mentioned somethin' about you marryin' her mother while we were doin' the supper dishes. It was just wishful thinkin', wasn't it, her bein' so fond of you?"

Wade stared at his feet. "I did ask Jane to marry me."

"Why, for heaven's sake? You couldn't possibly love her . . . in that way."

Wade shrugged. "I just thought it was the proper thing to do; make sure Amy always has a good home."

"But good Lord, you don't have to marry her mother in order for her to have a good home. She's Nella's granddaughter. I'll take care of her."

"I have been rethinkin' my proposal to Jane. The thing is, Ben didn't leave her anything in the way of money."

"No, I don't expect he did. I'm sure Ben grew into a fine man, but I doubt he was ever very ambitious."

Wade drew his legs up and took a drink of his whiskey. "Pa," he said, "I've always wondered why Ma left me behind when she took Ben and left us. Was I such a terrible youngster that she didn't want to bother with me?"

There was shock and pity in the look Jake gave his son. For the first time he realized how that nine-year-old must have felt at being deserted by his mother. In all likelihood he probably blamed himself for Nella's leaving.

"Ah, Wade." Jake shook his head. "I wonder how often parents unknowingly inflict pain on their children. Although it's many years late, I can ease the pain you must have suffered all these years.

"Your mother loved you dearly, Wade, just as much as she did Ben. The truth is, I wouldn't let her take you."

Wade stared at his father in confusion. "But you let her take Ben . . . the firstborn."

There was a small silence; then Jake said, "Ben wasn't my child."

"What?" Wade sat forward. "But everyone thought . . . *thinks* Ben was yours."

"Yes, I know. That's what we let everyone think." Jake rose and poured himself a drink. When he sat back down he continued, "You know that your ma and I came here from Chicago?"

Wade nodded, remembering how his mother always talked about that big city, how much she missed it, and then waited for his father to go on.

"When we fell in love and got married Nella had a baby boy only six months old. She was a widow, having lost her husband to pneumonia three months before the baby was born. When we moved to Laramie it was only natural that the people thought Ben was mine."

Several minutes passed before the full realization of what his father had said hit Wade. If he and Ben only shared his mother's blood, then he no longer had to fear the dreaded disease.

In a rush of words that sometimes fell over each other, he poured out to Jake the hell he'd lived in for over four years. He told of his love for Storm and why he wouldn't ask her to marry him, how the aching in his leg had convinced him that he, too, was afflicted by the disease.

Compassion for his son's suffering made Jake's eyes water as he said, "Nella's secret

405

has hurt you dreadfully, Wade. She and I have cheated you out of four years of happiness. But, God willin', it can be rectified. There are two things you have to do, and I hope I don't have to tell you what they are." He gave Wade a questioning look.

"No, sir." A wide smile lit Wade's face. "First I go to Doc and find out what's wrong with this leg; then I go to Storm, try to make peace with her, and ask her to marry me."

Wade was up early the next morning, anxious to get to the doctor's office as soon as possible, but Jane was up before him. She had a pot of coffee brewing by the time he rolled off the couch where he had been sleeping, and walked into the kitchen.

"Good morning, Wade," she said as she filled two cups with the strong brew.

When they had fixed their coffee to their liking, Jane spoke softly. "I overheard the conversation you and Jake had last night." She reached across the table and laid her hand on Wade's. "I feel bad about your suffering, but I'm very happy that now you can tell Storm about your love for her. The night of the party, I could see in her eyes that she loves you very much."

Wade turned his palm over and squeezed Jane's hand. "Thank you, Jane."

"I guess I'll start making plans for Amy and me to return to Chicago."

"Why would you want to do that?" Wade

scolded, releasing her hand. "Nothin' has changed where you and Amy are concerned. You'll live here with Pa just as we planned. Storm and I will want our own place."

"But, Wade, Amy is no blood relation to Jake. It wouldn't be right, us living off the kindness of his heart."

"If you don't want to break his heart, you won't take Amy away from him. Every time he looks at her he sees his Nella. I haven't seen him look so good in years. And no one need ever know that Ben wasn't Pa's son."

"If you're sure, Wade, I'd be ever so grateful."

"Don't be. Pa will be the grateful one."

It had stopped snowing, but the air was so cold it bit to the bone as Wade made his way to the small barn. He hardly felt it, though, as he saddled the black and led him outside. The elation of last night was still with him, his blood still pumping excitedly through his veins.

Renegade stamped his hooves against the frozen ground, anxious to run, to get his own blood flowing. Wade swung onto his back and gave him his head.

They arrived at Dr. Jacob's office just as the man was building a fire in the wood stove in his waiting room. When Wade opened the door and stepped inside, Doc asked in concern, "Why are you out so early, Wade? Is somebody sick at your place?"

"No, everyone is fine. I came in to have you take a look at my leg. It's been givin' me hell for some time."

Dr. Jacob gave him a stern look over the top of his wire-rimmed spectacles. "I've been wondering when you'd get around to having me look at it. Does the pain come and go, or is it more or less constant?"

"It's constant. Some days worse than others, but always there."

"Take off your jacket and we'll go into my office. It's warm in there."

Once they stepped into the small room, Doc ordered Wade to strip to the waist. "Hell, Doc, it's not my back that hurts," Wade said, unbuttoning his shirt.

"I know that." He ran exploratory fingers up and down Wade's spine. "Sometimes it's our back that makes other parts of our body hurt.

"Ah hah," Doc said, stopping his examination midway down Wade's broad back. "Just as I thought. I've seen it many times."

"Seen what, for Pete's sake?" Wade asked impatiently.

"A slipped disc pressing on a nerve in your leg. It probably happened when you were breaking a wild horse or lifting some overgrown calf out of a mud hole. How long has the leg been bothering you?"

"Close to six years. Can you do anything about it? I'm sure as hell tired of it hurtin'."

The doctor nodded. "I can help you, but you've got to follow my orders exactly if you want to be healed permanently."

"I'll do whatever it takes, Doc."

"All right then. What I'm going to do is give your spine a twist, forcing the disc back in place. Then I'm going to bind you up real tight until I can order you a brace from Chicago. When you're laced into it you have to wear the contraption for six months. Night and day for the first two months, then only in the daytime for the remaining four months. And you're to do nothing overly strenuous for the next two months . . . like overdoing it with one of your women." The doctor grinned.

Hell, Wade thought to himself, a fine honeymoon Storm and I will have.

Without further comment, Dr. Jacob slipped his arms up under Wade's shoulders, told him to hold on, and gave his torso a sharp jerk and twist.

Wade let out a yell, and sweat popped out on his forehead. "Damn, that hurt, Doc."

"Yes, I expect it did. And you're going to be pretty sore there as the disc settles in place and starts to heal. Now sit real still while I bind you up."

When Wade left the doctor's office 15 minutes later his body was stiff but he didn't limp.

Chapter Twenty-nine

The kitchen was warm and the water hot when Storm stepped into the big wooden tub and lowered her body into it. She reached for the washcloth and the bar of scented soap on the corner of the kitchen table and worked up a generous lather. As she smoothed the cloth over her throat and then onto her shoulders, her mind was on Wade. She hadn't imagined it that night, when she lay in a stuporous state, aware and yet not aware. Wade had been in her room, raging around like a mad bull. Why had he been so concerned about her? His actions were that of a man in love.

"Stop it!" her inner voice ordered. "You're doing it again. Time and again you've told yourself to stop pining over that man, and here you are once again building up your hopes on someone who is going to marry another woman. Surely you have suffered too deeply to ever be fooled by him again."

"You're right, of course," Storm muttered, stepping out of the tub and toweling her body roughly, as though punishing herself for slipping back onto that merry-go-round of "He loves me, he loves me not." She shrugged into the new robe Maria had given her for Christmas, tied it snugly around her narrow waist, and then brushed her hair. A fire burned brightly in the fireplace when she entered the other room. Storm had the house to herself as she curled up on the sofa. Maria had taken advantage of the cloudless day to visit her sister, and Jeb had helped Kane down to the stables to say hello to his mares.

Kane doesn't have to worry about the wild stallion stealing his mares anymore, she thought, half in relief and half in sorrow. The animal had been such a handsome fellow. The cowhands still hauled hay to his harem, and they reported that the mares were becoming quite tame. She knew by the interested gleam in Kane's eyes that he had plans for them.

Storm picked up a book she had been trying to read for two weeks and opened it at the bookmark she had placed there. She had read a couple of pages when the front door opened, letting in a draft of cold air.

"Kane, for heaven's sake, close the door," she called irritably.

Even footsteps approached behind her when the door closed, and she snapped her head around when a deep voice said, "It's not Kane."

Storm knew she was staring at Wade, but she couldn't help it. Despite his black eye, he looked ten years younger. The old sparkle of years past was back in his gray eyes, and the usually tightly held lips were relaxed and softly smiling.

Jane has brought that contented look to his face, Storm thought dismally, watching him slide out of his jacket and hang it on the back of a chair.

Adopting a light manner, she said cheerfully, "Well, Wade, you look like someone who beat the cat to the cream."

Wade carefully lowered his long length down beside her and, crossing an ankle over a bent knee, smiled at her in a way she hadn't seen since she was eighteen.

Steady on, girl, she silently reminded herself as her heart began to flutter. Don't forget how many times this man has set you on a seesaw. She kept her face carefully blank when he said softly, "You certainly look better than you did the last time I saw you."

"I feel better," Storm said.

A silence of repressed emotions and unsaid words grew between them; then they both started to speak at once.

"Go ahead," Wade said politely.

"No, you go ahead. What I was going to say wasn't important."

Wade paused for a moment before he said quietly, "Storm, there is so much I want to say to you, to explain . . ."

"Look, Wade, you needn't make any explanations. My dull-witted brain has finally worked things out. All these years I mistook brotherly concern for that of the love a man feels for a woman." She made herself look at Wade and added, "I'm sorry for all the times I must have embarrassed you."

A look of incredulity shot into Wade's eyes. "By god, Storm, you are dull-witted if that's the conclusion you've come to." His voice grew husky. "I haven't felt brotherly toward you since you were a girl of fourteen."

He stared into the flames. "You can't imagine what hell it was, wanting to make love to you every time I saw you, how I despised myself for lusting after a child." He picked up Storm's hand and stroked it, saying softly, "I think I've loved you since the day you were born."

Storm's eyes flew to Wade's face, a desperate searching in them. Surely she must be dreaming. And though her heart raced like a fire roaring over the plains, she forced her tone to be light when she said, "Oh, Wade, I'm sure tough little boys of twelve don't pay any attention to babies."

"I paid attention to you." Wade gently squeezed her hand. "I was fascinated by your soft, pink face and the big eyes that stared at me so soberly. Every time I could get away from Kane I'd sneak up to your room and just sit watching you."

He laughed softly. "One day your mother let me hold you. You looked up at me and gave me a wide, toothless smile and my heart has never been my own again."

Storm was suddenly laughing and crying at the same time. She flung herself into Wade's arms, declaring, "And you're never going to get it back."

She buried her face against his throat. "How could you have made me suffer all these years? You must have known how I felt about you. That day by the river, I'd have let you make love to me." She gave a small rueful laugh. "I'd have let you when I was sixteen. Fourteen, for that matter."

Wade reached into his vest pocket and pulled out the letter that had caused him so much agony. "I want you to read this, Storm. It will explain my actions."

The fire in the fireplace flamed and crackled, creating the only noise in the room as Storm pored over the letter. After a moment she let it drop into her lap, tears of bitterness and heartache running down her cheeks. Gathering Wade close, she sobbed softly, "How awful for you to bear such knowledge alone. Why didn't you show me this letter years ago? So much time has been wasted."

"I wanted to save you the pain Jane suffered, seeing her husband deteriorate mentally and physically. The disease causes a slow, painful death. I wanted you to hate me, that's why I treated you so shamefully."

"As if I could ever hate you." Storm's arms tightened. She was silent a moment; then she pulled away from him and said in a small voice, "Everyone thinks that you are going to marry Jane. It will break my heart if you do."

"I'm not going to marry Jane." Wade looked deep into her eyes. "I'm going to marry you."

"You are?" A wondrous light shone out of Storm's eyes. "What has changed your mind?"

Wade pulled Storm onto his lap. "I just came from Doc's office. It turns out, I don't have Ben's disease. The pain I've been suffering these past years was caused by a slipped disc pressing on a nerve in my leg." He took Storm's hand and placed it against his chest. "Feel that contraption? Doc has me strapped into it and I must wear it for six months."

When Storm finally realized that Wade wasn't going to die the way his brother had, she burst into tears again, but this time they were tears of relief. Then she wailed, "Six months? Do we have to wait that long to get married? We've waited so long already."

Wade slid a hand into her robe. Fitting a palm over a full, firm breast and squeezing it gently, he said huskily, "I agree with you. I figure next week would be a good time to tie the knot."

"Oh, Wade, do you mean it?" Storm's eyes sparkled. A frown worried her forehead then. "But what about your back? We mustn't take a chance of the disc sliding out of place again while we're making love."

A blaze of desire flashing in his eyes, Wade said wickedly, "There's more than one way of making love."

Storm slid off Wade's lap, tugging him up beside her. "Why don't you come to my room and show me some of those ways," she said huskily, a fire in her own eyes.

Wade must have shown Storm a great deal that afternoon, for five days before their ninth month of marriage Storm gave birth to a baby boy. They named him Ben, after the man their friends and neighbors still thought was Wade's brother.

SPECIAL SNEAK PREVIEW!

FANCY

Norah Hess

Young Fancy Cranson will do almost anything to keep her small family together. But the beautiful orphan will not sell her body to Chance Dawson or any other logger. Handsome, virile, and arrogant, Chance wants to claim Fancy for himself from the moment he lays eyes on her. The only obstacles standing in his way are her constant refusals to have anything to do with him. Yet amid the pristine forests of the Pacific Northwest, Fancy and Chance will discover a love that unites them in passionate splendor.

**Don't miss *Fancy!*
Coming in May 1995
to bookstores and newsstands
everywhere!**

Chapter One

The tinny, raucous sound of the scarred and slightly out-of-tune piano ended with the last chords of "Camptown Races." For the next 15 minutes the dance hall girls could rest their tired and aching feet and have a respite from the heavy logger boots that had been tramping on their toes for the past 45 minutes.

Nineteen-year-old Fancy Cranson limped across the sagging wooden dance floor, her short red dress swishing around her knees as she made for the roughly constructed benches lined against one wall. She sat down and leaned her head against the rough, unpainted wall of Big Myrt's dance hall with a sigh of relief. Taking a small lace handkerchief from the low

419

vee of her bodice, she dabbed at her damp forehead where short, pale blonde hair stuck to the smooth skin.

After a moment she leaned forward and kicked off her slippers, and after nudging them under the bench, safe from careless feet that might kick them across the floor, she began massaging her right foot through its black mesh stocking. Her arches ached from the height of her high-heeled slippers and her toes felt as if they were ready to drop off her feet from being tromped on by the heavy boots that laced to a man's knees that were worn by all the rowdy lumberjacks. She didn't know which hurt the most, her feet or her waist, where rough, callused hands had gripped tightly as she was hopped and swung around in a wild dance.

But there wasn't much Fancy could do about it. Any man who approached her with a ticket in his hand had bought the privilege of dancing with her for ten minutes, whether she wanted him for a partner or not. If she refused a dance, Big Myrt would show her the door.

And she needed this job, for a while at least. So she tolerated the drunks, the rough, bearded loggers who tried to look down the front of her dress, held her too tight, and made crude propositions to her.

Five weeks ago, when her father had been killed in a logjam, she had been devastated. To add to her overwhelming grief, when she counted the money they had kept in a cracked cookie jar she could have cried all over again had she had any tears left. The legacy left to her by big Buck Cranson was 21 dollars and 62 cents. That was not counting two horses, four rooms of furniture that had seen better days, and the care of her cousin Lenny, 21 years old.

All their logger friends had rallied around her, lending their support in whatever way they could, but Fancy knew she couldn't sponge off them the rest of her life. She had offers of marriage but turned them all down. Most of the men were as old as her father, and the others felt like family, she had known them so long. She couldn't feel romantic about them.

Her only hope was to somehow get together enough money for the fare to get Lenny and herself to San Francisco. Fancy's sister Mary lived there, along with her husband and young son. In Mary's letters, which arrived every month or so, she always urged Fancy to join her, writing that jobs were plentiful, and she would have no problem finding work in a restaurant or hiring on as a maid in a fancy house on Nob Hill. But city life didn't appeal to Fancy, and she hadn't given the idea any thought until now.

Fancy still wasn't enthusiastic about going to San Francisco, but it would be wonderful to see Mary after all these years. She knew life hadn't been easy for her sister; though she was loved dearly by her husband, Jason Landers was a drifter, moving from job to job. Fancy could always tell when things were tight with them: Young Tod would be put on a steamer and sent upriver to spend some time with Grandpa Buck and Aunt Fancy. After two or three months Mary would write that they should send her son home. She and her father would know then that the couple had managed to get back on their feet again.

It had been nice though, having Tod with them. Through the long visits they had gotten to know the little fellow, and they missed him greatly when he was gone. The last time he had been sent to them, around six months ago, he was a sturdy little fellow with a genial nature.

One thing had bothered Fancy a great deal: Why hadn't Mary come to their father's funeral? She had gotten a letter off to her sister immediately after the accident that should have arrived the same day. Mary would have had plenty of time to see her father one last time.

The only answer Fancy could come up with was that Jason had moved on to a different job, and the letter hadn't reached Mary. So what was Fancy to do now? she asked herself. She might not hear from her sister for months.

The answer came one day when she accidentally overheard a conversation between two loggers. "You ain't worth spit today, Sam," one of the men had complained. "I bet you was over at the Dawson camp dancin' last night."

"Yes, dammit, and I'm plumb tuckered out today."

"Used up a week's pay, didn't you?" the man said in disgust.

"Just about," Sam said with a sigh. "It don't take long to do it. A man has to pay pretty good to dance with them girls."

"Yeah, and they probably make more money in a week than you do bustin' your ass gettin' the timber cut and hauled to the sawmill."

"They make the money all right," Sam agreed, "but it sure is nice dancin' with them."

The next day Fancy had packed and made arrangements to have her belongings hauled to the Dawson camp. Two days later she had moved into a small house and become one of Big Myrt's girls. She had been dancing for two weeks now.

Fancy came out of her preoccupation at the sound of shrill laughter. She wasn't surprised to see black-haired Pilar come strutting from her room, followed by a thick-set, red-bearded lumberjack. As the Mexican dancer shoved several bills down the front of her dress, Fancy couldn't blame the men who thought that for a price she would take them to one of the rooms leading off the big hall and entertain them during the 15-minute break.

The old adage about birds of a feather ran through Fancy's mind. The men had naturally thought she was like the other dancers, who made most of their money that way; it was the main reason they were there. Pilar liked bedding the men and took one to her room at every break.

On the dance floor Pilar was vivacious, ever smiling. But the women who worked with her knew it was all a facade. Beneath those sparkling black eyes and that wide smile was a spiteful and vengeful woman to be on guard against. None of the dancers liked her; most hated and feared her.

Fancy disliked the Mexican woman intensely. They had clashed over a man recently—Chance Dawson, the owner of the lumber camp. Fancy scanned the milling lumbermen who waited impatiently for Luther, the piano player, to start pounding the keys again. She didn't see the broad-shouldered, whip-lean body of the man who was the reason Pilar had come after her with a knife. If someone had told her that disappointment flared in her eyes, she would have told them angrily that it was all in their imagination.

Of course he could still come, Fancy reminded herself. It was still early, early for the dancers, at least. They didn't start working until midnight, and the clock on the wall said it was only a few minutes to two. He might be playing poker with some of the married men in camp now and perhaps he would come around later.

As Fancy massaged her other foot she recalled the first time she had seen Chance Dawson. She had been dancing here for exactly a week when the handsome, brown-eyed man had approached her with a strip of tickets in his hand and a devilish twinkle in his eyes. She felt her heart slam against her ribs when he handed her the tickets and swept her onto the dance floor. Never before had a man made such an impact on her. Living in a lumber camp ever since she could remember, Fancy had known scores of men, but none had ever stirred her interest.

When he asked, "Where did you come from, angel face?" as he smoothly swung her around the dance floor, his hand light on her waist, she couldn't make her tongue move to answer him immediately. Finally she was able to answer him breathlessly.

"I come from Tumwater, about ten miles down the river."

He had looked down at her with a quizzical smile. "What made you leave that camp and come here? Don't they pay the men good wages there?"

Fancy wasn't sure she heard mockery in his voice so she answered, "I'm sure they get the same wages as the men here do."

"Then you must have fallen in love with one of the lumberjacks and he went away and left you, so you decided to move on. Am I right?" The slim fingers tightened slightly on her waist.

"You're partially right." Fancy's lips curved in a wan little smile, remembering how she had adored her big lumberjack father.

"So, you're grieving a lost love." The tone said that was no big deal, that love was of no great importance. He stroked a finger down her cheek, then lifted her chin. Smiling wickedly, he said softly, "I can make you forget that man ever existed."

Fancy shook her head, a sadness coming over her face. "There's not a man alive who will ever make me forget him. He will always be in my heart."

Fancy felt the logger's displeasure at her words by the way he jerked her up against his hard body and said curtly, "We'll see."

They danced in silence then, but she was still held tighter than she allowed any of the other men to do. It felt good to be held against a hard chest. That was another thing she missed since losing her father: the way he held her close when she was hurting about something, like the time Mary had moved to California.

It was almost time for a rest period when he whispered huskily in her hair, "Do you want to show me your room, cuddle a bit?"

Fancy caught her breath and looked up at him, hurt and surprise in her eyes. He thought she was like most of the other dancers, that her main reason to be here was to make contact with men who would pay to go to bed with them. "I don't have a room here," she answered coldly. "I don't live on the premises. I have my own little house."

"Hey, that's better yet," he said smoothly. When the piano music stopped on a discordant note he ordered softly, "Get your wrap and let's get out of here."

"I can't leave here until the place closes at five o'clock," Fancy answered stiffly, pulling away from him. "Big Myrt would fire me."

"Let her fire you." The grip he had kept on her arm tightened. "I'll take care of you. All you'll have to do is be waiting for me with open arms when I come in from the woods at the end of a hard-working day."

Anger gave Fancy the strength to jerk away from the possessive fingers. Glaring up into his warm brown eyes, she snapped, "I can take care of myself. I'll not be beholden to any man."

"The hell you say." The voice was harsh now. "You're beholden to every man you take home with you. You're depending on the money he'll put on your pillow before he leaves."

For a moment outrage nearly blinded Fancy. Then, hardly aware of her action, she felt the palm of her hand rocking with force as it connected with a lean cheek. As he stared at her, dumbfounded, she wheeled around and walked away.

The burly loggers stared after Fancy, hard put not to roar with laughter. They were wise enough, however, to bite their tongues and pretend not to have seen their boss get walloped by the new dancer that every man jack of them lusted after.

Chance Dawson—the owner of the lumber camp, Fancy later learned—started toward the door, his eyes black with anger and finger marks rising on his cheek, and was stopped by Pilar, her hand on his arm. "Didn't you offer her enough money, Chance?" she taunted him, loud enough for everyone to hear. "She's not

427

called Fancy for nothin'. She comes high."

Chance shook her grip off his arm and made no reply to the catty remark as he strode out of the dance hall and into the night. It was then, without warning, that Pilar had snatched a stiletto from beneath her garter and lunged at Fancy, screaming that she had better keep away from her man.

The raging dancer had been in for a surprise. For all her delicate looks and her slender body, Fancy was strong and just as swift as the woman bent on stabbing her. Relying on tricks learned from her dead father, Fancy grabbed Pilar's wrist, jerked it behind her back, and brought her arm up until the knife fell to the floor. Then she brought the screeching dancer to the floor, where she gave her a sound beating, blackening Pilar's eyes and cutting her lips.

When the loggers, who had watched delightedly, thought Pilar had had enough they dragged Fancy off her. The Mexican had given Fancy a wide berth ever since. Nevertheless, Fancy had been cautioned by the other dancers to keep an eye on the dancer, and to be very careful when she was alone; Pilar was sure to seek revenge one way or the other.

Luther, rail thin and somewhere in his fifties, came and sat down beside Fancy. Flexing his long fingers, he said, "I'm afraid I'm getting rheumatism, Fancy." Leaning his head back against the wall, he added, "I can't pound the keys like I used to."

Fancy liked the sad-eyed man very much and suggested sympathetically, "Your fingers probably only need a rest. Can't you afford to take some time away from the piano?"

Luther gave a short bark of laughter. "On what Myrt pays me? I can't afford to take one day off, never mind a couple of weeks or so. Besides, she would soon replace me with some other piano pounder."

"Are you sure about that? I've seen a softness in her eyes when she looks at you."

"Girl, you've got to be blinder than a bat if you can see any kind of softness in that woman. Did you ever hear the way she talks to me? Just like I was some kind of useless old dog that got in her way."

Fancy grinned and asked, "You mean like the way she sees to it that you get a big, hearty meal every night while none of us dancers get so much as a cup of coffee? It doesn't look like table scraps that you wolf down."

"That's because she knows she's paying me starvation wages," Luther muttered, a flush coming over his pale face. "She probably figures it's to her benefit that I have a decent meal every day, that I can move my fingers with more energy."

"But maybe she's feeding you for a different reason," Fancy pointed out with a teasing grin. "Maybe she thinks that a good hot supper every night will keep you here where she can keep an eye on you."

Luther shook his head, amusement in his

eyes. "You're quite a romantic, aren't you, Fancy?"

"No, I'm not; I just know what I see."

"Hah!" Luther snorted. "You can't see that Chance Dawson can't keep his eyes off you even when he's dancing with another woman."

"You're out of your head! He hasn't been near me since I slapped his face."

"That doesn't mean he wouldn't like to. It was his male pride you hurt, not the face you slapped."

When Fancy made no response Luther remarked, "None of those yahoos in here interest you romantically, do they?"

Fancy shook her head. "I'm afraid not. Anyhow, I'm not here to find a man to become interested in. I took this job to earn enough money to get me to California, where my sister lives. As soon as I've done that I'll be leaving."

"I'll be sad to see you go," Luther said sincerely. "You're the first lady I've been around in a long time. You don't see many of them in saloons and dance halls. You bring back memories of my youth."

"Thank you, Luther." Fancy patted Luther's hand, lying in his lap. "You're the only gentleman I've met since coming to this camp."

The loud clanging of a cowbell interrupted their conversation, signaling that the break was over. Luther gave Fancy a crooked smile, then stood up and made his way toward the piano. Fancy pushed her feet back into her slippers as a bearded logger rushed up and pressed a ticket into her hand. With a resigned sigh she allowed herself to be led in among the others, who were stomping and hopping to the tune pounded out by Luther.

She lost control of the many partners who shoved and pulled her around the uneven floor, but the small leather pouch strapped around her waist bulged with tickets. When she turned them over to Big Myrt at closing time she would receive a good amount of money in exchange, to be added to the old cracked cookie jar hidden in her small house.

Hours later, as Fancy was whirled around the room by a man whose face she hadn't bothered to look at, she glanced out a grimy window. A sigh of relief feathered through her lips: The eastern sky was turning pink. The cowbell would be rung any minute now, announcing to the loggers that the dancers would be leaving.

She thought of Cousin Lenny, who would be waiting outside to walk her home. He would have their little house nice and warm, and there would be water heated for her in which to soak her aching feet.

Fancy's lips curved in a gentle smile as she thought of the child trapped in a man's body. When Lenny was eight years old he had become ill with a bad case of measles that almost snuffed out his young life. And though he had recovered, his mental growth had been retarded, and his genitals were also affected.

Fancy thought the latter was a blessing: If he was always to be a child, it was good he would never desire a woman.

Now, at 21, he was big and strong, and yet very gentle. To look at his handsome face from a distance, one would never know of his handicap. Although his speech was fluent, he never spoke of things that would interest an adult. He was more apt to ask someone if he would like to play with him.

Lenny adored Fancy and would fight for her to the death. He was very affectionate, and some of the hugs he gave her when he was caught up in excitement almost broke her ribs.

Fancy remembered with sadness the day Lenny had come to live with her and Big Buck. He was sixteen, but his eight-year-old mind was filled with grief and bewilderment. His mother had run off and left her husband and son when Lenny was four years old, and now the father who had raised him had been crushed to death by a Douglas fir that hadn't fallen in the direction it was supposed to.

Fancy left off her unhappy reflections when, at last, Big Myrt rang the bell the dancer had been waiting to hear. Freeing herself from her partner, she got in line with the other girls to hand in her tickets.

Big-boned Myrt, with her painted face and red-dyed hair, was rough-spoken and rough-acting, but she was scrupulously honest with her dancers. She never tried to cheat them and didn't allow the loggers to paw them if the women were averse to it. She kept it strictly business between herself and the dancers, but she did have her likes and dislikes. She had liked and admired Fancy from the beginning. The young woman minded her own business, was a hard worker, and was dedicated to her simple-minded cousin.

Myrt disliked Pilar intensely. That one was a vicious troublemaker, man hungry and lazy. She intended to get rid of her before winter set in.

Fancy stood in the doorway for a moment before stepping outside, sniffing the odor of sawdust and pine bark drifting up from the mill yard, down by the river. She was reminded of her father and her eyes grew moist. She determinedly pushed the memory away and stepped outside. She looked toward the corner of the roughly built building, and as she had known he would be, she saw the shadowy figure of Lenny waiting for her. Fancy waved to him, and he came forward like a friendly puppy, asking her if her feet hurt as he put an arm across her shoulders.

"They're killing me, Lenny." She said what he wanted to hear. "Do you have warm water waiting for me to soak them in?"

"Oh, sure I do, Fancy," the big man assured her as they turned down the path that led to the small house tucked in among a stand of tall Douglas fir. "And I put salt in the water just like Uncle Buck used to put in his footbath. Remember how he'd always say that it drew the tiredness out of his feet? I sure miss him, Fancy."

Leaning on Lenny's strength as she limped along, Fancy said with a catch in her voice, "I know you do, honey. So do I."

"Don't cry, Fancy," Lenny coaxed anxiously, hating to see her cry. As though to console her, he added, "I've got a pot of coffee brewed and eggs and bacon laid out ready to fry as soon as we get home."

"You're a good fellow, Lenny Cranson." Fancy smiled up at him.

Lenny's pleased laughter rang out as he and Fancy entered the house and closed the door behind them.

Chance Dawson, on his way to the mill, had paused among the towering pines in the hope of catching a glimpse of Fancy as she left the dance hall. He despised himself for lurking around like a green boy wanting to approach a girl yet not doing it for fear of rejection.

Never before had he been so drawn to a woman, and he had known many in his 30 years. And he wasn't the only man in camp who practically drooled every time he saw her. Half his crew went around like lovesick puppies. Every time he saw one of his men dancing with her he wanted to smash the man in the face. He knew the thrill they were experiencing. He had known it, too, that one time he had danced with her. Her body had been so soft and supple, molding perfectly with his. She had smelled fresh and clean, with just a trace of rose scent in her hair; not like the heavy, cloying odor of cheap perfume the others wore, trying to cover up the odor of an unwashed body.

Chance realized now that he shouldn't have rushed the new dancer; had he given her time to get to know him she might be in his house— his bed—right now. But his rashness had been brought on by the unacceptable thought that one of the other men might find favor with her first.

Finally his long wait was rewarded. Fancy stood in the doorway. She stood there for a moment, and in that instant he made up his mind to approach her, to apologize for acting like an ass the first time they met, to ask her if they could start all over. When Fancy stepped outside he moved forward; then he came to an abrupt halt, a dark scowl coming over his face. A man had emerged from the shadows and was walking hurriedly toward her. The distance was too great for him to hear what was said between them when they came together, but he could clearly see the arm that came around Fancy's shoulders.

"So," he swore under his breath, "she doesn't want to be indebted to a man, does she? It sure

as hell looks like she's depending on that one."
And who was this man? Chance asked himself
as the pair moved away, the man's arm still
around Fancy's shoulders. Where did he work?
He wasn't one of Chance's crew, and the next
camp was nearly 20 miles away, down near
Puget Sound.

A thought occurred to Chance that made
him swear again. Maybe the man didn't work
anywhere. Maybe slender, delicate Fancy sup-
ported him. There were women who loved their
men so much they'd do that for them.

Chance's hands clenched into fists as he
watched the pair move off through the pine,
Fancy leaning into the man, and him looking
down at her, smiling and talking. When he
threw back his head and laughed at something
Fancy said before they entered her house and
closed the door Chance wheeled around and
strode away. He was torn between wanting to
put his hands around Fancy's lovely throat and
planting his fist in the handsome man's mouth.

An hour after returning home Fancy lay in
bed, her stomach pleasantly filled and her feet
aching a little less. She listened to the distant
sound of a saw biting its way through a huge
pine log. It was a sound she loved, a sound she
had grown up with.

Did Mary miss all the racket that went on
around a lumber camp? She wondered again
why Mary hadn't attended their father's funeral.

Fancy's lids grew heavy and soon she was drifting off to sleep, lulled by Lenny softly singing "My Old Kentucky Home" as he cleaned up the kitchen.

Chapter Two

The morning was crisp and clear, and a sharp wind blew through his jacket as Chance looked down on a logjam in the river. Breaking up logjams was a dangerous business. He had lost his father to such an operation in '53.

He had buried the loved and respected man next to his second wife, who had passed away two years before from pneumonia; then, after staying on alone in Placer County for a year, Chance had moved on.

It had been such a day when he stocked a canoe with enough provisions for a few weeks and headed upriver, looking for a likely timber camp. After a week he had found this spot and sent for his ax men. Timber men, like cattlemen in the early 1800s, paid little attention to who might own the land on which the great trees grew. To those hardy men's way of thinking, whoever got to a place first owned it—or, at least, the timber. They weren't interested in the land.

Winter wasn't far off when Chance's four men arrived, and the first task he gave them was to build a shelter for the crew that would come later: teamsters, choppers, scalers, sawyers, and swampers. It took a week to put up the long building, and though there was nothing attractive about it, it was well built, with tight caulking between the logs and a roof that wouldn't leak.

In the center of the room the men had built a large fireplace that gave off heat in three directions, and above it they had cut a hole in the roof so the smoke could escape. Berths were built along two walls, and at the end of the long room they had knocked together three rough tables and benches to go with them. Later a grindstone would be placed in a corner. It would get a good workout once the choppers, with their double-bitted axes, began to fell the huge Douglas fir. Across from the emery wheel a water barrel and a bucket would be installed in which the men would wash up in the cold weather.

The day the loggers' quarters were finished the schooner that piled the river connecting the communities around Puget Sound delivered a load of heavy equipment, and a sawmill was set up. Arriving with the gigantic saw were teams of mules and oxen and Chance's stallion.

And some thoughtful person had added a cow to the lot. Many of his crew were married, most of them having children. The mothers would be thankful for the daily milk that would be provided for their children.

The axes were put to felling more trees, which were dragged by oxen to the sawmill. There the logs were sawed into lumber, one tree yielding enough boards to build a four-room house.

The cookhouse went up first, a building almost as large as the crew's quarters, for there had to be room for the cook's bedroom, not to mention a space for the big cookstove that would arrive with the cook, plus a worktable and shelves to hold plates, cups, and platters. All his cooking utensils would be hung on the wall next to the stove.

Chance's house went up next. It would be larger than the others that would be springing up among the tall pine for the married men. His place had to have office space where the men could come to express grievances—of which there were always many—settle arguments among themselves, and where they would receive their wages at the end of each month.

Before the men started on the small houses where the men with families would live, another large building was erected. This would be a dance hall, the domain of Big Myrt, a longtime friend of Chance's, and her dancers. This structure would contain Myrt's quarters and a series of small rooms for her girls, who would be arriving shortly after the crew did. The rest of the place would be the dance hall where, for a price, the loggers could be with the young women.

Now, a year later, as Chance let his gaze sweep over his camp, noting the smoke rising from the chimney of each building, he thought of his own cold quarters, where he hadn't bothered to light a fire to ward off the chill. He was seldom in it; mostly only to sleep. With the exception of old Zeb, his cook, and Big Myrt, he had no close friends. He got on well enough with his men during working hours, but other than that he seldom socialized with them. The emptiness of his life hit him. All he did was eat, sleep, and work.

But that wasn't the case with his men: They seemed to live full lives. This was a close-knit camp. Interposed with their hard work they found time to visit each other in the evenings, have gatherings on Sundays when the sawmill was shut down, picnics in the summer and small parties in the winter, when the winds blew out of the north and snow lay a foot deep on the ground.

Although he was never invited to any of their doings, Chance was proud of his men and their families. The wives were decent women, and most were hard-working. Some had found ways of earning money, an extra income for the family. Some washed the bachelors' clothes, Chance being one of the men to avail himself of the aid, while another wife who was handy with needle and thread mended the loggers' shirts and trousers, which were always being torn by brush or branches of fallen timber.

There was even a new bride among them who had been a schoolteacher before marrying a scaler. When the men went off to work each morning, leaving their quarters empty, she held classes for the eight school-age children. Her students would be coming along any minute now; the little girls with faces bright and eager would be hurrying, while the boys would be dragging their feet, their faces scowling.

Chance broke off his amused smile to give a wide yawn. He had stayed up late last night, playing cribbage with three loggers who were short of money until payday and couldn't afford the price of dancing with Myrt's girls. Those men who could buy tickets had napped from after supper until midnight, when the hall opened. They would have had sufficient rest then to put in a hard day's labor when the place closed at dawn. It was his habit, also, when he knew he was going to dance a few times with the girls, to take one of them to her room during a rest period.

But he hadn't gone there often lately. He knew with certainty that he should stay away from the place. He doubted if he could stay away from Fancy Cranson even if it meant taking a chance of getting his face slapped again. She entered his mind a dozen times a day, and his nights were filled with dreams of her, dreams that were so erotic, he would awaken with a hard arousal in his hand.

Also bothering Chance, Fancy reminded him of someone; a woman he knew, or had known. Maybe a girl from his youth, maybe the first one he had ever slept with. They said a man never forgot that first one, but he was pretty sure his had been a whore, and a man never remembered them.

"Hey, Chance, how long are you gonna stand there starin' at them logs?" a cracked voice asked from the doorway of the cookhouse. "I can't keep your breakfast hot all day."

Chance turned around and looked at the wizened face of his cook, affection in his eyes. Old Zeb was more than a cook to him. He had been doctor, nurse, adviser, and countless other things over the years. He couldn't remember a time when the ex-sawyer hadn't been a part of his life.

Ten years ago, when the dreaded cry, "Whip the saw!" rang out everyone knew that a tree trunk was splitting. Men dropped axes and ran. The tree might not fall in the direction in which the sawyers had intended. And that had been the case then. On its way down the tree had hit another one, and the large trunk had whipped around as though it was a young sapling. When it finally lay still, the earth shuddering beneath it, Zeb lay on the ground, his legs pinned beneath one of the huge branches. When the men rushed forward, three of them lifting the tree limb off Jeb and two dragging him free of it, his left leg had been broken in two places. The nearest doctor was 50 miles away, and Chance's father had set the breaks the best way he could. The leg had mended, but Zeb was left with a decided limp. His days of working timber were over. Seth Dawson had persuaded his longtime friend to become the camp cook.

When Chance walked into the cookhouse Zeb placed a plate of ham and eggs and fried potatoes on the table before him. "Looks like we're gonna have a nice clear day for a change," he said as he poured coffee into the cup at Chance's elbow.

"About time," Chance answered; then he dug into the plate of steaming food. It had rained off and on for the past three days.

Chance pushed his empty plate away, drank the last of his coffee, and stood up. "I'd better go check on the men down at the river. There was quite a logjam there earlier."

"I expect it's been broken up by now. You've got an experienced crew workin' for you."

Chance mumbled a reply. His attention had been caught by the man who had just walked out of Fancy's house. He recognized the big handsome fellow, carrying a basket, as the same one who had met and walked home with her a week before. His eyes widened in a stare when the man placed the wicker on the ground, pulled a wet dress from it, and carefully spread it over a rope that had been stretched between two trees.

As he watched, disbelieving, two more dresses followed, then a pair of men's drawers. A dark

444

scowl came over Chance's face when delicate ladies' underwear was hung alongside them. As shirts and trousers joined the other articles of clothing, he looked at Zeb, a question in his eyes.

Zeb shrugged his shoulders. "I don't know who he is. All I know is that he came here with that pretty little Fancy girl. Keeps to himself, always stays around the house."

"He doesn't look sick or crippled. I wonder why he hasn't asked me for a job."

"Maybe he's just downright lazy. It don't seem to bother him that a woman is supportin' him. He sure is a handsome feller, ain't he?"

"Well, handsome or not, he's got no pride, that's for sure." Chance snorted his indignation. "You'd think he could see how beat Fancy is when she leaves that dance hall."

Zeb slid Chance an amused look from the corner of his eye. He'd never seen his young friend so riled up over a woman before. He turned his head away from Chance so the irate man wouldn't see the wide grin that tugged at his lips. It appeared that Chance Dawson had finally fallen for a woman—and had fallen hard.

Zeb managed to pull a semblance of sobriety to his face before responding to the muttered remark. "I agree," he said, "it ain't easy bein' a dancer, havin' your toes stepped on, makin' men keep their hands where they belong. But I reckon Fancy loves her man enough to do it. They seem awful fond of each other," he continued to jab at Chance. "He waits for her at the dance hall every mornin' and walks her home. They hug, and he keeps his arm around her as they walk along, with him talkin' forty to the hour."

"There's no figuring women," Chance said, disgruntled. "She's such a fiery little piece, I'd never in the world think that she would work so hard to support a big, strong, healthy man."

"I guess when the love bug hits a person it makes him do a lot of crazy things," Zeb said, sliding Chance another amused glance.

Chance gave a disgusted snort. "I doubt if love has anything to do with it." He stepped outside and started to walk away, then paused when he saw a horse and rider coming up the trail from the river. The stranger reined in beside the cookhouse and said to Zeb, "I'm lookin' for Chance Dawson."

"I'm Chance Dawson." Chance stepped forward. "What can I do for you?"

"Are you kin to Jason Landers?" the man asked.

Chance nodded, apprehension gripping him. What had Jason done now? he wondered before answering. "He's my stepbrother. Why do you ask?"

"I'm afraid I have some bad news for you."

Chance waited, his body tense.

"Landers and his wife drowned this morning, trying to cross flood waters down by Puget Sound."

The blood left Chance's face and his stomach clenched. He felt Zeb's supporting hand on his upper arm as he choked back the denial that sprang to his lips. It was impossible to believe that Jason's laughing and carefree face was stilled forever in death . . . and Mary, too, with her gentle ways.

He choked back the lump in his throat and managed to say, "They had a young son; is he gone also?"

The stranger shook his head. "He's all right. The way he tells it, the mare he was riding refused to go into the water, which was lucky for him. His ma and pa's mounts were caught in an undertow and were swept downstream. I'm sorry to tell you this, but it's doubtful their bodies will ever be found."

"How'd you know where to find Chance?" Zeb asked.

"One of the loggers in Al Bonner's camp recognized the Landers name and said he thought you were related to him." The man looked at Chance.

Chance pulled himself together and said, "I'll go get my nephew just as soon as I can saddle up."

"You'll find him at Al Bonner's camp, down near Puget Sound. Do you know where it is?"

Chance nodded and struck off running toward the shed where he kept his stallion.

The stranger turned to Zeb and asked, "Do you know where Fancy Cranson lives? The boy said she was his aunt, and that she was living in Dawson Camp."

"Yeah, she lives here." Zeb stared goggle-eyed at the stranger. "You say she's kin to the boy too?"

"Yes. The boy is all broken up about his parents and keeps crying for her."

"Fancy lives right over there in that little house." Zeb pointed to the one with the red curtains.